FAIRYTALES

Cynthia Freeman

BANTAM BOOKS
NEW YORK · TORONTO · LONDON · SYDNEY · AUCKLAND

*This edition contains the complete text
of the original hardcover edition.*
NOT ONE WORD HAS BEEN OMITTED.

FAIRYTALES
*A Bantam Book / published in association with
Arbor House Publishing Company*

PRINTING HISTORY
Arbor House edition published June 1977
Bantam edition / May 1978

ISBN 0-553-28116-6

Published simultaneously in the United States and Canada

---

*Bantam Books are published by Bantam Books, a division of Bantam
Doubleday Dell Publishing Group, Inc. Its trademark, consisting of the
words "Bantam Books" and the portrayal of a rooster, is Registered in
U.S. Patent and Trademark Office and in other countries. Marca
Registrada. Bantam Books, 666 Fifth Avenue, New York, New York
10103.*

PRINTED IN THE UNITED STATES OF AMERICA

KR   23   22   21   20   19

To Dominic Rossi
whose enormous spirit never
ceased to amaze me

Fairytales

1

It was one of those glorious mornings in Santa Barbara that sojourners from the damp, dismal fog of San Francisco dream about, in fact, look forward to every year. The men were already waiting in teams of twos and fours to get on to the green lush golf course. It was the promise of a great day for eighteen holes of golf as they stood swinging their clubs limbering up, but Catherine Rossi couldn't have cared less as she lay alone in the middle of the luxurious oversized bed, in the luxurious oversized room reserved at the Biltmore for herself and her famous husband. The famous Dominic Rossi. Famous stud. that's what he was as far as she was concerned. He'd given her seven famous children, hadn't he? Well . . . this morning Catherine had it up to here. Every time she thought about last night she did a slow burn as her anger smoldered . . . How dare he not remember to make arrangements for her to be seated at the speakers' table alongside of him and all the other dignitaries? Good question . . . how come? Wasn't that where the future United

States senator's wife belonged? . . . he'd better believe. That's where she and four of his famous children belonged . . . but where were they seated . . . at a round table in the shadows, in the corner like paying guests. She doubted if anybody knew she was present, but more important, did anyone give a damn? Especially Darlin' Dominic standing up on that platform making speeches with such dramatic flair that would have made Marlon Brando look like a piker . . . why he could easily have won an Academy Award and knowing Dominic, he would have accepted it. Well, there was one advantage . . . in case of fire she was so close to the exit she sure as hell would have had no problem getting out fast . . . why the very idea . . .

How dare he treat her like she was some insignificant Sicilian wife cooking pasta. Well, the odds were eight would get you five in Las Vegas that Dominic Rossi would be the next U.S. senator from California, that he was a winner, invincible. No contest. There was no one that could come up against him and place, much less win. But that's what *they* thought. There was one person who could beat him. Indeed there was. And by God, she would even if it meant her marriage. What marriage? Why she hadn't had a husband in the last six-and-a-half years. He'd gone off this morning to pursue his quest on the campaign trail without her, and Catherine Antoinette Frances Posata Rossi was tired of taking second place and today, more than any other day, she remembered who and what he was when she married him, a starving young attorney from San Francisco. But angry as she was, Catherine wanted to be fair, if even begrudgingly, with herself (and at this moment, it was damned hard to be perfectly fair). He hadn't been exactly poor, since his father and all of the Rossi brothers from Sicily had made it big in fish, or produce, or booze, or whatever they made it in after one generation. But nonetheless, he wasn't her equal when he'd come down to New Orleans that summer to meet her. Bet your little Sicilian ass he wasn't. Why her family had been

American born for three generations. Southern born, and they were rich, *really rich.* However they got rich, by now they could afford to forget that Pasquale Posata had jumped ship at New Orleans without papers and melted into a society struggling in a civil war. So with all that going on, who noticed an immigrant from Sicily? His heritage of survival from the old country had trained him well, he found a very lucrative business in rumrunning for the North and gunrunning for the South. He did anything and everything that was illegal or illicit, but the most important thing was his shrewdness to stay out of jail and above all, not to get deported. As far as he was concerned, it didn't make one damn little bit of difference who won, as long as he came out in the end with more than he had started and *Mama mia,* that he did. When the dust had settled, and the fray was over, Pasquale Posata decided to remain in this most divine, magnificent country of opportunity because where else in the world, but in America, could anyone become a millionaire over night from a revolution. When he thought about it, he laughed. In all the twenty years of his life, he'd known nothing but chaos and revolution in the old country, but out of that, one either found himself dead or starving, and here, from revolution, you could become rich.

Now he decided to become respectable and a gentleman. He changed his name to Peter and married an impoverished southern belle of Italian extraction with a crumbling dilapidated mansion and a ruined plantation. But he needed her and she needed him. Not only did he restore the mansion and eventually yield the greatest harvest of tobacco in the state, but he produced four sons and two daughters and Peter Posata was a very happy man. Life had been good to him. *Mama mia,* had life been good to him. He would even have been happier had he been able to foretell that, from the Sicilian earth from which he had come, four generations later, out of his loins would emerge a woman of prominence and distinction.

But this morning, Catherine Rossi wasn't concerned with her lineage nor her great-great-great-grandfather, her mind was filled with the past which didn't go back quite so far. It went back to a lavish garden party given by her parents, who lived in a house one hundred and fifty years old in perfect repair, one of the best in the Latin Quarter, furnished with the most elaborate antiques, and there she met, for the first time, Dominic Rossi, fresh out of Harvard. The meeting was more than casual or coincidental, although it was made to appear so. However, the Rossis of San Francisco and the Posatas of New Orleans had met on many occasions through mutual friends and relatives in their travels and through the years had developed a strong bond of friendship and it was they who had decided it was important the two young people meet. When Catherine's mother, in her most diplomatic, gracious manner, mingled with her southern accent, mentioned that Dominic Rossi was to be their houseguest for a time, Catherine exploded. "You mean, Mama, you're bringin' him here so as I can marry him, and that's the truth . . . isn't that the truth?"

"Now, Catherine, that's no way to talk to your Mama."

Catherine's Sicilian blood, of which there was more than a little residue after all the generations, bubbled. "Maybe not, Mama, but that's why you're havin' him come. Why, you'd think I was an old maid."

And that's what Catherine's Mama really thought. With the few eligible Italian young men in New Orleans from the best families, for some reason Catherine, pretty, petite five-foot-three, brunette, brown-eyed little belle that she was, had more beaus than one could count, but not one proposal. She was going on twenty-five and not one on the horizon and Mama knew why. It was because Catherine lacked her southern, quiet, coquettish style. Instead, Catherine was blunt and outspoken, half scaring, if not discouraging, the young men, and Mama swore it had to come from the Posata side, not hers. Rosa Ann was like *her*. She

4

knew when to say yes at the right time, how to appeal to a man's ego which was the only way to grab a man at the right time, and that was why Rosa Ann, who was only eighteen months younger than Catherine, was married and expecting her second child. Well . . . God almighty, somethin' had to be done even if it took importing a northerner, or more to the point, a westerner who was two years younger than Catherine, but Mama had read *Gone With the Wind* and decided she would think about that tomorrow (as Scarlett had suggested). But when Catherine saw Dominic Rossi for the first time, entering the garden with the orchestra playing softly, with his father at his side, her blood did bubble, not from anger this time, but from passion. He was virile, handsome, six feet tall with a shock of dark auburn hair, with a clear light complexion. His charm and smile were captivating as was his amazing wit which added to his allure, but he also had made a name for himself as best halfback of the year at Harvard. However he wasn't all brawn, there was a brain so keen and exceptional it had taken him to Harvard at the age of sixteen, from where he graduated first in the top ten, magna cum laude. Yes, sir, the moment she saw him, she could have swooned (if that were the sort of thing Catherine did) as he approached her, standing in that celestial setting with the violins playing in the background, dressed in the most exquisite, most expensive apricot silk organza dress (that Mama or money could buy) with lots and lots of ruffles and on her pretty little feet were four-inch heeled silk shoes to match. Her hair was coiffed to perfection (because Mama always knew a woman's crowning glory was her hair). She pursed her lips in a rather Mona Lisa style, crinkled her eyes as an inner smile tickled her. Yes, sir, by God, Dominic Rossi had met his mate in Catherine Posata and she made up her mind then and there she was going to marry him, make no mistake about that. In spite of his size, she was every inch the woman to handle him. The two fathers embraced one another around the shoulders as Catherine and Dominic looked into each other's eyes for a moment. The spell was broken as Angelo Posata said with enormous pride, taking Catherine's diminutive hand in his, "May I present my daughter, Catherine ... this is Dominic Rossi."

He answered smiling (beautiful teeth, she thought), "I can assure you this is a pleasure I've looked forward to for a very long time."

"I wouldn't be at all surprised," Catherine answered in her most extravagant southern accent, narrowing her eyes and thrusting back her chin.

For a moment, he inclined his head to one side as though he hadn't heard her, then looked her squarely in the eyes, smiled and laughed as she joined him in the laughter. The two fathers walked away, leaving them alone. "Would you like to dance?" Dominic asked.

And Catherine answered, "Would you rather dance or make love to me?"

This time he stood speechless and for Dominic Rossi, that was a rare situation. He took her by the hand and led her to the furthest part of the garden where he sat her down on a stone bench, half laughing, and said, "You know, beyond a doubt, you're the most curious girl I have ever met. I'm not sure if you're happy or unhappy to have met me."

"Well, I kinda think that's sort of an accomplishment if I can keep a big lawyer guessin' what my motives are."

"Oh ... well, in that case, I want to make love to you." He took her arm and gently stood her up.

"Now, you just hold on for one minute. What makes *you* think I want to make love to you?"

"Because you asked me."

"That's right ... I asked you a question, but all questions require answers and my answer is I wouldn't let you make love to me," she responded with that Mona Lisa smile.

"Oh, I'm not so sure of that," he said, holding her close to him, but she pushed herself back.

6

"Now, you listen to me. You know, as well as I do, that this is nothin' more or less than an arrangement, an arrangement made between our parents, expectin' me to say 'Yes' and 'how sudden all this is,' when the time came for you to pop the question and I should be coy and all nervous-like and excited. Well . . . for your information, Mr. Barrister, I want you to know I don't enjoy playin' these kinda games and I want you to know from the very beginnin' I'm gonna say yes because I do want to marry you. I didn't think I would, but I do. So anytime you want to ask me, don't hesitate."

Dominic started to laugh. Not at her and she knew it, but at her complete candor and lack of inhibition, then quite seriously, looking at her, he said, "You know, when I came down here, I had the same doubts and reservations, but of course I wasn't aware you knew why I was coming. Suppose I tell you something?"

"Yes, please do."

"Beyond a doubt, you're the most staggeringly honest person I've ever met. In fact, you're overwhelming and in these few minutes, I probably know more about *you* than most people do who go together for a long time. And can I tell you something even funnier?"

"Yes, please do."

"I know it's crazy, but I think I'm in love with you. Is that possible, just like that?"

"It's possible, but I wouldn't worry too much about it. If you don't now, you will before you leave."

They both laughed, then quietly and gently he took her in his arms and said, "Catherine, will you marry me?"

She said, with unmistakable languor in her voice, "I thought you'd never ask."

~

The next few months found Mama Posata as close to heaven as she'd ever come in this world, with all the excitement and frenzy of the impending nuptials. There was trousseau shopping which was not only expensive, extensive and endless, but there was china, silver, crystal and linens to be purchased. After God and church, there was nothing Mama loved quite so much as spending money, clothes, luxury, finery and parties. The whole thing was just about the most exciting thing that had happened to her since Rosa Ann's wedding. But for Catherine, her firstborn, after all, she wanted this to be one of those weddings the likes of which New Orleans had never witnessed. The largest chapel in the Cathedral was filled with an assortment of Rossis who had descended upon the city for days now. Like locusts, they had come all the way from San Francisco. And the Posatas hadn't been Catholics for that many generations not to make their enormous presence felt, with all the uncles, aunts, cousins, nieces, nephews, distant relatives and near, and with a select number of friends, handpicked, there were five-hundred people at the Posata-Rossi wedding and reception. If Garibaldi had the amount of food and champagne that was served at that dinner, he could have united Italy a lot quicker.

Dominic was so dashing and handsome that every girl breathed a little harder when they saw him dance, holding his new bride, all shimmering and soft and satin and lace. When he smiled down at her, tightening his hold around Catherine's thin waist, bringing her closer to him, it was certainly obvious to anyone observing, the promise of what would be theirs later tonight.

2

Catherine sighed deeply and nostalgically in that darkened, lonely room. Yes, sir, what a night it was. The promises of love, devotion, fidelity. Oh, my God, the things people tell each other in moments of passion. How the hell could she ever have predicted at that moment her life could possibly have turned out the way it did? As for love, in or out of bed, well . . . there'd been little of that in the last ten-and-a-half years. She sighed again, ran her tongue over her dry lips . . . she felt lousy this morning. How else could she feel, after last night when she had stolen quietly away, unnoticed, from that overpeopled, overheated, overfed multitude, listening to the great Dominic Rossi expounding all the virtues, panaceas, solutions and promises for saving that most grand sovereign state of California and all its inhabitants from the iniquities of the Republican Party. He stood like the messiah delivering the Sermon on the Mount. Catherine wanted to throw up.

9

She was in bed with a terrible headache when he returned finally, well after midnight, all charged up, exhilarated, excited and confident that California was his oyster. Switching on the bedside lamp, he sat on his side of the bed, taking off his shoes and socks, then undressed. Going into the bathroom, he showered, then brushed his teeth. By God, he felt good . . . his batteries were so charged up by the time he got into bed, he found it impossible to sleep. Turning off the light, he lay in the dark with his hands behind his head and reviewed the evening. Yes, sir, he'd made the right impression, said the right things, scored the points . . . in fact, he had them all eating out of his hand. Catherine moved closer to the edge of the bed away from the candidate for the senator from California, as far away as she could without falling out.

God, where the hell did he get his stamina? He had enough of that to fortify twenty men and here his family, his wonderful, marvelous, devoted family, who all adored him so, worried about his health, saying that Dominic was taxing himself to the point where they thought if Dom kept up this pace, he'd have a heart attack. Heart attack . . . Hell, what a laugh! He was strong as a horse. His family . . . there sure was no love lost there. Even from the very beginning when she'd come to live in San Francisco as a bride (already two weeks pregnant) with her young struggling husband. And the feeling was perfectly mutual, they couldn't tolerate her any more than she could them, putting on such airs, never letting them forget she was an heiress. She made sure, from the very beginning, that the custom of the Rossi clan getting together constantly was going to stop, if she had anything to say about it and she did. Eventually the invitations dwindled. In no uncertain terms, Catherine made it perfectly clear she had married *him* and not his family and if he wanted to pursue his long familial attachments, it would have to be without her. Naturally, Dominic didn't take that without a few rebuttals,

which didn't make her yield one inch, and after all the
fights and arguments had run their course, Catherine
achieved her point. Dominic saw less and less of the
family, which they regretted, but knew why, which
only intensified the animosity they already felt for her.
However, Catherine's southern Sicilian background
had taught her not to dwell upon things of unimpor-
tance, so she simply shrugged her shoulders and ignored the fact that Dominic was more than terribly
chagrined, embarrassed and unhappy when he attended family affairs, of which there were many . . .
especially engagements, weddings, communions, grad-
uations, birthdays, etc., etc., usually alone, always
having to give the same excuse that Catherine was not
well or had taken a little holiday back to New Orleans
to visit her family. His voice startled her, suddenly
interrupting her thoughts in the silent dark room. Oh,
if he'd only stop talking. My God, she had a headache . . .

"Well, how do you think it went tonight?" he
asked. He wasn't really asking she thought, only
loving the sound of his own voice.

She could have killed him, but she narrowed her
eyes, tightened her lips, caught her breath, swallowed
hard and mumbled, "Just the way you planned it . . .
right?" He laughed robustly, while to herself she said,
you'd better laugh tonight because this will be the last
laugh you'll have for a little while in view of the fact
I have a little plan of my own all mapped out for
tomorrow, your majesty, your royal highness . . . your
royal ass.

She was seething inside. Dominic had breakfast
early in their room, eating heartily while she, still in
bed, observed her husband over the rim of the coffee
cup. When he finished, she turned her cheek as he
pecked it lightly and quite matter of factly, said his
arrivedercis, saying he would meet her later in San
Diego, then left. Well . . . that was it. Finished, *finito*,
and all because he had forgotten last night or didn't

11

even remember she was alive and well and sitting in the back like some morganatic wife not quite good enough to be seated with the king . . . that's right. Okay . . . two can play the game . . . How? . . . Well, I'll tell you, Your Majesty, although I do feel a little ashamed 'cause it's not original on my part . . . I'm just not smart enough to ever have thought of runnin' away from home . . . wish I had, but it sure as hell was the most ingenious idea any political wife had invented up to date so far as I'm concerned, to make a husband realize she was alive and that he owed her a little courtesy . . . so . . . I'm gonna follow the leader . . . gonna do what that brilliant Angelina Alioto did . . . of course she went to the missions . . . so I can't do that, it just wouldn't be cricket to steal her stuff and besides I gotta have a little imagination of my own, so I'm goin' to the Farm . . . well . . . that's not really so unique or original 'cause I've been doin' that for years whenever I needed a rest, but what makes it so excitin' and intriguin' is the runnin' away without lettin' anyone know. . . . That's why I think what Mrs. A did was so smart . . . without lettin' anyone know. . . . Talk about fact bein' stranger than fiction. Well, ain't that the truth. All I can say is . . . God bless you, Mrs. Alioto . . . you sure did emancipate a lotta ladies by showin' us the way. . . . Two can play the game. *Ciao.*

Catherine hopped out of bed into her size four satin slippers, went to the bathroom, bathed in an aura of excited anticipation of what was about to happen. When the ablutions were over, she splashed herself with lots and lots of expensive Parisian cologne, made up her face (which did not diminish the deep circles under her eyes), dressed in her new Givenchy creation, put on her jewels in profusion, packed her Gucci luggage and called down to the desk clerk to have her bill forwarded, then left through the rear entrance, got into her rented Mercedes Benz and headed straight for Scottsdale, Arizona, and the Farm.

Although guests were only admitted on Sundays, for Mrs. Rossi, however, there was always a room waiting at any time on any day, since she had mentioned (facetiously, of course) on numerous occasions that her contributions had been so enormous with the frequent visitations through the years, that undoubtedly she had more than paid for the sauna. Sometimes she felt like a missionary, giving to that great and glorious cause . . . that mecca . . . that holy spa dedicated to the proposition that any woman who could afford fifteen-hundred dollars a week (plus gratuities) and wanted to get away from the kiddies and their husbands (who were driving them MAD, MAD, MAD) or the drudgery of telling the cook how many were coming to dinner this evening . . . or to avoid another dreadful, boring, horrible cocktail party all for the benefit of helping the old man get a few more votes at the next election, could find a haven here. Who said you never got another chance? Well, not in politics. If it wasn't assemblyman there was supervisor. If not that, then there was mayor, or senator, or governor, or even president. Sure. Why not vie for the highest position in the land, why not, Catherine thought. Well, at least *she* had a place to retreat to, to contemplate, to . . . to . . . to meditate, to restore her spirits. Yes, thank God, for her there was always room at the inn.

Arriving at seven in the evening, and knowing every nook and cranny, she made her entrance through the side door, went up the backstairs one flight, then walked quickly along the narrow corridor to Mrs. Van Muir's office, opened and closed the door immediately, slumped down in the pastel blue velvet chair, let her legs go askew and kicked off her shoes as her feet felt the cool, soft, lush deep piled blue carpet, then lay back wearily as her eyes wandered about the blue silk walls . . . to the blue damask draperies. Finally, her eyes came to rest on the enormous life-sized portrait of the patron saint (who founded this sanctuary) standing regally dressed in blue flowing chiffon. Even the fragrant scent of the room smelled blue. How divine, how quiet and relaxing in the atmosphere of the dim light that shone through the blue satin shaded lamp, that sat on the blue Venetian desk. Ah . . . oh, so tranquil, like a shrine . . . truly like a shrine. How long she had been dozing was indicated by the blue French clock ticking away on the blue desk. It was seven-thirty when Mrs. Van Muir gently took Catherine's hand in hers and said quietly, "Mrs. Rossi?"

Catherine opened her eyes slowly, blinked, sat up and looked into the concerned face of Mrs. Van Muir. "Oh, my dear, how are you?"

Catherine answered tearfully, clutching Mrs. Van Muir's hand, "You don't know how happy I am to see you."

"And I, you, my dear Mrs. Rossi, but you don't look well . . . not at all."

"Oh, I'm not, really I'm not. In the last few months, this campaign of my husband's has simply been too much for my nerves to endure . . . it's been plain hell, I tell you . . . just hell," she cried, almost hysterically.

"There, there, my dear, we're going to do everything in our power to help you through this most trying time," Mrs. Van Muir said, patting Catherine's hand, "now you just re . . . lax." Quickly, she thought, should I offer our sainted disciple a little drinky-poo or not? Should I risk it? . . . since booze is strictly a no-no, verboten. Oh, what the hell, it would certainly do no harm to be in the good graces of the more than probable wife of the next senator from California. Who knew when one needed a favor . . . a new job. Throwing caution to the wind, Mrs. Van Muir said, "Mrs. Rossi, I know this is most irregular, but I received a bottle of cognac at Christmas which I've been meaning to throw out but have forgotten to do so. However, since I was so negligent, would you care for a little pick-me-up?" She smiled reassuringly.

"Yes, that would be nice, thank you."

Mrs. Van Muir went to the closet where she kept a large stock of cognac for her own use, that she drank at the end of each weary day, which she needed badly

14

after catering to all those neurotic bitches. Taking out a bottle she uncorked it, poured some of the lovely amber liquid into a brandy snifter and handed it to Catherine, who sipped slowly. It felt warm, soothing and relaxing after being on the road for nine-and-a-half lousy hours. God damn, it had been hot. Mrs. Van Muir sat down behind her desk and watched, wishing *she* could get bombed, but business before pleasure. When Catherine had finished, she was offered another which she gratefully accepted . . . then another, as poor Mrs. Van Muir's mouth watered. By this time, Catherine was not only relaxed, but her words became slurred as she began to confide in Mrs. Van Muir, giving out with a tirade of complaints about the abuses and tyranny she had been subjected to by her husband, the public, the press and the Republican Party. That's why she was seeking refuge here. But it had to be in the strictest of confidence. She had run away from home. No one knew where she had gone, and if anyone inquired as to her whereabouts (as she knew the family would, since this was the first place they'd suspect her to be when they got around to realizing she was missing), Mrs. Van Muir was advised in no uncertain terms that she was to say no one had seen hide nor hair of Catherine Rossi. Mrs. Van Muir unequivocally answered that Catherine's secret was as sacred and secure with her as it would have been if told in the confessional at the Vatican, whispered in the ear of Pope Paul. However . . . there was only one place in the complex where Mrs. Van Muir knew Catherine would have maximum security, and that was in the old towers. Although it was still being cared for and Catherine would be provided with the same luxurious surroundings, there was one problem; an air-cooling system was going to be installed but not until a little later in the year. Apologetically Mrs. Van Muir asked if Catherine would mind the inconvenience of the overly heated quarters. At this point Catherine would have settled for the boiler room. Catherine

sighed with great relief, knowing she could depend on
Mrs. Van Muir's discretion . . . her dear and trusted
friend of long standing. Now dry eyed, Catherine continued (but not without first asking for another cognac): the plan was to be this . . . she would not go
down for her meals, instead everything would be sent
to her room and no one, but no one, was to know she
was here. Not the help, not the guests. She was to be
notified by Mrs. Van Muir before her suite was to be
cleaned each day so that she could go down the
service elevator to wait in Mrs. Van Muir's office
incognito, dark glasses, bandanna . . . *sans* jewels, *sans*
Givenchy, *sans* eyelashes, *sans* makeup. *Sans* all the
window dressing, her chances of detection were less
imminent that she would be recognized in the first
place. There was one other thing Catherine almost
forgot . . . when her meals were served (and to hell
with the diet at the Farm), the cart was to be wheeled
in by Mrs. Van Muir, so that the Lady of Mystery
wouldn't have to go scurrying off to the bathroom and
wait until some waitress took her leave. Catherine
narrowed her eyes in studied contemplation. Had she
forgotten anything . . . no, that was about it. Now,
she wanted to retreat to her quarters, plunge into a
warm tub before her dinner of steak, baked potato
with sour cream, chives and bacon bits, buttered string
beans, small salad with French dressing and coffee
was served . . . oh yes, and a napoleon for dessert if
that could be managed? No? Maybe not. Well then,
whatever, she wasn't too difficult to please, a piece of
lemon cream pie or whatever goodies could be had.
Damn, damn, she should have thought of buying a
bottle of her favorite wine before coming, but for
heaven sakes, a body couldn't think of everything,
especially when one was under such stress and strain.
Tomorrow she would steal away during the siesta
period, being sure not to be seen, and drive to the
liquor store and buy enough for a few weeks, and
while she was about it she would also purchase some
other things for little late night snacks. Let's see, now,

crackers, nuts, potato chips, sardines, cheese, those little triangles and cubes wrapped in foil in those darling little boxes, a large tin of Danish cookies and . . . and oh, yes, a large jar of those enormous green olives, stuffed with pimentos. Oh hell, why hadn't she brought that gorgeous box of Barricini chocolates instead of giving them to the chambermaid. But then, that was one of her greatest faults, always giving things away, always letting her heart rule her head. Oh well, no one was perfect. She'd just have to buy whatever chocolates she could find. One should be prepared at all times for any eventuality. From now on, she would be alone for some time to come, God only knew how long it would take for all of them to realize she was *really* missing and the prospect was a little frightening. Suppose it took months? Was that possible? Oh, come on, now, Catherine, don't let your imagination play tricks on you. You know better than that. Why, within a few days Dominic will have the Foreign Legion out scouting when you don't show up.

That evening, Catherine turned off the light by ten-thirty, feeling the effects of her "long day's journey into night," closed her eyes, but sleep eluded her. The full impact of what she had done, running off without telling anyone, suddenly began to nudge her conscience. But why, she thought adamantly, should she feel that way when she had been literally ignored by her husband and children in these latter years. Oh, damn, if only she had something to soothe her nerves. Was it too late to steal down to Mrs. Van Muir's and confiscate that bottle of cognac? Without another thought, she hopped out of bed and into a silk robe and slippers, let herself out without fear of being seen, since by now, everyone was in their room either asleep or sequestered for the night in view of the fact that the rules were rigidly enforced in this fabulous overpriced prison for the overweight, the indulged, the pampered. She walked to the service elevator which took her to Mrs. Van Muir's office. For a moment, she hesitated before knocking, then she tapped twice and waited, but when there was no response, she gently turned the knob and let herself in. What she found was Mrs. Van Muir in a horizontal position, stretched out on the blue velvet sofa, snoring and the bottle of cognac, half empty, sitting on the coffee table while the brandy snifter dangled from her hand. Why not, thought Catherine. What was there to do in this fat farm for excitement? In fact, Catherine could identify and empathize with poor Mrs. Van Muir and why not? After all, neither one of them had husbands. The only difference was Mrs. Van Muir's husband was dead, but mine, Catherine said to herself, was running off into the jungle of politics like Tarzan in search of Jane, but the results were the same; they were both alone, unhappy and terribly lonely. God, what a curse loneliness was. Catherine would certainly never inform the establishment that poor Mrs. Van Muir was undoubtedly a silent night drinker (which up to now she never suspected), but if anyone found out, she'd have her little size eight fanny in a sling. Well, enjoy . . . enjoy, Mrs. Van Muir. After all, there are so few pleasures and rewards in this life . . . enjoy.

So as not to awaken the sleeping directress of the Farm, she tiptoed to the closet, opened the door carefully and took a bottle of cognac. Holding it close to her, she tiptoed out, just as quietly, closing the door behind her and hurried back to her room. Once there, she poured herself a stiff slug of cognac, settled herself in the large chair and sipped herself into oblivion.

The next morning, she awoke with a dreadful hangover. She called Mrs. Van Muir on the phone (who was just as cheerful as a squirrel gathering nuts). "Mrs. Van Muir," Catherine said, barely able to speak above a whisper, "this is Mrs. Rossi."

"Yes, my dear, what may I help you with?" she answered almost lyrically.

How could she sound like Little Mary Sunshine after being bombed last night? Catherine felt irritated when *she* had such a headache. "I'm not feeling well this morning and I don't want any breakfast . . . in fact, I'm not sure about lunch and don't bother to have the room straightened . . . I want to be left strictly alone."

"Oh, my dear, you really don't sound well. Isn't there anything I can do?"

"Yes, on second thought, bring me some aspirin . . . oh . . . and a pitcher of tomato juice . . . and . . . and a large pot of black coffee."

"Oh, my poor dear, Mrs. Rossi, you're really not feeling at all well . . ." She was about to say more, but Catherine couldn't even stand the sweet chirping of birds this morning, much less the sound of a human voice saying, my poor darling. She was sick to death of everything, including the solicitude of dear Mrs. Van Muir.

Abruptly, she interrupted, "Look, just bring up what I asked for . . . I have to go to the bathroom," and hung up, doing just that, where she upchucked last night's cognac as well as her dinner, she was sure. Then feebly, found her way to bed where she lay weak from the ordeal, perspiring. God, she felt simply awful. But it wasn't just the liquor, it was her nerves and the accumulation of a lot of things she had harbored for a very long time.

When Catherine heard Mrs. Van Muir turn the knob on the door, she shut her eyes and pretended to be asleep. Quietly, Mrs. Van Muir placed the tray down, turned around, then paused for a moment in total disbelief when she saw *her* bottle of cognac sitting half-empty on the table. Wouldn't a mother recognize her own child? You bet she would and she knew that was *her* bottle. Well, I'll be damned. How and when did she get that. Quickly, she realized that dear Mrs. Rossi must have come to her office while she was sleeping in a state of inebriation last night and merely heisted it. Quite disgruntled, she decided from now on, she would be sure and lock her door when day was done. After all, she needed a little privacy too and this was the first time any of the old biddies had done anything like that. With those thoughts, Mrs. Van Muir left, happy that her cognac had not lain too lightly on Mrs. Rossi's delicate stomach. The moment she made her departure, Catherine left her bed, barely able to get out, and poured some tomato juice into a glass, unscrewed the top of the aspirin bottle, then popped two into her mouth and washed them down with the juice. Weakly, she sat in the large chair and drank some hot coffee, as her hand trembled slightly, then just sat breathing and sighing deeply. So far, this little escapade hadn't been nearly as exciting as the ones Mata Hari had had. But it was only her second day . . . things would look up, but no more cognac . . . well, maybe, but not in that quantity.

When she gathered enough strength, Catherine went to the bathroom, turned on the water taps, added a packet of blue fragrant crystals, and watched as they turned into thousands of tiny iridescent bubbles. How beautiful they were, how delicious. Wouldn't it be wonderful if life could only be like that. One great big beautiful bubble . . . oh, to hell with it. As she brushed her teeth and looked at herself in the mirror, she was shocked . . . My God, she thought, I look like a witch this morning with all the eyeliner and mascara running under my eyes and how ludicrous, with one eyelash off. It must be in bed. Putting her hands up to her cheeks, she stretched up gently. What a difference when she let go. My God, the crevices were really deep. There was no more jaw line, it had all gone slack, just jowls that really sagged and bags that were really bulging and dark under the lower lids . . . and the uppers were all crisscrossed lines that fell into folds as did her throat. She winced painfully, observing herself with yesterday's stale makeup. The lipstick was all smeared. That was something she hadn't done in a long time . . . forgotten to remove her makeup; she looked like a clown. Catherine started to cry uncontrollably. Oh my, how much she had aged in the last few years and nothing could prevent that from happening, not man, not money and God certainly wasn't going to intervene with mother nature (the bitch) to knock it off on behalf of poor little Catherine Rossi. Nothing could prevent the process of erosion, not even plastic surgery. That was only temporary. Good Lord, what was going to happen to her in a few years from now. She cringed when she looked at her hands. Suddenly, she became infuriated at the thought that this was Dominic's fault, all his fault. She was young and beautiful until he had gotten into those goddamned politics and her anger became heightened when she thought that he looked so young for his age. He had a skin like a baby's behind, not a wrinkle in sight. God damn it . . . he should've looked ten years older according to the pace and race he was in. But no, not him, why he didn't even had a gray hair, son of a bitch, and here she'd been bleaching hers for fifteen years because graying prematurely was a family trait. She needed something to soothe her nerves. Going back to the bedroom, she poured a stiff belt of cognac into the tomato juice, sat down sobbing and sipped as the tears ran down her cheeks into her mouth, unaware she was swallowing them along with the drink. When the acute emotion had subsided, she picked herself up unsteadily and went back to the bathroom where the water had almost reached the rim of the tub and was ready to overflow.

Catherine had one remarkable quality and that was to make emotional transitions rapidly. One moment she could be in utter despair and the next totally elated. In an effort to restore the self-esteem that had been so devastating to her a few moments ago, she threw back her shoulders, walked across the enormous bathroom and sat down at the mirrored dressing table. She deliberately looked at herself, almost as though defying the fates, and aloud she said to her image in the looking glass, "You haven't lost your glamor nor your looks, not by a damn sight, so don't fret . . . just need a little body work, that's all, and a good face job and no one will ever guess the mileage we have on us . . . will they?" Resolutely, taking the bottle of cleansing emulsion, she unscrewed the cap and poured the thick creamy liquid into the palm of her hand. With very gentle, upward strokes, she massaged her face. Already her spirits were lifted. She tissued off the grime, washed her face with a very, very special soap, then rinsed it off in tepid water, dried it and applied gobs and gobs of moisture lotion. She looked and felt a hell of a lot better than she had a few minutes ago. That's what every woman needs . . . a little tender love and care . . . saying out loud to herself as she stepped down into the sunken tub. Lying back, her head resting on a rubber bath pillow, she simply relaxed and let the beautiful blue bubbles take over.

In spite of the way it had started out, the day did not progress too badly. By one, Catherine found she was hungry after all. Calling Mrs. Van Muir, she asked if lunch could be served to her immediately . . . why, of course, what was Mrs. Rossi's desire? Oh, let's see . . . a chicken salad with avocado, asparagus . . . the large white tips, hot rolls and butter, coffee and a napoleon . . . ha, still no napoleon. Oh, well, whatever.

After lunch, she felt drowsy and fell asleep. Awaking at four, she sat up in bed, drenched in perspiration. The room had become stifling with the Arizona sun beating down on her windows. She got out of bed, opened them wider and stood looking down at her fellow inmates sitting around the pool, dressed in bathing suits, chatting as they applied sun lotion to their chubby extremities. Suddenly, the inner composure she had fostered earlier diminished as she became lonely for some companionship. Whereas Catherine had never been a woman who had ever encouraged the friendship of other women, still, she envied the ones below who seemed so casually to be enjoying each other's company. Come to think of it, Catherine had never been able to sustain a meaningful relation-

ship with a friend. In fact, she had never had a really
close girl friend in whom she could confide. Strange,
when she thought about it . . . people always thought
of her as very outgoing and gregarious, as indeed she
was. Being born southern somehow gave a girl a special advantage. She was taught how to smile broadly
and say 'How ya all, darlin', but with a built-in charm
that was warm and captivating . . . Catherine was no
exception. She could charm the pants off anyone if it
suited her purpose. But the impression she projected
was far from what she was really like. The truth was,
the moment she felt a friendship becoming too close,
she backed away. Why? . . . she'd never been able to
analyze completely and she wasn't trying to do so
now. Still, maybe it had something to do with the fact
that when she looked backward at her childhood in
New Orleans, rich as the Posata's were, socially they'd
never been accepted into that part of old upper-class
society where position and one's past heritage counted,
not money. And for Catherine, it was important, terribly important, to be accepted, almost to the point of
obsession. Now, that's the truth isn't it, Catherine
thought. You bet your sweet ass. No use trying to
pretend it wasn't as you used to do. Italians living in
the deep south, no matter how many generations, were
looked down upon. Wops . . . plain old dagos, that's
what they were considered. And how many suitable,
wealthy families were there at the time she was growing up to choose from? Thirty, maybe, but all in the
same social boat, and just maybe it had left Catherine
with a feeling of immense inferiority. Somewhere
down deep she knew the feeling of discrimination
which had never left her. It made her suspect everyone. Who could you trust? How could you be sure that
in someone's mind they weren't sayin' wop . . . wop
. . . Catherine recalled only too well never being invited to the cotillion or the important parties even
though she had attended the best girls' school in New
Orleans, which Daddy paid for through the nose by

adding a new wing to the library. The tears long past, still stung when she recalled how hard her father had tried to see to it that Catherine made her coming out. He donated to the right causes, contacted people whom he felt could bring their influence to bear. But when the time came for her to be sponsored, Angelo Posata was discreetly and tactfully told they were so, so terribly sorry, but not this year. Sooo . . . Catherine cried a lot and abandoned the idea of ever being presented in that beautiful white dress with all the tulle draped so demurely around her shoulders, carrying the long-stemmed red roses and having her picture appear in the society column as one of the most exciting young debutantes of the year. Oh dear, the tragedies and memories of youth. She remembered wanting to die . . . but she survived. Angrily, she stood, shaking her head. Well, New Orleans would regret what they had done to her . . . yes, *she, Catherine Posata Rossi* was going to be the next senator from California. No . . . not the senator . . . the senator's wife. Hold on a minute, Catherine . . . just one cotton pickin' minute, a small voice within her whispered, yesterday you said you'd beat him at the polls . . . now that's the truth, isn't it? Yes, she screamed, but that was yesterday . . . today, I've decided I want him to win. However, he's goin' to shape up and I'm goin' to be the power behind the throne . . . if I have to wait this out till next Fourth of July.

Refreshed, she dressed, put on a pair of dark sunglasses, a bandanna and left the room that seemed to be closing in on her, went down the hall to the elevator, made her departure from the building, got into her rented Mercedes and drove to the liquor store.

It had been a long, emotional, tedious day and by eleven o'clock that evening she felt drained. Going to the bathroom, she prepared for bed, lubricated her face and hands after brushing her teeth, then her shoulder-length hair. She put her fingers up to her head and parted the blonde strands; there was about a half-inch of dark outgrowth. Funny, the things one

24

simply forgets in times of anger. She had a standing appointment every ten days for a touch-up and this was what . . . Tuesday? Oh, dear, Thursday was her day to be beautified. Well, no matter, she'd manage somehow. She'd managed things more difficult than this in her life . . . you bet, why, she could write a book. Turning, she went back to the bedroom and wearily climbed into bed, switched off the light, shut her eyes and there she lay waiting, praying for sleep to overtake her. But try as she might, tired as she was, she twisted and turned from one side to the next. It was impossible to get comfortable. Catherine punched the pillow hard. The room was oppressively hot, and the perspiration ran down her forehead. In desperation, she got out of bed, sat on the edge with her arms stretched out at her sides as her fingers clutched the mattress. She'd gotten dizzy for a few moments. Maybe it was the wine she had for dinner . . . maybe it was her nerves . . . maybe it was Dominic waiting for her in San Diego. She would have given anything to know his reaction when he found she was not present today or this evening. Was he angry . . . did he huff and puff and say, I'll blow your house down? To hell with you, Mr. Senator. Catherine walked quickly back into the bathroom and showered (bathing three to four times a day had been a compulsion of hers since childhood, as was her frantic aversion to disorder, especially when she was upset). Vigorously, she wiped herself dry. Nude, she returned to the bedroom, took the bottle from the ice hamper and poured herself a large glass, then sat down after turning on the Johnny Carson show, just in time for Ed McMahon to say, "and *here's* . . . *Johnny*" . . . Applause . . . Applause . . . And that's the last attention Catherine paid as she sipped her wine. The more she sipped, the greater her emotional fever rose until she cried out: What really happened to us, Dominic, we were happy, weren't we? In the beginnin', when you brought me as a bride to San Francisco? We were happy . . . God, I loved you so. She sobbed . . . then a sip . . . another sip and another and another . . . as she sat nude with the flicker of the television picture reflecting its color upon her body in the dark room. But her thoughts were now drifting . . . drifting. I was young and carryin' Dominic's first child. Oh, my, the joys that went into the conception of that child. Delirious, overwhelming, wild joy of being one. Catherine could look back and see it all so clearly, that first two-bedroom flat they had taken. How much was it? $85.00 . . . $95.00 a month . . . something like that. She laughed, but not happily at this moment, with the tears streaming down her face. Dominic really couldn't afford it. Not just startin' out in private practice, the way he did. Sure, he could've gone to his father. In fact, his father said it was foolish to struggle when there was no need . . . hadn't he struggled enough in his life for all his children? But Dominic wouldn't accept a dime, not a dime. Not because he was too proud to take . . . he didn't have to be proud, not with his papa, but he wanted to prove that he could also struggle . . . that a little of the old Sicilian dust had rubbed off on him. Dominic . . . Dominic, so handsome, so brilliant . . . so . . . so virile. No wonder his family resented me. They were jealous . . . just plain jealous that he'd married an outsider. And you, Dominic, loved them so, with such devotion, *you* made me feel like an outsider, too. No, that's not fair . . . I mean about you, it was them, them that always interfered between us, tryin' to pull us apart, tryin' to make me feel as though I were different . . . Oh, I don't know, but 'course, I was. I was a lady with a proper upbringin', proper and suited to be your wife . . . Oh, pooh, what do they mean, they never really mattered at all. It was just Dominic and me that first year as far as I was concerned. I don't know, maybe I did make mistakes. God, I'd never let him know I was aware I made 'em. Not even now would I do that, but between me, myself and I, I did sorta start out wrong. I mean by buyin' all those things, those elegant things for the house. I just couldn't wait . . . no, not me . . . spoiled rotten, given everythin' by my Mama and Daddy. But maybe I shouldn't have done it to Dominic. It really offended him, sorta like takin' his manhood away. I suppose that's really what it came down to. I remember so clearly him sayin' "Look Catherine, I really don't want to deny you and I know this is going to be difficult for you, but you knew when you married me you were going to live within my ability to support you in the best way I can." "I know, Dom, but I want us to have all the pretty things now . . . Why, for heaven's sake, I can afford 'em . . . you'd think I was doin' somethin' wrong. After all, I'm your wife, what's mine is yours—don't you know that, darlin'?" I remember how his eyes grew dark, not angry, mind you —good lawd, he was such a little boy, twenty-three after all.He took my small hand in his big paw and held it for a moment, then he said, "That's very kind, Catherine, and generous, but don't you see, *I* want to be able to give *you* all the things you want and are used to and I will, but just be patient for a little while. What I need now is more than money or beautiful things from you—I need your trust and belief in me; you're going to have to wait for the things you want— and if you just trust in me, I'm going to give you everything . . . so instead of things, Catherine dear, give me time—time to build my practice. Help me, stand by me and I'll buy you the moon—will you do that?" "Oh, yes, Dom, my darlin', darlin', Dom, I'd do anythin' for you." I still can feel that kiss that could always fire my passion. Oh dear, what a night of love-makin' that was. I was content for a little while and I meant to keep my promise to Dom, I really did, but —here I was stuck with all those gorgeous table linens, the Crown Derby china and that sterlin' silver, to say nothin' of the hundreds of gifts that Mama was sendin' out west to me. I simply had to have the place and space to store them, didn't I? So, I sashayed myself down to W. and J. Sloane's and bought a little furni-

27

ture ... well, I can tell you, I was as nervous as a wet hen until it arrived. And just as I expected, Dom hit the ceilin'. It was our first fight ... really big first fight, sayin' all sorts of mean and nasty things—just so as we could hurt one another ... and we did just that. My God, the things Dominic said positively shocked me. In fact, I get mad right now when I think about that night ... over thirty years ago. Callin' me a spoiled, possessive, uncontrolled, undisciplined bitch ... and 'course I wasn't about to take that kinda sass from him, not for one cotton pickin' minute, so I called him every name in the book I could think of—and in Italian it sounded even better. I ended by sayin' I hated him—and at that moment, I sure as hell did. But as though that wasn't enough, I threatened to pack my bag and go home—and I meant *that* for damn sure. I think what hurt me worse than anythin' was when Dom said he'd help me pack. Then I really got so damned mad, I threw somethin' at him—let's see, what was it? Oh, what difference does it make now, but I did hit him so hard, right in the stomach, he doubled over, then fell down on the floor, hittin' his forehead on the corner of our new coffee table. My God, did my heart pound—why I thought I'd killed him. I can see it all so clear, me runnin' over to him, takin' his head in my arms and rockin' him back and forth as the tears streamed down my face. "I'm so sorry, Dominic, darlin', I'm so heartsick, I really don't know why I do these things." Finally, he recovered and I washed away the blood. Like all quarrels, the makin' up was sweeter than ever—if that's possible. But it was—why, we found things to say to one another durin' our lovemakin' we'd never said before ... such sweet tender things—I really gave myself to Dom that night ... and did I ever give myself to him!

Catherine drank the last drop in the wineglass, sighed deeply. Weary, and a little light-headed, she roused herself as though out of a dream and looked at the television. The only thing on the screen was the big white silent blob staring back at her. Quickly, she got up and turned it off. She was so tired of thinking. Once again, she returned to bed, and this time, fell into a deep sleep which took her far into the third day of her self-imposed exile. When she awoke, it was one in the afternoon.

The day seemed endless, although she tried to busy herself with unimportant things. After lunch she manicured her nails, then applied coat after coat of pink polish which seemed never to dry. She flipped on the television, turned the knob from station to station, but everything bored her. Shaking her head she thought, wasn't total isolation dreadful. Never before had she known anything like it in her life. Funny—at one time, she would've given anything for a little quiet and peace—what with raising those seven rowdy, and at times, unmanageable children. But, oh my, how she and Dom had loved them. Taking the box of chocolates, Catherine carefully observed the contents. Reaching for a cream, she popped one in her mouth. Nothing like Barriccini's, but not bad for plain old store-bought. With the box of chocolates she lay across the bed and selected a nougat this time. Eating was such a sensuous delight; in fact, it could be downright comforting, with nothing else to do. Wait a minute, there was the radio. She turned it on, then lay back, popped another chocolate in her mouth, stared up at the ceiling and listened to the soft music play . . . wasn't that pretty . . .

My dear, sweet Jesus, only you know how I needed a friend that first year of my marriage. Now wouldn't you expect my own husband would understand the difficulty I had adjustin' into his new world? He had everythin', this was the place he'd been born, he had a brand-new bride and a baby on the way. But what about me, I'd left everythin' behind, all my loved ones, my traditions, the familiarities, the customs I'd known all my life, the place of my birth and my birthright. I missed the long, lovely, hot summers, sittin' out on the tree-sheltered piazza, just whilin' away a lazy afternoon with Mama and Rosa Ann, gossipin' and drinkin' cold lemonade. How wonderful it was when my relatives would drop in for casual visits on Sundays and stay for supper . . . the fun we had. Lawd, the food Mama would serve. That marvelous southern food . . . well, you can't leave all that behind and not have a few pangs of nostalgia. Goodness, how I missed and adored New Orleans at Mardi Gras . . . especially at Mardi Gras, with all the excitement of make-believe. It wasn't easy cuttin' myself off . . . everythin' was so different, so changed. The weather, so damp and cold in San Francisco, it burrowed right into the marrow of my bones, and I thought those damned foghorns would drive me crazy at first. But when I think back to the beginnin', Dominic never took time out to try and understand how lonely I really was. He used to get . . . oh, so upset when I'd tell him I didn't have anyone or anybody to talk to. He'd always give me the same kind of argument over and over. "You could, if you wanted to. There's nothing wrong with my family, they'd be only too happy to befriend you, but no, you keep your distance with them, I don't know what the hell's wrong, I really don't." "I've told you, Dominic, time and time again, I just don't feel comfortable with them. We're simply not the same kind of people." "Well, what the hell *kind* of people do you think they are?" "You're not tryin' to understand what I'm sayin', Dominic." "Alright tell me . . . what are you saying?" "I've told you before . . . we just don't have anythin' in common." "Now, what the hell is that suppose to mean?" "I mean we're just from two different worlds." "Two different worlds? Really, is that a fact? Well, let me tell you something . . . in the seven months we've been married, not once did you make an effort to have my family here and don't think for one minute they don't understand." Then I'd get mad, really mad and ask, "What are they supposed to understand?" "That you have some sort of an inflated opinion about yourself

. . . that you think you're too good for them." "Is that what *they* think?" I'd scream. "Yes," he'd scream back. But that wasn't the truth . . . it was unfair for him to say things like that to me, "Alright, if you must know, I do resent them, wantin' to hang on to you so tight, to smother you, to keep you tied to them. That's what I resent." "Is that so, is it really . . . well, let me tell you something, my family are fine, simple, down-to-earth people, and if you gave them half a chance, they'd embrace you like one of their own." "See, there you go . . . always takin' sides against me . . . defendin' them against me." I'd cry, as though my little heart would break. "You love them more than you love me . . . I just want to die . . . and I don't have anyone here . . . no one . . . not even you." With that, I'd run into the bedroom and lay down sobbing. Dominic would wait, holding down his temper I suppose, then come to my side, take me in his arms and hold me close. Finally, he'd say softly. "There's no one in this world I love more than you, don't you know that, Catherine . . . but you mustn't be jealous of them. They're no threat to you as far as I'm concerned." "I'm not jealous, really, I'm not," I'd answer, the tears streamin' down my cheeks, "I only want us to belong to each other, that's all, Dominic." "We do, darling, we do, please believe that." Then he'd dry my tears and I'd feel better, much better, knowin' I had Dominic seein' things my way.

Well, the next two months were a joy . . . growin' bigger and bigger with Dominic's child inside me. Soon I'd have somethin' of my own . . . my very own, my baby . . . then I wouldn't be so lonesome anymore. And Dominic couldn't have been more devoted. He'd call me three . . . four times a day . . . hard as he was workin', tryin' to get started. Like yesterday, I can remember that morning when my water broke. I had gone to the bathroom and suddenly, like all hell broke loose, I stood there with my legs apart watchin' what looked to me like Niagara Falls. Nervously, I called

31

to Dominic, who rushed into the bathroom. He was breathin' hard and tremblin'. "Oh, my God, it's happened . . . wait here till I get something," he said . . . as though I were goin' anywhere. With that. he ran from the room bumpin' into the door and stubbin' his toe. He swore under his breath. but came back limpin' with a pail which I straddled while he went to call the doctor. frantically. After the flow of water had subsided sufficiently. Dominic bundled me into a coat and away we went to the hospital Three blocks from our flat, Dominic remembered he had forgotten my overnight case and was about to turn back when I said he could pick it up later. I happened to look down at his feet and noticed that he had put on a blue sock and a beige. Laughing, I said, "And Dominic, when you go back, change your socks." I don't think he paid any attention to what I'd said. When we arrived at the hospital. I was taken to my room immediately and prepared. Dominic never left my side . . . only for the times when Dr. Vincente said he had to examine me. Then Dominic was back. holdin' my hand. I screamed and hollered I shamefully admit, more than was necessary in the beginnin', but I felt he should know how much a woman went through in presentin' her husband with his child Well, the hours went on . . . by now, I had good reason for screamin' and hollerin' and I wasn't thinkin' about Dominic or anythin', just gettin' this child born. Finally, after six hours, I was taken to delivery, and greedily, I breathed in the gas anesthetic . . . one more hard push and there it was, that chubby little red baby boy, black-haired and dark-eyed. I swear, from the moment he saw the light of day, he looked just like *my* Daddy. What a baby . . . nine pounds, two-and-a-half ounces . . . he was so big, I thought he was gonna get off that table and walk right out of that room. I couldn't believe, for all the world, that I could've been big enough to give birth to a baby that size, tiny as I was . . . or thought I was, but the doctor said, "You're a born mother, you have

the perfect build for it." Then I was given somethin'
for sleep. When I awoke, Dominic was there, standin'
over me. He stroked my hair and held my hand. How
touchin' it all was, watchin' that big man with tears
in his eyes. "Are you happy, Dominic, darlin'?" "Oh
God, Catherine, you have no idea what I feel . . . to
think of what you've given me." I smiled weakly and
said, "It's been a pleasure doin' business with you,
Mr. Rossi."

When I look back on that first year, in spite of
all the quarrels and the makin' up and adjustin' to
married life, I'd say all in all it hadn't been any
different or more difficult than most young newly
married people have. Sure I took things seriously and
maybe overreacted at times and blamed Dominic for
a lot of things because I wanted him to be what I
wanted, and what I wanted was for Dominic to
keep reassuring me I was his whole life. But I suppose for a man that's not quite what he needs—to
make a woman his whole existence. A woman is different, she needs that, because, for all her emancipa-
tion, or her so-called independence, she really just
stepped out of the stone age. Bein' pulled out of
a cave by the hair wasn't so long ago and to walk
out of *that* into the Steinem age is kind of a hard
thing to come face to face with. I've been readin' a
lot about this lady lib stuff lately, in search of myself.
But that lady lib stuff didn't have one little bit to
do with me when I was a new wife and mother.
Sure, I'd fight back to try and defend myself against
Dominic Because he could be very persuasive when
he wanted to be, and had I allowed it, he could have
submerged me and my personality. I had to fight him
hard all the way to try and stay a woman in my own
rights . . . not that I did a very good job of it in
the beginnin'. I'm sure I never would've won any
prizes from the lady libbers. The truth is, that here
I was with money of my own to do with as I wanted,
and Dominic with his male ego would fight me for
spendin' what was mine. However, I did as I damned

well pleased, buyin' some of the things I wanted anyway, but he never knew how guilty he made me feel—which is not exactly what Gloria is advocatin' . . . but that's the way I always felt . . . *guilty*, guilty, guilty. But then Gloria Steinem wasn't in love or married to someone like Dominic Rossi . . . I was, and please forgive me, lady libbers of the world, I was never as happy or content as when I was pregnant. At these times I felt Dominic was mine, all mine, and lovin' him as I did, I saw to it I was pregnant just about as often as I possibly could be. I never did get around to wearin' my trousseau.

Eighteen months after baby Dom, I gave Big Dom another son. Salvatore, whom we called Tory.

Although Dominic's practice began to gain some momentum, he still wasn't makin' just gobs of money and we needed a new house. When we looked, everythin' I wanted was more than Dominic could afford. And as always, the problem of my money reared its ugly head. "Dominic, I'm just not goin' to move into one of those ugly old houses just because you're so damned stubborn." "Goddamn it, Catherine, we go through this all the time. I'm giving you the best I can for the time being. For Christ's sake, can't you just wait?" "No, because it's not the best *I* can afford and I'm not gonna raise my children like poor white trash." Dominic answered, "I'd hardly call this living like poor white trash. Who the hell do you think you are, Catherine de Medici?" "No, I'm Catherine Antoinette Frances Posata Rossi and I'm gonna live in a style I'm accustomed to. I've had enough of livin' in a place like that awful flat we're gettin' out of. Maybe that's good enough for your family, but not for *me*." Dominic went into a rage, "Well, goddamn it, you should've married a millionaire, not me . . . and leave my family out of this." "Maybe I should've done just that," I screamed back. For a week we didn't talk, then finally, Dominic calmed down and by that time I was so utterly miserable, I guess I'd have moved into the city dump if it could've been with Dominic. So we compromised . . . we bought that five-bedroom Victorian on Scott Street . . . but I furnished it.

In the meantime, Mama and Papa came out to see us. They hadn't seen the children because poor Daddy couldn't travel since he had had a severe heart attack and in the last year, he'd been doctorin'. It broke my heart that I couldn't go back to New Orleans. but I couldn't leave Dominic alone with little Dom and Tory and I was expectin' . . . so those telephone calls flew between San Francisco and home. It set us back a pretty penny, I can tell ya. But when Mama saw the house, I thought she was goin' to faint. *Her Catherine* . . . livin' in a place like this? "Well, Mama," I said, jokingly. of course, "you picked my husband for me . . . it's really your fault marryin' me off to some strugglin' lawyer." She smiled and answered, "I guess we have to be sensible . . . after all, Catherine, you're not married to a house, you can always sell it. But Dominic's a young man with a good future . . . and I truly believe, in my heart, he's a man of destiny." I've thought about that many times and wondered if Mama really realized how very profound she was or if she was just sayin' that to make me feel better . . . but she really hit the nail on the head, didn't she?

By George, no sooner had Tory turned one, I found myself pregnant again. But this time the nine months were miserable, really miserable. In the beginnin' I threw up constantly. Nothin' agreed with me, I felt sick and weak most of the time. I simply had to get some extra help in to assist with little Dom and Tory, and this time Dominic didn't complain, not once. In fact, I think I felt closer to him durin' that pregnancy than almost at any other time in our married life. His solicitude was so reassurin' and comfortin'. I'll just never forget it.

By this time, he was just about to the point in his practice where he was makin' a good livin'. In fact,

Dominic's name was beginnin' to appear in the newspaper as havin' won a large injunction against a major corporation. And always, there were little things said in the article about Mr. Dominic Rossi bein' the most promisin' young attorney that had come along in years . . . and naturally I was proud. In fact, I began to make a scrapbook of all of his clippin's. I'd buy an extra paper and send the article for Mama to see. But with all he had on his mind and as hard as he was workin', he managed to call me several times a day, if only for a minute before rushin' off to court.

Well, the months passed slowly and toward the end, my belly looked like one of those New Orleans overripe watermelons. I had the worse time gettin' in and out of bed. During the night, I would moan when I had to get out and go to the bathroom . . . and Dominic would wake up and help me. I can tell ya, I wondered many times how he could go into court bleary-eyed with hardly any sleep with me gruntin' half the night tryin' to turn from one side to the next. Finally with the help of the dear Lord, my time had come. And what a surprise that was. Heaven help us! We had twin boys. Angelo and Anthony . . . those adorable little pink chubby babies, whom we came to call Angie and Tony. Well, you'd just think no one in this entire universe had ever been the father of twins, the way Dominic strutted around and crowed. I swear, he was just about the proudest man alive. I just hate myself for admittin' that I could've had a . . . a mild case of jealousy over those poor little innocent babies. No, not them really, it was all the attention and lovin' they were receivin' from everybody and somehow, I felt neglected, especially after Dominic was so terribly concerned about me durin' those nine months. Suddenly, it seemed to me that all I was good for was producin' his inventions. I had the feelin' of bein' a conceivin' machine, poppin' out one child after another. Good Lord almighty . . . I'd never let a soul know I ever harbored such thoughts, why people'd think I was downright wicked

... I don't know ... maybe I am just a little, but who hasn't got faults for heaven sakes. I got mine but I do believe most faults are inherited and there's not much a body can do about that except admit to yourself you're just human. But I do think I showed my character by gettin' over those feelin's in a hurry and no one was the wiser. By the time *me* and the babies came home, we were one big happy family again.

Things really began to sail along for Dominic. I have to admit no one worked harder than he did. Those first few years he was almost like a mechanical man, wound up. Runnin' here, runnin' there, in such a big hurry. He didn't really have to, not with the income I had comin' in from all the inheritance my poor sainted Daddy left me. That was just about the saddest time in my life and the first time I left Dominic and the babies to fly home for that awful agonizin' event. It's just not to be believed, the things one can endure. In my state of bereavement, mingled with all the pain, I was never more angry with Dominic because he wouldn't leave that damned practice to go back with me ... he would have, but reluctantly. Why? Because he was smack in the middle of the biggest trial he'd had up to then and had the nerve to say there was no one to replace him. "No one to replace you," I said lettin' him know how hurt I was, "why, who do you think you are? No one is irreplaceable. Presidents and kings die and the country goes on and you've got one lousy case and can't leave it when my Daddy is laid out in his coffin?" He bit his lip and said, "Alright Catherine, I'll leave ... I'll go, if that's what you want." "No, sir ... you're not gonna put me in a position of blamin' me in the future for your losin' that case as I know you will. I don't want you to come ... I wouldn't have you come now." Well, I made that mournful trek back alone. And I stayed with Mama for three weeks ... I will say this, Dominic called just about every night, and like most women, I'm sure I was cold and remote and downright nasty the first week. Maybe, a little less so the next, and by the end of that third week, I was so lonesome for Dominic and those sweet darlin' babies of mine, I really couldn't wait to fly back into Dominic's arms when he asked in a sad and soulful way, "When do you think you're coming home, Catherine." Of course, I wasn't about to let him know my desires were greater than his, so holdin' back, tryin' to give the impression of reserved consideration that I was makin' a great sacrifice, I answered, "Soon as I get things straightened out for Mama. After all, you've got the babies for comfort and your family who, I'm sure, are hoverin' about seein' that things are in order." "Please, Catherine . . . please, darling, I know you're under a great strain, and I don't want you to be upset more than you are, but my family are not here. The help are managing more than efficiently. I know you're still hurt and angry at me for not going home with you and I can't say I blame you and I apologize as I have before. As I've said before, nothing would have kept me from going with you under different circumstances, but this case was so terribly important to us . . . will you just try and understand?" "For *us*?" "Yes . . . for *us*, for our future." "But I already have a future. My Daddy left me more income property than I'll ever be able to spend . . . won't *you* try and understand?" There was silence on the phone for a long time, but I could hear Dominic's breathin'. "Dominic . . . are you there?" Softly, he answered, "Yes, I'm here." "Well?" "Catherine, this is not the time nor the place to discuss this . . . and besides we've been through it so many times before." "Then let's go through it one more time . . . tell the truth, so help you God . . . just like you make those people swear that get up on the stand with a Bible in their hand . . . why do you refuse to share with me what I got? Is it that damned male ego surfacin' again?" "Okay, Catherine, you just won't let it alone, will you . . . alright, I will not take your money and feel like a pimp. I'm a man . . .

a proud Sicilian who's still got all those peasant corpuscles running through my veins. My father made it on his own and supported his wife and family as best he could, but he was a man and do you know what a man is? Don't bother to answer, I'll tell you. A man is only a man when his wife makes him feel like one. I will not take your money . . . I will not be beholden to you or anyone. I'm going to be my own man and do the giving . . . now, Catherine, just one more time . . . when are you coming home?"

This time I paused for a lone, long moment while Dominic waited, but I knew he'd never ask again. Finally, I was compelled to say what any woman would've said, "I'll be leavin' tomorrow morning." Of course, I knew right then I'd lost the ball game. That Dominic was not gonna bend like a willow, not when it came to bein' his own man. Of course, I really didn't want to dominate him . . . or domineer over his ambitions . . . but he thought I did, I guess. I only offered it to him outta the goodness of my heart and for us to have a little more of the nicer things in life.

As sure as I'm layin' on this bed and daydreamin' . . . I can see that day as if it was yesterday. My goodness, how young I was and pretty too, as I stepped off that plane dressed all in black. It was the least I could do for my Daddy for whom I mourned (and would for a long time). But when I saw Dominic lookin' down from the window at the airport, holdin' the twins and little Dom and Tory standin' on chairs, all wavin' to me, I thought I'd die, my heart pounded so. Good Lord, I loved and missed them more than I even realized. I walked as fast as I could down those landin' stairs, then ran as fast as I could down to the buildin' where my own little family waited. There was somethin' in the way I felt at that moment . . . a feelin' I can't explain, but I needed them all at that moment so very, very much . . . like they were all makin' up for my great loss. The next thing I knew, I had my arms around little Dom and Tory . . . how adorable they looked runnin' to meet me, callin' "Mama, Mama." I kissed and hugged them as though I'd never let 'em go. "My two precious lambs, you've really missed Mama haven't you, and oh dear, how Mama missed her little sugars. I'm just never gonna go way and leave again . . . never." I took them proudly by the hand to meet Dominic, but when I came face to face with him, the tears just spilled over. I couldn't control myself nor did I want to. It was my way of showin' Dominic how much I loved him. He gave the twins to Anna, our nursemaid, and I clung to him, weepin' and sayin', "Dominic, my Dominic, I'm home."

He answered, "I'm glad, we missed you."

Then I took the twins and smothered them with kisses, "Look at my babies . . . my little Angie and . . ."

"No, he's Tony," Dominic said, laughing.

"Oh, lawd, how am I ever gonna tell the difference?"

That night after the children had been put to bed, Dominic and I went to our room. We had a lot of time to make up for. The three weeks separation had seemed like a century. Oh God, how good he felt layin' so close to me, breathin' hard. It was like we just couldn't get enough of each other. The feelin's that man could evoke in me. Each time was almost like the first . . . even better. Then we were quiet, listenin' to each other's breathin' in the silent room. I was the one who broke the silence, "Dominic, did you miss me?"

"Terribly."

"What did you do in my absence?"

"Just worked hard. Of course, I saw the children before they went to bed every night."

"Oh . . . and did they ask for me?"

"All the time."

"Where'd you have dinner? . . . at your mother's mostly?" I was just jokin' him, but he seemed to resent that, which was surely apparent by his answer.

"Now, why do you ask me that, and what difference would it have made, since you were away?"

"No difference, just curious, that's all . . . just wanted to know if my sugar was eatin' well, that's all . . . did you take the babies over?"

Dominic was so sensitive, his voice was a little irritated. He raised up on his elbow, held his face in his hand and said, "I didn't say I had dinner at my mother's."

"I know you didn't . . . but I was just wonderin' . . . did you?"

"Yes."

"Did you take the children?"

"Yes."

"Why you gettin' so worked up, darlin', after all, I'm a wife and mother, it's only natural I'd be wonderin' how you'd be spendin' your time . . . now, that's not so unreasonable is it?"

"No . . ."

"Well then . . . lay back, Dominic, and put your arms around me. I've missed them so." After Dominic took me in his arms, we clung together, at least I did . . . always so ready to receive him. One thing I never had was a headache when he wanted me. "Dominic?"

"Yes?"

"Do you love me?"

"How can you ask me that?"

I laughed, "That's a funny thing for a big lawyer to do."

"What's that?"

"Answerin' a question with a question."

"It's not any funnier than asking me something you should already know."

"I don't think so . . . every woman has to be sure and from time to time, she just wants to hear it said."

"I tell you all the time I love you."

"No, you don't . . . not always."

"Come on, Catherine, that's just plain nonsense."

"Now don't get into a snit, sugar . . . it's just because I've been away so long . . . Dominic?"

"Yes?"

"Why'd you marry me?"

"Well . . . that's just got to be the goddamndest question you could ask."

"Hold on now, Dominic . . . don't let your Sicilian corpuscles start pulsatin' through your veins. I just asked a simple question, why'd you marry me?"

"Because I loved you, Catherine."

"Oh . . . and what was so redeemin' about me?"

"Really, Catherine, this sounds so damned childish . . ."

"To you maybe, but not to a woman. What was there about me you fell in love with?"

Dominic laughed sorta strange. It wasn't really a happy laugh, but he said, "I fell in love with you because you're beautiful . . . I didn't analyze it. Love is something a person feels. I don't know, Catherine . . . how the hell can you explain love . . . there was just something about you, the way you talked, being southern, so different from anyone I'd ever met. You were simply adorable and provocative."

"And rich."

"What the hell is that suppose to mean?"

"Oh . . . oh, Dominic, you're gettin' mad."

"Of course I am. You're also so damned irritating at times."

"So, the fact I had money didn't impress you, one little bit?"

"Yes, it impressed me totally, that's why I married you . . . is that what you want me to say?"

"If that's what you felt . . . yes, there's nothin' wrong with a *little* honesty . . . is there?"

"Nothing at all wrong with a *lot* of honesty . . . do you know what I think as long as you brought up the subject?"

"Yes . . . I'd like to hear."

"Okay, you ready for this?"

"I surely am."

"Fine . . . you've got a problem."

"I have, have I, and what's that?"

"Your problem is . . . you simply can't believe anyone could love you in spite of your money . . . you've got an obsession about it. Catherine, why can't you believe you're a beautiful and worthwhile person?"

"I do, Dominic, I mean the worthwhile part that is."

"No, I don't think so, Catherine."

"Dominic, don't say that to me. I know what I think . . . I couldn't have given you those four beautiful babies if I wasn't worthwhile . . . now could I?"

"We're not talking about the same thing. Giving birth . . . the act of childbearing has nothing to do with character. I'm not talking about motherhood."

Now I was really irritated and I wasn't about to take that lyin' down, so I said, "Look here Dominic, I really resent that. You surely must've thought I had plenty of character when you married me or you thought I had plenty of *somethin'*."

"I did think you had character and an inner strength which I admired when I first met you . . . I didn't know however that you had a complex . . . an inferiority complex."

"How dare you say that to me!"

"Because it's true. When someone has to be re-assured as often as you do, it can only mean one thing . . . that they feel unsure of themselves. Catherine, why can't you believe you're a worthwhile person, a lovely, lovable, beautiful woman whose husband married her because he loved her . . . *her* and not *her money*. Forget your money and learn to give . . . give of yourself, that's all I want . . . why you didn't even ask how the trial came out."

"I was gonna, but what with all the excitement of seein' the children and wantin' to love you, I haven't had time."

"Well, you've got time now."

43

I really was peeved at Dominic for sayin' those things to me, but as a dutiful wife, I asked, and very kindly I must say, "How did the trial come out?" But I'll be damned if it isn't a man's world . . . he was angry at me! Imagine, after he had let me know I didn't quite measure up to his expectations. But the thing Dominic was unaware of was my bein' a lady with the kinda breedin' I had . . . so as a dutiful wife I asked again, "Dominic, how was the trial?"

"Fine."

I swallowed my pride and overlooked his sullenness and asked again, "Did you win?"

"Yes."

"Oh, Dominic, I'm so proud, I really am."

"I'm so glad," he answered . . . without kissin' me or sayin' another word. Then he turned around and fell asleep after all the lovemakin' we'd had earlier and left me layin' awake there in the dark.

Well . . . as I could've predicted . . . me with my ability toward fertility, I was expectin' again. But this time, Dominic and I prayed it would be a girl, however I couldn't fight those Rossi genes. It was a boy . . . eight-and-three-quarter pounds . . . We called him Bobby which was pretty Anglo-Saxonized for Roberto Pasquale Mario Posata Rossi. Oh my, the weight I put on with that *one* . . . about forty pounds, give or take . . . and if there's anythin' I loathe is havin' to deprive myself of a most pleasurable delight such as eatin' and the kinda food our Stella could make . . . I declare. She was the best Italian cook this side of Genoa, that heavenly pasta. I have to chuckle when I recall her sayin', "Youa gonna eata signora *per gli nuovo bambino*." I took her advice (in half-Italian and half-English). I did just that and the result was . . . I simply hate to think about it. I once wore a size six and weighed about ninety-nine drippin' wet. Not that I was jealous, mind you, but Dominic was still too young and handsome for me to let myself go, especially with those cute little secretaries he now had in the office . . . well, it wasn't exactly for *them* or *anyone* for that matter that I decided to go on a diet; it was *my* pride that led me close to starvation that year. I can say this even if it is only to myself . . . talk about strength of character.

No sooner had I gotten myself down and begun to buy a new wardrobe, there I was pregnant again and this time I held the most adorable, precious little baby girl in my arms. For all my sons, there's somethin' so special about a daughter, especially my Gina Maria. And Dominic . . . I thought he would go mad with excitement. Good Lord, an Italian father with a daughter. I can remember my darlin' Daddy bein' so protective havin' to know just who I was goin' out with because no one was gonna get their grubby hands on . . . or climb into the hay with *his* little Catherine without the benefit of clergy. Oh, Daddy, if you could see the anguish your sweet little Catherine is goin' through now, you wouldn't have been so anxious to marry me off to that Italian import from the west with all the Sicilian corpuscles runnin' through his veins.

Catherine was brought up sharply from her long excursion into the past by a persistent knock on the door. She rallied herself to the occasion and barefooted, went to open it. There stood Mrs. Van Muir ready to wheel in the dinner cart. The room was in total darkness. Quickly, Catherine switched on the bedside lamp.

"How are you this evening, Mrs. Rossi?" Mrs. Van Muir asked, full of solicitude.

"Just fine," Catherine answered trying not to reveal her inner turmoil. Casually, she asked, "Did anyone inquire about me?"

"No . . . no, there were no calls."

Damn it all . . . have a family, a husband, and nobody gives a damn. She could be lying at the bottom of Grand Canyon as far as any of them were concerned. When Mrs. Van Muir left, Catherine poured herself a large glass of wine and sat down to dinner. It was really the only solace she had at this moment. Removing the silver domes from the platters, she sniffed. The roast beef was done to perfection with all the au jus gravy poured over it, the small new potatoes, buttered and parsleyed, made her pick one up and bite into it as she observed the salad and soup. The hot rolls smelled yeasty and fragrant and at last . . . at long last, there it sat as cozy as anything, a chocolate frosted napoleon. The only thing that was missing was a little soft music and candlelight. *That* she couldn't accommodate herself with, but she turned on the radio. It played softly as she launched into the salad . . . so crisp, the dressing was positively fabulous. She'd have to ask for the ingredients. The soup was one of her favorites, vichyssoise, cold and subtle. The rest of the dinner was sheer ambrosia and the pièce de résistance, the dessert, so flaky and delicate. Nothing like a scrumptious dinner, polished off with cognac to soothe the savage soul, was there . . . no, nothing, except a husband to share it with . . . Goddamn it, Dominic, get out of my thoughts. That's all I've done in the last hours is think about how nice it might've been if you were only content to be like other husbands, coming home after a hard day at the office and shuttin' out the world . . . but not you . . . always runnin' after another dream, reachin' for a higher star. You should've been the first man on the moon. And you could've, without Cape Canaveral. She settled back in the large chair and sipped the cognac, but Dominic still was there to haunt her. What the hell was he doing tonight? Wasn't he the least little bit worried about why she hadn't followed him to San Diego? *Calm down,* Catherine, the little voice within her sounded loud and clear . . . it was like the Mahony boys running after her with pitchforks. Times have changed, Catherine . . . not like it was a few years ago when you'd go dashin' off to the Farm trying to punish Dominic for his negligence . . . or screamin' and threatenin' you were goin' back home to New Orleans . . . then waitin' for him to call, which he finally usually did after a week . . . naturally angry in the beginnin' because he said you were drivin' him out of his mind. But did that make me feel guilty? Not a bit. Why? I'll tell you . . . for two reasons. First the children were all grown and second I no longer had to worry about him havin' a lady love in his life 'cause once he got hooked on politics he neither had the time . . . the urge . . . nor would he risk the chance of any possible scandal . . . not like some, I'll say that for him . . . One thing about Dominic, he's a man with a hell of a lot of discipline when it comes to somethin' he wants and he wanted to be a politician and eventually a United States senator no one could point a finger at . . . untainted, no stains, that's our Dominic . . . wouldn't jeopardize his name for no one or nothin'. Yes siree, so I guess for that reason I took him for granted in these last years, not having to worry about where he was spending his nights. Oh come, Catherine, give the devil his due. . . . He was never really a card-carryin', dyed-in-the-wool womanizer. So that's not what's botherin' you at this moment . . . no . . . what's botherin' me is that he would never face the fact that I'd pleaded with him not to get involved in politics. I said it would be bad for our home life . . . I told him. Did he listen? No. But I have to reiterate . . . it's a man's world, and that's for damn sure. I'm askin' what do you do when you try to make a man realize he's destroyin' you with his strength, self-importance and ambition. Well, I'll tell you, my darlin', you do a lot of crazy foolish things when you're dealin' with a fool . . . and I say he is a fool, because he traded me for the limelight and tried to push me aside when he could've had the world in me and the children. We could've been like a safe harbor. But here I am, ramblin' on and on like I was losin' my mind. I don't know, sometimes I think I am . . . I get so aggravated when I think nothin' I ever did worked . . . like leavin' Dominic when he started in politics to come to the Farm . . . I'll never forget the first time . . . I really had him . . . because he was frightened . . . a politician needs a wife and I had the advantage over him but was too dumb to see it . . . that was the time, yes, sir . . . I could've said, look, I'll make a deal with you, Dominic, give up the race and I'll come home and you wouldn't have to be beggin' anymore . . . or if you don't, I'm *through* with you . . . Hear? But did I say that . . . ?No. When he called I acted just like any other woman, but I was so damned lonesome hearing the sound of his voice sayin' "Catherine, come on home and we'll talk about it. In fact, we'll do more than talk. I'm taking you to Rome and I don't want you to say *no*—not this time."Maybe *this* just might be a new beginnin' . . . except the grapes don't get sweeter just 'cause they been hangin' on the vine a long time . . . imagine, him sayin' that just threw me into a state of complete confusion. I wasn't thinkin' straight. If I was, I would've stuck to my guns and held my ground. But no, dumb dodo that I was, I succumbed. "I don't want you to say no . . ." That's all it took and there I was goin' home . . . where did it get me? Back to the Farm after that glorious Roman holiday . . . with my little ass in a sling. You know why? Because the trip didn't solve a thing . . . and now it's like the boy who called wolf just once too often. My goin' away no longer disturbs Dominic like it did in the beginnin'. . . . That's why he hasn't bothered to inquire about me. You don't think it hurts? It sure as hell does, 'cause I'm just not important to him any longer in any way . . . and that doesn't lift a lady's spirits, now does it? Well, Dominic . . . you don't know it yet, but I got a great big surprise in store for you. This is a new ball game. Slightly embarrassed, red-faced and plenty ashamed you're gonna be when it comes out how I've been abused and mistreated. Everybody's gonna know who

I am . . . make no mistake about that, Dominic, my darlin' . . . so you can look all you want after you've come to the realization I'm really playin' for keeps this time . . . I won't come back, if and when you simmer down long enough to realize I'm missin' . . . not this time . . . not if I have to wait until hell freezes over.

Catherine's righteous indignation really boiled over the more she thought about it. She had to get out of here . . . everything was choking her. Quickly, she changed into a sleeveless dress, flats, and ran from the room . . . then from the building and finally into the Mercedes and away in a cloud of dust until she disappeared onto the main road where she drove and drove for miles. By the time Catherine returned to her room, she was weary, but much of the frustrations and hostilities she had felt earlier were dispelled. After drawing the bath, she poured herself a glass of wine, sipped as she went back into the bathroom and undressed, then slipped into the bubbles that covered her slightly plump body and there she found comfort as she reached for the glass of wine that had been placed on the edge of the tub and continued to drink slowly. Relaxed, she dried herself, applied some night cream, then slipped into bed. It was one o'clock before she turned off the bedside lamp and fell asleep almost immediately. At four, she awoke from a dream which she couldn't remember, but it had been dreadful, and now she lay wide awake in the dark. It was impossible to turn off the avalanche of thoughts that invaded her mind . . . and they took her back to that mansion perched on the edge of a cliff overlooking San Francisco Bay and the Golden Gate Bridge. She would never forget seeing it for the first time. It was magnificent with all its nine bedrooms, plus maids' quarters. The marble foyer with its imposing, regal, winding staircase . . . that enormous living room with the solarium adjacent . . .

then across to the dining room, a perfect size for a family as large as they had acquired . . . and the kitchen was almost as large as the dining room, but the garden was the thing that Catherine loved almost more than anything. Although there was nothing about it that resembled that garden back home, somehow being in front and enclosed by a high brick wall, the beautiful trees and shrubs which sheltered it from the winds that came off the bay, made her pause reflectively. This was the house of her dreams and she was going to have it. She was expecting her seventh child and the house on Scott had become obsolete long ago. Not only had she loathed it from the beginning, but it had only five bedrooms.

Dominic's practice had grown tremendously in the ten years since their marriage, so that he was on his way to becoming not only a man of wealth, much of which he invested in property, but an outstanding attorney who had acquired a reputation as probably one of the best corporation lawyers in the country. Now, Catherine wouldn't wait any longer . . . she bought the house without Dominic knowing it or seeing it; in fact, negotiated a very good deal on the price. She knew there was going to be a confrontation, but was ready for it. This time, Dominic wasn't going to force her into a compromise as he had done in the past with the old house and she knew if she had shown it to him in advance, he would have tried, since it really was a little more than he could afford at this time, in spite of the fact he was doing so well. But so what, they were going to live in it for the rest of their lives.

Catherine waited for what she felt would be the best psychological time (which Mama had always said was at the height of a man's passion and Mama's advice seemed extremely sensible in this case) . . . so that night, she made sure her femininity was alluring. She bathed and drenched herself with perfume, put on her most exquisite sheer gown, looked at herself sideways in the long mirror . . . her tummy was still fairly flat, although she was close to four months pregnant. Her hair hung below her shoulders (which was the way Dominic loved it . . . in fact, he said when she wore it loose, it made him sexy as all hell). She got into bed alongside of Dominic and snuggled close to him, ran her fingers through his hair, then gently down his back. Soon the desired results of all her attentions were felt as they shared that rapturous moment. Just at the culmination of their sharing, Catherine held Dominic even closer and whispered, "I love you, I really do."

And Dominic answered in staccato whispers, "I love you, too, darling."

Catherine whispered breathlessly, "Do you really?"

"Oh, yes, *mia cara.*"

"Would you give me anything I wanted?"

"I'd buy you the world."

"Would you really, my Dominic?"

"Oh, yes . . . yes . . . yes . . . yes . . . yessss."

After they lay quietly for a while, Catherine said, "You've made me so happy darlin', you really have."

"That makes me happy, Catherine, knowing you're content."

"Oh, I'm more than content, I'm positively ecstatic . . . there aren't many women whose husbands would give them the world, especially since there's just one."

"I would, if I could, believe me."

"Oh, I believe you, Dominic, but I think that would be a little too expensive . . . even for you. So you know what I did?"

"No, what?"

"I let you buy me a new house instead—who needs the world?"

Dominic thought for a moment, then laughed, "I don't get it . . . you let *me* buy *you* a new house?"

"That's right, darlin', you don't know it yet, but you bought me a house today."

Dominic moved his arm away, switched on the light and struck the same pose he had so many times in their married life. Up on his elbow with his hand cupped around his chin, looking at Catherine as though he were afraid to ask what it was that she had done. Finally, he asked, "Okay, let's hear what this is about?"

"I just told you, Dominic, we've got a new house."

"We've . . . got a new . . . house?"

"That's right, darlin'."

Dominic bit his lower lip, "Alright, let's start from the beginning . . . slowly."

"There's nothing much to tell, Dominic. This house is simply too small for us . . . it has been for a long time, you know that and I haven't complained till now, so I saw a house I knew would be perfect and bought it . . . that is, I put down a large payment and have made arrangements for the loan which, of course, you're gonna have to sign because of those crazy community laws you got in this awful state."

"You did *what?*" Dominic exploded.

"I just got through tellin' you, Dom, just as slowly as I could . . . we got a new house."

Dominic jumped out of bed. The muscles in his jaw tightened as he began to breathe hard and pace the floor. Finally, he turned and stood staring down at Catherine, the anger written clearly in his eyes. Mama was right, but Catherine was wrong. Her timing had been bad . . . she should've told him in the midst of their rapturous moment when he was on fire with lust. Catherine had never seen him quite so furious, and for a moment she recoiled within herself, but just as quickly she rallied to the occasion. Once and for all, he was going to understand that everything was not going to be his way so she stood her ground when he screamed, "Goddamn it, Catherine, how could you do such a thing as buying a house without my knowledge or permission?"

"What do you mean *your* permission? Since when am I chattel . . . you don't own me . . . they freed the slaves a long time ago."

"You little bitch, didn't you think I should have been consulted?"

"No, *I did not*, because if I had, it would've been the same as before and don't you *ever* . . . *ever* call me a bitch again . . . you hear? Why, I have to laugh . . . just a few minutes ago you wanted to buy me the world and now you're blowin' your brains out because I asked for a new house."

"That's just the point, you didn't ask, you took it upon yourself to go out and buy one on your own. A husband and wife talk about that sort of thing."

"Oh, really? . . . well, the last time we talked about *that sorta thing*, I ended up livin' in what you wanted and hatin' myself for it."

"You sound like you've been living in the ghetto. A lot of people would give their eyeteeth to have a house like this, but if it wasn't *grand* enough for you, well, it's the best I could afford and then some."

"But it's not now."

"Then in that case, why the hell didn't you come to me and sit down and talk it out?"

"Because I knew what you'd say . . . that it was too expensive and that you had all your money tied up in stocks and bonds and property and God knows what. No, sir, Dominic, my children aren't gonna keep on livin' in a place like this. I'm gonna live a gracious life with all the comforts I was accustomed to when you took me from my home."

"Okay, you can have all the comforts you're accustomed to, since you feel I've deprived you so . . . but you can live there without me. Do you hear, Catherine, because I'm leaving. I've had enough of this for ten years."

"You shouldn't have married me! Should've married someone like your sister Theresa."

"You're absolutely right." With that, he hurried into his clothes, grabbed a suitcase from the closet and began wildly to pack.

"And where the hell do you think you're goin'?"

He didn't answer, just kept on packing.

Catherine jumped out of bed and stood in front of him, "Dominic, I'm warnin', don't do somethin' you're gonna regret . . . I'm warnin' you."

"Get out of my way."

"No, goddamn it, you aren't gonna leave this house."

He pushed her to one side. Suddenly, Catherine was on the floor where she had slipped and fallen. She let out a scream in pain. Dominic knelt down and picked her up, then put her on the bed, "My God, Catherine, are you alright?"

All the anger was forgotten in that moment. "No, I think . . . I think I'm really hurt, Dominic . . . I think I'm bleedin'." She cried out, "Oh, Dominic, I don't want to lose my baby, I couldn't bear that."

"It's alright, Catherine, I'm going to call Dr. Vincente." Dominic was shaking as he spoke to the doctor and explained there had been an accident. Dr. Vincente did not question him as to how it had occurred, but said he would be there immediately, then Dominic went back to Catherine. He pulled up a straight-backed chair, sat next to the bed and held her hand. My God, if anything happened to this child, he'd never forgive himself. How could he have been so bereft of all his senses as not to have remembered Catherine was expecting. He bit his lip as Catherine moaned.

"I'm gonna lose my baby, Dominic," she wept.

"No, darling, everything will be alright . . . it will be alright. Please don't cry, please darling."

"I'll just die if anythin' happens."

"Nothing's going to happen. Dr. Vincente is on his way. Please try and stay calm if you can." God, why the hell wasn't Dr. Vincente here yet? If anything . . . but Dominic could not finish the thought as he heard the door bell ringing. Getting up quickly, he ran down the stairs two at a time, then followed the doctor up to where Catherine was. He remained outside pacing the floor back and forth. He turned around when he heard a small voice behind him, "Papa, is Mama sick?" Tory asked.

"Just a little, Tory, just a little."

"You're crying, Papa."

Dominic picked the little boy up and held him close as the tears ran down his cheeks. Then he wiped them with his sleeve and looked at the child. He must have been out of his mind to say he could leave. No wonder Catherine had tried to hold him back. No matter what she had done, it hadn't given him the right to walk out on her and at a time such as this . . . what kind of man did a thing like that? . . . with small children and expecting? She had faults, so did he. If only he could remember Catherine was a spirited woman that wouldn't be controlled or bent to his will. She simply wasn't that way and wasn't that the very trait he had fallen in love with. Of course, she was petulant and spoiled in many ways . . . and of course, a great many of their problems stemmed from the fact that Catherine refused to yield, thinking that if she did, it would make her subservient.

What he wanted was for her to be a simple, understanding, loving wife who thought about his life and his welfare and his wants . . . and if that's what he wanted, he should never have married Catherine. But goddamn it, wasn't that the most selfish attitude a man could have. So, Dominic thought, the very thing I'm accusing her of is the thing I'm guilty of . . . thinking only of my needs. Beating himself mentally he was making all kinds of excuses in Catherine's defense.

"Everything is alright, *mio figlio*," Dominic said reassuringly to his son as he took the child down the long hall back to his room. When he entered, Dom was sitting up in bed.

"Is Mama alright, Papa?"

"Yes, Dom," he answered as he tucked Tory in.

"But I heard Mama crying," Dom answered apprehensively.

"Yes, I know. She fell down, but she's alright now."

The children must have heard them arguing and how frightening and insecure that can make a child, Dominic thought. Swallowing the hard lump in his throat he bent down and kissed the boy on the cheek and said, "Don't worry, Dom. Mama's fine. Now, go back to sleep . . . both of you . . . I'll see you in the morning."

"Good night, Papa," they said as he closed the door softly behind him.

He sat on the Victorian red velvet settee against the wall, with his head buried in his hands, and started to cry. Why did he allow his temper to become so fever-pitched. Catherine could make him so angry at times, he really wanted to choke her . . . no, not really. She had so much that was good in her. There wasn't a more loving and devoted mother, an exceptional housekeeper and it couldn't have been easy for her in the beginning. Of course she rebelled . . . she wasn't accustomed to being denied. That wasn't her fault, it was the way she'd been brought up. He was going to accept the things about her he didn't like and try very hard to overlook them. It wasn't easy to control one's impulses when he was angry. "But I've got to learn to deal with Catherine for the sake of the children . . . for the sake of our own personal tranquility . . . for the sake of our future. I must. Dearest God, let Catherine have this child, born healthy and whole, please, I beg you." Suddenly in his guilt Catherine emerged in his mind with all the virtues and none of the vices.

He was startled when Dr. Vincente put his hand on Dominic's shoulder and said, "I think everything is under control, I've stopped the bleeding. However, Dominic, I can't say for sure that we're out of the woods. We'll know in the next few days . . . naturally Catherine is very upset which doesn't help, but I've given her an injection for sleep . . . I suggest it might be more comfortable if she could have the bed to herself. Now, Dominic, get some rest, you look tired. I'll be here early in the morning. Good night."

"Yes. You'll forgive me if I don't show you out?"

"Go in to your wife, that's more important."

"Thank you for everything."

"What for? Get some rest," he said as he descended the stairs, but Dominic did not wait until the front door shut as he hurried to their room.

Entering, he heard Catherine's voice weak and unsteady, "Dominic, please sit here till I fall asleep."

"Yes, darling." He seated himself once again in the chair beside the bed and held her hand.

"Dominic?"

"Yes."

"Your eyes are red . . . have you been cryin'?"

"Yes."

"Oh, my dear . . . you do love me, don't you."

"Very much, Catherine."

"I don't know why I question you at times."

"Darling, Dr. Vincente said he'd given you something for sleep . . . we can talk another time."

"No, Dominic, please, I'm really not sleepy. Dominic?"

"Yes?"

"I'm really wicked at times, I know it . . . I'm impulsive and in spite of knowin', I go right on doin' the very thing I know is gonna make you angry. Why do I, Dom?"

"Because it hasn't been easy for you . . . I know at times you feel frustrated. I've been so busy, trying to make a name for myself that I can understand you feeling neglected. But Catherine, I don't know how to stop trying. . . . I just can't back up now at the most productive time in my life. Darling, all I can say is, I love you very much. I just wish we understood one another better. For all our sakes, especially the children's, and become a little more tolerant of each of each."

"I surely hope so, Dominic . . . I'm gonna try, I really mean I'm gonna try."

"So am I, Catherine. Now, darling, go to sleep." Dominic remained until Catherine fell asleep, then went downstairs and slept, uncomfortably, on the couch.

The next few days were filled with a great deal of anxiety and although Dominic was in the middle of a large negotiation, he put off whatever he could in order to stay close to Catherine's side. After watching Catherine carefully, Dr. Vincente said to Dominic, "I don't think we have to worry any longer. If Catherine hasn't aborted by now, I feel almost certain she will carry the full term, but she's going to have to be very careful and rest a great deal."

"Thank God," Dominic answered, sighing deeply. The worst was over.

Since Dominic had still not seen the new house, Catherine said, when she felt stronger, "Darlin', take me for a ride."

"I don't think we should . . . yet."

"It's alright. I asked Dr. Vincente and he said I could."

"Fine. Where do you want to go?"

"To show you *your* new house."

"Okay, can I help you with anything?"

"Just have Anna get the children ready."

"Are you sure you don't want to go alone . . . just the two of us. It might be too much of a strain having them all come."

"No, darlin', I want my whole little family to share this one glorious moment. It's a happy day, Dom . . . we've survived so much together, I think we should all share in the joy, don't you?"

"Yes." He smiled, kissed Catherine, holding her close, then went and gathered his brood.

The children squealed with excitement, running all over the huge house. Little Dom slid down the bannister with Tory not far behind. And the twins were outside trying to climb a large tree, while Bobby, just turned four, was in one of the bathrooms, running the water in the tub and splashing his stockinged feet. By now, he was wet to his underwear . . . but it was such fun. Gina Maria hung onto her father's hand. Even at two, the devotion she had for Papa was a thing that was to last all of her life. Excitedly, Catherine led Dominic from one room to another, then they stood before the large window overlooking the blue bay and the green hills of Marin. "What do you think, Dominic?"

He was thinking he'd have to sell some of his investments in order for them to live here, but he owed her this. Smiling, he answered, "It's magnificent, Catherine."

"You really like it?"

"How could I help it."

"Dominic?"

"Yes."

"You're not angry anymore?"

"Oh, no, darling . . . no. In fact, I'm happy, now that you bought it. This is where you belong. I know it more than ever before."

"You mean it . . . really mean it . . . not just sayin' that to appease me?"

"No, Catherine, I mean it."

"But you said, *I* belonged here . . . you didn't say *we*."

"I meant we . . . yes, *we* do belong here."

"Oh, Dominic, we're gonna be so happy here, I just know it . . . feel it in my heart. It's a place for the children to grow . . . for us to grow. Nobody knows better than I how important one's heritage is and I want our children to have that . . . I also know you're makin' a lot of very important friends and I want you to be proud to bring them here. I haven't begun to show my potential as a hostess. Dominic, you're gonna be so proud of me. I'm gonna be what my Mama trained me for."

Dominic looked at his wife, his eyes narrowed

slightly in contemplation. Then, ever so fleetingly, the thought of Catherine's Mama vanished. He smiled, "Catherine, just be you."

"I'm gonna be, Dominic. I surely am gonna be me for the first time in a long time. And the kinda wife I've dreamed of bein' in a house like this." Then she walked quickly into the marble foyer where her happy voice echoed in the vast empty mansion, "Where're my babiés . . . Dom and Tory, get off that bannister and go look for your brothers." When she saw Bobby soaking wet, Catherine laughed so hard, there were tears in her eyes. Then gathering them all around her, and with a grand sweeping gesture, she said, "This is *our new home* . . . it is indeed and this is where we're gonna have the best time of our lives. I'm just about the luckiest woman in the world . . . and that's a fact."

From that day until her seventh month, Catherine spent almost all her time at the new house with the contractor who was remodeling the kitchen and bathrooms, complaining about the costs, and taking their good old time to do the work. And the painter quit in the middle of the job because Catherine kept after him while he spackled the walls, watching for every tiny crack, but what broke the camel's back was she decided the colors he had applied were not the same as she had chosen. Angrily, he walked off the job.

At this point, she became irritable and terribly fatigued. Each evening, after the children were put to sleep, she would collapse exhausted on her bed and fall asleep immediately.

Dominic was away on a case and would be for a few more days. At eleven o'clock that night, Catherine began to have excruciating pains. Her breathing labored, she called Dr. Vincente on the phone and told him to please come immediately. He was there within minutes. After examining her, he said, "Catherine, I'm going to take you to the hospital."

"No . . . no . . . I can't go. I'm only in my seventh month; Dominic's not here and I know I'm gonna die," she screamed hysterically.

"Now, Catherine, listen to me," he answered as he put his arm around her shoulders, "you're not to think of such terrible things . . . many women have premature babies. You're a healthy young woman. Now, you must be calm, everything is going to be fine, just trust me."

"I do, but it seems everythin' has been against me with this child and now, when I need my husband more than ever, where is he . . . ?"

"Catherine, you're not thinking rationally. Dominic had no more idea that this would happen than we did. I'll phone him later. Where is he staying?"

"The number is on my nightstand."

"Fine, now I'll get your coat and we'll go."

"No, I want to see my children first."

"We don't have time for that. I'll just tell Anna. Now rest for a moment." He hurried from the room and was back before she could protest.

The delivery was terribly difficult, and in her agony, she screamed out for Dominic. For a while, Dr. Vincente wasn't sure if the baby was alive . . . he had lost the heartbeat.

After eight hours, finally, she was taken to the delivery room where at last her child was born. He weighed only four-and-a-half pounds and was placed in an incubator. In the interim, Dominic had been notified by Dr. Vincente. For a moment, he could not recover from the shock of being told.

"Is she alright? Tell me everything."

"Look, Dominic, let's not waste any time . . . just get here as fast as you can."

"How is she," Dominic asked, afraid of the answer.

"She'll be fine, but it's not very promising for the baby."

"Oh, my God," Dominic cried out, "I'm leaving immediately."

"When do you think you'll be here?"

"In about six hours if I can get a plane . . . tell her I love her."

He arrived just in time to see Catherine being wheeled out of surgery to her room. He followed behind, but was asked to wait since Mrs. Rossi was under sedation and that the nurse had a few duties to perform. Nervously, he paced the floor. When Dr. Vincente tapped him on the shoulder, he was startled as he turned around. "Come, sit down, Dominic."

Taking out a cigarette, he drew the smoke deeply into his lungs. With fear in his voice, he asked, "How is Catherine?"

"She'll be alright."

"And the baby?"

Dr. Vincente shrugged his shoulders, "I'm not so sure, Dominic, he's very tiny and we had a difficult time trying to start the breathing. For a while, it was nip and tuck, but we'll watch him very carefully."

Dominic broke down and sobbed. Finally, he said, "It's a boy."

"Yes . . . and he's alive."

"Thank God."

"Thank God, indeed. It's nice to know he's on my side when I need him and in this case I sure did."

"I'm just sick that I wasn't here."

"How could you have known this would happen anymore than I did. Everything seemed to be going so well."

"I'm away so much. I know I'm missing a lot."

"Come on, Dominic, don't punish yourself. A man does what he has to do. Everybody makes compromises, trades one thing for another, including doctors. Now I think you can go in and see Catherine."

Dominic stood by the side of the bed and waited for Catherine to awaken. When she opened her eyes and saw him standing before her, she said, "I missed you."

He kissed her, then answered awkwardly, "I'm
. . . I'm so sorry I wasn't here."

"I needed you, Dominic."

He just shook his head. Maybe he ought to give
up and go into real estate . . . forget the dreams
and the ambition. It seemed to be destroying them.
His thoughts were interrupted by Catherine saying,
"Dominic, have you seen the baby?"

"No, darling, my main concern is you. I love you,
Catherine, I love you."

He pressed her hand gently and swallowed hard,
"What can I say?"

The next ten days passed slowly and sadly for
both of them, and when it came time for Catherine
to leave the hospital without her child, her youngest,
her Vincente, she was devastated.

That first night was simply dreadful. Dominic
tried to comfort her as best he could, but she would
not be consoled . . . in fact, her nerves were so taut
that she accused him of being responsible for the
early birth, an accusation he knew was unfair, but
nevertheless felt guilty about.

He wanted to say, if you hadn't made me feel
impotent I wouldn't have had any reason to leave,
but he suppressed the desire to lash back. Quietly,
he said, "No, Catherine, I don't think that my leaving
had anything to do with this."

"Then you're sayin' that I'm to blame."

"Catherine, please . . . nobody's to blame."

"But you are blamin' me, I just know it down
deep in your heart."

"Oh, Catherine, please . . . how could I blame
you for anything. It's just something that happened
. . . an act of God. Please, Catherine, stop crying, it
isn't doing you any good. Now let me give you a
sleeping pill and try and get some rest."

"If anythin' happens to that child, I'll never
forgive you."

In the next weeks, she fell into a depression so
deep that she refused to leave her room except to

go to the hospital. When she returned home, she would collapse on the bed and cry. The children brought her no solace nor did Dominic. All she could think of in her confusion was what he had done to her. She couldn't stand having him in the same bed.

It wasn't until a month later when the baby finally was strong enough to be brought home that her attitude changed. To add to her joy of the moment, she held in her arms the last child she knew she would have and took him to the nursery of their new home. She was overwhelmed with the feeling that somehow this new precious life was an omen that their lives would have a new beginning.

But it didn't quite turn out that way, did it, Catherine thought to herself as she watched the dawn break over the Arizona landscape. No, you're damned right it didn't. It was six and she hadn't shut her eyes all night. She felt empty, spiritually, emotionally and gastronomically. Getting out of bed, she went to the bathroom, brushed her teeth, washed her face and hands, put on some moisture cream and hand lotion, then went back into the bedroom. It was too early to call for breakfast so she opened a can of sardines, which she ate with crackers, peeled the foil off of the cheese and popped a cube in her mouth, then polished off the early morning snack with a few Danish cookies, which she dunked in cognac. Nothing was more tranquilizing than a little antipasto . . . that wasn't exactly what Dr. Atkins would have approved of, but what the hell, thought Catherine. "Sardines in the *morning*, Mrs. Rossi?" "Yes, Dr. Atkins." Let me give you a little of my expertise . . . doctor dear . . . you may know your carbohydrates, but I know what's good for someone who's ailin' from a broken heart. Now, for instance, how's your diet gonna help a woman who allowed her husband to get away from her . . . I ask you? Sure, you'd approve of the sardines and the cheese, but the crackers, the cookies and the cognac? Strictly against the rules, you say? Well, be that as it may, strictly between the two of us, who plays by the rules? Huh? Can't answer that, right? Well, don't feel too badly. I'm not so sure I can. Because all I know is I think I gave a lot to my husband, raising his children. Between the chicken pox, the mumps, the bumps and the rashes, I had my hands full, I can tell you. And while I was dashing off for fifteen years to the orthodontist, the obstetrician, the pediatrician, dancing school, the Boy Scouts, gettin' the boys off to summer camps, the Girl Scouts, piano lessons . . . Whew! And tryin' to furnish a beautiful house for Dominic to entertain *those* important people in, bein' a charmin' hostess and smilin' when all the time I resented it because it was all for *him* . . . long before he ever thought of runnin' for U.S. senator. Well, it wasn't easy, I can tell you that, and while all this was goin' on, Dominic was runnin' in twenty different directions. Sure, he asked me to go with him, but he knew I couldn't leave. In the beginnin', I was so damned consumed with those seven kids and my house, I didn't have time to notice how important he was becomin'. Then, all of a sudden, I woke up one mornin' and Baby Dom was nineteen and away to school at Harvard and Tory was goin' next year and the twins were fifteen, Bobby was thirteen and somehow different than the rest, in a way I couldn't quite understand. He wanted to be by himself a great deal and read all kinds of weird books. I was a little worried about him, but I tried to be understandin', knowin' he was goin' through an adolescent stage . . . and Gina Maria loved her Daddy so much, it made me feel absolutely superfluous. And Vincente was another source of worry because he was too small for his age and I kept taking him to a specialist for shots, but a lot of good that did. The doctor explained that he took after my side of the family, which didn't satisfy me one iota. I knew all the time why Vincente was so small. The memory of my pregnancy was still pretty well fresh in my mind. And where was Dominic? Gettin' richer and more powerful all the time. Do you think he appreciated what I was doin'? When I asked, "What you doin' all this for, Dominic?" He'd look at me as though I were askin' if he was gonna bomb the Pentagon, then he answered, "What do you want me to do?"

"Oh, come, Dominic, let's not play that game again. You know damned well what I want."

He got red in the face and answered, "Well, what you want, I can't do."

"Yes, I know . . . that sweet smell of success, as the sayin' goes, really invaded your nostrils, didn't it, Dominic?"

"Look, Catherine, I'm going to tell you something, for a long time you've tried to hold me back and I tried to understand and be patient. Your problem is you can't stand not being first. You'd like to have dominated me. I knew it . . . I wasn't blind, I could have been a very satisfactory husband and made you happy. But you're not going to dictate to me. I've given you the best life I know. You're the most extravagant woman I've ever known, all you want are *things* . . . and I've gone along with you to keep peace but that wasn't enough. You've pushed too hard . . . you're trying to strangle me. It's ironic, you once accused my family of holding on to me . . . Some joke. You've done the same thing with the children. Whenever I disagreed with you about anything, you always told me to stick to my business, that they were your children and this was your home. Your home . . . your children. What the hell is mine. You've played the part of the great martyr . . . but what have you done for me except complain about the difficulties you've had raising *my* children. They become *my* children when it suits you. Now, I'll tell you one more thing. You're jealous. I know that sounds crazy, but you're actually jealous of my success, and you know something else? You're mixed up because my success is yours, and if you weren't so blind you'd know that."

"Okay . . . Okay . . . Dr. Freud. Go ahead, who else can you use? You've told me so often about the problems I have. Now suppose I tell you somethin' since you haven't spared my feelin's. You're a selfish son of a bitch who was never around long enough for me to have a life with. What the hell do you think I have except things? I've dominated and programed my children, have I? Well, they turned out fairly well for someone who controlled their existence, didn't they? Dom's at Harvard followin' in Papa's footsteps. The only difference is, I'm gonna try and see that he has a little bit more responsibility toward a wife of his. I'm gonna try to impress him and my other children that their wives come first. Why, you were never here when they had a toothache or an earache or a bellyache or any other kind of ache. It was all over by the time you unpacked your suitcase. What kind of life did you give me, always dashin' off hither and yon . . ."

"Well, if I hadn't been dashing off hither and yon, as you put it, I wouldn't have been able to provide all the gracious living you needed so badly to become a *grand* lady. A grand lady, so accustomed to the finer things in life, the things your Mama trained you for."

"Dominic, you're a liar, a goddamned liar. Remember I've lived with you for twenty years and I know what makes you tick. I also know your little tricks. You didn't do any sacrificin' for us. You did it because you wanted people to say, *There goes the great Mr. Dominic Rossi* and that's a fact and you know it. You gave me *things* to pacify me . . . why, I didn't need things from you. I could have bought and sold you . . . *and don't you forget it.*" With that, I got so mad . . . so mad, I ran over to Dominic and slapped him square in the face, a thing I shoulda done long ago, but he grabbed my wrist so hard, I thought he was gonna break it and that's a fact. His face turned beet red and he had a wild look in his eye. Well, sir,

I surely expected him to beat me, but if he did, I swear I woulda shot him . . . I mean it.

"Don't you ever do that again!"

But I wasn't scared and I screamed back, "What if I do . . . you gonna stop givin' me *things?*" I suppose because he was afraid of himself and his Sicilian corpuscles pulsatin' through his veins . . . he ran from the room, down the stairs with me runnin' after him shoutin' as I leaned over the bannister, "I'm goin' home . . . you hear?" I don't think he heard the last of my words because he was out and slammin' the door behind him.

Well, I packed myself up and with my children, went home to Mama with a heavy heart, I can tell you. But thank the dear Lord, it was June, I guess providence was watchin' out for Catherine because school had just let out. Funny thing about life . . . the illusions and delusions . . . Thomas Wolfe was right, you can't go home again. I'd been away from New Orleans for so long that the lovely hot summer exhausted me . . . and the lazy afternoons, sitting on the piazza gossipin' with Mama and Rosa Ann bored me. I was like a fish out of water, my life had changed me so, I didn't even realize how much of a stranger I'd become . . . imagine, in a place I'd thought of all these years as *home*. What I missed . . . really was *my home*, my *own* home where I was the mistress. I longed for that marble foyer and the antiques. I missed the feel of my own bed, the feel of cool linen against my body, my room. The excitement of overseein' meals, directin' things, tellin' the help how I wanted them done . . . I missed Dominic . . . of course not in the very beginnin'. I was too angry at first to even allow myself to think about him . . . I refused to regard him as an essential to my life. That's why I was glad I could deprive him of the children . . . let him rattle around that big empty house without a soul to talk to . . . and I knew he would be hurtin' when he was home, but, like all things, nothin' is forever . . . time heals the wounds. It even gets rid

of the anger and hatred until you begin to forget
what you were so mad about in the first place . . .
and o'course when you been livin' with a man for
twenty years for better or for worse, as the sayin'
goes, it's hard to get him out of your system. I wasn't
fool enough to think that Dominic was gonna be callin'
like he had once before when I was a young wife
and mother and him beggin' me to come home. "Not
tonight, Josephine," as Napoleon told his lady . . . it
was a man's world even then. But after two and a
half months, I couldn't stand the silence. I called,
after swallowin' my pride. As I waited for the phone
to ring, my heart pounded for fear Dominic wouldn't
be home. It jumped and skipped a few beats. You'd
better believe I wondered what he'd say when he
heard it was me. I was about to hang up when Stella
answered, "It's a de Rossi residenta." Good Lord,
how good she sounded, just hearin' her voice, like
money from home and that's no lie.

"Stella, this is Mrs. Rossi, how are you." I laughed
nervously.

"Oh, *Signora, benissimo grazie, e lei?*"

"Fine, Stella. Is Mr. Rossi there?"

"*Si, Signora, un momento.*"

It seemed forever before Dominic answered. His
voice was strained, but he said, "Yes?" coldly. Nothing
had mellowed him.

I had to brace myself against the wall and take
a deep breath before I responded to his aloofness.
Finally, with my composure intact, I said, "Dominic,
I'm comin' home."

"Fine."

"Is that all you've got to say?"

"That's all."

"You not even gonna ask how we've all been?"

"No. I don't think you worried too much about
how I've been while you were drinking all those
mint juleps out there on the veranda."

"That's not true, Dominic, and you know it."

"Sure."

"Look, Dominic, I know what happened was nothin' more than happens between married people. I'm sure we're both sorry for what we said . . . now, I think the time has come when we've got to act like grown up, mature human bein's. For heaven sake, we can't go on bein' mad for the rest of our lives . . . now can we?"

I didn't think he was gonna answer, but he said, "Do what you want."

"Is that any way to talk, when I'm humblin' myself."

"Yeah, that'll be the day."

"There you go, Dominic . . . when I'm tryin' to make up our differences. I'd think you'd realize how difficult this is for me, your bein' so cold and all."

"Look, Catherine, I'm not going to argue with you. This is your home, the children's home, so do what you want."

"I'm not gonna come home if you keep freezin' me out. Don't you have any feelin' or consideration for me at all?"

"It's a little bit difficult after what happened, then suddenly, you call up and that makes everything alright after almost three months."

"Two and a half."

"Oh, so you're counting?"

"Dominic, please . . . I wish you could hear yourself, I honestly do. It's just plain childish stubbornness . . . If I did anythin' so unforgivable, I'm truly sorry."

"Oh, my God, if you did? You're not even sure about that. You bet you did."

"I hadn't meant this to be a contest, Dominic, but you're provokin' the subject. You said some pretty awful things to me, you know, which I'm not holdin' against you."

"I think that's very generous of you, Catherine."

"I know you're bein' sarcastic, but I'm gonna overlook it. Now, Dominic, I've got to come home and get the children ready for school and I fervently pray that by the time we come back, you can forget our differences, so that we can have harmony once again. Will you do that . . . Dominic, darlin'?"

There was a peculiar sound I took to mean as a laugh, but I wasn't sure, then Dominic answered, "Fine . . . sure . . . okay. I guess that's about all then, right?"

"Well, only for one more thing . . . I'll call you before I leave so as you and Dom can meet us at the airport."

"Fine."

"I hope you mean that."

"What?"

"That everythin's fine."

"Oh . . . yes, of course. Well, I guess that's it, then."

"One thing, Dominic, Gina Maria wants to say somethin'."

I handed the phone to my only daughter and stood there with tears of relief in my eyes as I heard her say in that sweet voice, "*Buona Sera, Papa,* I miss you."

I could almost feel Dominic swallow the lump in his throat and see him wipe the tear from his eye as he answered across that long span of distance, "*Grazie, mia cara.* I miss you more than you know. I'm so happy you're coming home."

"Me, too. Papa. *Arrivederci.*"

"*Arrivederci,* Gina Maria. . . . *arrivederci.*"

Oh, God, Catherine sighed, there was so much to remember. What are we but our memories and bein' alone as I am now leaves me with nothin' to do but think and thinkin' at this time is a most distressin' thing. I've simply got to get some rest, but I can't seem to turn it off. As she got up and walked wearily to the bed and lay down, she thought, the years are like yesterday, so vivid, like mental portraits hangin' on a wall. All the light and shadows of the past indelibly painted in the recesses of her mind. Something that happened ten years ago crept into her consciousness like a foe that would not leave her at peace. Before dropping off to sleep, her last thought was about Dominic. Did he remember what he had done to humiliate her ten years ago, which was an unforgivable thing she had never ever been able to forget. Did he remember . . . did he . . . ever . . . re . . . mem . . . ber . . . .

There were times Dominic did remember, and those times were as bittersweet for him as Catherine's were angry and hostile. Of course he remembered, how could he ever forget when Catherine had gone off and left him that year taking the children with her and leaving him completely alone, drained emotionally, with plenty of time on his hands to do his own thinking in the wee small hours of the morning. His thoughts were bitter and the whole of their lives made him feel trapped. Here he was, forty-three, married twenty years and seven children later with nothing left but a marriage on the rocks. Had the fault been his? Had he really failed Catherine? Be honest, Dominic. Were you an understanding husband? Did you do all you could to make your marriage work? Because what marriage requires is hard work, constantly. It's a continual reaffirmation time and time again. Marriage is not a one-shot thing. Think hard, search your conscience . . . did you?

Maybe, Dominic thought, we plead our own cases in our own behalf and delude ourselves because we have to preserve our own image, our own self-esteem, that precious little corner of our egos. Maybe it's totally impossible to see and evaluate ourselves as we really are or how we appear to other people. That being the case, he tried with all his integrity to step over the hurdle of self-deception and come face to face with the past. To begin with, he had married young, married a girl whom he knew for a very short while and although he thought he was astute enough at the time, he really didn't know Catherine at all. Certainly there was a sexual attraction. She was beautiful, different and spirited with a provocative uninhibitedness. In the beginning, he made excuses for her possessiveness, her demands upon him which later he felt, in all honesty, were unreasonable. To have no more illusions is a devastating thing. To see someone as they are is a shattering experience and when he could no longer blind himself to Catherine's caprices, he took a long . . . long look and what he saw under the facade of her external self was a woman without understanding of how to take or give in a marriage. She even mistook the act of childbearing as a gift to him, feeling that she had immortalized his being for posterity. She did not consider that having children was, in reality, the sacred culmination born out of the love of two people. Dominic tried with all his might to be honest in his evaluation of Catherine, but in the end, he could not delude himself. She had tried to carry on a traditional Italian household, perpetuate in the children a pride of their heritage, and as a mother, although she was possessive and demanding, she was devoted and loving and made them the center of her existence. But Dominic felt that his function as a father had ceased after the birth of Vincente. Catherine battled him all the way, as though she begrudged his success. When the thought first came to him, Dominic tried to fight it down saying he was imagining it . . . but the thought persisted until he could no longer deny it. What bothered him almost more than anything was her unwillingness to be with him when he was away. Naturally, he knew it would have been impossible for her to travel with him constantly, but never once did she seem to feel her obligation toward him. If the children had not been provided for with loving care, then he could have understood, but that wasn't the case. . . . The residue of all his reflections left him with one painful reality, that his marriage was a failure from which he could not escape, because not only was he a devout Roman Catholic, but he had seven children and how could he walk away from them. He was trapped, beholden to an illusion of his youth. . . .

3

The balance wheel of destiny turned and where it stopped was at the door with the name of Henricks, Wilcocks and Lang. Dominic, indeed, had his memories. In his desperation to escape the lonely absence of children's voices echoing in his ears, he attended a cocktail party his friend, Lawrence Henricks, was giving, having just moved into the penthouse suite of the Hills Tower building. At first, he disregarded the invitation, feeling in no mood, so he tore it up and sent a flower arrangement with a note of congratulations, as well as regrets for not being able to attend. But at the end of the day he sat in his office, listlessly, wondering how he was going to endure the evening. Catherine had been away for a week and the walls of that house seemed to close in on him. He swiveled in the large red leather chair with a pencil between his teeth. Impulsively, he reached for the phone and dialed his mother's flat, but in that split second before the ringing started, he hung up, thinking no, he couldn't go through the pretending tonight. Knowing his mother would guess something was wrong since he had not taken the children to see her after mass on Sunday which was what he did every week in view of the fact that it was the only time she saw them. He had made some ridiculous excuse, knowing she was not taken in, but at that moment he simply couldn't bring himself to say Catherine had taken the children and gone home. So that still left him adrift tonight. He placed his elbows on the long hand-carved Italian desk, buried his face in his hands and saw a kaleidoscope of images emerge out of his mind. Suddenly, Lawrence J. Henricks became a part of the fabric of his imagery. He looked at his watch . . . it was seven. What the hell, he had nothing else to do. So, without another thought, he went into the small washroom, shaved with his electric razor, applied after-shave lotion, combed his thick auburn hair, changed into a clean shirt (which he always kept a number of in the office), then quickly left. Once out in the street, he felt slightly better at least. On the way toward Montgomery Street, he thought maybe he would have Dom come home from summer school so they could be together, but just as quickly, he dismissed the thought as being selfish. Besides, what would happen when he had to be away on business. It would mean Dom would be alone during the day if he were to take him along. He'd just have to accept things as they were and God only knew how long Catherine would be away, or more to the point, what her final intentions were. Maybe she would decide on a permanent separation and stay in New Orleans, knowing how much she missed her own people. She had always thought of that as home. Okay, Dominic, that's enough, trying to second-guess life. Just go have a few drinks and get a little high . . . or better still, even plastered. He entered the building and got into the elevator, where he pressed the button to the penthouse. When the doors opened, it seemed to him that the immediate world was present. He heard his name being called above the sounds of voices and laughter, "Dominic, come over here," Lawrence Henricks called out as he held a glass of champagne in his hand. Dominic weaved through the crowd. When he approached, Henricks said, "I'm glad to see you, Dom . . . thought you were busy tonight."

"I . . . was, but my conference ended much earlier than I expected."

"Glad you could make it . . . here, let me see if I can get you a drink . . . scotch, bourbon, champagne?"

"Bourbon on the rocks, please."

"Good enough." With that, he was away.

Soon Dominic found a glass in his hand, served by a Negro waiter. As he started to walk toward the windows, he was stopped by a dozen different people, exchanged a few brief hellos, glad to see you, what's new . . . fine, fine . . . fine . . . thanks . . . thanks. He smiled his best smile, but inside he had never felt more alone in his life. Finally, he stood staring out at the panoramic view. Fleetingly, he thought, this building wasn't here when I was a kid growing up in North Beach, imagine, how the city had changed . . . just about as much as my life has changed, Dominic thought, but he was brought up sharply. "Enjoying the view, Mr. Rossi?" He turned around and saw Victoria Lang, beautiful as ever . . . her hair was soft blonde, streaked with golden highlights, worn simply. Her figure, slim with just enough fullness above to make it exquisitely feminine, as indeed she was. The white raw silk suit embellished the fine creamy texture of her suntanned face and her eyes were amber, the color of warm brandy. She was thirty-five and divorced six years, which to all outward appearances, seemed to have left no scars. She was a junior partner of the firm, having won her priorities the hard way, in spite of the fact her father

77

was Lawrence J. Henricks, a name she no longer carried and which, in a sense, pleased her since she no longer felt the need to trade on her father's reputation. Dominic looked at her standing against the background of the city lights that sparkled as she did, and for the first time, he realized how truly exquisite Victoria Lang was. There was a gentility about her . . . an inbred poise that came from the genes of distinction, but she was also a phenomenon of beauty and brains. She had graduated from Vassar and Stanford, had cut her eyeteeth on the law and could pit her brain against any man while remaining a woman.

"Yes, I am enjoying the view . . . it's really magnificent," he said, not able to take his eyes from her.

"I wasn't sure, you seemed so . . . well, so lonely, standing here . . . here, let me refill your glass. What are you drinking?"

"Bourbon on the rocks."

"Now, don't go away, I'll be right back, if I can get through this obstacle course," she said smiling as she left.

Within minutes she was back and handing Dominic his drink. "Here's to every happiness in these marvelous surroundings."

"Thank you, Dominic, I'll drink to that."

"Congratulations on winning that civil suit last week. Your picture in the paper was lovely."

"Thank you, for both compliments . . . and you're not doing too badly in the press department either."

He laughed and suddenly, he felt happy . . . or light-headed or something. "That suntan certainly didn't come from the San Francisco fog . . . it's most becoming."

"Again, Mr. Rossi, my thanks, but no, I just had a few well-earned days in Hawaii."

"Did you enjoy it?"

"Oh, yes . . . I adored it, especially Maui."

"I know what you mean."

"You've been there, I take it."

"Yes, but not in a long time."

"You sound so sad," she answered lightly.

"Did I?"

"Just a little, sort of longing, perhaps . . . you should go, Dominic."

"You're right, I should . . . talk about going, what are you doing for dinner this evening?"

"Nothing."

"In that case, may I have the pleasure of taking you to dinner?"

"I'd love to, this place is getting to sound like Grand Central Station . . . wait till I get my coat and say good-bye to L.J."

"I'll go with you."

"Alright, but don't push too hard through this crowd or you'll get stampeded."

They had dinner at Trader Vic's. The food was marvelous, the conversation stimulating, and Victoria Lang was enchanting. Then just as suddenly, his mood changed when it came time to leave; a peculiar loneliness settled over him. When they stood before Victoria's door, he wanted to ask for a nightcap but thought better of it. Afterward in his room, he found Victoria had not left him . . . he could almost feel the touch of her hair . . . smell the haunting fragrance of her perfume . . . she was such a totally fascinating woman and indeed she was a woman in every sense of the word. He slept badly that night, barely able to control the impulse to call her even at that hour . . . but of course he didn't. The next day, he had difficulty concentrating . . . Victoria Lang was all he could think of.

No longer able to control the impulse, he finally dialed her number on his private phone. When he was connected, he heard himself saying, "I can't tell you how much I enjoyed last night."

"It's mutual, Mr. Rossi."

"What about tonight, are you busy?"

"Yes and no."

"That wouldn't stand up in court, Miss Lang. I want an unequivocal yes."

"No, Mr. Rossi. but thank you for asking . . . another time, perhaps."

"What do you mean, perhaps . . . and what do you mean by no . . . Before, you said yes and no."

"Well, I wish to rescind the original yes and no . . ."

"Please, Vicky, I'm really lonely. I'd love you to go to dinner with me . . . please?"

"Love, Mr. Rossi? That's a very strong word, just for dinner."

"Stop teasing me . . . I'm really at loose ends, will you?"

"Dominic. I really would, if I didn't have to work on a brief that is very important."

"Can't it wait?"

Victoria hesitated. then said, "I don't know why I feel so sorry for you, Mr. Rossi, but I'll say yes, although you're interfering with my discipline."

"Thank you, Vicky . . . really. When may I call for you?"

"Let's see . . . say, about seven. And Dominic, it will have to be an early evening because tomorrow is going to be frantic."

"Again thank you." Dominic hung up like a schoolboy. Excited at seeing Victoria again, he could scarcely wait for seven . . . and when seven came, he was at Victoria Lang's apartment, ringing the bell. When he saw her looking so lovely in her cerise silk frock. he wanted to take her in his arms and hold her against him, but that's where the feeling remained . . . only wanting.

He'd never had an affair before. For a moment Catherine crossed his mind. An affair? The thought startled him. making him feel uncomfortable.

"Dominic, would you be a dear and help yourself to the bar—the ice is in the bucket—while I get the hors d'oeuvres out of the oven," she said, going to the kitchen. Then she called out, "I'll have scotch and soda."

Dominic poured the drinks and soon Victoria was back, placing the silver plate on the coffee table, in front of the velvet sofa. Dominic handed Victoria her drink and settled back observing the room. It looked just like its mistress. In the most exquisite taste . . . simple and elegant. The view was much the same as the one he admired last evening.

"It's so lovely . . . the apartment, I mean."

"Thank you, Dominic. it's been such fun doing it."

"You have so many talents."

"Now, you are flattering me."

"No, it's far from flattery. it's true. There's a tranquility and a quietness about this room that makes one forget there are any problems in the world . . . that's rare, Victoria."

She peered over the rim of the glass as she took a sip. There was something so gentle. so lonely, so poignantly sad in his face. Trying to keep the traces of what she felt within herself, casually she said, picking up the tray of hors d'oeuvres, "Dominic, have one of these while they're still hot."

"They are delicious . . . you're even an excellent cook."

Laughing, she said, "I'm afraid not . . . these are frozen . . . Why? Are you that fond of home cooking?"

"I suppose . . . remember, I have an Italian mother."

"Well . . . I have a Jewish mother. I imagine that explains why I love chicken soup."

They both laughed and the laughter seemed so good, especially for Dominic. "Here. let me refresh your drink." Victoria said, taking the glass from Dominic. As she stood at the large brass bar cart, she asked suddenly, "Dominic, how would you like to have dinner here?"

"Are you sure . . . no, I wouldn't hear of it. It's too much trouble."

"No, it isn't, not really . . . remember my Jewish mother? I have a freezer full of goodies."

Dominic smiled, "That would be nice. You're sure now?"

"I'm sure . . . turn on the stereo and amuse yourself while I go back to the kitchen and start thawing out."

After dinner they sat on the sofa drinking their black coffee. Dominic said, "This has been a great evening."

"That makes me very happy."

He looked at her.

"Dominic . . . it's very strange, I've known you, how long?"

"Since you went into L.J.'s office. How long ago was that?"

"About ten years . . . that's a long time, isn't it?"

"I can't believe it . . . you've hardly changed."

"Of course, I've changed, we've all changed . . . but what I started to say was that people don't really know each other, do they? I never really knew you, the image you project, especially in court, because I've seen you in action. You're truly brilliant, decisive and articulate. We've seen each other at social gatherings and you're so witty and gregarious, but tonight I find a man so humble, lonely . . . you are lonely."

"Yes . . ."

"Why?"

He hesitated. "People can be very lonely together." He was shocked at himself, revealing his private life to someone he'd known for years but only under the most impersonal and professional circumstances.

"How well I know. I went through that once, but then I suppose it's different when one has children."

"Very . . . one can love one's children a great deal, but unless you're happy you can feel so obligated that you no longer know where the man begins or ends."

"You do love your children, though?"

"Of course . . . I was only making an observation."

There was a long pause. "Dominic, let me fix you another drink."

"No, thank you . . . please, just sit here, Vicky. I haven't spoken this way to anyone . . . I don't really believe I ever did . . . and you know something else?"

"What, Dominic?"

"I've never really known you. You're a lovely woman. You're more than just beautiful, you're a whole person. I've always noticed you, but never the way I have the past two days . . . Victoria . . ." he hesitated, and almost painfully the words tumbled out, ". . . I love you . . . and I have no right, no right at all to say that."

It was a night of discovery for both of them.

"Oh, Dominic, you have a right—"

"I should go while I still can, but I want to stay, not because my wife is away, but because I . . ."

"Oh, Dominic, you're so dear, how easy it would be to love you."

He took her in his arms and held her tight. The feeling was impossible to sustain. He kissed her passionately . . . hungrily . . . lingeringly, then carried her into the bedroom and there they made love as though it had never happened before, for either of them . . . ever.

Dominic's life had taken on a new dimension, and although the fire that had ignited his desire for Victoria that first night remained as intense, in fact, it became more urgent with each passing day, he found in her more than just the need for release. It was her quiet serenity, her willingness to listen . . . no demands were made, no strings attached, no barters, and as a result he found himself falling more and more deeply in love with her. After the excitement and passion of the moment had spent itself, she would lie quietly in his arms. Words were unnecessary for either of them. It was as though they were one with one single thought. For Dominic, it was wonderful to be loved, loved in a way that brought a sanity into his life.

The weeks that followed brought with them a

renewal of spirit that had been smothered, buried deep within his consciousness for so long. It awakened within him a kind of hope which up to now he had not only lost, but had accepted as part and parcel of his marriage. Now in Catherine's absence, he tried to obliterate her from his mind and pretend that life with Victoria would go on forever, and for the three months she was away, he almost succeeded. The times he found difficult to live with himself were when his thoughts drifted to the children, and in those moments he felt enormous guilt that what he was doing was so absolutely wrong, but when Victoria lay in his arms, the feelings were dispelled, convincing himself that he was entitled to this small part of heaven, a thing he'd been deprived of in his life up until now. When Catherine called and said she was coming home, he felt desolate. This could mean the end of his life with Victoria. How could he possibly give her up now. It would have been different if this had only been an *affaire d'amour*, but he loved her so deeply that the thought of never seeing her, holding her in his arms, awaking in the small hours at dawn and looking at her, sleeping so contentedly . . . just the sight of her sent joy coursing through his heart and his body. The breakfasts, the dinners she prepared, the quiet evenings, the intimacies of living together these last few months had meant so much to him that they had become a part of his sustenance, his life.

That day, he found it impossible to work, to concentrate, to find a place within himself to hide from the torment that this evening he would be compelled to tell Victoria. But how . . . what could he say, and the answers to which there were none left in its wake a feeling of complete devastation. No longer able to function at the office, he left at four, going to Victoria's apartment where he let himself in with the latchkey she had given him. He poured himself a large bourbon, dropped a few cubes of ice into the glass and listened to the sounds of their clinking. Turning on the stereo, he seated himself on the sofa and listened to the haunting strains of "Clair de Lune," just as he listened to the sounds of his own thinking. The music only served to heighten the thoughts so poignantly running through his mind that this could be the last time he might be here . . . here, in this place that had brought him the only happiness, the only comfort . . . the only solace he'd known and now he would have to return to oblivion, living with a wife he no longer loved. My God . . . he took a long swallow and laid his head back against the soft velvet cushions and stared up at the ceiling. He did not hear Victoria enter. Soon she was standing before him. "Dominic?" she whispered. He looked at her without saying anything. "Dominic, you're upset about something, darling. What is it?"

He just sat, looking at her, unable to rally enough courage. But somehow, instinctively, she knew, "It's her, isn't it?"

He didn't answer, there was no need to.

"Do you want to talk about it?"

He hesitated for one moment longer, then said, "She's coming home."

Victoria got up and poured some scotch into a glass, then came back and sat once again near Dominic. "Well, darling . . . without ever speaking of it, we knew this was inevitable, didn't we?"

"Yes . . . although foolishly I didn't know how painful it would be. How can I go back to living with her after what we've been to each other? After the things we've shared together, loving you as I do, can I pretend you don't exist? You must know how my life will be without you."

"Yes . . . but is that how you want it to be?"

"How can you ask me that . . . How?"

"Because you said, without me."

He took a swallow, stood up, paced the floor, turned and faced Victoria. "You've become my life, but what can I offer you . . . nothing but loneliness."

"I have no world without you, Dominic. But if you have to walk away, I'll understand."

He sat down and drew her close to him, holding her tight. Stroking her hair, he said, "You're the only woman I want . . . or ever will. But, darling, I'd be asking you to sacrifice yourself for me."

"Sacrifice! What else do I want in my life? Darling, listen to me . . . I'm a big girl and I went into this with my eyes wide open. That's the risk a woman accepts when she falls in love with a married man." She took a sip of her drink. "Look, Dominic, if you can possibly live with yourself without feeling you're doing something terribly wicked, then you don't have to live without me. On the other hand, there are no strings attached. I have no claim on you and if you walk out that door, I'll know it's not because you love me less, but because you feel in your heart you had no other choice."

He took her face between his hands. "What makes you what you are?"

"Oh, Dominic, all of us are what we are, I just happen to love you enough to want you to be happy."

"But what about you?"

"Memories are wonderful things, too, Dominic . . . and what we had briefly together will be the sweetest thing that ever happened to me. Nothing is forever and sometimes people get caught up in circumstances and situations they have no control over. We didn't plan to fall in love . . . It just happened. I have no regrets. I'd do it over again."

"You know what it will mean if we go on like this?"

"Yes."

"Are you sure, absolutely sure . . . because I won't be as free as I've been. There will be times, no matter how much I want to be with you, I won't be able to, and what will happen to you, what kind of a life will that be, waiting for a man to telephone? Having an hour or two whenever it's possible . . . is that enough?" They sat silently. "I don't know, Victoria, I just don't know."

"Then until you do, we'll pretend just for tonight

... tomorrow will be time enough for decisions. Now, darling, change the record to something more gay. 'Clair de Lune' is only lovely when you're happy ... then fix a drink while I fix dinner, and later I'll love you as though there were going to be no tomorrow."

Dominic and his oldest son watched from the windows of the airport as Catherine and the children descended the landing steps, then walked excitedly toward the building. Gina Maria saw her father and she waved furiously, calling out to the others, "There's Papa and Dom." She began to run so that she was the first in Dominic's arms. "Papa ... Papa, I'm so glad to see you. I missed you."

Dominic held and kissed the little girl so tenderly, so lovingly. How good she felt in his arms. God, how much he had missed her. One by one, the older boys held Papa by the shoulders and Vincente's arms were around Dominic's waist. The excitement at seeing him was overwhelming, as Catherine stood to one side and observed. The thought entered her mind at this moment, how much they loved him, almost more than her, it seemed. A peculiar kind of resentment mingled with jealousy rankled within her that for all her devotion, her being there when they came home from school, plus the millions of other attentions she gave them, they prized Dominic as though he were some kind of a god. The thing she found so difficult to understand was him being away so much of the time, when did they have the oppportunity to develop such fatherly affection? The whole thing was simply a puzzle to her. But she stood by, smiling as though she were enjoying the fatherly demonstration. Finally, Dominic said, "Let me look at all of you," as they clustered around him. "I can't believe it, you've all changed so this summer ... Gina Maria, you're a young lady." He laughed at the sight of them. By God, they were handsome kids, so lean and tanned and healthy looking.

If nothing else, that was something to be damned proud of. Then the laughter ended as he looked at Catherine smiling at him.

"Dominic, darlin', you look simply wonderful . . . seems a little celibacy hasn't done you too much harm. You're just as handsome as ever . . . I'm happy to be home, Dominic." He thought, well, here we go again, it's starting all over, with the little southern subtleties. She reached up, wanting to kiss him on the lips, but he turned his cheek. She disregarded the rebuff and continued as though she had not noticed. No matter . . . she'd be bigger than him. He was still licking his wounds, but he'd get over it just as soon as they got back to the business of being a family again. She turned her attention to Dom and kissed him. "Let me look at you . . . I swear you're lookin' more like my Daddy every day. How was school, sugar?"

For Christ's sake, why did she have to call him by that ridiculous name. "It was okay, Mama . . . fine."

"I'm glad to hear that . . . my goodness, Dom, I did miss you, but thanks for sending the cards . . . not as often as I would'a liked, but considerin' how busy you must have been, I was grateful for the few. Now, let's all get started. I think it's time we went home."

And home for Catherine had never seemed quite so sweet. She walked from room to room savoring the joys and beauty of all her past efforts. It had been a long and tedious job, furnishing this place, but it paid off. It was her . . . the way she wanted it, not some decorator. The few she had tried threw up their hands in despair, leaving her with her drapes down. She fought with them, saying in no uncertain terms, "This is my house and it's gonna reflect my personality" . . . And it did! The colors were vibrant. The gold damask silk paper ran rampant on the walls. The marquetry, heavy with bronze ormolu, was in abundance. The Sevres, the urns, the Capo-di-Monte, the candelabras, the Dresdens, the paintings, the statues sitting regally on their pedestals and the crystal fixtures. Catherine's house had enough to stock an antique store. It was a never-ending project that went on . . . and on . . . and on. As her eyes wandered about, she knew the dining room chairs could stand recovering although they had been done last year, but what with the wear they received . . . oh, well, it would be fun, why have to have reasons for everything. She hurried into the kitchen to see Stella. In Italian, Catherine said, "Stella, we'll have something very special tonight. Remember, this is our homecoming and I want everything just perfect. *Perfetto.*"

"*Si, Signora.* You had a good time with your Mama, huh?"

"Oh, yes, Stella . . . but there's nothing like home."

"*Si, Signora.*"

"Stella, how was Mr. Rossi while I was away?"

"He was fine, *Signora.*"

"That makes me happy . . . Stella, did he have dinner home every night?"

"No, *Signora* . . ."

"I don't mean every night, but was he home often?"

Stella hesitated. She, too, was Sicilian and it took one to know one and she knew Signora was pumping her, but with her allegiance a little more toward the Signore, she answered, "*Si, Signora,* he was here often except when he was away for business."

"Was he away often . . . on business, I mean?"

"Ah . . . *mezzo* . . . *mezzo, Signora.*"

"Ah . . . I see, half and half. You think he had dinner with his *madre?*"

She shrugged her shoulders and turned the palms of her hands up, "I don't know, *Signora.*"

"I see . . . well, Stella, make a grocery list of what we need. Prosciutto . . . do we have everything in the house for the antipasto?"

"*Si, Signora.*"

"That's good . . . now, melons with the prosciutto. I think maybe three large honeydews will be enough . . . and we need sweet butter, cream and parmesan cheese for the fettuccine . . . and Stella, we'll have

scaloppine di vitello al Marsala with pine nuts . . .
Signore Rossi loves that . . . so I'll order veal, olive oil
we have, but we need fresh mushrooms, lemons . . . the
Marsala wine we have . . . parsley and zucchini . . .
you'll stuff them. Now, let's see. I think six butter
lettuces will be enough for the salad, with olive oil and
wine vinegar. Fresh fruit for the centerpiece . . . and
. . . oh . . . Stella, do we have cheeses for the dessert?"

"*Si, Signora.*"

"That's good . . . and for the zabaglione . . . eggs,
sugar, the wines we have . . . so, I think that's about
all." Catherine took her pencil and pad and went
through the pantry shelf by shelf and jotted down
things she would order in addition to this evening's
meal.

When she left, Stella began to make the pasta
with the little machine Catherine had ordered from
Italy and as she turned the handle and listened to the
gears mesh, she thought *Mama mia,* if the *Signora*
knew that the *Signore* had spent his evenings . . . more
important, his nights in the bed of another woman,
oh! *Madonna mia!* Stella cringed, it would be like an
explosion . . . worse than the *bomba atomica.* But her
lips were sealed . . . never would she breathe a word
that when she sent his suits to the cleaner, there was
the sweet fragrance of perfume completely unfamiliar
and different than that of her *Signora's.* And how
much of a detective did she have to be when a man
stayed out all night, returning at eight in the morning
to change his clothes . . . and how sophisticated, when
she found the bed unused every day.

4

Dominic sat in his swivel chair and stared out of the windows to the view beyond. But today it was lost from his sight. Seeing the children this morning had disturbed him more than he would ever have imagined. In Catherine's and their absence, he had been able to handle the guilt he felt about his affair with Victoria. Two thousand miles away made the feelings more subdued. However, after seeing them, holding them close to him, and the way they responded to his embrace, he was sick with turpitude, feeling what he had done was reprehensible. His mind was filled with so many regrets and mixed emotions he found it impossible to work. As the day wore on, he became more and more confused, his feelings overlapping. What about Victoria. He still loved her . . . what about that? There were no simple answers. How could he say he would never see her again? The prospect was too painful and yet if he continued, how would he be able to live with himself and face his children knowing he was committing adultery. And Catherine would expect him to sleep with her and what excuse could he make. O.K., once . . . twice . . . three times, he could say he was tired, but not forever. It was the first day in almost three months he hadn't spoken to Victoria or heard that lovely lilting voice. More than once he'd found his hand on the phone, but just as quickly, he'd said no. He could think of nothing else except the kind of hell she must be going through. Oh, God, what should I do?

He got up, pushed a button which separated the sliding panels of the hidden bar, poured himself a stiff drink and swallowed it in one gulp. Then he paced the length of the large room, no closer to the answer than he was since this morning. He pressed the intercom and told his receptionist he was leaving for the day.

How he got to his car, he couldn't remember. All he knew was he was driving wherever his instincts directed him. Finally, he brought the car to a halt at Baker's Beach under the span of the Golden Gate Bridge and there he sat behind the steering wheel gazing out at the blue Pacific. Victoria . . . Victoria, what do I do, he asked himself. My children are important, I'm responsible for them . . . I helped give life to them, do I forsake them, in my heart for you . . . or do I forsake you for them? I don't think I can have the best of two worlds, not because I'd be the first man in history to have a mistress, but because I'd stand in my own way. It's me . . . something in my psyche that somehow holds me back. If only you had been a broad that I slept with, zipped up my pants . . . said it's been nice knowing you, it would have been different, but unhappily for me, that's not the case . . . I love you. But the more he dwelled on it, he finally came to the realization that no matter how much Victoria meant to him, he would have to live without her. He simply couldn't play the game, it wasn't his style. Quickly, he started up the engine and drove to the first pay station he found, got out of the car, then stood in the booth waiting for Victoria to answer as his heart pounded. When he heard her voice he didn't think he had sufficient strength to tell her, but he steeled himself, saying, "Victoria, how are you, darling?"

She didn't respond immediately, then answered, "Sad . . . terribly sad because I know why you're calling. I can tell from your voice."

"What can I say . . . except that I wish life had been different for us."

"A little late for that, isn't it? I understand, in fact I knew last night it was over . . . you have no other choice, Dominic."

He wanted to say, You don't know what this is costing me . . . giving you up, but the words stuck in his throat.

"Actually," she went on, "it's worse for you . . . You have to live with a woman you no longer want. At least I don't have that kind of thing to contend with."

"Victoria, what can I say to you?"

"Nothing. We'll both go on living, surviving. It just wasn't meant to be . . . no woman can compete with seven children. The odds against that are too great . . . so, darling, I'm going to hang up now. But as a last good-bye . . . I love you, I always will."

"And I love you and I always will."

"Good-bye, Dominic." He held the silent receiver in his hand for a moment, then replaced it on the hook, leaned against the wall of the small enclosure and wept.

That night at dinner the platters were passed, family style. As Dominic helped himself to the fettuocine, Catherine said, "I swear nobody, but nobody makes pasta like Stella." There was no answer required as everyone continued to eat. If only she'd keep her mouth shut, Dominic thought. "How beautiful it is to see my whole family assembled together. I think we should all toast our blessin' and to Papa's health."

"*Saluté* . . . Papa."

"*Grazie, mio bambino, grazie.*"

As the dinner progressed, Dominic listened to the happy voices of his children as they spoke in Italian just as Catherine wished them to do when in the intimate circle of the family. Much as he loved them and was happy they were all together, he felt uncomfortable and ill at ease. He missed Victoria . . . he simply couldn't help himself. He ate almost mechanically, not really knowing or caring what dinner was like. His mind kept wandering off wondering how Victoria was spending this evening alone. He could guess. We're both alone, he thought, I'm sitting right next to you in that lovely serene room, holding you close.

"Dominic, I planned this dinner especially for you . . . havin' Stella make everythin' you love."

"I'll buy you a Ferrari, thanks." Oh Christ, why couldn't she leave him alone.

"You enjoying it, Dominic?"

"Yes."

Finally, with thanks to heaven, dinner had come to an end. The children went their separate ways. For a while Dominic sat at the table alone, drinking his wine. The thought of having to share the bed with Catherine tonight was a little more than he was up to. But after a while, he walked wearily up the marble stairs to their room. He undressed and showered, rubbed himself dry, put on his pajamas, the first he had worn in three months and got into bed, stared up at the ceiling. I suppose the end of an affair is more difficult in the beginning . . . it's always that way . . . the loss of a person is shattering. What he felt was almost as painful as when his father had died . . . almost . . . there was that hollow feeling . . . that void that something was missing which was lost forever . . . it would take time . . . just time . . . tomorrow, it might be a little easier. But my God, Victoria was alive and living not more than ten minutes away . . . that was almost worse, wasn't it? He was so deep in his thoughts, he hadn't heard Catherine come into the room. She was saying something about Mama sending her love, and how hot the weather was and Rosa Ann's daughter was expectin' her first child, and that her relatives couldn't have done more for her and the children.

They thought the twins looked just like him and that Bobby was the spittin' image of her and that Gina Maria was going to be a positive enchantress, and imagine, Tory going off to Harvard next year when it seemed to all of them that it was only yesterday she had been a bride ... and ... and ... and ... and the next thing Dominic knew, Catherine was lying next to him in her black sheer nightgown smelling of perfume, her hair loose and her breathing a little too deep. "Dominic, you don't know how I've missed you," she said passionately and seductively. How could he go on with this; if only she'd leave him alone. "Didn't you miss me just a little?" Catherine purred as she moved closer to him and ran her fingers through his hair. After all, someone had to make the first overture, she thought ... three months ... that was a long time for a man like Dominic. But she was stunned as he said, getting out of bed, "Look, Catherine ... nothing has been resolved just because you came home ... what is this supposed to be, a reconciliation, a roll in the hay and everything is forgotten ... Well, nothing has changed. I'm still the same lying son of a bitch you accused me of being three months ago. I haven't changed and do you think I've forgotten that slap across the face ... not for one minute, no ... or taking the children and going *home* ... back to Dixie ... it's taken me a little longer to get over that and don't think I'm going to protest if you threaten that you're going *home* again because frankly, my dear, I don't give a damn. But the next time you pull a stunt like that, you'll go alone, because those children are as much mine as they are yours and don't you forget it. *Beggin' your pardon*, the bed's all yours." With that, Dominic hurried from the room, slamming the door behind him, went to the storage closet, grabbed a blanket and pillow, walked quickly down the stairs to his study and locked the door.

No sooner had he settled himself on the leather sofa ... he heard Catherine knocking frantically, "Dominic, open this door!"

"Get away, there's nothing to talk about."

"Dominic, open this door, I'm warnin' you."

He didn't answer.

"I'm warnin' you, Dominic. If you don't open up, I'm gonna get a hatchet and bash the door in . . . and I never meant anythin' more sincerely in my life."

Dominic knew she'd do just that, so what the hell, he had no choice. Opening the door, she stormed in with her hands on her hips, stood before him, "Now, you tell me what the hell this is all about?"

"I told you upstairs. You can't come home and butter me up as though you'd just gone off on a holiday to visit Mama . . . I'm sick and tired of catering to your whims. I'm sick and tired of fighting you about how badly you've been neglected. I'm an ambitious man who's going to achieve as much as he can, and I'm not going to allow you to interfere with that. If you had loved me, you'd have been proud of what I've accomplished in twenty years. Instead, you've been a pain in the ass, constantly telling me the same damned thing over and over again . . . well, a man gets his belly full of that and I've had just about as much as I can take from you."

"You have, have you. Well, what do you propose to do about it?"

"I think we should stay out of each other's way as much as possible. It'll be best for both of us."

"Is that a fact . . . Well, let me tell you, Mr. Rossi The Great, I didn't have to come back and don't think for one moment I hadn't thought about it. Contrary to how you think my understandin' should be about the great contribution you're makin' to the world's cause, my life hasn't been easy with you . . . I have felt I've taken second place in your affections and in your life . . . but with all of that, if I hadn't loved you, do you think I would have humbled myself to you tonight . . . I tried sincerely and honestly to make up for whatever wrong you think I've done. Now, what do you want me to do, live the rest of my life beggin' your forgiveness . . . get down on my knees in sackcloth and ashes. Well, I'm not gonna do that because I've got a few memories of my own. You said some pretty rotten things to me that night which seem dismissed from your mind and if you must know, it was you tellin' me about my faults that brought on the whole miserable affair."

Dominic interrupted. "Listen, Catherine, we've been through this over and over again. I don't know how to resolve my life with you, I really don't."

"You don't because you lack the understandin' I need. You think only of your needs. Well, I've got mine, too."

With that, Catherine sat down on the chair and wept uncontrollably. She looked like a broken, bewildered child. Dominic bit his lower lip and shook his head. Even though he no longer loved her as he once had, still she was a distraught woman and seeing her cry as she was doing now evoked enormous pity.

Finally he said quietly, "Don't cry, Catherine, please don't cry."

"I'm cryin' because I do love you . . . in my way. I know you don't believe that, but I do and when I think I'm losin' you, I do and say things I know I shouldn't ought to, but I don't know how else to get your attention. And I go about it in the wrong way . . . I know it, Dominic . . . I really do know it." She stood up and clung to him, burying her head against his chest. "I love you, Dominic, truly I do."

Awkwardly, he put his arms around her, "I know, Catherine, I know."

"Well, can't you say you love me?"

Painfully he swallowed and said, "I do."

"Then come back to bed where you belong. I'm your wife, Dominic, and that's where you belong, not layin' down here alone on this cold sofa, but next to a warm wife who's been away for a long time."

They went up the stairs together with Catherine's arm in his and at this moment, he wanted to be anywhere else in the whole world. Getting into bed, Catherine put her arms around Dominic and waited for him to respond. When he did not, she kissed him over and over again, trying to arouse his passion, but it served only to inhibit him. Finally, after a struggle to give Catherine what she so badly needed, he gave up, leaving her unsatisfied and unhappy. "I'm sorry, Catherine, but I guess I'm just too tired tonight. Please forgive me."

As he turned over with his back toward her, he felt her frustration. In spite of the rejection she said, "That's alright, Dominic, I understand . . . sleep well, there are other nights."

The scene at home seemed, for Catherine, a normal simmering down of the past events. Once again, she took up her roll as mistress of her ménage. Dominic had performed his duty as a husband in bed only once in the ten days since her return and it had culminated much too quickly for her. It was not enough after her abstinence, but it was a beginning. Feeling sure that eventually he would recover entirely from their recent conflict, she felt comforted with that token. The chairs went out to be recovered, the draperies were sent to the cleaners, she shopped for the children, getting them ready for school, directed the household and now, once again, Catherine was doing the things she had missed. But for Dominic, life was not so simple. The night he had been forced to submit to Catherine's advances, he had no alternative. But the only way he could accomplish an orgasm was to think of Victoria. And he had never stopped thinking of her . . . to such an extent that when he was in a conference, his mind wandered off to things they had shared. Remembering was a shattering thing that haunted him like a ghost he could not escape from. To make matters worse, he bumped into her, leaving court today. His pulse raced and his heart pounded as he said, "How are you, Victoria?"

"Fine, Dominic, and you?" she answered, smiling.

"Alright, I suppose."

It was impossible not to notice the change in her
. . . the deep circles around her eyes made her appear
tired and wan, she had lost weight. And although she
tried to be casual, her hand trembled when Dominic
lit her cigarette. They stood awkwardly, looking at
each other, then Victoria said, "It was nice seeing you,
but I have to dash back to the office."

"Victoria?"

"Yes."

"Oh, nothing . . . just stay well."

"I'll try," she answered as she raced to the elevator
while Dominic watched her disappear.

After court, Dominic went back to his office and
sat in the silence, where he remained until everyone
had gone home. He was lonely beyond anything he
had ever felt before. It kept digging into his consciousness. He wanted to scream or pound the walls. In final
desperation he called Catherine and told her he would
not be home for dinner since he had a client who had
come into town unexpectedly. She was disappointed,
but said she understood, which to him, mattered not
at all. The only thing that mattered was Victoria. Seeing her today made him realize even more how impossible his life was without her. Quickly, he got up,
left the office, then drove aimlessly around the city.
When he shut off the ignition, it was in front of the
building where Victoria lived. He sat in the car, de-
bating with himself, even though he already knew the
answer. The doorman came out, "Good evening, Mr.
Rossi," he said, opening the door on Dominic's side.

"Good evening, John, is Miss Lang in?"

"Yes, she is."

"Thanks," Dominic said as he got out. Nervously
he pushed the button to the fifteenth floor, got out
and walked to Victoria's apartment. He stood staring
before ringing, then his finger pressed the bell.

Within a moment, it was opened and he saw Vic-

Fairytales

toria standing before him dressed in mauve silk loung-
ing pajamas. The shock at seeing him was written in
her eyes. In fact, she could not find her voice.

Finally, she said, "Come in, Dominic."

Entering, he closed the door behind him and
stood facing her . . . without a word, he drew her to
him and held her close. She trembled in his arms.
Then he lifted her face to his and gently, tenderly,
kissed her, then passionately, then hungrily, until they
clung together as though they were one. He whispered, "How could I ever have thought I could live
without you? God . . . oh, God . . . oh, God . . . I love
you so."

"Don't talk, darling, you've come back. That's all
that matters."

He picked her up and carried her into the bedroom and there they loved each other with a need so
great nothing existed in the world except this moment.
When they lay quietly in each other's arms, Victoria
did not question him about why he had come back . . .
it simply didn't matter. It was Dominic who broke
the silence. "After seeing you today, I knew it was
no use . . . no use at all . . . it's been bad, hasn't it?"

"Yes."

"Sweetheart, you know I said I never wanted to
hurt you, but I did, didn't I?"

"*You* didn't hurt me. It just overwhelmed us."

"How can I ever make up to you for what I've
done?"

"But you haven't done anything, dearest. Let's
not even talk about it. Our time together is too
precious . . . we're here and that's more than I ever
hoped for."

The urgent passion spent, he kissed her, feeling
her warm body next to his. Nothing quite equaled
what he held in his arms.

"Dominic?"

"Yes, darling?"

"I'll bet you didn't have any dinner?"

"You're right," he laughed.

100

"See, I can make one transition to the next. First, I can make exquisite, delicious love to you and then just like that, I become a Jewish mother . . . did you eat?"

"Oh, God, you're marvelous. I am hungry, now that you ask."

"Okay . . . you fix a drink while I make an omelet . . . your robe is still hanging in the closet."

As they ate he said, "This is the best thing I've ever had. But it can't be too Jewish with all the green peppers, shrimp, ham and mushrooms." He smiled that magnificent smile that lit up a room.

"No, Mr. Rossi, it's half and half. The eggs are Jewish and the other things are Protestant."

He laughed, "God, you're wonderful."

"I know it," she answered, matching his laughter, "and you, Mr. Rossi, are the most exciting, the most virile, the most exceptional . . . the most fabulous . . . the man of the year with the most animal magnetism . . . you're the most."

"Can't you think of one nice thing to say about me?"

"I would, if I could think of anything."

"Oh, Victoria, I love you," he said, taking her hand and leading her to him, where she sat on his lap as he kissed her.

Then time became their nemesis. Dominic dressed as Victoria tried to keep the conversation light, but when it came time for him to leave, it wasn't quite so easy. "This is the most difficult part . . . the thing I knew would happen."

"Now, look, Dominic, my Jewish mother taught me if you can't have the whole matzo ball, you savor the part you have. Dominic, let's savor the part we have."

"I'll try, but God, I wish it could be different."

"So do I . . . but in time it will be easier. Now, darling, go home. It's getting late and we have enough to worry about. I love you."

"I adore you. I'll call at the office tomorrow and if you're free, we'll have lunch, okay?"

"Okay, Mr. Rossi, I'd love that. Now, goodnight, darling."

When Dominic left, Victoria straightened up, put the dirty dishes into the dishwasher, went back into the living room, poured herself a drink, turned on the stereo and listened to it play "Clair de Lune" as the tears ran down her cheeks.

The next morning at ten, Dominic called like an excited school boy, "May I speak to Miss Lang?"

"Who's calling?"

"This is Mr. Rossi."

"One moment, I'll see if Miss Lang is available."

While he waited for Victoria to answer, he hummed "the most beautiful girl in the world makes my" . . . "Victoria, darling."

"Yes, Mr. Rossi, darling, how are you this fine day?"

"Couldn't be happier . . . what about lunch and where?"

"Meet me at the office at twelve, if you can, and where I'll tell you later."

"The answer to the first is I can . . . and the question of the latter, I'll leave up to you."

"Twelve then. The door to my office will be open. Oh, and remind me to tell you I love you, Mr. Rossi."

"I intend to, Miss Lang."

When Dominic entered, Victoria was on the telephone. She motioned to him to be seated, gestured, holding up her index finger that the conversation would be over in about a minute, give or take.

"Yes, Mr. Friedman . . . yes, of course I can understand how you would take that attitude."

Dominic walked to where she was seated behind her desk, took her hand as she stood, then he seated himself with her on his lap, kissed her on the neck, unbuttoned the front of her blouse and felt her firm warm breast as her nipple distended . . . "The only problem . . . is . . ." holding her hand tightly over the mouthpiece, she said, "Stop that, Dominic, how can I concentrate with you doing that. This is a very important client. . . . No, Mr. Friedman, I don't think there's a chance they'll settle out of court . . . yes . . . yes, I know, but I believe that's in our favor . . . with the proper jury . . . Yes? How do you mean? . . . Dominic, stop biting my ear . . . Of course, I absolutely agree it will be a different story when we take their deposition." Trying to release Dominic's hand, which was very disconcerting, she said, "Fine, that's exactly the way we'll proceed and I'll be in touch as soon as I have a few more answers from the opposition . . . Fine . . . yes . . . not at all . . . no, Mr. Friedman, I don't think it's very good strategy to show them we're too anxious . . . alright, I'll keep you posted . . . of course. . . good-bye, Mr. Friedman."

Hanging up, she said, "Dominic, you're incorrigible. How do you expect me to carry on an intelligent conversation with you . . ."

He kissed her over and over again.

Breathlessly, she said, "If you don't stop that, I'll have you on the couch and then you'll be sorry because I have something for lunch that won't keep."

"I dare you. Go ahead and see if I'll be sorry and besides, I don't think I can keep till after lunch."

"You'll have to . . . now, come on," she said, taking his hands. They walked to Victoria's car and drove along the Embarcadero where Victoria turned onto a deserted pier where she brought the car to a halt. "Where'd you find this spot?"

"I've had my eye on it. In fact, I'm thinking of buying it just for us."

"Okay, I'll chip in a dollar and a quarter."

"That'll help. Now, darling, I have to get something out of the trunk rack."

"What?"

"You'll see."

Dominic took the keys and opened the back, got out a basket filled with sourdough bread, cracked crab, cheese, olives and wine, and brought it back. They ate looking out to the blue bay as the ships slipped past them. Victoria picked the white plump crab from its shell with a small fork and handed a piece to Dominic, then took one for herself. Nothing ever tasted so good. The wine, that had been chilled in a small ice container, Dominic poured.

"Victoria, this is the most marvelous thing. How did you ever think of it?"

"Just clever, I guess."

"And that's no exaggeration."

"I know."

"I believe it."

"You can believe anything I say, Mr. Rossi."

"I do."

"Including the fact I adore you and you make me happier than anything in the world."

"Me too," he said, kissing her. "Victoria, do you think you could leave for a few days . . . I've got to go to Chicago on Thursday."

"Umm . . . I don't know, darling, I'll have to see what's on the calendar."

"Try. Will you?"

"Yes."

"Oh, God, wouldn't that be wonderful."

"Simply wonderful, but let me see what I can work out."

"Try?"

"If I can make it, you won't be able to keep me away and then you'll be sorry you asked."

Drawing her close to him, he whispered hoarsely, "I'll never be sorry where you're concerned . . . Vicky, I want you so badly now."

"Can you hold on for about five minutes?" she said, releasing herself gently, then starting the ignition.

"I'm not sure," he answered smiling.

"Discipline yourself, Mr. Rossi, we'll be at the apartment before you know it." . . .

When they'd finished loving, tenderly, Dominic stroked her hair, "I didn't know anything could be so wonderful between two people."

"Nor I, Dominic."

Then suddenly, Victoria sat up in bed, "My God, Dominic, do you know what time it is . . . two-fifteen, and I have a two-thirty appointment." She picked up the telephone and dialed her office. As it rang, she said, "Dominic, you're interfering with my livelihood, a struggling lady lawyer has to . . . Hello, Jenny, Miss Lang here . . . look, I've been detained, but I should be there in about twenty minutes. Hold down the fort." She kissed Dominic on the forehead and jumped out of bed, rushing to the bathroom.

When she finished, she came back quickly to the bedroom, where Dominic was still in bed. "Alright, sir, the bathroom's all yours and I would suggest, if you want to hitch a ride back to your office, you'll have to be ready in about five minutes."

"Come and get me."

———⌄———

After an exhausting and hectic afternoon, Victoria was happy to be home. She undressed, then sat on the edge of the bed taking off her stockings. When the phone rang, she lay back nude. Her free hand ran over the bed where Dominic had lain earlier today. More than sure it was him, she said, "Hello, darling."

He laughed, "How did you know it was me?"

"I could tell from the sound of the ring."

"You're even psychic."

"That's right, but only about you."

"And I'm more than psychic about you. I can't get you off my mind and I had to call before leaving the office. What are you doing?"

"Well, I'm lying in my favorite spot, dressed in the same outfit I had on the first day they spanked me on the bottom and dreaming about earlier today with you."

"I miss you."

"Same here."

"Wish I could be there."

"Well, Mr. Rossi, nobody can have everything. Don't you remember when you were a little boy and found out there was no Santa Claus?"

"I remember and I cried a lot."

"Did you really? How sad . . . that can be traumatic for a little boy . . . but I'll try and make up for that shattering experience."

"You've already helped . . . about Thursday, can you go?"

"Yes, darling . . . I shouldn't, but I'm going."

"Oh, my God . . . there is a Santa Claus."

"That's what I've been trying to tell you."

"Got the message . . . what about tomorrow for lunch?"

"What time and where?"

"Twelve-thirty at Paoli's . . . can you make it?"

"I may be a few minutes late."

"I'll wait. I love you."

"Me, too, Mr. Rossi." She hung up with the sound of his voice still in her ears, feeling warm all over, wanting him terribly after this afternoon. . . .

At eleven o'clock that evening, Dominic stood brushing his teeth in the bathroom and observed himself in the mirror, but the image he saw was not of himself. but of Victoria rushing nude into the bedroom earlier this afternoon. The glow of today still remained with him. The anticipation of what lay ahead for them filled him with an excitement he could scarcely contain. Imagine being with her alone, just the two of them away from everything familiar, like going into a world of enchantment. When he lay in bed with the lights off and Catherine alongside him, he said, "I have to go to Chicago for a few days."

"Oh . . . and when will you be back?"

"Sunday night."

"Dominic?"

"Yes?"

"I've been thinking."

"About what?"

"That the time has come when I can leave the children . . . and go off with you."

Unable to catch his breath, he thought he was going to faint. He couldn't believe it. He shook his head in the dark. What was he going to say to Victoria? He could fight enormous corporations and win, but he didn't know how to handle this one. Then his mind began to play tricks on him . . . Did she know? . . . Did she suspect? . . . for Christ's sake, how could she? Logically, he realized Catherine must have reconsidered their positions, coming to the conclusion that maybe she should be with him a little more, since their so-called reconciliation. But why . . . why now, at this time in his life? Years ago . . . yes, but that was a different time . . . It was altogether different.

"Catherine," he said, trying to keep his voice even, "you know I won't have much time to devote to you. This is strictly business."

"I don't care, Dominic. You're not gonna work night and day."

"That's just the point. Sometimes these conferences go on and on into the early hours of the morning."

"I'll worry about that when we get there."

"Look, Catherine," he said, switching on the light and sitting up in bed, "this could be very boring for you . . . I'm only saying it for you. What will you do with yourself all day?"

"Don't you worry your pretty little head about that. I'll find things to do. After all, Chicago has lots and lots of gorgeous things to buy. I could spend the entire day at Marshall Field's alone."

Oh boy . . .

"You do want me to go, don't you, Dominic?"

"What . . . oh, yes, of course."

"You're not to concern yourself with me. It'll just be nice bein' together." Dominic wasn't listening, just thinking. "What'll the weather be like? Cold, I suppose?"

"Uh-huh."

"Dominic?"

"Huh?"

"I asked you what about the weather?"

"What about it?"

"I just asked . . . do you think it'll be cold?"

"Oh . . . oh, yes, very, very cold."

"Then I'll take my mink coat and hat, a few woolen suits, maybe one or two dresses for dinner and . . ."

"Look, Catherine," making sure he didn't sound as though he was protesting too much, that could be the kiss of death, "knowing how much you dislike the cold . . . it's *cold*. In fact, freezing in Chicago this time of the year. Why don't you wait until I go some place more pleasant where the weather is better?"

"No . . . Dominic, you'd be surprised how accustomed I've become to the cold. I never thought I would, but do you know I was so uncomfortable in New Orleans this summer, I thought I'd die . . . now, would you believe it?"

"Believe what . . . ?"

"Dominic, you're not payin' attention. You got so much on your mind, sometimes I think I'm talkin' to myself . . . I said the weather down south was so hot, I couldn't stand it."

"Oh, really . . . is that a fact?"

"That's a fact. Mama couldn't get over it."

"I believe it." I can believe anything after this, Dominic thought. Catherine was fast asleep when Dominic got out of bed at two in the morning after not shutting his eyes. Going down the stairs, he went to his study and poured himself a large bourbon, then stretched out on the sofa and thought about Victoria. He knew she was a woman of extraordinary patience and understanding, but how much could a woman take . . . how long would she be able to endure the strain of what she was being subjected to. He was really devastated. Drinking himself into oblivion, he fell asleep. That morning at six he awoke groggy with a headache and a terrible taste in his mouth. Going to the small adjacent bathroom, he brushed his teeth, then went into the kitchen where Stella was just preparing fresh orange juice.

"*Buon giorno, Signore,*" she said, continuing in Italian, "You're up so early."

"Yes, a little."

"*Signore,* would you like breakfast?"

"No . . . no, Stella, just strong black coffee *per piacere.*"

Putting the palms of her hands up, she asked, "*A tutto?*"

"*Si grazie, a tutto.*"

"No orange juice?"

"Just coffee."

"I'll bring it into the dining room in a few minutes."

"*Grazie,* Stella." With that, Dominic seated himself at the dining room table and waited with his head in his hands, trying to stop the throbbing in his temples.

"*Buon giorno,* Papa."

Dominic looked sideways. It was Bobby. "*Buon giorno,* Roberto. You're up early too."

"No, I'm always up early, Papa . . . Sometimes I think sleep is such a waste of time."

"It can also be a blessing, believe me, Roberto."

"You look tired, Papa, like you haven't slept at all."

"You're right. I had about four hours."

Without hesitation, he said, "You know, Papa, I'm not going to be a lawyer like the others."

"You made up your mind? At sixteen?"

"Yes, Papa, I did."

In spite of the pounding in Dominic's head, he laughed mildly, "It's funny how sure you can be at sixteen. I'm forty-three and not sure about a lot of things."

"You're *sure,* Papa."

There was a peculiar sound in Bobby's voice . . . almost like condemnation. "What do you mean by that?"

"I mean you're sure about the things you want."

"Really . . . and what do you think I want?"

"You want to be famous . . . important . . . rich."

Dominic looked at his son as though he were seeing him for the first time. He seemed so old . . . so mature . . . too mature for his age this morning. It was a little disturbing. "And what's so bad about that?"

"It's alright if that's what you want . . . but not me."

"No . . . ? What do you want?"

"I want to be free."

"Free? And you can't be free and want all those things?"

"No."

"And what makes you so smart and wise?"

"I'm not so smart and wise. I just don't want a lot of possessions." Stella brought in the coffee and put it in front of Dominic. As he started to take a sip, Bobby continued, "Possessions and power are the worst evils in the world."

Dominic choked as he swallowed. Finally, with a gulp, he asked, "Where are you getting all these ideas, Bobby?"

"From philosophy."

"From philosophy? What kinds of books are you reading?"

"Nietzsche . . . Marx, Engels."

Once again, Dominic choked, but this time a fine spray of coffee spewed from his mouth. "Nietzsche, Marx and Engels? Listen, Roberto, those books are not for you now. Not now. Wait until you're older and can understand them. Do you hear what I say? . . . They were all crazy, paranoid misfits."

"I don't think so, Papa. They were men of vision, who saw how oppressed the masses are."

"Is that a fact . . . well, you don't look too oppressed."

"That's just it. Why should we have so much when other people are starving?"

"Because I worked goddamned hard to see to it that you wouldn't be oppressed."

"Yes, but you didn't do it for humanitarian reasons, you did it only for us."

Oh, my God, he didn't have enough to think about this morning with Victoria and Catherine, he had a junior Commie on his hands who had no idea what he was getting into. "Listen, Roberto . . . this discussion is over. Now, I'll call Stella to get your breakfast. On a full stomach the world doesn't look so bad."

"Listen, Papa, there's one thing I've been meaning to tell you."

Dominic was afraid to ask what . . . maybe he was joining the Communist Party . . . maybe he'd get a medal from Stalin for being the youngest member in existence outside of Russia. "Okay, Roberto . . . what have you been meaning to tell me?"

"I don't want to go to school anymore."

"What the hell kind of nonsense is this?"

"It's not nonsense. I want to go to Europe and study sculpting in Florence."

"Are you crazy? First, you'll finish school, then we'll talk."

"See, that's what I mean by being free."

"At sixteen, you don't have to be free . . . at twenty-one, you'll be free."

"No, Papa, a person has a right to *be* from the time he's born . . . he was born with that inalienable right."

Oh, for Christ's sake, this was really too much for him this morning. "Besides, your mother would never permit it."

"I've already spoken to her about it."

Slowly, Dominic asked, "And what did she say?"

"She agrees."

"*She agrees?*"

"Yes."

Oh, my God, he had to get out of here before he lost his sanity. "You're not going and that's final. When you get older, you can save the world, your mother and yourself." With that, Dominic got up from the table, his head pounding worse than before and hurried up the stairs. As he went up, he knew he'd discuss this with Catherine, but not this morning . . . he simply wasn't up to it.

There were two doors that slammed almost simultaneously. The front door where a very angry Dominic hurried out and a door to a very hostile Roberto's. Immediately Catherine jumped out of bed and walked rapidly down the hall. Standing before Roberto's room she paused before entering. Knocking gently she waited, then entered before asking to be invited in. She was a mother who understood her son and what he was feeling. Roberto was lying on top of the unmade bed staring up at the ceiling. Quietly she sat on the edge and observed the face of her son. So young, so beautiful, so full of longing for a life that belonged to him . . . one he was fighting so desperately to explore. Taking his hand in hers she asked, "Darlin', tell mama . . . what happened?" He bit his lip hard and breathed with contempt, his eyes studying the ceiling.

Finally he answered with unmistakable bitterness, "What's to tell?"

"A whole lot, Roberto . . . if you have a problem the problem's easier if it's shared."

"Sure . . . Sure . . . that's a lot of baloney . . . that's baloney. I tried that with Papa and you know what he said . . . you ready for this?"

"I surely am, darlin'."

"Well, dig this . . . he thinks I'm some kind of a weirdo Commie . . . would you believe that. From your own father? What the hell kind of understanding is that? You got to think his way or it's no go."

"Listen, Roberto, to your Mama. Now don't think I'm takin' sides with Papa, I'm not . . . but the truth is he really wants the best for you . . . but it's difficult for him to understand the needs of people like you . . . like us, really. When it comes down to it, darlin', you and I are so much alike . . . I do believe more alike than all the others, although I love you all the same . . . but I understand *you* because we're both reachin' out for love and understandin'. And it's just somethin' people don't seem to sense in us. It's confusin' . . . I know in my case I got a lot of love to give but it seems to me there's no one to receive it all . . . like livin' on an island. That's why I understand your needs . . . your dreams and, Roberto, you're gonna have 'em and . . . maybe I will too."

Roberto looked away from the ceiling and into the face of his mother. It was like seeing her for the first time. with tears in her eyes, and for the first time he realized what she was saying . . . *look at me, please look at me. . . .*

At five minutes of twelve, Dominic was seated at a table in the corner waiting for Victoria. This was a rendezvous he did not look forward to. In spite of the hangover he had earlier, he sat drinking a Bloody Mary . . . the next was a double. When he looked up, Victoria stood before him, smiling breathlessly . . . exquisite in her navy blue suit and the soft, pink silk blouse beneath it.

"Darling, I'm so happy you went on without me. I'm sorry I'm late."

"You said you might be. It's alright."

The waiter came and Dominic ordered scotch and soda for Victoria, but she said, "I'm going to have the same as you, a Bloody Mary."

"Fine, make that two."

"How did your day go, darling?" Victoria asked.

Dominic laughed, putting his hand up to his head. "You wouldn't believe it, you honestly wouldn't."

"I know, darling . . . I suppose we're in the worst profession in the world."

Before he could answer, the waiter was back with their drinks and asking if he could take their orders.

"What will you have, sweetheart?" Dominic asked.

"The sole amandine."

"Make that two."

They drank their drinks and spoke about unimportant things, then lunch was served which Victoria ate with relish, but Dominic couldn't get it down. She stopped eating, "Darling, are you worried about something?"

"Yes . . . you could say that."

"What is it?"

"I . . . I don't know how to tell you this."

"Tell me what?"

He hesitated. Victoria asked, "Did you rob a bank?"

"I wish it was as simple as that."

"Then where did you bury the body?" She laughed, "Nothing can be that impossible to tell me."

"This is." His words had a very sobering effect . . . was he breaking off with her, was that possible? No, she mustn't even think a thing like that.

"Alright, Dominic, whatever it is, I'll understand."

"I'm afraid you won't understand this."

"Okay, test me."

For a moment longer he put it off, then said, "We can't go on Thursday."

"We can't? . . . well, I suppose it couldn't be helped . . . your plans changed, that's par for the course."

"No, that's not it at all."

"It's not? . . . Well, then?"

"Victoria," Dominic said very slowly, "my . . . wife insisted on going."

Victoria's mouth dropped open in stunned disbelief as she sat staring at Dominic . . . there were no words . . . simply no words. Trying to hold down the anger, she shook her head and finally asked, "Why now . . . I simply don't understand, Dominic, I simply don't. You've told me she never wanted to go with you. Why . . . just this time?"

"I know . . . that's what I asked myself last night over and over again."

"And?"

"And I realized the stupid irony of this."

"What's that, *tell* me."

"That she feels since our reconciliation, which is strictly on her part to be sure, she apparently felt it was her duty to go with me. Now, I ask you, is that ridiculous?"

"That's putting it mildly. I suppose you had to tell her . . . ?"

"Of course, I did, sweetheart . . . I've never gone away, without saying where I was going to be."

"I know . . . I know . . . that was a stupid question to ask, but I'm so upset, I can't think rationally."

"Oh, darling, don't you think I know what you're going through . . . my God, I seem to always hurt you . . . and I love you so . . . I'm really sick about this."

But Victoria seemed not to hear the words as she rambled on, "Yes, I can see that, but since I'm not likely to be sainted, I'm going to tell you, I went through all kinds of hell so we could go away. Poor Wilcocks was going to carry the load. I'm just devastated—"

"Darling, don't you think I realize how crushing this is for you?"

"I'm sure you do, but at this point, I don't know whether to scream or cry. I feel as though I'm living on the edge of a precipice, ready to fall over."

Dominic reached for her hand and held it firmly.

"Tell me, what can I do?"

She bit her lip to hold back the tears, "I don't know, Dominic . . . I really don't, but at this moment, it seems almost impossible."

"Please don't say that, Victoria . . . please . . . if I pressed her too hard, you know what that would mean."

"Did you try and talk her out of it?"

"Of course, but how could I say she can't go . . . what else could I do when she insisted?"

Victoria saw the agony in his eyes and suddenly, she knew how impossible it was for him and she was badgering him, just like his wife. She sighed, "Funny,

Dominic, I really felt, in the beginning, I would be able to cope with anything, but I'm so in love with you and so tied up in knots, I'm not thinking. Of course, you couldn't help it."

"Thank you, darling . . . God, I'm so damned miserable about this."

"I know you are and so am I, but next time, check it out first with your spouse before asking me to make any plans."

"You're right, except I never expected her to go—"

"I know . . . I know, dear, and I am sorry we won't be together."

"What will you do?"

"The same thing you did when you found out about Santa Claus . . . cry a lot."

⌒〜⌒

When Sunday morning finally came, Catherine was only too happy to go home. The past three days had been exactly what Dominic had promised. It had been miserably spent for her. The days of shopping and having lunch by herself had not been too bad, but the nights were dreadful with Dominic not returning until well after midnight, and she had hoped that this could be a second honeymoon . . . a new start, but nothing happened in spite of the fact she waited up for him in bed all bathed, smelling from the scent of Christmas Night. He fell asleep almost immediately, not from exhaustion, but from weariness. His business was usually concluded about six . . . seven in the evening, at which time he would go to dinner with his clients until nine, give or take, but after dinner was over he would walk aimlessly around the city, finally coming to rest at some bar, have a few drinks and listen to the piano player while conjuring up thoughts of Victoria to whom he spoke every night. No sooner would he hang up, he had an impulse to call back, just to hear her voice again . . . *just to hear her voice again,* although they had said all the sentimental things that lovers say to each other, but she left him with a feeling of complete emptiness. He would have listened to her reading the classified section, if the conversation could have gone on and on. The results of his deliberate neglect of Catherine had exactly the effect he had so carefully planned.

She had decided that from now on, she would not go on business trips with him again, but sitting on the early morning flight, she said, "Dominic . . . I think next summer we're going to Europe."

When a man had taken on a mistress, it was better not to start any deliberate confrontations. Guardedly, he said, not wanting to argue with her, "I'm glad you brought that up."

"Yes, Dominic, what's that?"

"Bobby told me you and he spoke about quitting school . . . I'm absolutely opposed to that."

"Why?"

"Why? Well, for God's sake, Catherine, you can't be serious. A boy, not quite sixteen, with no education, what kind of future could he have?"

"The thing you have to understand, Dominic, is that Roberto isn't like the other boys. They all want to go into the law, but Roberto, of all our children, is a dreamer and an artist . . . an idealist."

"Even an idealist has to have an education."

"I don't agree. With all the readin' he's done, since I can't remember, he knows more about things than the other boys . . . he's brilliant and I'm gonna see to it that we don't inhibit his creativity."

"Catherine, he's only sixteen . . . by the time he's eighteen, he'll want to be a surgeon . . . a tightrope walker . . . a million things. You can't take this too seriously."

"That's where you're wrong. I don't want to bring up anything unpleasant about the past, but really, Dominic, you haven't been around long enough to ob-

serve the children. Roberto's a dreamer . . . so are you
. . . in a different way, of course, but you've had your
dreams same as him and I'm gonna encourage him."

You never encouraged my dream, he couldn't help
thinking.

"Look, Catherine, I think this is a big mistake."

"No, Dominic, I've made up my mind. Roberto's
gonna be a great sculptor and I'm gonna do everythin'
in my power to see to it he has his chance. Now, next
summer, we're gonna take him to Florence so he can
study with Amileo Segetti . . . and that's a promise I
made to him."

"I'm still against it."

"I feel real sorry about that, Dominic, but I'm
gonna have to insist." The subject was over; to Florence they would go . . . no use trying to move a
mountain.

It was one o'clock Sunday afternoon when the family all settled down to lunch . . . all were present except
Dom who was away at school. Dominic looked around
the table at his children. Catherine was right about
one thing . . . he hadn't really realized how different
Bobby was from the others. He always had a remote-
ness about him that the others didn't. He even dressed
differently, not casually, just sloppy. Why didn't Catherine do something about that, but his thoughts were
interrupted by Tory saying, "Papa, do you think it's
possible for me to make law school in two years
instead of three?"

"You could if you went to summer classes, forgot
about girls, weekends and . . ."

Angie interrupted, "Not me. When it comes to
girls, I'm going to take my good old time."

"You can say that again," his exact replica, Tony,
chimed in, laughing, while Bobby grimaced and continued eating.

"Papa," Gina Maria said, "I think I'd like to go to
Harvard . . ."

"No, I'd rather you go to a girl's college . . . Wellesley."

"But why?"

"Because it's traditional."

"I think it's a stupid tradition . . . see, that's one example of freedom . . . in Russia, women are treated equal," Roberto answered.

"Well, this isn't Russia," Dominic answered a little too quickly, "this is a democracy."

"What's so democratic about a country when a girl can't go to the school she wants to, or if you're black or a Jew or—"

"Listen, Roberto, I'm warning you—"

"Now, just a minute, Dominic," Catherine interrupted, remembering New Orleans . . . the cotillions . . . the wops . . . dagos, "Roberto has a right to voice his opinion."

"I'm not saying he didn't, but he's way off base. His whole total concept is one-sided."

"You mean radical . . . isn't that what you want to say, Papa?" Roberto said, defending himself.

"Please don't tell me what I want to say. I'm reasonably competent at articulating what I mean."

"Sure you are, but this is not a court of law."

Dominic turned red while the others sat stunned. Catherine said sympathetically, "Roberto, you have a right to your opinions, but darlin', don't get so upset."

"Of course I'm upset, the courts are so corrupt and Papa's defending a corrupt society."

Tory answered, heatedly, "That's damned unfair, Bob, and you know it."

"Sure . . . very unfair because you're a member of the great decadent American society."

"Come on, Bob, knock it off," Angie shouted.

"Is this the way my sons behave to one another when I've taught you love?" Catherine said above the voices.

But Tony was so angry, he didn't hear. "Well, let me tell you, Mr. Marx, this decadent society is going to send you to Florence so you can bum around . . . all expenses paid for."

"That's enough, all of you," Dominic pounded on the table.

Roberto got up abruptly, slamming down his napkin, upsetting the wineglass which ran red over the table linen and left, running upstairs with Catherine going after him. Everyone sat in awkward silence. Finally, Gina Maria came to Dominic's side and put her arms around his shoulders, crying. "Bobby shouldn't have said those things to you. I'm never going to forgive him, never."

He stroked her hair and wiped her tears, "It's alright *cara mia*. Roberto will learn. He's just growing up . . . as all of you are."

Dominic was deeply disturbed. Maybe some of the arguments Catherine had raised through the years had a ring of truth in them. Children needed the strong hand of a father's guidance. And of course, he couldn't be in two places at one time and the times he should have been home, he wasn't, which left Catherine in complete command. If she had seen this happening, apparently she did not seem to realize how serious the situation with Bobby was. But he wasn't blaming her; for that matter, never had he. Going to his study, he sat silently, deep in thought. After he was alone for some time, Catherine came in and stood before him, "Dominic, you handled that situation with Roberto in the worst possible way imaginable."

"Look, Catherine, I don't want to talk about this . . . I'm too upset."

"Oh, are you really . . . well, let me tell you, Roberto is a very, very sensitive boy who has a whole set of ideals you don't understand."

"And what you don't understand is he's turning into a radical, a Commie radical."

"How dare you say that about your own son?"

"My God, are you so blind or deaf you didn't hear or see what happened?"

"I heard and I saw . . . and it's nothin' but a phase that all children go through. Where's your understandin'?"

"I understand that the others aren't like that. Now, how do you account for that?"

"It's because you want to think of them as livin' in your image, followin' in your footsteps . . . that's why you can't believe one of *your* sons could be a free, independent soul."

"Oh, for Christ's sake, Catherine, wake up, that boy's becoming a nutty radical."

"No, he's not."

"Okay, Catherine, if that's what you want to believe, okay . . ."

"Well, I have a deeper perception . . . a more esthetic value of sensitivity than you do."

"Fine . . . fine, but I'm warning you, if we don't try and straighten him out, I'm afraid to think of what he's going to become."

"Well, I can tell you what he's gonna become . . . an artist of whom I'm gonna be very, very proud."

"Then, you don't think anything's wrong in his reactions."

"No, I don't."

"And you're not going to try and help straighten him out?"

"There's nothin' to straighten out . . . he's an individualist who's got to have room to breathe and I'm gonna give him that room."

Dominic shook his head. "Alright, fine, but I'm going to try to talk some sense into him. At least, I won't have a guilty conscience."

"You listen to me, Dominic. If you do one thing to destroy his ideals, I'll fight you tooth and nail."

He glared at Catherine. Angrily he said, "Okay . . . Now, if you don't mind, since this is Sunday, I'm going to see my mother."

"Fine . . . be sure and give her my love."

He stopped the car, got out at the first telephone

121

booth he came to and called Victoria. Thank God, she was home. He heard her say, "Hello?"

"Darling, how good you sound."

"Oh, Dominic, I'm so happy you're back."

"That makes two of us. Are you busy?"

"Never, not for you."

"I'm coming over."

"I can hardly wait."

When he let himself in, Victoria ran to his waiting arms. "Oh, God, how good you feel," he said, kissing her on the neck, her lips, her face.

"Darling, I've missed you so," she said, barely able to catch her breath, "it seems like you've been away forever."

"I have been." Then with the greatest urgency, they made love . . . violently, greedily, then tenderly, and then quietly until all the need was spent and they lay there in each other's embrace.

Dominic broke the silence, "Sweetheart, I have to go back to Chicago in ten days on that same case, and this time, come hell or high water, you're going too."

"Did you clear it with the board of directors?"

"Yes." He laughed. "I don't think the board of directors is about to ask again in a damned big hurry." Momentarily he remembered Florence and next summer, but pushed it aside, refusing to dwell on that. When the time came, he'd face it.

In the month that followed life took on a pattern for Victoria and Dominic, accepting those moments together as the most special, important things they had. Whenever it was possible for Victoria to leave her practice, she went with Dominic. It was those times that compensated for the loneliness which, naturally, she felt, but life and love was good between them, so that even during the absences Victoria tried to hold close to her heart the souvenirs of their last encounter. And the memories did sustain her. But—then the months slipped away and it was June once again, and when it came time to tell Victoria why he had to go to Florence, she was shaken. No matter how logically one accepted things, when it came to affairs of the heart, it wasn't simple to be completely reconciled in situations without regret. However, she said her good-byes with as little outward display of emotion as possible, which was far from what she felt. And then in the month that Dominic was away she tried to involve herself in work even more than usual and accepted every invitation. She called friends whom she had neglected for some time, played bridge, went to the symphony . . . anything to try and keep her equilibrium, but the most difficult times were those moments when Dominic called via long distance or sent letters which she read over and over, crying all the while.

As for Dominic, he tried speaking to Bobby, father to son, patiently, trying to reach him, but in the end doubted it did any good. Catherine, on the other hand, felt Dominic was merely confusing a young boy of sixteen, trying to turn his mind around to Dominic's ways of thinking.

After remaining in Florence for a week, they left Bobby in the care of the great Segetti, much to Bobby's relief, and flew to Rome.

As Dominic lay in his bed, he thought life is like one great big boomerang. What he had done to Catherine in Chicago was coming home to roost. He was completely miserable with her. She had him in a position where there was no compromise. He wasn't tired, he had no clients and he had no excuses. As for the days, Catherine shopped like the Italian lira was going out of style and Dominic sat on the Via Veneto, sipping campari, watching the Fiats go by.

Finally, the two weeks slipped by, all too slowly, but Dominic's reprieve was almost at an end. A week in Paris was all that had to be endured and there it didn't seem too bad. They spent a great deal of time with an old classmate of Dominic's from Harvard who was practicing international law. The Rossi's were wined and dined royally. In fact, the Herbert Hills (formerly of Great Neck, Long Island) thought Catherine was positively charming, stunning and so stimulating with her knowledge of art. They found it almost unbelievable that Catherine had seven children . . . imagine, someone as diminutive. Catherine adored the attention, but sitting on the plane going home, she said to Dominic, "I swear, your friends are the most borin' people I even met . . . you'd think with all the culture they'd been privileged to they'd be more sophisticated."

"You certainly seemed to enjoy them."

"Well, I had to give that impression . . . after all, Dominic, they're *your* friends."

"Really? Well, I'll be a little more careful next time I subject you to such an ordeal."

"Now, Dominic, that's just downright sarcastic and you know it."

"No, Catherine, I mean it. Someone who has your background and knowledge of the finer things shouldn't have to be with such plebeian people."

"Why is it, Dominic, you never seem to agree with anything I say?"

"But I am agreeing with you. If you feel they're boring, that's your privilege."

"Thanks a lot, Dominic . . . knowin', of course, you don't mean it. I know you found Gloria Hill most impressive."

"Well . . . yes, I do think she's a very gracious lady."

"And pretty too?"

"Umm . . . yes, in her way."

"Well, I thought she was absolutely drab."

Grateful beyond belief to American Air Lines— like an angel sent from heaven, the stewardess interrupted their conversation and asked, "What will you and Mrs. Rossi have to drink?"

"Catherine?"

"I think I'll have a campari over ice."

"Thank you, Mrs. Rossi, and you, sir?"

"I'll have a double bourbon on the rocks."

"Thank you," she said and proceeded down the aisle.

Dominic turned the newspaper to the financial section. Catherine interrupted, "Dominic?"

"Yes," he answered, still scanning the columns.

"I wonder how she knew our names?"

"Who?"

"The stewardess, naturally."

"I suppose because we're in first class," he answered vaguely.

"I'm not so sure of that," Catherine pursued.

"Is that so?" he continued.

"No. I think it's because your picture is in the papers so often. Winnin' all those big injunctions. That last one in Chicago was news, I'll tell you. The San Francisco *Call-Bulletin* said it was the largest fee an attorney had ever received."

"Did they really?" he mouthed, scarcely listening.

"They did indeed. That must make you very proud."

"Huh . . . very."

"You can imagine my pride."

"I can imagine."

"Dominic?"

"Yes . . . ?"

"Don't you get lonesome when you're away?"

"Of course." . . . Let's see, Standard Oil was up two points . . . and R.C.A. . . . down to . . . umm . . .

"What you do with your free time?"

"What . . . ?"

"You're not listenin'."

Poising his finger on the stock he was about to explore, he looked at Catherine. Quickly, his mind clicked . . . was she interrogating him, trying to be subtle . . . did she have any idea at all about Victoria making that trip with him? "I'm listening," he answered, taking a large swallow of the bourbon.

"What did I say then?"

From the valley of his mind, he called up the

vestige of her former question. "You asked about my free time."

"Yes."

"Well, as you know from being with me in Chicago, I don't have much of that, remember?"

"You bet, I do . . . but for heaven's sake, Dominic, it's like livin' in a monastery."

"To a degree . . . yes."

There was silence, thank God, but somehow Dominic had the feeling it wouldn't last forever. He could almost feel the wheels turning in Catherine's mind and he was right. She asked, "Dominic, tell me the truth . . . now be honest . . . I'm just askin' . . . don't you ever get the urge to have a little hanky-panky?"

Goddamn it. He was almost sure she suspected something. If only he could see inside that little mind. She's never questioned him quite this way before. May God forgive me . . . he answered evenly, although his pulse was racing a litle too rapidly, "No . . . never."

"Never? . . . never even thought about it?"

"No, Catherine, never . . . my work is too consuming and demanding."

"Oh . . . ? Now, forgive me, Dominic. I don't mean this in a derogatory way, but I had the feelin' you thought Gloria Hill was a terribly attractive woman."

Oh boy . . . "I think she's a very nice woman."

"I didn't ask that. I said attractive . . . didn't you think so?"

"I didn't think about it."

"Oh, come on, Dominic . . . you got eyes . . . you must've thought somethin'."

"Catherine, I've already told you."

"I know, but somehow I don't believe you didn't notice her. You were so friendly."

"For Pete's sake, she's the wife of a dear and old friend. What did you want me to be, cold and aloof?"

"Why is it, Dominic, you always have to get so angry?"

"Why do you always have to make a mountain out of a molehill?"

"That's kind of funny . . ."

"What's so amusing?"

"The play on words."

"What the hell are you talking about?"

"Molehill . . . Gloria Mole Hill."

Catherine laughed but Dominic shook his head, "What do you want me to say?"

"I want you to say what you thought."

"I thought Gloria Mole Hill was gorgeous. . . like Gina Lollobrigida . . . satisfied?"

"I wouldn't go that far."

"You wouldn't, huh?"

"No . . . I think she was most drab and unattractive, and terribly fortunate to have such a handsome husband who seems to adore her."

"Yeah . . . well, I guess some people are more blessed than others."

"That's right, Dominic, you hit it right on the button. It seems the dear Lord is a little partial, givin' some people so much and others so little. I wonder why?"

"You'll have to ask him." Dominic released the back of his seat so that it tilted, shut his eyes and pretended to sleep.

5

Dominic had never loved San Francisco quite as much as he did at this moment, in spite of the fact he had been born and raised here, knew every street and alley from North Beach to Pacific Heights It was like coming home to the arms of a beautiful woman. A woman as beautiful and warm as Victoria. Their first meeting after the long absence went beyond anything either of them could have imagined.

"I thought about you constantly," Dominic said later, holding her in his arms.

"And I tried not thinking about you, but it was impossible."

"Strange . . . when I'm here with you like this it seems we've never been apart."

"That's true, Dominic."

"The trip was miserable."

"Did things work out with Bobby?"

"I doubt it . . . I have the feeling he's lost."

"Maybe not, Dominic, after all, he's only sixteen. You can hardly write him off as a failure."

"I'm not so sure. The trouble is, he's encouraged to be a bum."

"Dominic, do you think that's fair?"

"You sound like Catherine . . . please forgive me. What I mean is, she encourages him."

"Darling, is it possible she does see something in him that you're missing?"

"I don't know . . . possibly, but I don't have to pretend with you. I think Bobby's never going to amount to anything."

"He did want to go to Florence to study. That counts for something."

"No, I don't see it that way. I think it's an excuse to leave home."

"Maybe not, Dominic."

"I don't know him too well . . . that's sad, but I don't."

"Maybe you're expecting too much of him."

"Maybe . . . but what the hell is all the rebellion about?"

"It's against you, obviously."

"Against me? Why?"

"Perhaps he doesn't think he's able to compete."

"Compete? Why do my sons think they have to compete?"

"Because it's difficult to live in the shadow of someone else. I think I can identify with Bobby."

"You can? Why's that?"

"When I first went into law, everyone reminded me how simple it was, being L.J.'s daughter. But it wasn't simple at all. In a sense I had more to prove because I was compelled to top him, if that's possible, and it is a terrible burden for someone who wants to make it on their own."

"So what are fathers supposed to do . . . be hod carriers?"

"Of course not, just be patient."

"I don't understand it."

"I think you do, Dominic . . . just don't expect them all to conform."

He sat up in bed and looked at her, "By God, you do sound like his mother."

"I wish I were," she answered quietly.

"I wish you were, too . . . God, how I wish that. Now, enough of my children. I don't want to think about them or anything else except us." He settled back and took her in his arms again.

"Darling, do you realize we had an anniversary? We met a year ago last June," she said.

"It's funny you should say that because I sat one afternoon on the Via Veneto and suddenly remembered we had met that night a year ago."

"Did you really?"

"Yes, and I wanted to buy you something, but of course, because of customs, I couldn't." Getting out of bed, he went to his jacket that hung over a chair and took out a small box. Getting back into bed, he handed it to Victoria.

She looked at it, then at Dominic. "Darling, why did you do this?"

"Because I love you. Now, open it."

Carefully, she took the wrapping off and inside the jewel box was a gold and diamond watch. When she released the cover, it was inscribed, 'Time is the most precious gift one can give another. With my deepest love, thank you for sharing it with me.' Victoria's eyes brimmed over with tears, "Oh, Dominic . . . Dominic, how truly beautiful that is," and when she looked up, there were tears in his eyes too . . .

As the months slipped away Victoria became his joy. A marvelous contentment settled over Dominic so that even Catherine became tolerable to him. He was able to tune her out like turning down a hearing aid.

However, it was not so with Catherine. There were things that began to disturb her which she could not entirely articulate. Dominic seemed so satisfied, so easy, so tranquil, so patient . . . there were no arguments, no rebuttals, which in itself she not only missed but wondered about. He worked much, much later with clients and more often. He seemed to travel less frequently, delegating out-of-town trials to his partner (which, at one time, would have pleased her beyond measure) because, by now, he had become nationally known, if not internationally, and had even mentioned opening up offices in Paris and Rome as soon as Dom was through with school. There were little subtleties she could not fathom, which didn't quite seem to hold together.

One morning, on returning from marketing, she found Stella coming into the kitchen with several suits of Dominic's which surprised her . . . in fact, shocked her since Stella never went upstairs. It wasn't her duty to attend to anything except the cooking.

"What are you doing, Stella?" Catherine demanded in Italian.

Nervously, frightened, guilty Stella stammered, "Nothing . . ."

"What do you mean, nothing? What are you doing with the *Signore's* suits?"

"Waiting for the cleaner," she answered as her hands shook.

"Since when do you send the *Signore's* clothes out . . . Anna or I do that," Catherine said, angrily.

"But Anna was so busy. I thought I'd help."

Catherine shook her head, "Oh . . . I see. You don't have enough to do, taking care of a big family, cooking, cleaning a large kitchen and dining room . . . you're lying to me, Stella . . . Why?"

"I'm not lying, *Signora* . . . on my mother's grave, I swear I was trying to help."

"Help? In what way . . . to take a few of the *Signore's* suits? In all the years you've been with us, I find you stealing . . . Why? I took you in as an immigrant and this is the thanks I get . . ." She grabbed the suits away from Stella, who began to cry.

"I wasn't stealing, please, believe me, I was trying to help."

But while Stella was pleading and crying, Catherine sniffed a strange scent from Dominic's clothing and as if a dam had burst, in that moment, Catherine knew. Sitting down, stunned, with the suits in her arms, she looked at Stella without saying a word. She knew . . . How could she have been so *stupid* not to have suspected Dominic. Of course . . . everything began to fall into place. She ran her tongue over her lower lip. "Stella. How long?"

Stella wept, crossing herself, *"Madonna Mia . . .* I swear I don't know what you're talking about."

The suits fell to the floor in a heap as Catherine got up and slapped her so hard across the face that Stella staggered as she stood against the drain board for support. "Don't swear on the Virgin's name or you'll go to hell where you belong," she yelled, shaking Stella. "Tell me or I'll have you deported. Remember, you have no papers."

"Signora, please, in God's name, I meant no harm."

"In . . . God's name, you meant no harm? I want you out of my house today . . . *You hear?* . . . today!"

"But *Signora,* I have no place to go."

"You should have thought about that when you lied to me . . . you ungrateful bastard . . . pack and get out of my house." Catherine ran from the kitchen, up the stairs to her room and flung herself upon the bed and wept, uncontrollably. When the tears subsided, she sighed, heavily, trying to catch her breath. Her eyes swollen and red from crying, she went downstairs to the solarium, poured herself a large brandy and drank it down in one gulp, then sat down. Shaking her head, she said to herself, "You'll pay for this . . . you'll pay, Mr. Rossi . . . you'll pay . . . but first, I'm goin' to let you have your fun. When I find out who *your amante* is, then I'll deal with you . . . I can wait as you've made me wait." Taking the telephone book, she looked for the number of detective agencies, her finger stopping at the one everyone knew . . . the most famous, and dialed the number. After having given all the information asked for, she ended by saying, "I want a report on everythin', startin' this minute."

"Yes, Mrs. Rossi, we'll get on the case immediately."

Hanging up, she went to the kitchen once again to see if Stella had left. She had, and Catherine savored the moment . . . bitch . . . she had known, but for how long? She telephoned the employment agency and put an order in to hire a black cook, knowing Dominic wanted only Italian help. She then went upstairs and let the water run into the tub while she undressed. After the bath, she felt refreshed and for all her seething anger, she would play the game . . . would she ever. . . .

At three o'clock the door bell rang. As Anna went to the door, Catherine intervened, "I'll get it, you go to your room, Anna." Catherine smiled.

Opening the door, she stood before a stout, black, immaculate woman in her forties, who held a white employment card in her hand. "I'm Willie Mae James, the . . ."

"Yes, I know. Come right in." Willie Mae followed Catherine to the kitchen where they both sat at the kitchen table. Catherine questioned her about her last employment . . . why she left . . . how many years she had been employed. Everything seemed satisfactory. Willie Mae was shown her room which pleased her, then they discussed the pay and when she could start. Whenever Mrs. Rossi needed her. Would today be too soon. No, in fact, Willie Mae was not accustomed to being unemployed, but since her former employer had passed on, she wanted to get into a situation immediately.

"That's good," Catherine said. "Can you be back by four-thirty?"

"Yes, I'm sure I can be."

"Fine . . . I hope you'll be happy here . . . we're a large and lovin' family, Willie Mae, and don't you fret about makin' Italian food . . . I think a little southern cookin', which I've missed for a long time now, will suit us just fine."

"I'll do my best to please you, Mrs. Rossi."

"I just know you will."

After Willie Mae left, Catherine went to her room,

looked through her closet, and selected a flowered chiffon hostess gown she bought at Pucci's in Rome and placed it on the bed, then sat at her dressing table and prepared her face to perfection . . . taking special pains with the black eyeliner, applied the false lashes, arranged her hair on top of her head with a cluster of curls, put on her most extravagant emerald jewels, slipped into a silk dressing robe and called the florist for a table arrangement, to be sent by four. Of course, Mrs. Rossi, anything to accommodate our most gracious client. Then she went down to the dining room and selected a large lace cloth, the Old Amari Crown Derby china and set the table, knowing Willie Mae would have enough to do when she got here. After finishing, she called Dominic's office and waited for him to answer. "Hello, Dominic, darlin'," she said, her heart pounding, "I've got a lovely surprise for dinner this evenin'."

"Catherine, I'm a little busy just now."

"Oh, I see, well, I just wanted to make sure you would be home no later than seven."

He hesitated, then said, "I may be a little . . ."

But Catherine interrupted and in her voice there was a slight betrayal of her feelings that made Dominic realize she meant it when she said, "Darlin', I would suggest you try."

"Alright, Catherine, I will." When he hung up, he sat staring at the silent phone, his fingers poised around his mouth.

Catherine met Dominic entering a little after seven as she regally descended the stairs. "Dominic, darlin'," she said, extending her hands, then kissing him, "Come into the solarium and have your drink . . . you look so tired, darlin'."

He looked at Catherine, she was so elegant, so dressed up. "Who's coming to dinner?"

"Why do you ask?"

"I don't know . . . you seem so festive."

"Why do you say that, darlin'? I want my very own husband to always find me attractive." Dominic had difficulty putting the pieces together. Something was out of focus. He followed Catherine into the solarium where she fixed him a bourbon on ice. "Now, you just relax, darlin'."

"Thank you," he said, taking the drink.

"Now, how did your day go?" Looking at her again, he thought, I don't know, maybe I'm going out of my mind, but the whole thing seems so unreal. "I asked, Dominic, how was your day?"

"About the same."

"About the same as what, darlin'?"

"As usual ..."

"Meanin' it was difficult?"

"Yes, that's it, difficult ... as usual."

"Oh, my ... one thing I'm happy about is you have such wonderful people to take some of the burden that would fall heavily upon your poor overworked shoulders."

He just sat, shaking his head. For a moment, he wanted to look around to see if he was in the right house ... "That's very kind of you, Catherine."

"Why not at all, after all, a good wife should be concerned about her husband's welfare."

"Yes ... well, that's very nice. Have you gotten a letter from Roberto or Dom?"

"From Dom ... which I planned to show you later after you've relaxed, but from Roberto, it's a little soon and besides, he's not too big on letter writin'."

"I wouldn't think so ... where are the children?"

"Gina Maria's doin' her homework and Tory too, but the twins are havin' dinner at a friend's."

"When will they be home?"

"About ten ... I told 'em no later and Vincente's at Boy Scouts. Here, let me refresh your drink," Catherine said, taking the glass from Dominic. "Now, you drink that while I go see about dinner." When she left, Dominic wondered if it was a birthday or an occasion he had forgotten. Hard as he tried, he could think of nothing. Then he heard Catherine call, "Gina Maria ... Tory, dinner's ready."

Soon they came down, "Papa, *buona sera.*"

"*Buona sera, cara mia,* and you, Tory."

"*Grazie, Papa.*"

They sat down at dinner . . . the crystal goblets glistened in the candle lit room. Tory asked, jokingly, "Didn't we pay the light bill this month?"

"Now, Tory," Catherine mildly reprimanded, "where's your manners?"

"Well, it's so dark in here, Mama."

"Tory, you're gonna have to learn that everythin' isn't just money and power . . . there are other things in life like beauty and esthetics . . . appreciation for the exquisiteness of life. Roberto, at his age, has that quality."

"I know, but why does it have to be so dark while we find out?"

"That's quite enough, Tory . . . now, eat your salad."

"I can't see what I'm eating."

"Not another word."

I can understand how Van Gogh cut off his ear . . . he was probably eating in the dark, Tory thought. Since Mr. Marx went to Florence, we all have to develop a sense of appreciation. Holy cow, he couldn't wait until September to get to Harvard.

"You enjoyin' it, Dominic?"

"Yes, yes, it's very good."

"Are you ready for your next course?"

No wonder she had to ask, Tory said to himself . . . she couldn't see in the dark.

"Yes, anytime, Catherine." She picked up the small dinner bell and rang. A moment later, Willie Mae came out dressed in a black uniform over which she wore a white starched short apron. Dominic, Tory and Gina Maria sat stunned, staring as Willie Mae began to remove the salad plates.

"Willie Mae, this is Mr. Rossi and my daughter, Gina Maria, and my son, Tory. The others, you'll meet tomorrow."

"Pleased to meet you," she said softly, going back to the kitchen.

For a very long moment Dominic couldn't quite understand what had happened. "What's wrong with Stella?"

"I didn't want to tell you before dinner, knowin' how difficult your day was, but poor Stella had a terrible thing happen to her."

"What do you mean . . . what happened to her?" Dominic asked apprehensively. After all, she had become one of the family after almost twenty years.

"Her last and only brother died and unfortunately, she received the letter this mornin'."

"And you didn't let me know?" Dominic asked angrily.

"Why, Dominic, I'm surprised at you, shoutin' at me like that."

"Well, why didn't you call?"

"Because you're always so *busy*."

"Where did she go?"

"Home."

"Home?"

"Yes, back to Italy."

"When?"

"This mornin', she packed and said she was leavin' . . . well, what could I do with the poor thing half out of her mind."

"Who does she have to go back to?"

"Her sister-in-law."

"Her sister-in-law?"

"Yes . . . she pleaded with Stella to come and comfort her."

"Well, I'll be damned . . . after all these years."

"Yes, I simply felt devastated."

"How did she get the tickets and all?"

"Why, Dominic, I'm even surprised you should ask . . . why I took care of everythin'. Even drivin' her to the airport."

"Did she have any money?"

"Did she have any money? Well, now, you don't think I was gonna let a faithful servant leave without takin' care of her, did you?"

"I don't know what to say . . . she was like a mother . . . gave us all those years . . . did she say she was coming back?"

"Not exactly, but I assured her there would always be a place for her here all of her life, if she wanted to come back."

Dominic drank his wine. "What are you going to do about—?"

"What?"

"You know damned well."

"But on such short notice, I simply had to get someone. I really think Stella could've stayed until I did . . . but when all is said and done, a servant is just a servant . . . they have no loyalty."

"Don't say that, Mama, about Stella," Gina Maria said, on the verge of tears.

"I'm sorry, darlin', but after all, I was the one that went through the ordeal today and it wasn't easy . . ."

"I know, Mama, but the house won't seem the same without her."

"We'll get over it, baby . . . nothin' is forever and the sooner you learn that, the better . . . there are many bitter pills to swallow in life, aren't there, Dominic?"

He didn't answer. Soon Willie Mae was back. Only Catherine ate the fried chicken, corn fritters, thick country gravy and the black-eyed peas while Dominic scarcely touched his, as did the children.

From the beginning to the time Dominic retired, the evening had been more than disturbing. He couldn't quite understand why he felt so uncomfortable. Of course, Stella's leaving had a great deal to do with it . . . but not altogether. Catherine's entire behavior seemed so bizarre, her solicitude, when first he had come home, then being dressed like the queen of Rumania, the elaborate floral arrangement, the new colored maid dressed so formally . . . Stella used to wear a plain white cotton uniform and dinner was a happy, exciting thing with all the children around, laughing, arguing, just the sound of all their voices filled the room with buoyancy and tonight, except for Gina Maria and Tory, they were all away, one place or another. How much he had missed while they were growing up . . . but on the other hand, when he had been home, he enjoyed them so . . . but they couldn't remain children all their lives . . . still he wished that somehow he could turn back the clock, taking them all to mass on Sunday, then going to his mother's for Sunday lunch . . . but on the other hand, time stood still for no one and in a few years they would all be away one place or another and Catherine and he would be alone in this enormous house, just the two of them, sitting at that long vacant table . . . he at one end and she at the other and the prospect made him shudder . . . why hadn't Stella called him to say good-bye . . . her leaving so suddenly left him with a feeling of deep loss . . . The entire situation this evening had left him reeling. When he saw the shaft of light appear through the door as Catherine entered, he shut his eyes and pretended to be asleep. Enough was enough. Tonight, he couldn't stand the sound of her voice . . . or the explanations . . . or the small talk. Not tonight.

That night had left him with a feeling he somehow could not dismiss, but as always Victoria gave him the relief he so badly needed. She was there. He spent more time with her than before. When he went to Washington, D.C., she arranged to be there on a case. She sacrificed her own career in order to go with him, but for her, nothing was as important as Dominic.

In September, Tory went to Harvard amid tears of good-byes and both Catherine and Dominic shed theirs for different reasons.

Then in October, Victoria had a birthday. She said to Dominic the evening before, "Well, how does it feel to be in love with an old lady? You sure you don't want to trade me in for a new model?"

"No," he answered, laughing, stroking her hair, "I have a mother complex."

"Thank you for the compliment."

"It is a compliment. You're the only other woman I know, outside of her, that has what it takes to make a man feel whole . . . now, for tomorrow, what do you want to do?"

"Be with you."

"I would hope so . . . but where do you want to go for dinner?"

"To our favorite restaurant . . . DeLucci's."

"Alright, I'll call for a nine o'clock reservation."

While Victoria and Dominic were making love, in the shadows across the street stood Hank Woods. He had been there since Dominic arrived earlier that evening and then later trailed at a safe distance behind him. Hank Woods took out his black notebook and wrote: subject returned home at eleven. Then drove away . . . returned at seven in the morning to take up his post again down the street from the Rossi residence.

That evening, Dominic arrived at eight, only to be greeted by a more than radiant Victoria. She had never looked more exquisite than at this moment, dressed in a black velvet dinner suit with jeweled buttons and smelling of the fragrance of Joy, his favorite perfume, which only matched the dozens of red roses that filled the room and which he had sent earlier today.

"Let me look at you," Dominic said, holding her at arms length. "You're magnificent."

"And you're magnificent. Did you ever see anything so beautiful?"

"Yes, you."

"Oh, Dominic, this is the happiest day of my life . . . I'm filled with something so special, I can't explain it. There are no words."

"We don't need them. At a moment like this, words get in the way."

Kissing him, she said, "You're right, you know, darling."

"Yes . . . I do know."

For a moment they looked at each other, then Victoria said, "I had better get us a drink or we won't go out to dinner . . . go sit down." Soon she was beside him. He drank to her health and long life together, then he took a small brown paper bag out of his pocket and handed it to her. "What is this?" she laughed, "tomorrow's lunch?"

"Yes . . ."

She unrolled the folded top and took out a box wrapped with silver ribbons and a seal attached that read Tiffany's. "Dominic, I don't want to open it . . . please, I have so much with you."

"Open it for me . . . I've been so excited all day."

When she took the box top off, inside was a diamond and emerald bracelet . . . she was speechless. Finally, she said, "I . . . I have never seen anything so magnificent."

"Here, let me put it on."

"And while I make a wish we stay as much in love and as happy as we are at this moment."

At nine, while the two lovers sat in their secluded corner, Hank Woods stood phoning from a booth inside DeLucci's, observing them. "What a lousy way to make a living," he thought as the ringing began. I should have bought that candy store in . . . "Hello," he heard on the other end.

"This is Hank Woods . . . the subjects are at De-Lucci's now. They arrived at nine."

"What are they doing?"

"The waiter has just served their cocktails."

"I see . . ." Catherine steadied herself: "I imagine they'll have dinner?"

"I would guess."

"Do you think if I got there in about an hour, that would be about right?"

"I would say so," he answered reluctantly. "Mrs.

Rossi, I have no right to say this, but the restaurant is packed, do you—"

"Listen, I haven't paid you for any advice. You just do your job and watch."

"Right." As he hung up, he thought, what a fucked-up business . . .

"Victoria, I hadn't mentioned it before, but I think I'm going to open an office in Paris. I've begun to represent a number of American interests abroad and this summer I saw a friend who encouraged me . . . what do you think?"

"I think it would mean a lot of traveling and a tremendous challenge. It would also take you away from your children even more."

"Well, let me tell you something strange . . . I realized, suddenly, the boys are all growing up. They won't be home in a few years anyway. Next year, Dom will be through and he'll come into the office, and in a few years Tory will have his name on the door, then the twins, and before you know it, they'll be a battery of Rossis, and I have a feeling Dom would love practicing abroad. Are you against it?" he asked.

"No, as a matter of fact, knowing you as I do, I think you need the excitement for your vitality . . . which, Mr. Rossi, I would say you have an overabundance of."

"I take that as a compliment . . . I think?"

"It was meant to be."

"Of course, I'm going to be selfish and expect you to be ready on a moment's notice."

"Are you really?"

"Yes . . . I'm a demanding Italian husband . . . who feels as married to you as I'll ever be."

"Thank you, Mr. Rossi, but if you research it out, you'll find bigamy is an offense that could get you twenty years."

"I know, Miss Lang, but not if it's mental bigamy. There isn't a court in the land that would convict me."

"I rest my case, Mr. Rossi." Their special waiter was standing by.

"What do you feel like having?"

"You do the ordering."

"Alright . . . Louie, we'll have scampi . . . tortellini
. . . veal piccata, and the wine you know."

"*Grazie*, Dominic."

Dominic said, "Do you know how long I've known
Louie?"

"No, how long?"

"We were raised in North Beach together. It's
hard to believe we've been friends that many years
. . . where did they go?" Dominic said, as though the
sight was yesterday, so fresh and vivid. "God, those
were wonderful days. We were all so poor and we
didn't even know it. Talk about food, you never smelt
anything like Columbus Avenue about 1920."

Victoria smiled. "Do you know what I adore so
much about you, Dominic?"

"My tremendous charm?"

"No, I'm trying to be serious. For all the achieve-
ments there's still that little boy in you from North
Beach with the enormous pride in your origins. I always see that little boy going after school to visit his
nonna. There's not an arrogant thing about you. I've
never heard you drop a name or talk about the accom-
plishments—"

"Some people would say I'm damned ambitious—"

"It's not true . . . you just have the greatest drive
of anyone I know . . . but more important, you never
forgot where you came from."

"Wait a minute, Miss Lang . . . let that rumor get
out and you've ruined my whole image."

For a moment Victoria wasn't sure if he was kidding or not. "Then I wish more people knew you as
I do . . . as you really are."

Dominic looked at her. I'm the same man I always
was, but I look different to a hundred different people
. . . strange.

"What are you thinking, Dominic?"

"That I'll gladly settle for you seeing me the way

you do . . . I feel as though it's *my* birthday . . . Now, darling, here's to you."

Louie had just placed the veal piccata in front of Victoria at the very moment Catherine drove up in front of DeLucci's. When Giuseppe, the doorman, saw her, he didn't know whether to run inside and try and get word to Dominic that his wife was obviously hunting him down, but between the thought and the deed, Catherine was out of the car and swinging open the door inside of the restaurant. Giuseppe wasn't the only one shocked and nervous when seeing Catherine. Adolfo, the maitre d', thought he'd faint. Oh, *Mama mia!* This was all they needed with a room full of people and a jealous wife.

"Where is he?" Catherine said, as Adolfo took her hand and tried calmly to say, "Who do you mean, my dear Mrs. Rossi . . . ?"

"Don't pretend to be so innocent, you know goddamned well who," she said, abruptly pulling her hand from Adolfo's sweating palm. She scanned the dimly lit room, trying to adjust to the light, then, suddenly, she saw Hank Woods, sitting at the bar. He pointed to the place where Victoria and Dominic were sitting. Catherine walked rapidly, weaving in and out between the tables, then she stood in front of the lovers who held in their hands the wineglasses, ready to drink to each other, but the toast was never begun as Catherine began with her tirade of obscenities. "You goddamned son of a bitch," she screamed in the now silent, stunned room with the other diners looking and listening. "If I had a gun, I'd kill you, and you . . . you dirty whore, takin' my husband away from me." She rambled on, incoherently, as she reached for Victoria's hair and began to pull, then she slapped her across the face, so hard the imprint of her fingers remained. It had all happened so quickly that before Dominic could stand, she threw a glass of wine in his face, tipped over the table as everything came crashing to the floor. She kicked at Dominic, scratched him, and he couldn't control her because the wine had temporarily blinded him. The waiters tried to hold her back, but she struggled loose, kicking one in the groin, then took off her shoe and threw it at Dominic, hitting him on the forehead. In all the confusion Adolfo led a devastated Victoria out through the kitchen, hailed a taxi and helped her in. "Miss Lang, are you able to go alone?"

She didn't hear him. Again he offered his assistance, but this time she shook her head, yes.

"Where to, lady?" the driver said.

"Clay and Jones."

They drove off while Adolfo returned to the bedlam that was still going on inside. By now, Dominic had wiped his eyes and rallied himself. He grabbed Catherine by the arm and said, "We're getting out of here."

"No, I want the world to know what a bastard, a *bastardo* you are."

He clamped his hand over her mouth and pinned her arm back, then dragged her through the kitchen as he said to Adolfo to have her car brought around to the side. Obeying Dominic's command Adolfo first picked up Catherine's shoe and slipped it onto her foot as she struggled, then ran out to Giuseppe.

Once out in the street, Dominic said, "How could you do such a thing, washing our dirty linen in public, coming in like a madwoman."

"Keep your goddamn mouth shut, I've known every time you slept with that slut. What do you think I am . . . stupid? I shouldn't air our dirty linen in public? I'm gonna do more than that, darlin'. Everyone is gonna know what a whorin' bitch she is. I'm gonna blacken her name and yours too, then we'll see who's . . . "

"Catherine, for God's sake, you've gone crazy."

Getting into the car behind the wheel, she answered, screaming, "By the time I get through with you, we'll see who's crazy."

"Catherine, please, let me talk to you."

"*Talk* to me? I'll see you in hell first."

145

"Please, Catherine, listen, will you?" He tried talking above her.

As he tried to get into the car, she slammed the door in his face and locked it, saying, "Go talk to your *amante!*" and turned on the ignition. There was the sound of screeching brakes as she wheeled around the corner, leaving Dominic watching, his suit wine soaked, torn, and the scratches on his face red and bleeding and the welt on his forehead swollen, but for a very, very long moment he was unaware of how he looked. All he could feel was an empty hollow void . . . it was as though the world had shattered and splintered into a thousand fragments. It was the throbbing in his head that brought him back to the reality of what had happened. The worst of his hell, at this moment, was the humiliation of what Victoria had been subjected to. He turned immediately and went back into the kitchen where Louie waited.

"Dominic, come with me. You look terrible, like after the rumbles we used to have on Filbert Street."

Dominic followed Louie to the lavatory in the corner where he offered Dominic his shirt and tie hanging on a hook. Dominic bathed his face, changed, thanked Louie, then left the way he had come in, walked to his car, and drove to Victoria's apartment.

When he let himself in, he found her sitting silently. Vaguely, she looked up. Without a word, he took her in his arms and held her like a broken child. Finally, he took her face between his hands and said, "How can I ever make this up to you?"

"Please, Dominic, don't talk . . . not right now."

He remained silent and placed her head against his shoulder. After a long silence, Victoria said, "Dominic, what's going to happen to us?"

"I haven't had time to think about much of anything . . . but one thing I know is, I'm not going to give you up."

"Oh, Dominic, let's be realistic, how can we go on?"

She started to cry softly. "I feel that all the beauty

we had between us has been made to look so sordid and distorted. I feel dirty and cheap. There were so many people in the place tonight that must have thought I *was* a whore. . . . Oh, God, I can't stand the sound of that word. It keeps ringing in my mind."

"I know . . I know . . that's the thing that hurts more than even her finding out."

Getting up, Victoria said, "Please, darling, I have to be alone . . . forgive me, but I simply must."

"Let me stay for a just a little while . . . I can't leave you like this."

"No, really, I must be alone to think this out."

With that, reluctantly, he got up, kissed her, then said, "Forgive me for bringing you this pain."

Clinging to him, she answered, "Forgive you? Darling, you've brought more happiness into my life than I can ever say . . . but somehow, down deep, I always knew something like this had to happen. I just never let myself think about it . . . but this evening is something that's going to take a long time to recover from."

He had tears in his eyes as he held her. "My God, if only you could have been spared this—"

"Please . . . dearest, go home. Maybe something can be salvaged . . . try for your children's sake."

"You sound so final."

"I don't know how I sound. It's like a nightmare."

"I love you beyond words."

"And I do, too. What a pity that something like the thing we had was . . . " She couldn't finish for fear of becoming hysterical. "Go home, darling . . . please."

"All right, but I'll see you tomorrow."

"Yes, all right . . . tomorrow."

Dominic put his latchkey into the lock, but the door would not open. He tried and tried again, finally realizing it was bolted from the inside. Going to the back door, he tried, but with the same results. He broke a window in the basement. Climbing in, he scratched his hand on a jagged piece of glass. Taking out his handkerchief, he wrapped it around to stop the bleeding and went up the stairs which led to the kitchen, then into the central foyer and up the stairs to his room. Catherine was in bed. When she saw him, she jumped out of bed and everything she had felt earlier was aroused. "How dare you come into *my* house you bastard . . . you're not fit to be the father of my children, you *patrone* to a whore."

He grabbed Catherine by the wrist and said, through clenched teeth, "Don't you ever call her that again."

"Let go of me . . . I should kill you."

"You did that a long time ago. You killed everything that I ever felt for you. If I turned to another woman, it's because you drove me away."

"I drove you away? You lyin' bastard . . . what did she do, give you a few *thrills* you couldn't get from me?"

"What kind of mind do you have . . . you're vile."

"Vile, am I?" She bit him on the wrist and grabbed the bedside clock, then threw it, but it grazed past him, crashing to the floor.

He rushed to her and threw her on the bed, holding her down. "I blame you for this . . . I came home to try and talk, to explain how and why this happened . . . but who can talk to you with your violence, your impossible temper."

Looking up at Dominic, she said, "I'm warnin' you, let go of me. You wanted to explain how and why this happened. Let me tell you how it happened. When you had no more need for me after I gave you *your* children, you had everythin' from me you needed. You used me and on top of it, you had an ally. Stella knew, everyone else must have known. You've made a fool of me and nobody does that . . . you hear . . . I'm throwin' you out the way I threw Stella out into the streets where she belonged."

He stood up and looked at Catherine, disbelieving, "You threw Stella out?"

"Yes, and without a quarter . . . the ungrateful bitch . . . after all I'd done for her . . . as good as I was to her, she betrayed me just like you did."

Dominic stood stunned, shaking his head. Finally, he said quietly, "You're ruthless. . . I had no idea how ruthless until now."

Catherine laughed, "And what are you . . . a whoremaster, a . . . "

But Dominic had heard enough. He drove around the city aimlessly. What had happened to his life? Victoria . . . Victoria . . . He had to see her. It was one o'clock when he rang the bell. This evening, he could not let himself in. When she answered the door, he stood before her. "Vicky, forgive me, but I had to come . . . I had to."

"Oh, God, Dominic," she cried, "how much I wanted you." He closed the door behind him, and took her in his arms . . .

After Dominic left, Catherine picked up the phone and called her mother. She needed an ally too. This was one thing she couldn't endure alone. "Mama," Catherine cried, "you've got to come. Dominic's left me."

Mama took the early morning flight and arrived at the San Francisco airport at five the next day, where a very subdued Catherine met her. They embraced amid tears and kisses. "Mama, what would I do without you?"

"My heart breaks to think anythin' like this should have happened."

"You don't know what I've been through."

"I know . . . we'll talk later."

And later that evening, Catherine told her mother the whole story. "Mama, how could Dominic have done such a thing to me, disgracin' me like this . . . havin' no respect for his children. I've given him my life . . . always tryin' to make him happy . . . enter-

tainin' his friends . . . devotin' myself to his needs . . .
his wants . . . everythin' I did was for him."

"I know how hard this is for a woman—"

"Yes . . . but Mama, he even tried to make it seem
that I was the one at fault . . . when I found out he
had a mistress, I went crazy . . .what woman wouldn't?
Then he said he wanted to try and talk . . . imagine, to
talk! How does a wife talk about her husband's love
affairs?"

"Listen to me, Catherine . . . please."

"What are you gonna say, Mama . . . that I
shouldn't have gotten angry?"

"No . . . but there are things a woman has to learn
to live with."

Catherine looked at her mother, "Do you think
any woman could endure that kind of embarrassment?"

"Yes . . . "

"I'm stunned, hearin' you say that . . . of all people, I thought you would understand."

"I do, *cara mia*, I do."

"Mama . . . I just got through tellin' you, Dominic's got a mistress."

"I know . . . now, let me tell you something I never
thought I'd ever tell you." She hesitated, then quietly
said, "Your father had a mistress too . . . for a little
while."

"Daddy? I don't believe it."

"I know, but believe it."

"And you knew?"

"Yes."

"For how long?"

"From almost the very beginnin'."

"And you did nothin'?"

"No."

"I loved my Daddy . . . but how could you accept
that?"

"Because I loved your father . . . but above that,
I knew he loved me."

"None of this makes any sense, Mama."

"It makes a great deal of sense. Do you think because a man sleeps with another woman, he stops lovin' his wife . . . no. Because a wife is a wife and that's more important than bein' his mistress. She has his name . . . his children and no mistress in the world can take that away."

"I'm shocked . . . simply shocked at your attitude, Mama."

"Catherine, Italian men, especially Sicilian men, don't take their mistresses too seriously and if a woman is smart, she'll look the other way because nothin' that isn't sacred can last forever."

"But suppose he really loves another woman . . . truly loves her, then what?"

"An affair can't last indefinitely . . . impossible. I don't care how it is in the beginnin'. It can't last because it can only go one place . . . and that's to bed. When it's all over, he comes home and eventually, the other woman stays just that . . . the other woman."

"Mama, you sound positively depraved."

"Maybe . . . but think about it, Catherine. Women, especially that kind, become possessive, then they begin to make demands and when they do, a man grows tired and says to himself, what does he need that for, and it's the other woman who, eventually, sends him back to the arms of his wife, and if she's smart, she'll forget because it's only growin' pains he had in the first place."

"I can't believe I'm hearin' my own Mama sayin' she believes in adultery."

"You're not listenin' to me, Catherine . . . I'm not sayin' I believe in it, I'm sayin' it's a fact of life a woman has to learn to accept and if she loves her man, she realizes it's just like so much candy."

"And you'd be willin' for me to take Dominic back after what happened?"

"Yes . . ."

"I don't understand you . . . I swear, I don't."

"Maybe in a few months you will when the hot anger's gone and the loneliness sets in."

"Never . . . never . . . never. I'll never forgive Dominic for the way he humiliated me."

"Well, never is a very long time and after livin' with a man for twenty years, she's got a big investment. No, siree, I wouldn't . . . not without a battle to win him back."

"Well, Mama, you don't know your little Catherine if you think I'm gonna do that. I've humbled myself to Dominic enough times in our marriage and I'm not about to do that again, not if he came back crawlin'. In fact, I'm not gonna even allow him to see the children . . . especially, Gina Maria."

"Catherine, let your Mama say one more thing to you because it's gettin' late and I'm gettin' tired."

"What's that, Mama?"

"You're real mad now . . . and I don't say you're wrong, but what husbands and wives say in moments of anger can be forgotten when they begin to think of all the good things they had between them and as time goes by, it's only human nature to forget the bad . . . now, take my advice and don't try and turn the children against Dominic because if you do, they're just liable to turn out hatin' you . . . especially Gina Maria. Now you just digest that, Catherine, my baby and maybe you'll just find out your Mama's right."

Catherine had just turned off the light and lay in the darkness with her mama lyin' on Dominic's side. She'd always loved sleepin' with Mama when she had a heavy heart, even as a child, remembering now, how tender and comfortin' she was then, just as she was tonight. Nothing quite like a Mama . . . although she'd said a few things Catherine simply couldn't go along with. Still, there was something in the way Mama said it or explained it that never made you angry or resentful. She was just as feminine as ribbons and lace and violets and smellin' of sweet verbena, that hauntingly delicious smell which Catherine could never remember Mama not smellin' from, no matter how early in the morning. Catherine, or anyone else for that matter, had never seen her without her hair dressed to perfection or her face done up with delicate color. She was soft-spoken, and a lady . . . and that was no lie. She had impeccable taste, much better than I have, thought Catherine . . . not so flamboyant. Much more serene about everythin' . . . how to handle men. She'd kept Daddy happy all those years in spite of the fact he strayed, hadn't she? Which must've meant that for all the clingin' vine exterior and the appearin' to be so flighty, lovin' parties and clothes, underneath it all some steel. And Catherine had never realized how strong she was until tonight. Funny, when she thought about it . . . she didn't really know her Mama at all that well . . . now did she?

"Mama?" Catherine said softly. "You sleepin'?"

"No, baby . . . no, just layin' in the dark and thinkin' . . . same as you."

"Mama?"

"Yes, baby?"

"Mama, tell me the truth, now."

"I surely will, Catherine. No use bein' deceitful to your own children. What's your question, sugar?"

"Mama . . . you think I handled things wrong with Dominic?"

"Yes, I do, darlin'."

"How should I have done it? Knowin' he was carryin' on with that slut?"

"Well, now, lovin' heart, you always had one thing I wished you didn't have . . . not that I love you less for it . . . but your temper is like your darlin' Daddy's . . . and if I could say you had a fault, I would say it was that."

"I know it, Mama, it always gets me into the worst kinda trouble. There's just somethin' about it . . . before I can stop myself there I am, blowin' off like a storm . . ."

"And then you regret it . . . am I right?"

"How'd you know?"

"Cause you're just like your Daddy. You're so much alike, you coulda been one."

"I know, but yet he was so lovable."

"And so are you, sugar, except that you allow your anger to get in the way of your better judgment."

"Well, for heaven's sake, Mama, no one's perfect . . . I just expect the people I love to understand me."

"Catherine, baby, husbands aren't mothers. They're males that have to be nurtured along like hothouse plants."

"And if you're not willin' to give into every whim, then what?"

"You lose 'em."

"Now, Mama, that's a little silly because in spite of all your understandin' about men, Daddy strayed, didn't he?"

"Yes, but I never lost him, did I?"

Catherine seemed sobered by that fact. "And I've lost Dominic . . . that's what you're tryin' to say?"

"I don't know, darlin' . . . first thing you have to ask yourself is how much do you want him?"

"Well . . . I'd never admit this to anyone but my very own mother . . . I love Dominic in spite of the way he offended me . . . I really love him, but I saw red when I found out he had replaced me . . . makes a woman feel mighty inadequate. I wanted to get even with him. Now, that's not so difficult to understand, is it . . . ?"

"No . . . but you went about it in the wrong way. You sent him flyin' right back into her arms."

"Alright, you bein' so smart and all, what should I have done?"

"You should've made things so nice and comfortable for him, he never would've thought of this woman as a permanent fixture in his life."

"And how could I have done that . . . I did everything I could have in the past to make life happy for him . . . I gave him all those precious children."

"Catherine . . . listen to me. Husbands don't stay with their wives because of children. They stay because of their wives . . . now, I can't put my head on your shoulders, but you've got a way of diggin' and diggin' at a man until he wants to turn to someone for a little peace and quiet."

"Do I really do that?"

"Yes, you do, sugar. You're a little too forceful, too demandin'. Now, you can put a man on a long, long leash and let it out just so far, then gently pull it back."

"I don't know . . . I'm just downright confused about how to do that."

"Alright, let me give you a small example. Don't keep tellin' a man about the great gift of motherhood. He gets tired of hearin' it."

"Beggin' your pardon for interruptin', but Dominic said that to me."

"Well, he gave you the clue. Now, the point is, if a woman *listens* to what her husband says, she can have it all, if she lets him believe it was his idea in the first place . . . what she's really doin' is havin' it her way without him knowin' it."

"My goodness, Mama, you're just about the smartest lady I ever encountered."

"Why, thank you, Catherine . . . it's mighty nice to have your child admirin' you . . . but the thing I'm most interested in is how serious you're takin' all this and how understandin' you're bein'."

"I know one thing . . . what you're sayin' makes a lot of good old sense . . . how did you get Daddy back?"

"Well, in an odd kinda way, I never lost him. I simply played the game of make believe, keepin' up all the pretenses, givin' lots and lots of parties on Saturday nights, especially poker parties, which Daddy loved, you remember, and mistresses hate bein' alone on Saturdays. I got tickets for every show and theater, made plans to take a trip up north, out west, it didn't make one damned little bit of difference where we went, so long as I kept his mind occupied and away from her . . . and after a while I knew it was over because he said to me one day, 'Violet, I got a big surprise' . . . 'What's that,' I said . . . 'We're goin' to Italy for a long trip.'"

"I think that's wonderful, but my situation is a little different than yours. Dominic traveled so damned much through the years . . . handsome as he is . . . I don't know how many women he might've slept with."

"Alright, Catherine, that's the first mistake you made."

"And what do you mean by that?"

"Now, now, baby, this is Mama speakin'. Don't get mad . . ."

"I'm not, but I just can't be wrong about everythin', now can I?"

"I'm not sayin' that, Catherine, and I'm surely not sayin' that what Dominic did was right, but you should have gone with him when he wanted you to."

Catherine switched on the lamp and sat up in bed. "I'm surprised at you, Mama, knowin' I had little babies."

"But they weren't so little after a while . . . you still could have left them in competent care. Money was never the problem."

"And you don't think my first duty was to my babies?"

"No, I surely don't, Catherine," she answered softly, "I think your first allegiance was to your husband . . . like the Bible says, forsakin' all others."

"And you would have left Rosa Ann and me?"

"You can bet your pretty little pink foot I woulda, if it came to your Daddy."

"Well, I'm sure learnin' a lot about you I never knew."

"Maybe that's a pity, Catherine . . . perhaps if you'd known me better, you might not have lost Dominic."

Catherine's heart began to pound, "You think I've lost him . . . for good."

"Well, darlin', it wasn't more than an hour ago you said you'd never take him back."

"I know, but that was an hour ago . . . and after

talkin' this over, I think, for no other reason than that twenty-one year old investment, I shouldn't be too hasty. After all, why should Dominic have her and why should she, the dirty bitch, have my Dominic . . . I've learned a lot from you, Mama, I can tell you that."

"Have you really, baby?"

"Yes, indeed I have . . . now, tell me how do I go about gettin' Dominic back without him knowin' how many regrets I have about the things I did that night . . . which was not the kind of ladylike thing to do . . . I can see that, Mama, and I truly am filled with remorse. I showed myself in the worst possible light. I was so mad that I lost my dignity and that's something I hope I never do again."

"I hope so, Catherine, sugar . . . I hope so."

"I wouldn't, I promise you that . . . now, what do I do?"

"Alright . . . first, you let Dominic go on with this woman."

"Slut, you mean . . ."

"Now, Catherine, let's be calm . . . one can always strategize better with a clear head."

"Sorry, Mama." Catherine was beginning to enjoy the intrigue. "Go ahead."

"Alright . . . leave him alone . . . for a while. Don't you think, for one moment, that somewhere down deep, his home and family aren't somethin's he's gonna miss because he is . . . now, when a man carries on an illicit love affair in the beginnin' there's all the excitement of forbidden fruit that makes it excitin' . . . like doin' anythin' that's naughty, but given a little freedom, you'd be surprised how quickly the heated passion disappears because it's no longer wicked. And suddenly, he begins to feel cut adrift without an anchor."

"You sure?"

"I should know."

"Then how long does it take for him to begin to have all those doubts?"

"I can't say, but one thing I know is, if you give him enough rope, he'll have second thoughts."

"Well, what can I do to hurry it along? I don't want him with that disgustin' woman any longer than need be."

"Patience, Catherine, patience . . . alright now, in the next few weeks, you have the children start callin' and sayin' how much they miss him, then after a little while, you tell the children to ask Daddy home for dinner and when he comes, you act as sweet as can be. But not so sweet as to give him the idea that what he's doin' is wrong, just be natural and pretty soon he's gonna ask to come over."

"Do you really think so, Mama?"

"I surely do . . . then with your permission, I'm gonna visit *his* Mama and I'm also gonna call Dominic and see him . . . after all, I'm his mother-in-law and I never did or said a thing he ever resented."

"That's true, Mama. In fact, Dominic always had the deepest affection for you and Daddy."

"Alright, you just leave it up to me and I think if we do this right, Dominic will be home . . . happy to be."

Her Mama had given Catherine hope that things were going to work out, except one thing still bothered her. "Mama, I know you're tired and we've done a lot of important talkin', but let me ask you a very delicate question."

"Yes, sugar?"

"Can you ever make love again knowin' your husband slept with someone else?"

"Of course, if you remember that his sleepin' with a strange woman was just like takin' a hot shower . . . when it gets that hot, he's got to turn on the warm, then the cold and when the affair's cold . . . it's cold."

"Like it never happened?"

"You're learnin' . . . now, good night, sugar . . . or should I say, good mornin'?"

"Good mornin', Mama, I sure do love you."

"And I sure do love you, but that's what Mamas

are for . . . now, shut your pretty little eyes and don't you fret. I'm gonna stay here till I see my baby happy once again with her husband."

"Mama . . . my darlin' Mama, if only Dominic could see me as you do. I know I do silly things and act independent and all . . . but that's really a defense. The truth is, Mama, I love that man so much, I'd really go to hell and gone if I could only reach him, if only I felt I mattered. What I'm sayin' is, a woman's got to feel needed and wanted and when it comes down to it, she's got to feel number one and I never felt any of that with Dominic . . . why? Just please tell me why?"

"Well, baby, I can't answer all the questions, but one thing I can quote . . . It might not be the kind of comfort you're needin' just now, but a very smart man once said . . . I think his name was Oscar Wilde . . . The quote might be a little wrong . . . but never mind that, he said, that to a woman, love is all but to a man love's a thing apart . . . that's the nature of man, Catherine baby . . . that's life and no one's been able to change the thing for five thousand years . . . so come over here close to your Mama, lay your head on my shoulder . . . no more cryin' and let's see how things look after we've had a little sleep."

6

It had been two weeks since that dreadful night and now Dominic and Victoria were free to live together. But a change had come over her that made her responsiveness to Dominic's lovemaking strained. The spontaneity was no longer the same. Not that she loved him less, but her self-esteem had been so crushed. One evening at dinner, he said, "Let's go away, darling, I think the change would be so good for us."

She toyed with her food, not looking at him. Then she said, "I'd love to, Dominic, but I really must be here until Thursday."

"Thursday?"

She looked up, "Darling, I do have a practice, after all . . . we're going into court."

"Couldn't someone else take over for a few days?"

"I don't think so, dear, not on this case. It's really my baby."

He hesitated, then finally said, "You don't want to go, do you?"

"That's not true . . . of course, I do, but I simply can't."

"You've left cases before."

"I know, but not this one."

"I see . . . Victoria, we've never held back with one another. Let's talk about this."

"Talk about what?"

"I think you know." She didn't answer. "That night affected you so badly you can't get over it, can you?"

"No . . ." she answered, biting back the tears.

"Vicky, just tell me what I can do."

"Darling, what can you do? It's just me . . . I've never felt ashamed before that night, but that name has rung over and over in my ears. I'm embarrassed to see anyone. I die . . . simply die, Dominic."

"Oh, darling," he said, taking her hand and guiding her to him until she sat on his lap, "do you realize how important that night was . . . if it hadn't happened, we wouldn't be together."

"I know, but the way it happened . . ."

"I grant you, that was unforgivable . . . and it doesn't make you feel any better, I'm sure, but the one that made an ass, a fool, a spectacle of herself was her. She acted mad . . . insane."

"But that affected me . . . us."

"No, it's made us even stronger, now we can be together—"

"But you miss your children."

"Of course I do."

"Then can you be happy with me alone?"

"Vicky, no one is happy about everything. One thing has to outbalance the other . . . I love my children, I always will, but they're going to be grown up soon and I want you."

"Oh, Dominic, it all seems so wrong . . ."

Fairytales

"Look, do you remember when we first met, you asked if I could share your life without feeling wicked. I'm begging you to accept what we have and somehow, someway, this will resolve itself."

"Do you think so, Dominic?"

"I know so, darling . . . now, please do this for me . . . forget about Thursday. Some one can take over for you and let's go to Hawaii."

"Oh, God, Dominic, maybe what we do need is to get away."

"I know it is. You'll go?"

"Oh, yes, darling . . . yes."

The week in Maui was the panacea Victoria needed so badly to restore her spirits. They swam in the surf, sunned on the beach, lunched on the terrace, dressed elegantly for dinner, danced in the moonlight and made love to the sounds of the sea caressing the shore. The world was beautiful once again with the fragrance of tropical flowers that wafted through the air. It was a paradise from which Victoria wanted never to depart, but she left with a feeling of renewed hope that somehow she would be able to cope with whatever challenges lay ahead for both of them.

When Dominic sat in his office the next day after their return, going through his mail, he found a message from Gina Maria . . . he looked at the date. She had called three days ago. He realized, in that moment, how much he missed her, in spite of the fact he had tried desperately to shove aside his feelings. Looking at his watch he knew she would be in school. He took out his private telephone book from the desk and found the number. Dialing, he thought next month would be Thanksgiving. This would be the first time the family would not be together. Roberto was away . . . Dom and Tory, of course, would be home, but like Roberto, he too would be in exile . . . this would be the first holiday in nearly twenty years that he would be spending outside the family circle . . .

His thoughts were interrupted by the voice an-

162

swering the phone. "Yes, this is Mr. Rossi, would it be possible to speak to Gina Maria?"

"Let me se what class she's in." Dominic waited. . . . "I think she's in calisthenics. Will you hold on?"

"Yes."

"It will take a few minutes."

"Well, then, could she return my call?"

"Yes, Mr. Rossi."

"Thank you."

"Not at all . . . it will be very shortly."

Dominic busied himself with his correspondence. When his private phone rang, he picked it up, immediately. "Hello, Gina Maria," he answered excitedly.

"Yes, Papa . . . I'm so happy you called. You've been away."

"Yes, *cara mia,* but I've missed you so much."

"Me too, Papa, every day. Papa, when are you coming home?"

He swallowed. "I don't know . . . has Mama talked to you?"

"Yes, but, Papa, please come home."

"I can't just yet, but ask Mama if I can take you to lunch on Saturday."

"I will, but Papa, I cry every night because you and Mama are angry at each other."

"No, we just had a misunderstanding."

"Are you going to make up?"

"Yes, darling, yes." He listened to himself lie.

"Then why don't you come home."

"We'll talk about it on Saturday . . . Okay?"

"Okay, Papa. Grandma's here and said when I spoke to you to say she loves you."

"Grandma? . . . Oh, that's nice. It must be wonderful seeing her."

"Yes, but not like you, Papa."

"But we'll see each other Saturday . . . Oh, ask Vincente if he wants to come."

"Papa, would you mind if just you and I had lunch this time . . . just the two of us?"

"No, darling, I'd love that . . . now, you'll be sure and let me know if it's alright with Mama?"

"She'll say yes . . . I know it."

"But you'll call anyway, tomorrow?"

"Yes, Papa . . . Papa, I love you."

"And I love my little *cara mia*."

"I'm not so little any more, Papa. I'm fourteen . . . almost fifteen."

He paused and cleared his throat. "Sometimes I forget."

"Good-bye, Papa, I'll call tomorrow."

"I'll be waiting." With all his freedom, how free was he . . . that's what Roberto had said about possessions. He, of course, had meant material things, but children were flesh and blood . . . the other possessions one could sell, rid one's self of, but children? His reprieve from such thoughts was the phone ringing . . .

Getting back to work was impossible for Victoria. The week away had left her unfulfilled, the memory still so fresh that she couldn't launch into the batch of mail and phone calls that lay on her desk. By eleven o'clock, realizing it was impossible to concentrate, she gave up, calling her secretary, saying she was going home and would be back in the morning. But home was not exactly where she was going. First, she stopped at Guide's, the greengrocers who also sold a vast assortment of Italian delicacies, where she purchased all the ingredients for the cannelloni, which she'd had many disasters at trying to fix, but with the aid of Mrs. Guide, she was now confident that tonight's would be superb. Excitedly, she proceeded to the poultry store where she bought a large tender four-pound hen, then to the florist and finally, to the bakery. She cooked, and cleaned the apartment, arranged the flowers, set the table. It was four by the time she had finished. Getting into a tub, she relaxed and lay back. How much she had changed this year. Once, she had thought of nothing except a career. In fact, it was so important to her that Tom Lang had taken second place. Victoria had warned him before they were married that she'd never let anything interfere with that and he had accepted it . . . for a while . . . but then he became tired of fixing scrambled eggs for himself or ordering Chinese food and one thing led to the next until the mild arguments began . . . that led to the larger ones until she said "I told you so, Tom," and he said "You did", and she said "I think it's best while we're still friends to call it a day," and that's what they did, went their separate ways. Of course, Victoria never said "I was right and you were wrong," nor did Tom. What had happened to two nice people was a case of college love and a difference of interests. He was an architect and she, an attorney . . . or maybe it had nothing to do with that . . . really . . . because the last time she saw him, quite by accident, he was happily married to a doctor, a pediatrician, no less and they had one little girl whose picture he showed to Victoria with enormous pride. The child was perfectly adorable and at the time, she could scarcely remember that once he had been her husband for four years. When she had met Tom, they were both in school and it wasn't like a marriage at all, just like two roommates. But suddenly, at thirty-six, she felt barren and life had no permanency. Her career no longer seemed so important nor her ambition so urgent. So today, doing what she did, cooking, cleaning, getting ready for Dominic to come home, seemed so much more worthwhile and rewarding than any case she ever tried and won. At seven, she could scarcely wait to hear the key in the latch and when she did, her pulse raced as she ran to greet him. The lights were dimmed, the music played softly, the wine was chilled, the candles glistened and glowed, the cannelloni was bubbling in the oven, the salad was ready to be tossed and the French bread was ready to be toasted. They exchanged the same kisses and embraces, then talked about unimportant things over their drinks before dinner, but something in Dominic's manner made Victoria say, "Dominic, you're very quiet."

"Am I . . . I hadn't meant to be."

"Did something happen today?"

"No . . ."

She did not press the issue, "I didn't stay at the office."

"You didn't . . . why?"

"Oh, just wanted to play hooky."

"That's not like you."

"I know . . . but I just wanted to play house."

He laughed, "And you did an excellent job . . . everything was so delicious and beautiful."

"Thank you, darling . . . I don't suppose the cannelloni was quite like your mother's, but I tried."

"Don't tell my mother, but it was better."

She lowered her eyes, then took a sip of coffee, "I won't . . . because I've never met her."

There was no answer. Obviously, Dominic couldn't say 'you will.' Instead he answered, "It was delicious, darling. I loved it . . . but you best of all."

"Do you, Dominic?"

"Yes, Victoria . . . I wouldn't think you'd have to ask me that."

"Oh, darling, I'm not really asking, of course, I know you love me."

Something had gone wrong . . . the questions, the answers didn't seem like them at all. There was a peculiar strain she felt all through dinner.

Later, as Dominic sat reading, he seemed so far away.

"Dominic, I've been so happy today . . . I hate going back to the office."

He stopped reading, "Do you really? That's a new Victoria."

"I don't know. Something has happened, I can't explain. I think I just want to be without obligations, no regimentation. I don't know what's come over me."

"I've felt that way myself when things get to be too much."

"I don't know, Dominic . . . I'm beginning to feel I've missed so much not having children. Do you miss *your* children?"

He took her in his arms and said, "Yes . . . but it doesn't make me love you less."

"Oh, Dominic, after being so happy all day, I suddenly feel so inadequate."

"Why? Have I made you unhappy?"

"No . . . no, darling, it's just me."

"It's more than that, isn't it?"

"Yes."

"What?"

"Your mother . . . I think not being able to know her or ever meeting your children."

"Darling, in time all of that will change."

"How?"

"I really don't know just now, but one day it will be different."

"It all seems so futile."

"You don't really mean that, you couldn't."

"I don't, darling, I'm sort of confused this evening. I simply sensed something this evening I can't come to terms with."

"About me, you mean?"

"Yes, you seem so withdrawn . . . almost like you're pretending."

"You're right . . . you just know me too well."

"Something's on your mind, isn't there?"

"Yes."

"What is it?"

"Well . . . Gina Maria called."

"And you realized how much you wanted to see her."

"Yes."

"That's natural."

"I know, but it makes me feel guilty."

"Why should you?"

"Because I have a luncheon date with her and you can't be there."

She sat silent for awhile, trying to put down the feeling that this was a part of Dominic's life she would never be able to share. "But I have to see my children, darling," he continued, "what else can I do?"

"Oh, Dominic, you're making me feel so ashamed . . . as though you could read my mind."

"Much more than that . . . I can understand your feelings. You feel left out."

"Thank you for knowing me so well, but, darling, it has nothing to do with jealousy . . . only my foolish dream that I could've been friends with them, knowing, of course, that's impossible."

"Someday, darling, when they're older and have more understanding and realize how important you are in my life."

"I know, darling, I know you're right. Now, sweetheart, if you'll excuse me, I'm tired. I think I'll go to bed."

"Alright, but remember how much I love you, and need you."

"Mr. Rossi, your mother-in-law, Mrs. Posata, is on the phone," the receptionist said as Dominic sat shocked, wondering what the hell he could say to her.

Finally, he answered, "Yes, put her on."

"Dominic, darlin', this is Mama Posata. How are you?"

"Fine, Mama, and you?" he said evenly, trying to make his voice sound elated to hear from her, which was far from what he felt.

"I couldn't be better, Dominic . . . unless you were home so as I could see your sweet, shinin' face. What are you doin' for lunch this afternoon?"

He thought fast . . . should he, shouldn't he . . .

he'd have to see her eventually, so why procrastinate?
"I'm not busy at twelve-thirty. How would that be?"

"Just fine, Dominic, darlin'."

"Is there any particular restaurant you'd like to
go to?"

"Any place at all, darlin', where it's quiet and we
can talk."

He sighed, this was one lunch he could live without. "What about the Fairmont?"

"Why, that's just about my favorite place."

"Good, shall we say twelve-thirty then . . . in the
lobby?"

"That's just perfect and, Dominic, I can't tell you
how happy I am about seein' you."

"Thank you, I'm looking forward to it."

Well, twelve-thirty couldn't come around fast
enough to get over the ordeal of seeing his mother-in-
law. They sat in the quiet of the Camilia Room and
ordered. She was the epitome of charm and grace.
Not once did she refer to the separation which he knew
had brought her on this mission. She spoke about
everything else, about Bobby . . . how wonderful it was
for one of the children to show such cultural ability
and, of course, the others . . . my dear, what exceptional minds, just like his, she assured him, and Gina
Maria . . . well, that one was a beauty if there ever
was, "Why before you know it, Dominic, darlin', I
swear you'll be leadin' her down the aisle and what a
happy day for you. My goodness, I simply can't believe it, the way time is goin'. Why, Dominic, look at
me . . . I'm an old lady. Seems like only yesterday you
and Catherine were married. Time surely does march
on, doesn't it though?"

"I should say."

"And you're right, darlin', before you know it,
Christmas will be here and then the New Year always
follows and all us gettin' older. A funny thing, Dominic, I've been alone a long time now, but you know
somethin' . . . you never get over your first love. I

coulda married, but could you imagine *me*, tryin' to replace *my* Angelo? Oh, my goodness, the very idea is just simply ludicrous. Your *first love* is *your* first love and nothin' can come between that."

Dominic wiped his sweating palms on the napkin. He looked at his watch and said, "Mama, I can't tell you how wonderful it was seeing you . . . now, I really have to get back to the office."

"My goodness, Dominic, I had no idea I was detainin' you. I hope you'll forgive an old lady for ramblin' on, but I haven't seen you in some time."

"I regret that . . . it is a pity, but you're looking wonderful . . . you'll never grow old . . . you're just as lovely as ever."

"Why, thank you, Dominic . . . and you're my same handsome son. That's how I've always thought about you. Oh . . . I'm gonna have dinner with your Mama tonight. Yes, indeed, she's always been one of my very favorite people."

"She feels the same about you, I know."

"Well, we've been friends a long time."

Dominic shook his head. She took the last swallow of coffee, then said, "Darlin', you go on your way . . . I know you must be very busy."

"Yes . . . well, again, it's been very nice seeing you . . ."

She interrupted, "We're gonna see each other again, Dominic . . . you don't think I'm gonna remain in this city and not see my favorite and famous son-in-law, now, do you?" she said, smiling. "Why, Dominic, I'm the most proud mother in the world. I always knew you were gonna be someone of importance."

"Thank you, for saying that . . . it's very kind of you."

"Oh, come on now, you're just bein' too modest, Dominic."

He wasn't at all modest, he was just damned uncomfortable and couldn't get away fast enough. "Well, Mama, again, what a lovely surprise this has been."

She reached up and kissed him which he returned. As she saw him go through the revolving doors, she thought, I haven't even begun to surprise you.

The rest of the afternoon was filled with a million conflicting thoughts, all of which had been meant to achieve the desired results that Violet Posata had so carefully planned. He was aware of her strategy, making sure she made no mention of his separation from Catherine, but still, he had been uncomfortable, knowing that she knew all the reasons. At the end of the day he could hardly wait to see Victoria.

Saturday came and when he left, it was with tremendous ambivalence, but Victoria was sweet and casual, "Have a good time," she said.

"I hate leaving you."

"Oh, darling, please don't . . . after all, it's not for another woman."

She looked at him, smiling, trying to reassure him that she accepted this as part of their lives. But when he left, she sat down with a drink in her hand and thought if it were another woman, I think I could fight that, but how do you fight this, and yet, she reasoned, if she did or said one thing to discourage his relationship with his children, he would choose them. When he returned that evening, Victoria was dressed and waiting. No mention was made as to his afternoon, for which he was more than grateful. As she fixed him a drink he said, "How would you like to go dancing at the Mark?"

"I'd love it."

"Okay, we'll finish this, then get your coat. I think it's about time I took my best girl out to celebrate."

In the weeks that followed, he spent Sundays with the children, which always left Victoria at loose ends, but when he returned in the early evening, she would have dinner prepared and try to be recovered from the depression she had fought.

Then the week before Thanksgiving Violet Posata

171

paid Dominic a visit at his office, dropping in late that afternoon without having called in advance, hoping he would be able to see her. It was simply the chance she took and, as it happened, Dominic was just getting through with his last client for the day. He picked up the intercom phone when it rang. "Yes?"

"Mr. Rossi, Mrs. Posata is in the reception room waiting to see you."

Goddamn it, he thought. It was five and he and Victoria had theater tickets. He had promised her he would be home about six and he still had some paperwork to do before leaving. Angrily, he said, "Send her in . . . in about five minutes." He then called Victoria on his private phone and, when he heard her voice, his heart skipped a beat. "Sweetheart, I'm going to be a little late, I'm afraid, but something came up which might detain me."

There was a moment of silence, then she asked, "Do you think we'll be able to make the theater?"

"Oh, I'm sure and if it's alright with you, we'll have something to eat later."

"That's alright, I understand."

"Thank you, darling, but I'll be home as soon as I can get this out of the way."

"I'll be waiting."

He wanted to say I love you, but she had already hung up, leaving him looking at the silent phone. Mechanically, he pressed the button, "Have Mrs. Posata come in."

Standing up to greet her, it was difficult for him to try and be cordial, but if there was a trace in his manner that indicated his dismay, she certainly gave no indication as she said, "Dominic, darlin', I hope you'll forgive me for bargin' in on you, but I thought that maybe this was the best time after office hours."

"I'm glad you did. However, I have a business conference in about twenty minutes."

"Oh . . . well, I just would like to talk to you for just a few minutes, darlin' . . . may I sit down?"

"Forgive me, please do."

She sat across from him as he seated himself behind his desk. "You look a little tired, Dominic. Maybe you're overdoin' things."

"Today was a little hectic and long."

"I can imagine so, Dominic, I'm not gonna carry on a lot of sweet talk with you and get right down to the reason I wanted to see you." He sighed, knowing what was coming, but he remained silent. "Dominic, I know you're aware of why I'm stayin' with Catherine and, of course, I also know what happened between you. But before I begin, I also want you to know I'm not judgin' you nor puttin' the blame on you."

He looked at her, clearing his throat and running his tongue over his dry lips, "Thanks—but before you begin, would you like something to drink?"

"I think that would be nice, Dominic."

"What would you care for?"

"Anythin' . . . a little brandy if you have it."

"Yes," he said going to the bar, pouring a brandy for Violet and a bourbon for himself. He couldn't go through this without a little something to fortify him. Handing her the glass, once again he sat down behind the desk, took a swallow, then said, "I don't want to be unkind, but really, I think this is a subject I'm not quite up to discussing."

"Well, Dominic, the truth is, this is the kind of subject one is never up to discussin', but you're just gonna have to be a little patient with an old lady who doesn't really want to interfere, but, Dominic, it does seem to me that I think you're not takin' into consideration a lot of things."

"Yes, and what is that?"

"You know, Thanksgivin' is comin' and what do you suppose it's gonna be like for the children without their Daddy there?"

And what's it going to be like for Victoria and how in the hell could he face Catherine after that horrible nightmare? The wounds were too raw and deep

173

to even consider sitting at the same table with her. Obviously, she had discussed his spending the holiday with the family or else why would Violet Posata be here? "Mama, I don't want to offend you, knowing your intentions are meant for the sake of the children, but I regret to say, I simply could not do that."

Quietly, she asked, "Why, Dominic, is it your pride?"

"It goes a little deeper than that."

"Are you gonna sit there and tell me that what happened between you and Catherine goes above your responsibility to your children?"

He got up and walked to the window, looking out at the dusk that covered the city. Turning around, he said, "I love my children and I think I've been a good father, but there are some things a man can't do, not because of pride, but because . . . the situation between Catherine and me is completely over."

"When you have children, it's never over."

"I'm afraid that's one thing I'm going to have to deprive them of."

Taking a sip of her brandy, she said, "Dominic, I think you're one of the most exceptional people I've ever had the privilege of knowin' and I'm just a little shocked that someone of your stature can't rise above your own personal feelin's . . . not when your feelin's involve so many others. Whatever your problems are with Catherine, I'm not even concerned about . . . in fact, the two of you, at this moment, are unimportant . . . it's those children I'm thinkin' of. You brought them into the world and imagine, if you can for just one minute, what that day's gonna be like? Now, I'm not takin' you to task, you know that. No matter what happens, the future between you and Catherine is somethin' for the two of you to resolve . . . but, Dominic, think like the mature man you are. You can't avoid one another forever . . . not that I'm askin' you for one minute to make it up with Catherine, you two just aren't important . . . but those children are. Don't you know there are gonna be lots and lots of events in the future the two of you are gonna have to share . . . have you thought of that?"

"Yes . . . I'd be less than honest if I said I hadn't."

"Well, then, Dominic, be honest. Don't you think you should be sittin' at the head of your table with your children all around you?"

He sat down with his head in his hands and thought, much as he wanted to say, "I wouldn't, I can't," he could not dismiss lightly the things she had said. He was brought up sharply. "Dominic, darlin', I know you have to be goin', but you think about this . . . and whatever decision you come to, I'll still love you. But you consider the children. I know, before I go, that you'll do the right thing . . . Now God love you and I'll be in touch in a day or so."

He got up and kissed her lightly, on the cheek, and watched as she closed the door behind her, then he went back and sat for a few minutes. He swiveled in his chair and stared up at the ceiling. He knew the answer . . . that wasn't why he was procrastinating . . . how do you tell a woman you're living with, someone you love, adore, would do anything in the world for . . . except be with her on Thanksgiving . . . Christmas . . . Fourth of July . . . Sundays . . . etc . . . etc., and expect her to keep saying, "yes, darling, I understand . . . of course darling, I don't mind playing second fiddle to your seven little Neros." Oh, shit! It was easier before he left Catherine. Cockeyed as it was, the only problem it seemed then, as he looked back, was being unfaithful to a wife. He glanced at the clock on his desk . . . it was six. Getting up quickly he left with a feeling of being more unfaithful to Victoria than he'd ever been to Catherine.

That evening, he sat in the theater and heard not one word of what was going on. Instinctively, he laughed in the right places, applauded at the right time, said it was marvelous when Victoria asked. He had all the makings of Mr. Hyde, but the pretense was killing him. That night, when he lay next to Victoria, he felt like a louse for having made love to her that evening. It was almost the same kind of deviousness Catherine had perpetrated on him when she had tried to soften him first . . . the night she told him about the house she had bought without his knowledge, the only difference was that he weighed in the balance what Victoria's reaction would be.

He held her tightly and asked for the very first time, "Victoria?"

"Yes, darling?"

"Are you happy?"

There was a long, long pause, "Why do you ask?"

"Because I know this situation isn't easy for you."

"It isn't easy for either one of us, is it?"

"No . . . but my concern is you."

"I've never complained, have I?"

"No, never . . . but I'm sure there have been many times when you would have liked to."

"That's true, Dominic, but I've got to accept it on these terms don't I . . . what other choices do I have . . . or you, for that matter?"

"None, not really. I told you once a man doesn't belong to himself when he has children. You remember that?"

"Yes . . . and what you're trying to tell me is you're having a problem with yourself?"

"Yes, things like where my loyalties lie . . . my duties, obligations."

Victoria switched on the lamp and sat up in bed. "Let me understand this, Dominic, what kind of duties, obligations and loyalties are we talking about? Do I fall into the category of a duty . . . an obligation? Look, let me tell you this . . . my boiling point is very high. It takes a great deal to make me angry. I cut my eyeteeth on tolerance and never being sorry later for things I said in anger. At this moment, I'm not thanking my parents for giving me such sage advice because I think there's a great deal more to this conversation than you're telling me. Alright, Dominic, say it."

"Victoria, I can't stand it when you're hurt like this."

"You can't stand it? Well, at this moment, if you don't mind, I'm concerned about *my* feelings . . . you have something to say, then say it."

"I had a visitor today."

"Really . . . your children . . . your wife? The King of Siam?"

"This is not like you, Victoria."

"Don't you think so? Well, maybe there are things about me you don't know. Now, who was your visitor?"

"My mother-in-law."

Victoria started to laugh, until there were tears in her eyes. "Your mother-in-law? My God, there's no end to the parade. And what did the dear Southern patrician lady say? . . . No, don't tell me, I know."

"What do you think she said?"

"Dominic, I'm in the law, remember? Now, let's see . . . she said, Dominic, darlin' I really think it's wrong for a family to break up. It doesn't make any difference what happened . . . you're a *family* . . . Am I gettin' warm?"

He didn't blame her, she had a right. Quietly, he answered, "That's about right."

She got out of bed, and went into the bathroom, trying to hold on to whatever dignity she was still able to control because if she said another word, it would be like the night at DeLucci's with Catherine throwing things and that's exactly what she felt like doing . . . screaming but she washed her face in cold water, grateful Dominic had not persuaded her or tried to be soothing or comforting. At this moment, she had to be alone. Then, suddenly, a thought conjured up from the past when Dominic had pleaded with her not to become involved with him. Remembering his words, 'But what kind of a life will this be for you' and the rest of the words and conversation rang like a bell in her mind. He'd been right . . . hadn't he? But how sure she was that evening which seemed like a million years ago. 'But I'm a big girl,' she heard herself saying, 'and I know what I'm getting into . . . my eyes are wide open.' Isn't that what she said? My God, the promises people think they're equal to before the challenge. Victoria, you're acting like a jealous wife . . . be honest for God's sake, Dominic's torn between you and them. They came first, his duties and obligations *are* to them . . . it's tough, but that's what you're confronted with . . . Okay, now, how much does he mean to you . . . how much do you really love him . . . is the loneliness, the frustration, the feeling of being shut out at times, worth it . . . would your life be less complicated . . . That's a damned foolish question. Of course, it would . . . but can you have the love without the pain? Think . . . what would it be like without him Hell. Okay . . . dry your tears and wash your face and act your age and be a *woman*.

She went back into the bedroom and for a moment looked at Dominic, who could not meet her gaze. Of course she had become an obligation to him. Was that bad, she asked herself . . . no, because it was more than that . . . he loved her and that's why he couldn't face her at this moment. Getting back into bed, she clung to Dominic in silence for a while, then she said, "Now, I'm ready to hear what your mother-in-law said to you."

Softly, he answered, "She spoke to me about being with the children at Thanksgiving."

Victoria responded without emotion, "You've given it a great deal of thought?"

"Yes."

"And?"

"I feel it's the only thing I can do . . . "

"You're right, Dominic . . . forget a few minutes before. I simply had to blow off steam, but I, honestly, know this is right."

He held her closer. As she turned off the light, she felt his tears on her naked shoulder. Dominic was deeply shaken, knowing he was abandoning her. Finally she said, "Darling, I love you and that's all that matters." And almost believed it.

Dominic stood before the door, dreading to ring. How the hell could he see or much less be in the same place with Catherine. He felt like a stranger with his finger poised on the bell. Finally summoning enough courage, he pushed and heard the sound of chimes inside. Almost immediately the door was opened by Gina Maria who threw her arms around Dominic, kissing and hugging him saying, "I'm so glad you're home, Papa." Home? No, you're the only thing that makes it possible for me to be standing here, he thought and then she called out, "Papa's here." Soon the rest were surrounding him, embracing him like some hero returning from the wars. He looked at all his sons. They took hold of him by the shoulders. If only they had been Victoria's. Then the moment he had dreaded was standing before him dressed in a printed flowing matte jersey from Pucci's, her hair coiffed to perfection, bejeweled with earrings that hung like diamond chandeliers.

When Catherine took his hand in hers, he shuddered, but as though nothing at all had happened, she said, "Dominic, the children could hardly wait and I've got a few wonderful surprises. Now, come on in." He released his hand which she seemed not to notice as he followed her into the enormous sunken living room. There were autumn chrysanthemums in profusion. The aroma from the kitchen permeated the air with delicious holiday smells. And sitting in the large chair before a blazing fire was Dominic's mother. Shocked at seeing her, he said, "I spoke to you last night and you didn't tell me you would be here."

"We wanted it to be a surprise."

"I thought you were going to Theresa's . . . you go every year."

She smiled and shook her head, "So this year I decided to be here."

Catherine didn't overlook a thing, did she, he thought as he kissed his mother with great affection.

"And don't I get the same kind of a kiss from my

favorite son?" Mama Posata asked, dressed in her
favorite color, rose mauve lace.

"Of course," Dominic answered as Catherine
stood by smiling broadly.

"Now, Dom, you be the bartender while I go see
if everythin's going well in the kitchen."

Everyone was in a festive mood laughing and
chatting . . . all except Dominic and his mother who
both pretended to join the happy occasion. His mother
felt out of place since this was the first time Catherine
had been so cordial, extending her hospitality so gra-
ciously, which Mrs. Rossi knew was for the benefit of
Dominic. She also knew that Dominic had left his
home and was living with a strange woman. At this
moment, although her grandchildren made up for
some of the pain she felt, never before had she been
grateful that her beloved husband had been spared
the charade of this pretense. For Dominic, it was like
drinking hemlock, seeing Catherine, remembering all
too well what she was capable of and the crushing
humiliation Victoria had suffered, and she was heavy
on his mind, knowing that, although she was spending
today with her parents and a house full of friends, she
felt as alone as he. But he sat on the large sofa talking
to Dom and Tory about school when suddenly he
looked up and standing in front of him with a platter
of hors d'oeuvres was Stella. His mouth hung open
This was the second shock he had received today . . .
that's what Catherine had meant by a surprise.

"*Buon giorno,* Stella," Dominic said, feeling the
heavy pain in his chest, in fact he had to hold back the
tears knowing she had suffered because of her loyalty
to him. He truly loved this simple woman. How had
Catherine taken her back?

"*Buon giorno, Signore.*" She held the plate for him
to help himself. As he did so, she lowered her eyes,
then moved on to the others.

Catherine sat at ease and chatted casually with
the two mothers as though today was as natural as past
holidays had been. If she felt any tensions, they were

not apparent. After an hour, Anna came in and announced dinner. Dom took his mother's arm while Dominic assisted his mother on one side and Gina Maria on the other. Tory escorted Grandma Posata and the others followed. Everyone took their seats with Dominic uncomfortably sitting at the head of the table.

"Everyone'll be quiet while Papa says grace . . . Dominic?"

He lowered his head while his eyes rested on the dinner plate. For a moment he could not find his voice. Then quickly, shutting his eyes, he said, "We thank thee dear Lord for all we are about to receive which you have given us so abundantly." His voice faltered at the end, but all the children raised their glasses, as did Catherine and the grandmothers, and drank a toast (which Catherine had previously suggested they do) to Papa's good health.

Dom stood up with his glass in hand and said, "I drink, as I think we all should, to the love of our parents for having given us so much . . . for having given us the understanding and patience through all the years . . . to your health and happiness, I drink."

Each of the children stood. "*Salute* . . . Mama . . . Papa."

Dominic had tears in his eyes as Gina Maria went quickly to her father and kissed him, then to her mother.

Stella had outdone herself . . . the dressing was marvelous, the turkey moist and tender, as Dominic carved. The cranberry molds, the sweet potatoes, casseroles, the pies and pastries melted in one's mouth.

Catherine had been instructed by Mama to be gracious, but not overly so . . . to be casual with Dominic without seeming aloof. She played the part to perfection. The gracious, loving mother, the understanding wife, solicitous only when the occasion demanded, sure the innuendos intended were understood by Dominic.

Dinner over, everyone retired, more than full, but

happy, to the living room where Catherine said, "Gina Maria, play Papa's favorite song."

She sat down at the piano and began "Sorrento." Vincente came to her side and began to sing. Soon all the others joined in as Dominic sat observing them, while Catherine sat observing him and thinking, this is the beginning, Miss Lang. He'll be back and you'll be out.

The music continued with all the old Italian songs which Dominic loved so much. It was Dom who came to his father and whispered, "Dad, could I speak to you?"

Reluctantly, Dominic said, "Yes," knowing, of course, what the conversation was going to be about.

"Shall we go into your study, Papa?"

"Alright." The two left as Catherine watched, still singing along with the others.

When they sat down, Dominic took out a cigarette, lit it, watched the flame die, then said, "You wanted to talk . . . I suppose about school?"

"Well, that . . . but first, about something more important."

Dominic puffed on the cigarette and waited.

"Papa, Tory and I didn't know about you and Mama until we came home. In fact, when you weren't at the airport, we were shocked."

Dominic scratched the back of his head. "I didn't know when you were arriving."

"Oh, I see." There was silence. "Papa, I'm sure this is very difficult to discuss, but all I know is what I got from Angie and Tony."

"What did they say?"

"That you moved out."

"Did they say why?"

"Only that you and Mama had a terrible fight."

"This *is* very difficult to talk about."

"I'm sorry, Papa . . . but I think I have a right to know what happened."

Dominic hesitated and looked at his oldest son.

"You're right. In a family there should be no subterfuge."

"Okay, I'm waiting.

"Dominic, I don't know how or where to begin."

"Why not from the beginning?"

"Well, that goes back to a garden in New Orleans."

"I don't mean that, Papa. Let's talk about *now*. What happened between Mama and you?"

"What happened is that when people are completely different they have nothing in common . . . well, they fall apart. It's like a house without a foundation."

"And you have no foundation? Your children aren't a foundation?"

"Dominic, let me try and explain . . . I love my children and I think you all know that, but I find I can no longer go on living with the tensions between your mother and me. After all these years, just—"

"But we were a happy family. . . . I find it hard, Papa, to understand how you and Mama suddenly have nothing in common."

"That's just the point, it wasn't sudden . . . and may I say, Dominic, much as I respect you, I don't want to talk about all the differences between Mama and me."

"Why?"

"Because if I do, it would appear I was defending my position while making your mother seem wrong and that I wouldn't do."

"But you do feel she was wrong . . . wrong enough to leave her."

"Please, Dominic, don't push me into saying a great many things I believe are better left unsaid."

"So you're just going to leave it by saying you're incompatible and let it go at that?"

"Yes."

"Well, I'm not, Papa . . . I know there's a great deal more to it than merely being incompatible."

Dominic was trying to hold down his desire to
say, look, don't question me in that tone of voice, but
checking his impulse, he answered, "Since you want
to pursue this, say what you want to tell me."

"Alright, Papa . . . there's another woman . . .
obviously, isn't there?"

Dominic answered slowly, "Yes . . . since you
already know . . . yes."

"And you left Mama for someone else . . . I'm
sorry, Papa, but I think that's unforgivable."

"Dominic . . . up to now I've tried to be patient
and explain as best I could—"

"But you haven't explained a thing—"

"Alright, you listen to me, Dom, and carefully . . .
I didn't leave your mother for another woman, because
when two people have something important between
them then there never is a need for another woman.
In all the years of our marriage, I never cheated on
your mother once. It's only when there is no marriage,
a man goes elsewhere."

"What were the terrible differences you and
Mama couldn't resolve . . . I simply don't understand."

"That's because you're a son, not a husband."

"So give me something to understand . . . as a
husband."

"You're forcing me, Dom, to tell you things I
don't want to."

"What did Mama do that was impossible to live
with?"

Dominic, not looking at his son for a long moment,
said, "Alright. From the time we were married, your
mother fought me all the way on every important thing
in my life. I'm a man, Dom, a man who wants to go as
far as my abilities can take me. I've been poor, terribly
poor in my life. I've made a name for myself and I did
it the hard way, but your mother wanted me to do it
her way. I think you've known I always wanted to get
into politics, but I've stayed away because of her. She
would have made me into a dependent, frightened
little man if she could have, but our biggest and great-

est problem is both of us are too strong-willed and that's bad for a marriage. That's the dilemma in our lives."

Dom sat trying to see his mother in the role of the domineering woman, but somehow found he could not. All he could see was the good woman trying to make a home, raise her children and be a patient wife, remembering, during his growing up, that his father was away more than he was home. He loved his father, but in his heart he felt his father had misjudged his mother. "Well . . . I don't know what to say. Please forgive me, Papa, but I think you're making a terrible mistake. Maybe you don't realize it now, but I feel this woman has been a very great influence in your leaving Mama. I hope it's not one you'll regret."

"Dominic, *mio figlio*, this woman was not the reason . . . she was the result."

"Please, Papa, I guess I'm confused . . . but tell me, what does she have to offer you that Mama doesn't?"

Dominic laughed sadly, "Oh, *mio figlio*, you're asking questions to which I have no answers."

"There have to be some answers, Papa."

"The only answer I can give you is she gives me the peace I need in my life. . . . I know that doesn't satisfy you, but you asked."

"You're right, Papa, it doesn't satisfy me. . . . Papa?"

"Yes, Dominic?"

"You talked about politics before . . . well, you know under these circumstances, that would be out for you . . . The public doesn't take too kindly to politicians who have mistresses."

"Well, in that case, Dominico, I'll just have to content myself with trying to elect the men whose positions I would have liked to occupy . . . no one can have everything."

"Then you mean it's over between you and Mama?"

"I'm afraid so . . . my Dominico, I'm afraid so."

Dom got up and put his arms around his father, holding him tightly around the shoulders and said, "I still love you, Papa."

"And I love you, my oldest son, my pride . . . my name."

Mama Posata knocked on the door, interrupting them. "What's goin' on in here. You're missin' all the fun. Now, come on, the two of you," she said, taking Dominic by the hand and leading him back into the living room, where the singing still continued.

Dominic looked at his watch. It was ten. . . . Victoria would be home. He excused himself and went to the kitchen. Stella was just finishing when she saw him. The guilt written in her eyes . . . had it not been because of her stupidity, her clumsiness in being caught that morning, her signore would still be here, living in his house, the head of his table.

He, of course, would never know how frantically Catherine had tracked her down, living with her friends from Italy in North Beach, afraid to leave even for a breath of fresh air for fear she would be apprehended by the immigration department. But Stella went with the package if Catherine was to try and get Dominic back. So in Catherine's subtle way, she told Stella how much she regretted what had happened, that in no way did she hold Stella responsible for anything and what had happened *that morning* was simply the case of a distraught wife. She insisted Stella come back to the place where she was wanted and needed . . . *her home,* so with no other choice Stella packed her small belongings and returned.

"Stella," Dominic said, putting his arms around her, "I'm sorry you suffered because of me."

"No . . . no, *signore,* I have asked the Madonna for forgiveness because I was responsible for your pain . . . please forgive me."

Oh, God, this dear soul wanted to protect *him.* He let her go, then sat down at the table and wrote a check for five thousand dollars. She trembled when she saw it and refused to take it, but Dominic insisted.

Handing it back, he said, "Stella, you know where the bank is, California and Sansome."

"What bank?"

"Ours . . . you know the one."

"Yes," she said with eyes downcast.

He took her face in his hands and said, "Look at me, Stella, never be afraid to look anyone in the eyes."

"*Si, signore.*"

"Alright . . . don't tell anyone about this but I want you to have money of your own so *no one* can throw you out into the streets penniless again . . . you understand me?"

"*Si, signore.*"

"Good. Now, tomorrow I want you to open a savings account and I will continue to add to it . . . and the next thing, I want you to become a citizen. I'll take care of that, too."

"Why are you doing this for me, *signore*, I'm only a servant—"

"No, to me you are a very special lady . . . and a very good friend and that many friends we don't have in life."

She took his hand and kissed it.

"Please, Stella, my hand you don't have to kiss . . . only the Pope's . . . now, *arrivederci*, Stella, sleep well."

"*Arrivederci, signore*, and may God be with you."

"*Grazie*, Stella," he said, leaving the room.

When he sat in the car alongside of his mother, driving her home, he was grateful to her that she had said nothing about the way the children looked when he left or how wrong he was. She mentioned nothing except what a lovely day it had been, how happy she was they were together, but that was his mother. . . . Stopping in front of her flat, he came around to her side and opened the door. When she got out, she kissed him good night, "God bless you, Dominic. I'm proud to have a son like you," she smiled.

"And I'm grateful to have a mother like you." He waited as she walked up the stairs and disappeared.

Getting back into the car, he drove away with thoughts of Catherine, seeing her in his mind's eye. The way she had underplayed the whole affair, trying to copy her Mama, the gentle Southern lady . . . "Dominic, we're all so happy to have been together this evening," as he was leaving . . . he wanted to say, thank you, very much, Catherine, for your hospitality . . . it was really something I could have lived without. Shaking his head in the dark . . . yes . . . how well I remember your graciousness . . . whoremaster . . . *patrone* to a whore . . . come on, Dominic, knock it off . . . that's enough.

When he let himself in, Victoria was not home. Feeling deserted, he undressed and got into bed. Looking at the clock, he realized it was almost twelve . . . he began to worry if anything had happened . . . an accident . . . he got out of bed and poured himself a drink and sat down. Now it was twelve-thirty. The palms of his hands began to sweat. Where the hell was she, he asked the silent room as he paced the floor? If she wasn't home in another . . . then suddenly he heard the key being turned. It was one by the time Victoria opened and shut the door behind her.

"Hi, darling," she said, taking off her shoes. Flushed with pretended excitement, she kissed him. "Let's have a drink . . . oh, you already have one. In that case, I'm going to, too. Bet you had a wonderful time," she said as she poured herself a scotch. "I certainly did, with all my family and friends . . . it was simply great . . . best turkey and . . . the dressing . . . you wouldn't believe it, so festive. So terrific . . . so really terrific—or did I already say that?" She hiccoughed, "Excuse me, must have been something I drank . . . or ate." Dominic sat down and watched as she finished her drink, then poured another. "How 'bout you, darling, feel like a little refreshment?" she asked unsteadily.

"No . . . in fact, I think you've had enough."

" 'nough of what. . . . I think we should give thanks. It's Thanksgiving, Dominic . . . time to be 'appy . . . to *Thanks* . . . there I go again, repeating myself."

"Victoria, come to bed."

"To bed with you . . . you wench!" She laughed, "Dominic, you're *dominating* me."

"You're drunk, Victoria. Now, let me help you get into bed."

"Drunk! How can you say that?" she slurred, "insulting me that way. I was never inebriated in my whole life . . . in my whole crazy, stupid, mixed-up life." She laughed, and laughed until she cried.

Dominic took her in his arms and carried her into the bedroom where he lay her down, hovering over like a child.

The crying had sobered her. "Oh, Dominic, I'm acting so stupid . . . like a real ninny. How do you put up with me?"

"I'm the one who should be asking that."

"Oh, God, Dominic, I missed you so. How do I get over that . . . how do I reconcile myself to that . . . how?"

"I don't know because today was just as lonely for me. It's plain hell being without you."

"But what can we do?"

"I wish I knew the answer to that one."

"My mother was so wrong . . . I want the whole matzo ball and when I can't, I act like a spoiled, deprived infant who just had her shovel and sand pail taken away."

"Honey, you don't have to be so brave just because you got slightly tight tonight. It's little enough for what you have to put up with."

"But, Dominic, this moment with you is all the intoxication I need . . . wouldn't it be wonderful if we could just make time stand still?"

"And how many times I've wished that, but I think this is the toughest time of the year. If only we can get over the holidays, then we're going to Mexico for a few weeks on a cruise."

"Oh, Dominic, how wonderful."

"I've had it up to here with everything."

"Everything?" she asked, snuggling closer to Dominic.

"Everything, except you," he said, kissing her erect nipples, then holding her close, feeling her body yield to his, making them one.

7

The month of December came all too soon and once
again it was a time for Dominic to spend Christmas
Day away from Victoria. But this time she was resigned, thankful she had a family she could go to as
well.

The Rossi ménage was all assembled around the
huge tree, opening presents, and once again Catherine
played the role of the contented wife and mother pretending that nothing was different than in years gone
by, only this time, she took care to be ever so slightly
more attentive to Dominic than at Thanksgiving.

After dinner, she found Dominic in the study, relaxing with Dom and Tory. "What's goin' on in here
with all my men?"

"Nothing," Tory said, "just discussing politics."

"Is that what you're doin' . . . I think you ought to
let your Papa relax today and not have to talk or think
about such things . . ."

Dom stood up and looked quickly at Tory, who
got the message, then making some excuse they left,

191

leaving Mama and Papa alone. Dominic was not at all grateful for what they considered a time for estranged parents to be alone, but he remained.

Catherine looked all shimmery in her gold and green lamé as she seated herself across from Dominic. "You're lookin' fine, Dominic, better and more rested than I've seen you in a long time."

"Thank you," he answered, his voice flat, which Catherine pretended not to notice.

"How about a little Cointreau to settle your stomach after that sumptuous meal?"

"No thank you."

"Sure now?"

"I'm sure."

"Well, I think I'm gonna have a little . . . " Pouring herself a drink, she said lightly, "Stella's just gotta be the best cook in the world . . . don't you think so?"

"Yes . . ."

"Now, Dominic, tell me, what was all that about, all that politics and all."

"Well, like you said before, today's not the time to discuss world affairs."

"And you're right . . . what do you think of the boys . . . so grown up and handsome and brilliant . . . just like their Daddy."

"I think I will have that brandy," Dominic said.

"Why, of course." Handing it to him, she said, "Aren't the children just simply incredible?"

"Just incredible."

"Dominic, did you get a letter from Roberto?"

"No . . ."

"That's strange . . . I forwarded it to your office."

"Did you . . . well, I didn't get it."

"That's too bad. I suppose with the Christmas mail, you'll probably get it next week."

"How is he?"

"He's doin' just wonderful and happy as can be."

"I'm glad to hear that."

"Wait till you read the letter. It'll do your heart good."

"I'm sure." Then there was silence between them. Dominic gulped down the brandy.

"Here, let me get you another." Before he could protest, he found the glass filled and in his hand.

"Dominic?"

"Yes?"

"Dominic, I know this has been difficult for you comin' home like this . . ."

"Yes, it has."

"But don't you think enough time has gone by that we could be just a little more friendly when we have to see each other?"

"That isn't so easy."

"I know, but the children feel it, in spite of all the . . . well, pretense."

"I'm afraid that's the only way we're going to make it. . . . I can't cut myself up into a million little pieces. I can only be me—"

"But don't you ever remember the good times. Shouldn't that make you just a little more . . . friendly?"

"When were the good times, Catherine?"

"While the children were growin' up and we had all those wonderful holidays together."

He didn't answer.

"You mean all those years made no impression on you, you never recall . . . the birthdays, the happy times don't mean a thing?"

He sighed, "Look, Catherine, there's nothing to talk about, what I do remember are a lot of other things I'd rather forget—"

"I don't want to argue with you, Dominic. All I'm askin' is for you to try and forget the bad and remember the good."

"What I'm trying very hard to do, Catherine, is not to remember anything, except the fact that I'm here doing what is expected of me."

"You mean then, there isn't a chance that you and I can share at least what I remember as some of the happiest times of my life with you?"

193

"Catherine . . . you're not a fool and neither am I. What's past is past. It can never be relived. If we had those good times, as you put it, we wouldn't be in this position now."

"So you're totally through. Am I understandin' right?"

His shoulders slumped. Finally, he said, "Yes, Catherine, you're right. It's all over. It really was a long, long time ago."

She sat, thinking Mama was mistaken. She had underestimated human nature. Dominic was not Daddy and havin' a temper at this moment or a fit wasn't goin' to bring him back. He would do his duty, be the best father he knew how, but he was never comin' back and it would be childish to think he was. But she was going to remain the charming lady, if it killed her, "Well, Dominic, I think we should join the others." With that, her head held high, she walked ahead of Dominic across the marble hall back to where the festivities were going on and joined in, although she knew later she'd cry for a very long, long time.

～⌣～

Victoria stretched out on the deck chair in her bikini, feeling the delicious sun and sea breezes upon her body. How marvelous to be so completely relaxed. It was so peaceful and quiet as though there weren't a care in the world. She reached over and held Dominic's hand without saying a word, and there they lay, feeling the oneness of each other. At last she had come to terms with herself about Dominic's children, knowing what part they played in his life . . . not that she had ever doubted his love for her. And now she had come to terms with reality.

The next two weeks were paradise. But the ecstasy they'd known was coming to an end. Their last night out, Victoria lay in Dominic's arms. "Darling, I wish this could go on and on . . . I'm not ready to go home . . . how about you?"

"It's difficult to believe we've been away two weeks."

"But what a two weeks it's been . . . let's look at the pictures." Getting out of bed, she went to the dresser and took out an envelope of snapshots. With Dominic's arm once again around her, she snuggled up to him and together they looked. "Oh, Dominic, you with that great big sombrero, trying to get on that donkey with your legs almost touching the ground. Where was that taken?"

"Puerto Vallarta, I think . . . and look at this one with you eating that tortilla and all the juice running onto your new Mexican blouse. The expression on your face is priceless."

"Wait . . . look at this one when the zipper on your trousers broke and I found a safety pin in my purse. I think I'll keep that one for the opposition when you become president."

"And when will that be?"

"Probably at the next election."

"Really? Well, at least I'll have the smallest majority of one in history . . . look at this . . . remember when that Mexican boy in Acapulco snapped our picture together and the sun was in my eyes, I look like Ben Turpin."

They screamed with delight. "Oh, Dominic, you're not only the most wonderful man I've ever known, you do a very mean rumba . . . among other things," she said, kissing him.

"And you, Miss Lang, are the most beautiful, wonderful sexy woman I know . . . and you're also mine, *all* mine . . ."

Laughing, she said, "Aren't you lucky?"

"That's about the most accurate statement anyone ever made."

"Oh, Dominic, we're the luckiest people in the world."

"I know that I am."

"Thank you, darling. These few weeks have been very special for me."

"And for me . . . I don't know when I've ever been so completely happy—"

"But it's more than just being happy. Something wonderful has happened inside me."

He looked at her.

"What do you mean?"

"I've accepted things as they are."

"I'm not so sure that I have . . ."

"Why, darling?"

"Well, the fact that we can't ever marry—"

"It really isn't that important, darling, not anymore . . . because I feel *I am* married to you . . . not being able to be friends with your children . . . well, I've come to terms with that."

"No wonder I love you so much."

"Oh, darling, that's just it . . . if two people love one another the way we do, we can't allow the *impossible* to spoil what we have."

She moved even closer. "Dominic, I wouldn't trade places with any woman."

Kissing her, he said, "And I wouldn't trade you for anyone."

But tomorrow came and once again they were home, putting aside all the memories and momentos. After breakfast, Dominic drove Victoria to her office then went to his. When he arrived, his private secretary said, "Welcome home, Mr. Rossi. You look like you're still on cloud nine."

"Thanks, Margo, but I better get off from the looks of the mail sitting on my desk."

She hesitated, then said, "Mr. Rossi . . . Mrs. Rossi has been trying to get you since yesterday. She seemed quite upset."

"Did she mention what the problem was?"

"No."

"All right, get her on the phone."

When Catherine said, "Dominic, a terrible thing has happened," his heart began to race. His first thought was Gina Maria.

"What's happened?"

She started to cry. "Roberto's missin'."

He frowned. "Roberto's missing . . . what are you talking about?"

"Segetti called . . . there was so much static I could hardly understand him, but finally between shoutin' I realized he was tellin' me Roberto left all his things and hasn't been back for about a week now."

"Oh, my God, what else did he say?"

"That finally he had asked all of Roberto's friends about where he was, but they said they hadn't seen him."

"Did Segetti notify the police?"

"Yes, but he was nowhere to be found in Florence. I'm simply beside myself with grief."

"I'll be there in a few minutes . . . in the meantime, try and stay calm. I don't think anything terrible has happened. You would have heard if that were the case."

"You're just sayin' that to make me feel better and I appreciate it, but I have this gnawin' feelin', Dominic, I can't explain . . ."

"I'm leaving now and then we'll decide what we should do."

"Thank you, Dominic."

When Dominic arrived, he found Catherine worn from weeping and Mama Posata by her side trying as best she could to comfort her. In that moment, he felt honest pity for Catherine. Roberto, of all her sons, was her favorite and if something had really happened to him . . .

Trying to remain calm, Dominic once again questioned Catherine, but nothing new had been added. "Segetti simply said that Roberto had not been heard from for a week . . . now somethin' must have happened, Dominic. A boy just simply doesn't go off and leave his belongin's without sayin' a word . . . and he'd never do that to me . . . not let me know where he is . . . no, Dominic, I just know in my heart, somethin' *terrible's* happened to him . . ."

Dominic moistened his dry lips. He couldn't simply reassure her any longer, because what she said made sense. If the boy had been found, the police would have notified Catherine or Segetti. "Alright, Catherine, let me go back to the office and straighten things out and I'll pack a bag . . . the only thing we can do is go to Florence and try and find out what this is all about."

"God bless you, Dominic, for your understandin'."

"He's my son, too, Catherine."

Leaving, he went to his office, made a few very important calls, told Margo that he would be away for an indefinite period but would be in touch, then he called Victoria and told her to meet him at the apartment.

She entered and saw Dominic ash white. "What's happened, darling?"

"Roberto's missing."

"Missing? What does that mean?"

"It means he hasn't been seen nor heard from for a week."

"Oh, dear God."

"Darling, I'm leaving at four with his mother . . . it's sickening . . . I can't imagine what's happened to him."

"I know . . . here, let me pack for you, but first, go sit down and I'll get you a drink. You look like you need it."

He sat down heavily. Two weeks, just two lousy weeks had been his reprieve and now . . . this.

When he stood in the foyer, kissing Victoria, she said, "Dominic, I just know everything will be alright . . . I just know it."

"I pray to God you're right . . . I love you, and I'll try and keep in touch."

"Darling, don't concern yourself with me . . . please don't . . . just take care of yourself and when you find Bobby, let me know."

"I will." Holding her close, he said, "Life plays

198

games with us . . . I guess we just had too much for the gods not to be jealous, didn't we?"

"Take care of yourself, darling . . . I adore you."

～～～

Amileo Segetti was a short, rotund man whose belly rose above the wide leather belt that held his baggy corduroy trousers. The fringe that surrounded his rather large head was gray which contrasted startingly with his heavy black, bushy eyebrows. Just as startling were his pudgy, square hands which made it almost impossible to equate the exquisite masterpieces of sculpture that those ten fingers could create.

When Catherine and Dominic arrived at his studio, he was high above, standing on a scaffold which almost touched the obscure glass roof.

"Maestro Segetti," Dominic called out, looking up, trying to be heard in between the sounds of heavy chiseling as the marble dust flew.

Segetti looked down, "Ah, *Signora* and *Signore* Rossi. *Buon giorno* . . . I'm coming down." For all his eighty years, he descended from his lofty perch with the agility of a ballet dancer. When he removed his goggles, all but the area around his eyes was masked with pink dust as were his calloused hands. He wiped them on his dirty smock and shook both the signora's and the signore's hands vigorously.

In Italian, he asked, "How was the crossing?"

"A bit turbulent," Dominic answered.

"I would rather be up there chiseling than in the air. I feel closer to heaven and more safe, although my former counterpart, Michelangelo, would have argued with me had I been around at the time . . . now, come into my rooms and we'll have a capuccino while we talk about the reason you're here." Catherine and Dominic followed with rapid pace behind the maestro, until they were seated in the sparsely furnished room where Segetti called out, "Rosella, come, I want you to meet Roberto's parents."

A young woman in her mid-thirties emerged dressed in a black cotton dress. Her long, thick, black hair hung loose below her slim waist, above which was an ample bosom which had attracted Segetti to her more than ten years ago. In fact, Dominic saw in the strange, dark piercing eyes, why any man could find her more than alluring, although she was not beautiful in the sense that bore most descriptions. There was an underlying tempestuousness that only someone like Segetti could handle. She had been his *amante* for ten years now and loved him with a passion that defied any woman to challenge her supremacy. She smiled without warmth . . . in fact, rather condescendingly, which made both Catherine and Dominic feel quite uncomfortable, as though they had invaded her private domain, a place where only a privileged few were permitted. However, they both acknowledged the introduction, *"Buon giorno*, it's a pleasure to meet you."

She nodded sullenly while thinking, I could kill you with my bare hands for sending your *figlio* to my Segetti and upsetting him so that he couldn't sleep for nights and God only know he sleeps little enough.

"Rosella, go fix coffee . . . bring out the bread and the cheese."

She stood for another moment, her eyes narrowed on them, then she turned and left. When she returned, they were deep in conversation . . . "that's all I know . . . Roberto left without a word one day and hasn't been heard from since," Segetti said. "I must be honest . . . if he hadn't shown such promise as a sculptor, I would have thrown him out and sent him packing long ago . . . but he has such a gift, to waste his time wherever he is . . ."

Rosella was listening behind the open door, where she spit. Like a son Segetti had taken him in when others were pleading for the Maestro's time.

"And you have no clues?" Dominic asked while Catherine sat with tears in her eyes.

"None . . . we . . . the police and I have combed every corner of Florence. We went to the house of a young woman he had become involved with, but she swore angrily, cursing him, that she, too, had not seen nor heard from him and that's where the trail seems to end."

Dominic said, "Why do you think he left?"

Segetti raised his bushy eyebrows and said, shrugging his shoulders, "You see, *Signore*, a gift is only good if one has the will . . . the discipline to endure the ordeal and the pain which art demands. Without those things, the gift is wasted and sometimes providence makes its mistake by endowing someone like Roberto with the talent, but forgets to give him the nature that makes greatness. He has the talent, but lacks the desire. Perhaps it was I that drove him away by the ordeals I put him through, but he is soft . . . he is lazy, and I demanded. I pushed, hoping I could breathe the desire into him . . . I'm afraid I failed . . . but worst of all, he did not keep faith with the deity that gave him his gift . . . the greatest obligation of all. A man can learn to be a doctor . . . that is science . . . a man can learn from books to build a bridge, but the architect who has a dream . . . that is the human riddle . . . from where did it come . . . from the mind, from the soul, from the heart . . . who gives it? And why should it be given to one and not another? Why a Caruso . . . a Michelangelo . . . why a Picasso? . . . Why a Shakespeare? When the song is sung and the picture hung and the book read, it all seems so simple . . . ah . . . but no one knows the agony that went into the song, the picture, the book. And I must be truthful . . . Roberto is not deserving to have such a gift." Dominic and Catherine sat silently, captivated by this man. "Here, drink your coffee first and then we'll go to the chief of police and discuss what can be done to find Roberto."

The first and only thing a bewildered, subdued Catherine said was, "Maestro, when we find Roberto, will you take him back. After all, he's only a young boy who hasn't grown up enough to realize what he's done?"

He looked kindly at this mother . . . remembering he had never known his . . . she had abandoned him at birth . . . a bastard to grow up in an alien world, but he thought maybe had his mother been like the one who sat across from him, he might not be the Segetti he was. Answering her gently, "No, *Signora*, Roberto's youth has nothing to do with it. Michelangelo was eight when he came to Florence. I would not be able to take him back. He will never be a sculptor . . . never. It is not inside him . . . I am sorry . . . he should go home."

Dominic, Catherine and Segetti crossed the cobblestoned courtyard to *di Agenti di Polizia* where they were ushered into the chamber of the Chief's private office. There they waited silently until a door opened and standing before them was the head of missing persons. Segetti stood, "*Tenente* Batisimo, may I present Signora and Signore Rossi, all the way from San Francisco, California."

"Ah . . ." he said, shaking their hands, "from San Francisco, California . . . what a city. I've been there . . . as magnificent as anything in Italy." Seating himself behind his desk, he bent over the edge addressing his attention to Dominic, "You know Sausalito maybe?"

"Yes, Sausalito . . . it's across the bay from San Francisco."

"Ah . . . ha . . . that's the place . . . I have a cousin living there." Kissing his lips, he said, "What a place . . . so exquisite . . . so gorgeous . . . so . . . what can I say . . . I hated to leave . . . now, what can I do for you, my noble friend, Segetti?"

"These are the *genitore* of the missing boy, Roberto."

He sat looking at them with pain in his heart, remembering having lost a son in the war . . . that *bastardo*, Hitler . . . his Mario was a lover, not a soldier, but for this boy to do what he had done to his parents was unforgivable. "*Si, Signore*, you have come a long way . . . now, let me tell you what has been done up to now in trying to find out the whereabouts of your son . . . The last he was seen was in Rome."

Segetti interrupted, "And you, my friend, said nothing, knowing the anguish I've been through?"

"*Stampo da fonderia*, my friend . . . be calm . . . I said nothing because, by the time the Roman police found out where he was, it was already too late."

"Too late?" Segetti demanded, "too late for what?"

"He had left, taking a plane to Paris."

"And they couldn't apprehend him. . . . I don't understand us Italians . . . after *fare la seconda colazione*, we close the shutters and make *amore* and the police are no different."

"How can you say that, Segetti, we work twenty-four hours a day."

"Twenty-four hours a day you work? What happened in between the hours you got word from the Roman police till now? Couldn't you have told me that at least you knew something?"

"Please, Segetti . . . try and understand how exacting our work is. Suppose I had come to you and said, Segetti, we know the boy was in Rome, but got away. What could have been done when the police could not nab him in time?" Pleadingly, he asked, "Now, I ask you."

"At least I would have known he was alive."

Catherine was becoming hysterical, "Yes, why didn't you at least tell Maestro Segetti? That is unforgivable, makin' us suffer so, not knowin' what had become of our son."

Reflexively, Dominic took her hand and held it, "Catherine, please calm yourself. They're doing everything they can to find Roberto."

"*Grazie, Signore* Rossi, for your understanding, but then I understand from Maestro Segetti, you are a very great and important *avvocato* . . . now, I would suggest you go on to Paris . . . I have been in touch with the police there . . . they know about the case and it is believed that the boy will be found there."

Dominic asked, "When were you in touch with them last?"

"Only yesterday."

"And what did they say?"

"That they are searching, nothing else . . . but the Parisian police are like, how do you say . . . like the F.B.I. . . . that is correct?"

"Yes . . . now, thank you for all your effort. My wife and I appreciate all you have done."

"*Mille grazie,* for your patience. We have done everything we could . . . we have left no stone unturned. Unfortunately, we were unable to find the boy. I regret that this was the case."

On the way out, Segetti said hissingly to his lifelong friend, "The next time I have need, God forbid, for the police, I'll call a plumber."

The next few hours were chaos. First, Catherine and Dominic couldn't get a plane to Paris because there was a strike, Segetti explained, by the *fascisti,* the *bastardos.* Deciding in desperation to charter a plane, they found their luggage was lost which delayed them for another hour, which by now had Catherine prostrate. When they finally boarded, it was a one-engine plane that had originally been used as a mail carrier. There were only six seats, all on the right side in single file. Catherine counted the rosary beads as she sat trembling with Dominic seated behind her. Only once did the pilot say a word during the harrowing experience with the wind against them all the way . . . twisting and turning the slight aircraft like a kite in the sky. "We are over Orly airport, but it's impossible to land because of the visibility."

"How long do you think it will be?" Dominic asked, trying to remain calm.

"Who knows? As soon as I get word from the tower."

Dominic wondered if they had enough gas but the pilot, reading his thought, said, "Don't worry, *Signore,* I have six children and a half and my wife is expecting me for breakfast tomorrow morning. She'll be very angry with me if she has to waste the food."

Dominic almost laughed, but Catherine was repeating over and over again out loud, "Hail, Mary, Mother of God, Jesus, fruit of the womb, protect us, help us. Hail, Mary, Mother of God . . ." Her prayers were answered as the plane came bumping, thumping to the ground and with a jerk, stopped abruptly.

Paris was freezing and the rain pelted down on a frightened, exhausted Catherine as she stepped from the taxi into the lobby of the George V Hotel. Shivering, she waited, huddled in her sable coat, as Dominic registered for a suite of rooms. It seemed an eternity until they were finally taken up in the lift to their quarters. Sitting down heavily into a wing chair, she began to sneeze and cough, pulling her coat around her even tighter. The bellboy struck a match and lit the logs in the pink marble fireplace. Dominic looked disheveled, as though he had slept in his suit, the bellboy thought as he was being tipped . . . rich Americans can afford anything, even a two day growth of beard.

"Is there anything else, *Monsieur?*"

"Catherine, would you like something now?"

"Yes," she answered, her teeth chattering, "hot coffee and a bottle of brandy. I think I'm really sick."

Dominic asked that the order be brought immediately. When the door was shut, he said, "Why don't you get out of those clothes and go to bed . . . your coat is wet."

"Thank you, Dominic, but I'm really so ill, I don't think I can make it," she answered, wheezing.

"Come on, I'll help you." He held her arm and led her into her room across from his, being separated by the large sitting room. Helped out of her coat, she sat shivering on the edge of the bed, too weak to undress.

"Dominic, would you . . . please be kind enough to unzip me?"

"Of course."

"Thank you . . . and if you don't mind, I'd be ever so grateful if you'd get that small blue bag. I have my nightgown in it."

He brought it to her. "Is there anything else I can get you?"

"If you don't mind my sayin' it, Dominic . . . you're bein' awful sweet."

He felt uncomfortable and awkward. "We've been through an ordeal . . . and I'm sorry you're not feeling well."

She sneezed . . . taking out her handkerchief from her purse, she wiped her nose which was red and sore. "Dominic, do you think I could get some aspirin . . . I simply forgot to bring some."

"I'll go downstairs, there's a drugstore across the street, if I can't get any in the hotel."

"Thank you, Dominic, I really appreciate . . ." she sneezed again. On his way out, she said, "I think it might be a good idea to get a thermometer."

"Okay . . . I'll be right back."

In Dominic's absence, she thought about him . . . how he had rallied to her when she needed him . . . but don't put too much importance into it, she thought just as quickly. Dominic had a large stretch of goodness in him and when he wasn't mad you'd just never believe he was capable of any kind of temper. Did he ever get mad at . . . *her?* Catherine wondered . . . what was he like as a lover . . . with . . . her . . . And now in her mind's eye, she saw them making love, kissing, fondling and exploring one another as once *they* had done . . . once . . . once upon a time like a fairytale that ended in tragedy. But fairytales were supposed to end happily. The golden slipper . . . the handsome prince . . . the beautiful princess . . . from New Orleans . . . what happened to her? She was lying in a strange bed in Paris worried sick that her son was missing and her husband was gone . . . gone forever . . . into the arms of another woman . . . so it seemed fairytales didn't have happy endings after all.

The night had been dreadful for Catherine, alone

in her bed ill, when just across the room, Dominic, still her husband, lay sleeping. She would not allow herself to be foolish enough to indulge in the fantasy that the attention Dominic had shown her earlier was anything more than just a kindness he would have done for anyone who was not well. At two, she took her temperature . . . it was 102. Her head was throbbing and her pulse was racing. She had chills, her teeth chattered. My God, maybe she had pneumonia. For a fleeting moment, she wanted to call for Dominic, but thought, no, better not let him think she was trying to take advantage of their situation. After all, he was only here because of Roberto . . . he was his son too. But when morning came, her temperature had risen to 103. When Dominic came in, dressed, he could see the glazed look in Catherine's eyes.

"You're worse this morning . . . I think we should have a doctor take a look at you."

"Whatever you say . . . Dominic, I'm really not feelin' at all well . . . I guess it was sittin' in that terrible cold little plane. I must'a gotten a bug of some kind."

Dominic was on the phone calling the desk clerk. "This is Mr. Rossi, my wife is ill and I would be grateful if you would get us a doctor immediately." As ill as she was, she heard him say it . . . my *wife* . . . what a beautiful sounding word.

Within a half-hour, Dominic opened the door and let Dr. Monet in, leading him to Catherine's room. During the examination, Dominic waited in the sitting room and he recalled the night Catherine had slipped and fallen, almost losing the baby . . . what a night that was. Strange, when he thought about it . . . they had been through a great deal together, hadn't they? Seven children . . . all the fights and arguments . . . but during the years there had been some good memories too. Impossible to live with someone for twenty-two years and not remember a few good things . . . like the surprise birthday she had given him on his thirtieth. That was a lovely evening . . . yes, it was . . . and then there was . . . His memories stopped when Dr. Monet came out and said, "Mr. Rossi, I find a little fluid in the right lung, but it isn't pneumonia. At this point, it's pleurisy and I would suggest she be hospitalized."

Dominic was truly shaken. "All right, whatever you say."

"Fine, I'll make arrangements at the American Hospital . . . may I use the phone? I want to make sure we can get a room and also she should be sent by ambulance."

"Is it that serious?"

"It could become quite serious."

All the arrangements were made. Dominic thanked the doctor, then went to Catherine's room. She was breathing hard, trying to catch her breath. Dominic said, "Catherine, the doctor thinks you should be hospitalized for a few days."

"No, Dominic, please, I'm really not that bad," she answered him with difficulty.

"Catherine, please don't be obstinate. You should be where someone can take care of you."

"But what about Roberto . . . I should be helping to find him."

"It doesn't take two of us."

"But why should you have all the responsibility?"

"Listen, Catherine, you're not well and this could become worse, so tell me what you need and I'll pack a little bag."

She was too ill to protest. Her breathing labored. She said a toothbrush and the blue bag would be sufficient. As she lay quietly, unable to move, she almost whispered, "Dominic, you look tired . . . why don't . . . you have . . . some breakfast . . . sent up?"

"Don't worry about me. Let's just get you well."

She lay back against the pillows and shut her eyes. Trembling, she thought, maybe I'm goin' to die. I feel so ill that at this moment, I wouldn't even care . . . if I died, then Dominic could marry . . . this . . . woman. Wouldn't that be a blessin' . . . for him . . . so simple . . . solve all his problems . . . with me. But before she could think further, the ambulance attendants arrived and Catherine was taken by stretcher down the hall to the service elevator, then through doors to the alley where she was carefully lifted into the conveyance. Dominic sat on the side opposite her, listening and watching the oxygen mask as it ballooned in and out. He felt so many things on that drive to the hospital. Pity ... regret that their lives had not turned out ... guilt over her touching humility ... the anguish she felt over Roberto which had subdued her to the point he saw a different Catherine ... it wasn't love that he felt, but a deep compassion he had thought he was beyond feeling for her. When they arrived, Catherine was taken immediately to a large corner room overlooking the garden, which she neither saw nor could appreciate since she was semiconscious ... her temperature had risen to 104 and a half, and when the doctor came out after examining her, he told Dominic that by now she had pneumonia. There were rales in the right lung, which was a dangerous sign. Dominic shut his eyes ... The doctor assured him everything would be done. The antibiotics were given intramuscularly, she had been placed in an oxygen tent and was being fed intravenously. The thought of Bobby was forgotten for the time being, as Dominic waited through the long, long day well into the evening. The only time he left Catherine's bedside was to go downstairs to the dining room in the hospital and have dinner. By eleven that night Catherine's temperature had dropped slightly, but she still lay in a semiconscious state. Finally the special night nurse opened the door quietly. She discussed Madame's case with her friend and fellow worker who was now going off duty. After going over the chart, Mademoiselle Vredue left.

"My name is Miss Lavinna Middings," she said in perfect English, which for all of Dominic's concern about Catherine still surprised him a little ... American Hospital in Paris ... a nurse without a French accent with a name like Middings. Seeing the mild surprise on his face, she laughed softly, "I'm English and from London."

"Very pleased to meet you, and I'm Mr. Rossi from San Francisco."

"Pleased, indeed ... now, Mr. Rossi, I might suggest you leave since Mrs. Rossi seems to be resting comfortably and is in no immediate danger. And may I add, you look like you might need a little of the same ... rest, that is," she said slightly above a whisper, observing his heavy bearded shadow.

"I am tired, but do you think it's safe to leave?"

"I can assure ... yes. Should the occasion arise the hospital can contact you ... but I truly believe there will be no need for that."

Hesitatingly, he finally said, "Alright, but if Mrs. Rossi wakes up tell her I'll be here first thing in the morning."

"I shall, sir ... good night."

Dominic left, walking slowly down the hall where he took the elevator to the lobby ... and had the receptionist call a taxi which took him back to the George V Hotel. Wearily, he sat on the edge of the bed, looking at his watch ... it was now eleven thirty at night ... what was the time difference? About eight hours ... Victoria would still be sleeping. He picked up the phone and asked to be connected with the overseas operator and waited ... finally a voice ... he placed the call and waited once again. ...

"Hello?" a sleepy Victoria asked, rolling over on her back.

"Darling, how are you?"

"I'm fine, but how are you?"

"At this moment, I'm not sure."

"Speak a little louder. There's so much static, I can't hear."

"I said I'm not sure. Is that better?"

"Yes, can you hear me?"

"Yes."

"The line seems to be have cleared ... what do you mean you're not sure?"

"Well, so much has happened, I don't know where to begin."

"Have you found Bobby?"

"No."

"Where are you?"

"In Paris at the George V Hotel."

"In Paris . . . Why Paris?"

"It's a long story. I'll tell you when I see you, but here's where the police seem to think he is."

"Do they have a lead on him?"

"I don't know. I haven't seen them yet."

"You haven't?"

"No."

"When did you arrive?"

"Last night."

"What about today . . . why haven't you—?"

"Because . . . Catherine is in the hospital."

There was a long pause . . . "The hospital? Dominic, my God, why?"

"She has pneumonia."

"Pneumonia? How did that happen?"

"Darling, it's too long to go into, but she's quite ill."

"I'm so sorry to hear that. You poor darling . . . what you must be going through."

"Truthfully, I'm too beat to think about being anything tonight."

"What time is it?"

"About one in the morning."

"Oh, darling, how I wish there was something I could do to help."

"Just hearing your voice has helped."

"And I've thought of nothing else but you since you left."

"Thank you, sweetheart. If I can get through this, I think I'll live to be a hundred."

"I hope so . . . I love you, darling . . . try not to worry. I just know everything is going to be alright."

"I hope so, sweetheart. If you don't hear from me, you'll understand."

"Of course. Please don't concern yourself with me . . . I love you, Dominic, take care of yourself."

"I love you, too . . . Just hearing your voice, I feel better."

"Darling, can I do anything here for you?"

"No, dear . . . just be there when I come home."

"I will. You know I will . . . now, try and get some sleep. I love you."

After hanging up, he placed calls to Dom and Tory, then called home telling them Mama was not feeling well . . . just worn out and resting in the hospital for a few days . . . no, Roberto had not been found yet, but it was just a question of a few hours . . . why should he alarm them. More exhausted than he knew, he lay back fully clothed and fell asleep. . . .

Dominic slowly opened his heavy eyelids. For one brief moment, he seemed unable to orient himself. He looked down at his suit and shoes suddenly realizing he had fallen asleep so swiftly that he had not undressed. In spite of his stamina, this morning he was unable to move. The long, arduous journey had been much more strenuous than even he could sustain for all his vigor, and then Catherine's sudden illness . . . Looking out to a gray somber morning, he watched the rain pelt against the windows . . . the day matched his mood.

Arousing himself to full consciousness, he glanced at the small travel clock on the nightstand . . . it was six-thirty. Picking up the receiver with one hand he stroked his bearded stubble with the other while he waited for a response. It took so long, Dominic became annoyed. Ah . . . ha, a voice . . . someone was there after all. *"Bon jour,* what is your pleasure?" the desk clerk asked.

"Let me have room service."

"Oui, Monsieur, one moment . . ."

Again, a long . . . long wait. . . . *"Bonjour, Monsieur,* what is your pleasure?"

My pleasure would be to have you tied to a tree in the rain this morning for not answering the phone for fifteen minutes. "In thirty minutes I want my breakfast to be in my room . . . *vous moi comprende?*"

Stunned silence, then, "Of course, *Monsieur* . . . now what is your desire?"

"My desire is a large orange juice, two scrambled eggs with ham, toast and coffee."

Americans! Their taste for food, like peasants. "*Oui, Monsieur* . . . will that be all?"

"*Oui* . . . but remember . . . in one half-hour."

An indignant sigh . . . "But of course, *Monsieur.*"

Dominic got out of his clothes, went to the bathroom, bathed, and shaved. As he looked at himself in the mirror . . . he needed a haircut . . . and badly, well, that he'd forget about today. What was ahead of him, he didn't relish. Getting into his jockey shorts, he heard a loud knock at the door . . . see, it's thirty minutes, the knuckles were saying, as a reprimand. Quickly getting into his robe, barefooted, he opened it to a waiter, somber and arrogant, who wheeled in the breakfast table. He placed it in the center of the sitting room, then stood at attention. No *bonjour?* No nothing? This was the polite French? It apparently was the desk clerk who had told the order clerk, who told the waiter not to cater to the demanding, impatient American in room 1704.

Dominic sat down to breakfast which he ate without enjoyment. Finishing, he sat on the sofa and picked up the phone . . . again, silence . . . a long pause . . . and for this he was paying seventy-five dollars a day . . . "*Bonjour, Monsieur* . . . your pleasure?"

To get the hell out of this fine establishment, Dominic wanted to say, but instead, "Will you get me the American Hospital?"

"*Merci.*"

Dominic heard the ringing, then "American Hospital."

"Yes . . . will you connect me with Mrs. Rossi's room?"

"I'm sorry, but the phone has been disconnected."

Dominic's heart began to race, why was the phone

disconnected? Was Catherine much worse? "Connect me with the floor nurse."

"*Oui, Monsieur.*"

". . . Miss Doumont here."

"Yes . . . this is Mr. Rossi. Would you be kind enough to have someone go to my wife's room and tell the nurse I would like to speak with her."

"I am very sorry, *Monsieur,* but we are so busy."

Goddamn it, he was getting to hate the French more by the minute. "Listen, I want to find out how my wife is . . . do you understand me?"

"*Oui, Monsieur,* I understand, but there is no one who has the time . . . we are all very busy."

Dominic bit his lip to keep from cursing, "Do you know how my wife is this morning?"

"No, *Monsieur,* since she has private nurses."

He slammed down the phone, dressed quickly, put on his raincoat, a hat, grabbed his umbrella and left the room. Getting a taxi which took him across town unhurriedly, since by now the rain was coming down in torrents, he cursed under his breath . . . when he caught up with Roberto, he'd knock the hell out of him for putting them through this . . . but his anger was interrupted when the taxi came to a stop in front of the hospital. Paying the driver, he hurried into the building, shivering. Taking off his dripping raincoat and hat, depositing the umbrella in the receptacle, he walked rapidly to the elevator.

Once inside Catherine's room, he found her awake and feeling better this morning. The medication had done its work and she was remarkably improved since yesterday, though far from recovered. The nurse took his coat and hat, putting them in the bathroom to dry, then he looked through the transparent tent where Catherine smiled wanly, "How are you, Dominic?"

"I'm fine, but how are you?"

"Much better this morning. Yesterday, I thought I was gonna' die and then I was afraid I wasn't." She laughed, which started the coughing.

"Don't talk, just rest." He sat down. How did Mrs.

Rossi sleep last night, he asked a French nurse that had replaced Miss Middings.

"She did quite well."

"That's good . . . has the doctor been here yet?"

"No, but I expect him . . . he is probably making his rounds now."

Dominic sat, rubbing his hands together. Dr. Monet soon came in. "Good morning, Mr. Rossi," he said with a slight accent.

"Good morning, Doctor, how is my wife?"

"We'll soon see." Picking up the chart, he looked. "Better, much better . . . her temperature has dropped, her respiration is more normal . . . pulse rate better." Taking out his stethoscope, he placed the ends around his neck, pulled back the flap of the tent and said, "Good morning, Mrs. Rossi. You look better today."

"I am," she said.

"That's fine . . . now, can you pull up your gown so that I can hear what's going on?" Putting the stethoscope into his ears, Dr. Monet pressed the instrument against Catherine's chest . . . listened . . . then under her breast . . . listened. "Now, are you able to sit up?"

With the aid of the nurse, she lifted herself into a sitting position. "Try breathing in and out a little more deeply . . . do you have pain when you do that?"

"Yes, but not like yesterday."

"Fine . . . now, you may lie back."

"How long will I have to be in the tent? I hate it."

"Probably another twenty-four hours, but we'll take the intravenous away and you can have a soft diet."

"Thank you, doctor."

"You're doing fine."

"How is she?" Dominic inquired as Dr. Monet pulled the flap down again.

"Your wife's recuperative powers are remarkable. Her lungs are much clearer this morning . . . but of course we were fortunate that she was hospitalized before it became too bad."

"How long do you think she'll be here?"

"Oh . . . I would say about a week . . . if she continues to improve as she is doing now."

"Thank you, doctor, for all you've done."

"Not at all . . . I'll stop by this evening." He wrote out some added instructions and handed them to the nurse and was gone.

"Dominic?" Catherine called softly.

"Yes?" Dominic answered, coming to her side.

"Have you any news about Roberto?"

"Not yet. I wanted to see how you were first."

"Dominic, I'm only sorry I'm an added burden."

"Don't worry about that, Catherine, just get well . . . now, I'm going to the police and see what they have turned up."

"Please, God, they have good news . . . have you called the children?"

"Yes, last night. They're fine."

"You didn't say I was ill, I hope."

"I only told them you were in the hospital for a rest. That you're worn out."

"Oh, dear, I wish you hadn't. I don't want them to worry."

"I made very light of it."

"I'm glad."

Getting his coat and hat, he put them on. "I'm going now . . . is there anything you want me to bring you?"

"No, Dominic . . . Dominic?"

"Yes?"

"Well, I want to thank you again for being so kind to me—"

He nodded uneasily. "Well, I'm going . . . I'll be back as soon as I can."

And he was quickly out of the room and down the hall, waiting for the elevator.

8

"Monsieur Rossi, we believe we have found the whereabouts of your son Robert."

"Are you sure?"

"Yes, but he is an elusive little scamp," said *Monsieur* Blum, the head of missing persons. "When first he arrived in Paris, he registered at a most disreputable hotel on the left bank. As is the custom in France, everyone must register with the police as I am sure you are well aware."

"I take it he is no longer there?"

"Your assumption is correct . . . the next day he paid for his lodgings and left."

"Where did he go?"

"To a rooming house in the Montmartre district."

"Why didn't you apprehend him?"

Smiling and tilting his head to one side, *Monsieur* Blum said, "As an attorney, you should know we had nothing to apprehend him for . . . his papers were in order. He had committed nothing . . . so on what grounds could we question him?"

"I guess I'm thinking like a father."

"Natural, I can assure you . . . now, I'm sure you are anxious to see him."

"Indeed . . ."

"Here is the address . . . however, *Monsieur*, I warn you, the lodgings your son has chosen may come as quite a shock, judging from having met you."

"Nothing that one would do could shock me."

"Perhaps . . . but prepare yourself." *Monsieur* Blum handed the address written on a slip of paper which Dominic looked at, then put into his pocket and left.

It was a gentle, soft rain that now fell as the cab stopped in front of the building, where, undoubtedly, Bobby slept so peacefully at this hour of the morning in a rotting room he preferred to the mansion in which he had grown up. As Dominic got out and paid the driver, he looked up at the dirty crumbling facade. The shutters were closed on this dismal day . . . one hung unhinged, ready to fall, but flapped against the broken window patched with tape. Why? Dominic questioned himself. The feeling that somewhere . . . somehow . . . someway they, as parents, had failed Roberto plagued him. But why Roberto and not the others? The children had all been raised the same and showed no such hostility. He was no closer to the answer when finally in revulsion he opened the battered door and found himself standing inside the dark hall. At the end, beyond the stairs stood the form of a man.

"What do you want?" an old voice called out.

Walking toward the figure, Dominic asked, "Do you have a Robert Rossi living here?"

Narrowing his eyes and appraising him, the old man asked, "Who wants to know?"

"His father."

He was the police . . . there was always that unmistakable look about them. "There is no one by that name."

"I know differently . . . tell me what room he's in."

Again the old man denied there was such a person. Taking out a ten franc note and dangling it in front of the man's eyes, Dominic asked again, "What room is the boy in?"

"You are not the police?"

"No."

"Who are you?"

"A friend."

He grabbed the money and told Dominic to go up three flights, turn left and it was the last room at the end of the hall on the right.

With each creaking step Dominic took, his anger rose. He stood staring at the decaying door. The paint was peeling and blistered. He would not give Roberto the dignity of knocking. Turning the knob, he found the door unlocked. Opening it, he stood, revolted . . . unable to move. *Monsieur* Blum had warned him, but for this he was not prepared. The room was oppressive with the smells of sweating bodies . . . stale smoke . . . rancid urine that came from the bidet in the corner. The only light in the dark room came from the cracks in the slatted shutters. Clothing lay strewn about and a bottle of Pernod stood on the floor near Roberto's side of the bed where Dominic saw his son lying nude next to a young woman. He walked quickly to the bed, looked down at the sleeping bodies. No . . . Dominic was not going to be the understanding, appeasing father. He was feeling very Italian and very Sicilian. Throwing back the torn blanket, he grabbed Roberto by the shoulders and shook him. It was a frightened Roberto who woke up. When he saw Dominic, he screamed at his father.

"What the hell do you think you're doing?"

The girl alongside of him sat up, trembling, pulling the cover up under her chin to hide her nakedness. "I'll tell you what I'm doing here . . . but first, get that cunt out of here," Dominic screamed back. He picked up the dress from the floor and flung it at her.

"What the hell gives you the right to barge in here and give orders . . . she's not going."

Dominic raised his hand ready to strike Roberto, then dropped it, but shaking his large fist, he said, "I'm warning you . . . keep still . . . now, get out of here and fast." Quickly, the girl jumped out of bed, slipped into the flimsy dress, grabbed her coat which hung over a chair . . . as she did so, Dominic took out some francs and threw them on the floor. On the way out, she picked up the money and ran from the room, slamming the door after her.

"You've got a hell of a lot of guts calling her a cunt . . . like father, like son . . . I understand you're living with one. Vincente wrote me all about it and why you left Mama for a slut . . ."

Dominic's jaw tightened into a knot. Grabbing Roberto, he pinned him against the bed. "What's holding me back from knocking the shit out of you, I don't know . . . but you listen and listen carefully . . . don't you mention my life . . . do you hear? and don't press your luck, you ungrateful little bastard . . . what you've put your mother through, I *should* beat you to a pulp. She's been frantic not knowing what happened to you."

Roberto began to say, "What I've done! That's a joke . . . what the hell did you . . . ," but Dominic held him harder against the iron bed until he winced.

"I'm warning you, while I can still control myself . . . keep your mouth shut . . . now, get out of that bed and get dressed."

"Why? What makes you think I'm going anywhere with you after coming in like the gestapo and rousting me—"

"Because I'm your father . . . that gives me the right . . . but more important, your mother is in the hospital because you sent her there."

Roberto was stunned. "In the hospital?"

"Yes . . . goddamn it . . . you little bastard. Do you know what you put her through? How could you have done that to *her?*"

"How could you have done what *you* did to her. You feeling a little guilty?"

Under his breath, Dominic said, "Listen, I don't have to explain anything to you . . . it so happens whether we're living together or not, your mother's still my wife and unfortunately we had a son like you . . . let's talk about you. All right, you hate me. I did a terrible thing because I wanted to be rich so I can understand how you would want to punish me. I did a lot of harm to you giving you a good life which makes me decadent. I have all the vices you find so reprehensible . . . but your mother, why her? You're her favorite son . . . she loves you for the same reason you hate me, we don't stand for the same things . . . okay, but you hurt her so badly she wanted to die . . . now, you little bastard, get out of bed. You're filthy . . . get washed, you stink. I can't stand the stench in here . . . I'll wait downstairs . . . outside." Dominic left, slamming the door and ran down the stairs. He couldn't get out fast enough. The soft drizzle felt comforting against his hot face. Ten minutes later a disheveled Roberto stood, seething, at his father's side without saying a word. Dominic hailed a cab . . . Roberto stared out the window in one corner, while Dominic stared ahead sitting in the opposite corner. The first stop was the barber where Dominic could have bet Roberto would rebel . . . as he was doing now, but a determined Dominic said if he had to tie him down he would get his hair cut. Dominic being a little bigger . . . a little stronger . . . and a little tougher when need be, Bobby submitted. While Dominic sat in the chair next to his son's, he looked in the mirror. What the hell was he going to do with him? Was a psychiatrist the answer? He sure as hell knew Freud would be against the way he handled Roberto. He heard the voice inside his ear reprimanding him. What he should have said was, "Yes, Bobby, I understand your rebellion, your dislike of me. I represent the establishment, the decadent

221

society, so wicked ... the one that supports the charity wards and gives the poor back so much of what we were privileged to ... easy come ... easy go ... the hell it was, I worked my ass off so you could have what I never had ... and the funny thing is, I never hated my father, I loved him ... how about that?" The thing that bothered Dominic was taking a good long look at his children ... all of them came into view ... the thought of Vincente so close to Roberto was more than a little disturbing. He looked up to him, trying to be like him, wanting to be a free spirit, but it went beyond that, Dominic reasoned. Vincente, from birth, had not been as robust as his brothers and wasn't able to compete in sports as they did. Although Roberto could have been in their league, he hated sports. And Gina Maria, raised in a family of boys, was set apart, although they treated her with a special affection, she felt left out which Dominic knew must have made her frustrated and lonely many times. But it was Vincente, at the moment, that became his immediate concern ... afraid that the same problems they were having with Roberto might make Vincente think of him as the rebellious returning hero.

After the tonsorial battle was won, Dominic sat in the best men's shop watching Roberto as he rebelled against trying on suit after suit, all of which he rejected saying he refused to become the stamp of Harvard. Finally Roberto relented stubbornly and settled for a navy blue sports jacket and a pair of gray flannel trousers, a white shirt and a striped tie which he insisted was choking him, but an adamant Dominic said he was going to look like a human being when he saw his mother. There was much more Dominic wanted to buy, but Roberto resented the gesture so Dominic threw up his hands, saying to himself, the hell with it ... at least he accomplished the enormous feat of getting him to look human. On the way to the hospital Dominic bought a bouquet of flowers which he handed to Roberto to present to his mother, which again he grumbled about, but when at last he stood before Catherine, who was so greatly touched by seeing him, as well as having thought to bring her flowers, in this one case he was happy he had listened to his father.

"Roberto," Catherine said weakly, insisting the end flap be lifted by her nurse so that she could see him, "you look so handsome . . . Mama's so happy you're well and safe . . . you know, we were awfully worried about you . . . that something might have happened. It's just not like my sugar to run off and not say a word."

It wasn't a reprimand and Roberto felt truly guilty for having hurt her. The old man was right about one thing . . . why her? She'd always been his best ally and in his way he really loved her. "I'm sorry, Mama . . ." Roberto said with eyes diverted.

"I know you are, but you just weren't thinkin' . . . that's the way it is with gifted people . . . I understand the inner feelin' of artists, wantin' to have been one myself when I was young."

Dominic wished she could have only seen her darlin' shacked up this morning . . . *Mama mia.* Ashamed to take him shopping, looking as he did, in those sandals without any socks and smelling like a dead carp.

Reaching for his hand she said, "In my heart I knew you were the son I had raised. It means a lot when one has the background and the heritage behind them."

Roberto swallowed hard; changing the subject, he asked, "How are you, Mama?"

"Couldn't be better now that I've seen you . . . why, in a few days you're gonna be surprised how well I'll be . . . like nothin' happened."

"I hope so, Mama."

"You bet . . . 'course, you have no idea what a comfort your Daddy's been, darlin', takin' over the way he did when I came down with this damned cold

that laid me low . . . now, let's not talk about it anymore . . . what you did was just a prank that all boys
do one time or another."

Son of a bitch, thought Roberto, leaving my
mother for some whore.

"Did you call Maestro Segetti, Dominic?"

"Not yet, I haven't had time, but I will later . . .
has the doctor seen you since this morning?"

"Yes, he dropped in a little while ago and said I
was just comin' along beautifully and now, with my
dear son here, I'm gonna be like new in a few days,
you just wait and see. Roberto, did you have anythin'
to eat today?"

"No, Mama."

"Well, then go down to the restaurant in the hospital and have lunch . . . what about you, Dominic?"

"I'll eat later."

"Well, then, Roberto, you go . . . have a good
lunch . . . hear? I don't like you so thin." Roberto
hesitated. "Now go on, darlin' . . . I just love my boy
and I'm so happy you're here safe and sound."

"Thank you, Mama, I'm happy to see you." As he
turned to go, there were tears in his eyes.

"Well, Dominic, was it difficult findin' Roberto?"

"No . . ."

"That's good . . . where was he livin'?"

"In a bohemian apartment with an artist friend."

"You see, he's got it in his blood . . . artists always
seek each other out, isn't that the truth?"

"That's the truth."

"Did you have a heart-to-heart talk . . . like father
and son?"

"Naturally."

"Oh, Dominic, I can tell . . . the way he looked
when he walked in here, looking so handsome and fine.
I knew it was because you got to him . . . with your
convincin' logic."

Catherine would have died if she had known the
logic it took to get her lovin' boy here.

"Dominic, I've been thinkin' a lot lyin' here. We both know all the children are different and that's not so unusual in a large family, is it?"

"No."

"Dominic, I've thought that when I'm well, I'd like to go back to Florence and speak to Segetti. Somehow I feel if he could see Roberto and realize that what he did was just a childish prank, I truly believe he would take Roberto back."

"No, Catherine, I don't think so. To begin with, Segetti would never accept him back, no matter what you said. But more important than that, I know Roberto belongs home."

She looked at Dominic with tears in her eyes. She said softly, "Please forgive me, Dominic, for sayin' this, but a home constitutes a Mama and Daddy . . . not that I'm rakin' over old coals . . . believe me, I'm not. But a place in which there is no father makes a big difference in the attitudes of the children."

Dominic took a deep breath, then sighed, walking to the window, "Lots of people are separated and the children grow up."

"But how do they grow up, Dominic?"

"That I can't answer, Catherine. But we can't re-live the past. We're just going to have to do the best we can with the future."

She slumped back into the pillows, sorry she had brought up the issue that was long since gone.

That evening Dominic and Roberto returned to the hotel. Silently, Roberto went to Catherine's room and Dominic to his. Taking off his shoes, he lay on the bed and called Victoria.

"We've found Bobby."

"Thank God," Victoria sighed. "Was it an ordeal?"

"Yes, but at least he's safe and his mother's happy."

"How is she?"

"Better, much better."

"How long will you be away?"

"About a week or so . . . it depends on her . . . how quickly she can travel."

"I hope it will be soon. Darling, get some rest now that the worst is over."

"I don't know about the worst . . . but at least he's in the next room."

"He's just a boy, darling, he'll grow up."

"And while he's growing up, I'm growing old."

She laughed. "You'll never grow old. Now, get some rest and call when you can . . . I love you, sweetheart."

It was only nine-thirty and with nothing else to do, he put his shoes on again and went downstairs to the bar. When the drink was served he sat twisting the glass in his hand, then took a sip. Finishing, he ordered another. God, he felt lousy. Getting up, abruptly, he walked across the lobby out into the street. The rain had stopped. Although it was very cold, he did not bother to go back and get a coat. Instead, he walked along the boulevard for blocks, trying not to think. It was eleven when he put the key in the lock. First, he looked into Catherine's room to see if Roberto was there . . . he was and fast asleep. Then he went to his room, picked up the phone and called the overseas operator again.

"Will you hold on, sir, or shall I call you back?"

"Call me," he said, hanging up. Undressing, he prepared for bed when the phone rang. Quickly picking it up, he said, "Anna?"

"*Si, Signore* Rossi, how is *Signora?*"

"Much better, *grazie* . . . let me talk to Gina Maria."

"She's not here."

"What! It's only seven in the morning. She can't be at school."

"She's not."

"Then where is she?"

"Staying overnight with a friend."

"What friend?" Dominic asked angrily.

"A girl from school."

"What girl?"

"Wait, I call Vincente. He tella you."

"Hurry up. This is long distance."

"I'ma gonna go," she said, running up the stairs. "It'sa your Papa on'a the phone. Come quick . . . it'sa long distance."

Lifting off the receiver from his phone, he said, "Hi, Papa, how are you?"

"Fine and how are you?"

"Great . . . how's Mama?"

"Better . . . tell me, where is Gina Maria?"

"Sleeping overnight at a girl's house."

"What girl?"

"From school."

"I know that, but what's her name?"

"Pam McCormack."

"Who the hell is she?"

"I don't know. They go to school together."

"You don't know! Do you have her phone number?"

"Yes, hold on for a minute. I'll get it." Soon, he was back, giving Dominic the number.

Writing it down, he said, "This is the way you take care of your sister? Three grown boys in the house with a grandmother and you let her sleep at a girl's house you don't even know?"

"What do you want from me, Papa? It's only a girl's house she's at. From the sound of your voice you'd think she was being raped."

"That's enough . . . from now on, when we're away, I don't want any of you to sleep away from home . . . you hear? I mean none of you."

Big deal, Vincente thought, but it's all right for you to sleep with another woman. "Okay," he said sullenly.

Dominic caught the intonation in his voice. He was beginning to realize that since he had become the errant father, he was being more demanding with the children. "All right, Vincente," he said more softly, "be good. Take care of yourself and Gina Maria. I depend on you. Now, let me talk to Angie and Tony."

Vincente swallowed hard, "Papa . . . don't holler, but they're not here either."

"They aren't?" he asked, bewildered . . . it was too early for them to be in school. "Where are they?"

"Papa, please don't get mad now."

"What is it . . . tell me."

Slowly Vincente answered. "They're in Juvenile Hall."

Dominic took the receiver from his ear and looked at where it lay in his lap. Finally, putting it back to his ear, he said, "Juvenile Hall? Why?"

"You won't get mad?"

"I won't get mad . . . what happened?"

"Angie . . . now you're not going to get mad?"

"No . . ."

"Okay, Angie talked Tony into taking a motorcycle . . . now, wait a minute . . . it doesn't sound like it really was."

Long pause, then, "What was it really like?" Dominic asked.

"What happened is they were just goofing off with this kid's bike and drove away."

"And?"

"And they took it overnight."

"Don't tell me . . . let me guess . . . the kid thought they stole it, right?"

"Right, Papa . . . how did you know?"

"Because I'm psychic . . . then what?"

"Well, the kid's old man called the cops and said Angie and Tony swiped the bike . . . and when they got here they found it parked in front of the house." Vincente hesitated.

"That's okay, Vincente, I'm listening."

"Well, Papa . . . they handcuffed Angie and Tony, put them into a police car and took them to Juvenile Hall."

"Handcuffed them . . . took them to Juvenile Hall?"

"That's right, and was I mad . . . I called the boy every name in the book and told him the twins had only meant to borrow it and were bringing it back but he wouldn't buy that."

"He wouldn't . . . who is the boy . . . ?"

"Peter Owens. He called you a terrible name. That's when I swung at him."

"You tried to fight him?"

"Yes, but he was bigger."

"Did he hurt you?"

"Only gave me a black eye, but I wasn't going to let anyone call my father the Mafia."

Dominic put his hand up to his forehead to stop the pounding.

"Are you mad, Papa?"

"No, *mio figlio* . . . I'm proud of you . . . very proud . . . now, Vincente, call Gina Maria and tell her I called. I'm depending on you to take care of her. I don't want her to sleep in any girl's house, you understand? I'd call, but first I want to get the twins home. Don't tell Mama, if she calls. There's no need to upset her."

"I won't, Papa . . . did you find Bobby?"

"Yes."

"Is he okay?"

"Yes."

"Are you mad at him?"

"No . . . not anymore."

"I'm glad . . . give Mama my love and say hello to Bobby."

"I will . . . *grazie*, Vincente, we'll be home as soon as possible . . . you're the man now. Take care of everything."

"I will, Papa . . . *arrivederci.*"

"*Arrivederci*, Vincente." Hanging up, he placed a call to his partner's home.

"Dominic?"

"Yes."

"How's everything going?"

"Couldn't be worse."

"What do you mean . . . you still haven't found Roberto?"

"We found him . . . at the moment he's not my problem."

"You've got more problems?"

"The twins are being detained at Juvenile Hall. I want them released immediately."

"Juvenile Hall?"

"Right."

"On what grounds are they being held?"

"For . . . for borrow . . . for stealing a kid's motorcycle, which they didn't intend to keep. I want them out of there in a damn big hurry. *Comprendere?*"

"Right . . . I'll get on it immediately."

"Call me the minute they're home."

"Will do . . . how's Catherine?"

"Better."

"That's something to be grateful for."

"Yeah, right."

"Dominic, I know this is not the time, but I've got to say it . . . this is your nickel and you can tell me to mind my own business or to go to hell, but, Dominic, go home, make it up with Catherine . . . that's where you belong . . . the head of your house. If you were, maybe this wouldn't have happened. Now, don't blow your stack . . . I never said a word or tried to give you any advice when I found out about you leaving . . . but listen to me, Dominic, no matter how much you love this woman, your kids come first . . . now, tell me to keep my damn mouth shut."

Dominic sighed deeply and remained silent.

"Dominic? You there?"

"I'm here."

"Okay, I'm sorry I shot my mouth off. I suppose it's just the Sicilian in me . . . not that I've got much to brag about in the broad department, but when it comes to the Mrs. and especially the kids, that's a whole different ball game . . . Still friends?"

"Still friends . . . thanks. Now get the boys home."

"It's done . . . talk to you later."

"Good." Dominic hung up slowly. Jesus . . . his whole life had come crashing down on him. Who did he owe? The painful answer came rushing at him like a bulldozer, hitting him right in the pit of his stomach. Victoria . . . Victoria . . . I love you more than anything in the world. You're the best thing that ever happened to me, but I'm not Dominic Rossi . . . I'm the father of seven children whose lives have to be shaped . . . whose lives I hold in my hands . . . I can't turn my back on them . . . I love you, but I can't have you because I don't own myself.

The next morning Dominic sat across the table from Roberto having breakfast in their rooms. It was to an angry Roberto Dominic said, "Your mother was happy to see you."

"That's great . . . and so were you when you rushed into my room like gangbusters yesterday."

"I'm sorry about that, Roberto."

"Sorry? *You're* sorry?"

"Yes."

"That's very nice, but it doesn't excuse what you did."

Dominic said, "It doesn't excuse what you did either . . . running away."

"Maybe not, but I just got fed up with the whole fuckin' world."

Dominic was shocked to hear the word from his son. He said nothing. "What made you so fed up?"

"Segetti . . . putting me through the hoops like I was a circus performer."

"Do you know what he told us?"

"That I was a bum . . . a lazy bum, right?"

"Wrong . . . that you were a gifted sculptor, if only you had the discipline . . . in fact, he said your talent was extraordinary."

231

"He said that?"

"Yes, and much more about your ability, but that you lacked the incentive."

"What does he know about incentive? He thinks everyone is the same . . . can be driven the same . . . I'm not a machine. I have to work things out my own way—"

"And what way is that?"

"To work when the inspiration hits me. If it's in the middle of the night or in the middle of July, I've got to do it when I want to . . . I don't want to be told when to create. Maybe that's the way most artists work, but not me. Don't you understand . . . I'm a person . . . Papa, a person with my own ways."

Dominic shook his head. He was beginning to understand a great deal . . . "Okay, Roberto, what is it *you* want to do?"

Roberto looked at his father . . . it was the first time he had ever been asked. "You *really* asking, Papa?"

"Yes . . . I'm really asking."

Maybe the old man didn't want to make him over into his own image after all . . . was it possible the old man was growing up?

"Let's talk, Roberto . . . about you. We've never done that, have we?"

"No, did you ever give us the chance? Were you ever home long enough?"

"Well, Roberto, I'm sorry . . . but I have needs too. Whether they're the same as yours is unimportant . . . Now, about you."

For the first time, Roberto forgot his anger and set aside his hostility. "I want to go home . . . but not back to that big house . . . it suffocates me . . . what I want is a studio with a glass slanting roof, a bed, a table and a toilet. I want to paint . . . murals at four o'clock in the morning if I feel like it or all night or not for days sometimes . . . I want to explore myself. I don't want to conform . . . I don't like ties, Papa. They choke me . . . not my neck, my soul."

Dominic sat silently, listening for a long while. Catherine, in her way, knew more about their son than he did. Once she had said he needs room and that's really what Roberto needed. "Alright, Roberto, when we get back, you find a place and I'll buy it for you . . . that is, if it's not against your principles."

Roberto smiled . . . it was the first time Dominic could ever remember him doing so and, at that moment, he loved Roberto more than he could say, not only loved him, but admired him because he stood up for what he believed in . . . maybe they weren't so different after all. Both fighting for the things they wanted. Suddenly Dominic felt a strong bond between them. "It's pretty tough, Papa . . . trying to be a human being, isn't it?"

"That's pretty profound stuff, Roberto . . . and the answer is yes . . . very . . ."

Roberto looked at Dominic. "Funny, isn't it . . . to find out about your father in a few minutes when you've been living together all your life?"

"Sometimes it takes a real crisis to wake us up."

"Right . . . I sure caused one, didn't I?"

"You sure did, but maybe it was a necessary one . . . a new beginning for you and me."

"Maybe. I hope so, Papa."

"Okay, Roberto, go get dressed and we'll go and see Mama." Getting up, Dominic said, "If you don't want to wear the tie, don't."

Roberto smiled and answered, "I want to while we're here. . . ." Laughing, he added, "it's the least I can do to make up for the trouble I put you through." Dominic laughed back, then put his arms on Roberto's shoulders and held him close.

Catherine sat in the large chair near the fireplace, warming herself with a blanket around her knees. The George V Hotel wasn't home, but she was grateful for it. "Dominic, you don't know how good it is to be here . . . after eight days in the hospital . . . you certainly had your hands full."

"It wasn't that bad."

"Thank you for everythin'."

Dominic shrugged his shoulders as he sat on the sofa. "No thanks needed."

"I've noticed a great change in Roberto . . . he seem so changed, so calm . . . not at all like the boy we brought to Florence last year, I've noticed a difference between the two of you too . . . Dominic?"

"Yes . . ."

"You're quite a father."

"I wonder."

"Oh, you don't have to wonder . . . look at Roberto. It takes a father, I can tell you that. No matter how hard you try, a mother's just not able to handle children the same way . . . I suppose it's a different kind of respect they have."

The moment had come, a moment he'd thought long and deeply about, but the decision was hard and difficult . . . he was trading his own personal happiness . . . his love . . . his joy in Victoria . . . But there was no other way. He would have to be a husband once again with all *that* involved. "Catherine," he said, "you know with all that's happened in the past few weeks . . . with you being sick, and Roberto . . . well, I've done a lot of thinking and I've finally realized that when you're a parent you can't just think of yourself. Sometimes you can't think of yourself at all. What it boils down to is something you said. You're right. Children have got to have a mother and a father . . . So, in spite of what's happened between us, if you're willing, Catherine, to try again, I feel my place is with my family . . ."

Catherine shut her eyes and mentally put her hands together, pointing them toward heaven. Thank you, dear Mother Mary, for your blessings, I've prayed for this moment.

Dominic went on, thinking the decision was difficult for Catherine to make. "Would you . . . be willing to try again . . . ?"

Holding back the tears, she answered, almost whispering, "Yes, Dominic, I'll try."

"That's the most, or should I say the least, we can do for the children."

Thank you, God . . . thank you, Jesus. "Yes, Dominic, the very least." What about the other woman? But thinking she knew Dominic . . . he would never have asked if his intentions were not to break off with her.

"There is only one thing I feel we should understand," he said.

"And what's that?" an apprehensive Catherine asked. Maybe she had been too confident.

"Well . . . you know I've always wanted to get into public service. Since Dom will be through with school this June, he can assume many of my responsibilities. I'm going to take an active part in the party . . . there's a Senator DeKaye I want to see get reelected, which is going to mean a lot of campaigning. I'm telling you this because most of our past problems have come from my being away. Do you still want to try . . . knowing that?"

"You want me to be honest?"

"Yes—now's the time."

"I don't like politics, never did—but that's not important, now. What really matters is the family. Yes, Dominic, we'll try."

Roberto came back from walking. He was a welcome diversion.

"Hi . . ." he said, kissing his mother. "Hi, Papa . . . boy, is it cold out."

"Yes . . . but it's mighty warm in here." She smiled.

As Dominic looked at Catherine, the reality of his decision suddenly was like being hit in the gut by a sledgehammer. He still had to face Victoria. Indecision had always been difficult for him, but this . . . he had to be alone. Getting up he excused himself and said good night. Going to his room he shut the door quietly and stood against it, staring up at the ceiling. He walked to the window, flung it open and breathed the cold, raw night air. Turning abruptly away he stared at the telephone. Quickly he went to the bed, sat on the edge and clutched his hand over the receiver without picking it up. Looking at the silent phone he said, as though his thoughts could be transmitted, "Victoria, I'm sacrificing you as surely as anything was ever sacrificed before. I feel hollow and empty and selfish. I despise myself for abandoning you. I can't even excuse the fact that I'm doing it for my children but everything seems to be mine, and me. But what about you and the rest of your life? You've given me so much, and what am I leaving you with? Nothing. The last two weeks have seemed like a whole lifetime without you. What's the rest of my life going to be like without you . . . Again, me . . . my . . . mine. He put his head in his hands and gave up to the tears.

9

The day of their arrival held more excitement for the Rossis than they had ever known. The children were at the airport with flowers for Mama, and for Papa, the display was more than he could believe. Catherine had called and told her mother Dominic was coming home to stay. And Mama said I told you so and Catherine said Mama, you were right. There was no mention of love, Mama, but Dominic was coming home . . . and in time . . . time was the healer of all things. The other woman? Well, nothing was mentioned about her, but Catherine said she knew it was over . . . just as Mama knew the day Daddy was through.

But it wasn't quite so simple for Dominic as he sat through the special dinner prepared for their homecoming. Catherine sat at one end, observing Dominic . . . noticing he ate very little while the excited conversation went on around him. The children all sat in awe of Roberto . . . what he had done . . . where he had been . . . what he had seen. During dinner, mother and daughter glanced at each other. Mama's eyes saying, see, Catherine, I told you . . . just wait. And Catherine's eyes responded, you're just about the smartest lady in the world, Mama. After dinner, Dominic left, saying he had some important business to attend to and Catherine said, of course, Dominic, and Mama smiled, knowing where the business was that took Dominic.

An impatient Victoria waited for Dominic who had sent a cable earlier. When he opened the door, she was into his arms, kissing him again and again. "It's been a hundred years, darling," she said.

"More than that," he said, holding her tight.

Breathlessly she took him by the hand, "Come, sit down while I get a drink, then you'll tell me everything."

He sat down wearily.

"I can't believe you're back."

He shook his head, "I'm back alright."

Looking at him, she said, "You look so tired . . . here, darling, take this."

When she'd handed him the drink, he said, "Play 'Clair de Lune.'"

" 'Clair de Lune'?" she asked slowly.

"Please?"

"All right." Putting on the record, she sensed something was simply not the same, "What is it, Dominic . . . you seem more than just tired."

He sipped . . . How did he begin? "I am more than just tired . . . I'm sick . . . like you feel when someone's just died . . ."

Shaken, she sat quietly. After a long silence, she said, "Someone has . . . me."

He closed his eyes and drew her to him, "Oh, God, Victoria, I knew it was going to be difficult, but nothing like this."

Holding him to her, she said, "Dominic, my poor Dominic, I really knew someday it would happen, but in spite of that one is never really prepared.

"There isn't anything to say, is there?" Victoria

asked, shocked at her own composure. Later, she knew
she'd break things, scream in the silent rooms, but now
she sat quietly trying to comfort Dominic, knowing
what this decision had cost him. What good would it
be to ask the reasons. "Dominic, I love you."

"Only God knows how I love you."

"We both know, God and I . . . now, look at me.
You've given me a gift for the rest of my life. Don't you
know that? I once told you memories were also souvenirs to hold on to and when I long for you, as I will,
I'll try very hard to remember what we had between
us. They wouldn't be you, but in time I'll be able to
take out the pictures and look at them and remember."

"And I'll remember all my life without the pictures
that I've given up the greatest treasure a man could
ever have possessed." They sat silently, now, in each
other's embrace. There was nothing more to say . . . it
had all been said in the nuances of touch. She would
make sure that when he came for his things, she would
not be here . . . but for this last time, she would think
of nothing else but that she was in his arms.

Dominic's only reprieve from thought in the painful months after his affair with Victoria had ended,
was June . . . it was a time for great elation . . . a time
for pride . . . a time for joy. Dom was graduating and
the Rossi household was in a frenzy of excitement.
Not only was the entire family getting ready to attend
his graduation, but there was another reason for re-
joicing . . . Dom was engaged to the daughter of a
most illustrious and famous thoracic surgeon, Dr.
Andrew Stevens from Atlanta, Georgia. The family had
not as yet met Tish, but from her picture as well as
her voice on the telephone, it was almost as though
they knew her. Catherine was elated that Dom had
chosen a girl from the south with whom she felt an
immediate rapport . . . until she found out that Tish
was not Catholic. The fact that Tish was not Italian

was a thing Catherine could not alter, but, hopefully, Catholic, she could do something about. When Dom had come home during his last midterm break for a few days, Catherine spoke to him at great length. "I know we're gonna love her as our very own and more so because you love her, but one thing I'm gonna have to insist upon, Dom, is that she become Catholic."

"Look, Mama, Tish and I have discussed this at great length and she will not become Catholic."

"I'm real sorry to hear that because I *want my grandchildren to be.*"

"Mama, I love and respect you . . . but you've got to understand that Tish and I have to work this out our own way."

"I also respect your position and I've gone along in spite of the fact that all my life I dreamed when my sons married, they'd have the feelin' in their hearts to marry Italian girls. Well, I've been willin' to overlook that, but I cannot in all honesty give my blessin' to a marriage where my future issues will not be Catholic."

"Mama," Dom laughed at the incredulity, "I think you're forgetting this is a different era and as much as I'd love everything to be to your liking, there's one thing you've got to understand . . . the decision to marry Tish is mine."

Catherine was taken aback. "Am I to understand that *my* wishes mean nothin'?"

"In this case, Mama . . . yes."

"Well, I must say, Dom, you surprise me very much in view of the way you were brought up. The trainin' you were taught and given . . . I'm shocked to learn that my blessin' means so little and the decisions are all yours . . ."

"Mama, for God's sake, I love Tish. Why are you making such a big thing out of this?"

"Because I don't think a marriage can be a happy one when people don't have the same beliefs."

Dom sighed. What the hell did she want from him . . . There he was, marrying one of the most desirable and eligible girls to graduate from Vassar, who could have had her pick of anyone, and she had fallen in love with him. "Mama, let me tell you something."

"Yes, Dom," she said coolly. "What do you want to say?"

"That Tish's family weren't all choked up over the fact that I'm a Catholic Italian, but they didn't make a great big brouhaha over this . . . they're intelligent people who want their daughter to be happy."

"And you're sayin' I'm not?"

"I'm saying you're making an issue out of something that shouldn't be."

"Well, I resent that remark . . . I resent it very much because I want the same for you . . . to be happy and I'm entitled to my feelin' that religion is a very important thing for children."

"My children will be raised with religion."

"What kind? Baptist?"

"No. Mama, for Christ's sake, Tish happens to be Protestant—"

"Are you gonna become one of *them?*"

Dom had reached the end. "I'm going to work this out with Tish," he said, angrily, leaving the room and slamming the door behind him.

That evening, after dinner, Dom sat in the study, unhappily telling his father about the problem he was having with his mother . . . The whole thing had made him so unhappy and he was going to cut short his stay, in fact, he was leaving first thing in the morning.

"Catherine, I'm warning you, for your own good . . . don't interfere in this thing with Dom," Dominic said, lying in bed as Catherine undressed.

She turned around and faced him . . . "Let me understand this . . . you're warnin' me not to interfere . . . well, Dominic, I think it's my duty as a mother to try and advise my son that he might be makin' a mistake. Is that so bad?"

"In this case . . . yes."

Shocked, she said, "Well, Dominic, you're full of surprises. You who's been raised so devoutly, not to take a stand alongside of me."

"Not in this case because Dom has the right to make his own choice."

"Funny thing, you didn't think Roberto had a right to make a choice when he wanted to go to Florence."

"Well, this is a little different. He was sixteen. Dom's a man. Listen, Catherine, and listen well. If you press this issue with Dom, you're going to lose him and if that's what you want, then continue. I don't know what the hell you want . . . here he is marrying a fine girl from an old and distinguished family and you're not satisfied."

"Well, we're not so undistinguished. My family and I are fourth generation Southern born. My great-grandmother was from a fine, distinguished family. My heritage is pretty fine, I'd say."

"But mine's not. My father came from a fine old Sicilian family of dirt farmers . . . so don't throw your heritage around or you'll lose the ball game . . . now take my advice . . . drop it . . . be proud and happy that one of your sons made the big league in the society department."

That night Catherine lay in the dark thinking things over . . . maybe, just maybe there was another way. For heaven's sake, why was she getting herself into such a stew . . . Dom wasn't even married yet, much less having babies . . . when they were married, Catherine felt sure that she and Tish would become very good friends . . . buying lots and lots of expensive presents also made one very receptive to suggestions . . . not that Tish Stevens needed anything from the Rossis . . . but look, human nature being what it was, never had enough . . . and dangling a few baubles in front of someone's eyes didn't hurt the cause. Her grandchildren would be Catholic if she went about it in the right way . . . patience, my dear, as Mama would say. With those happy thoughts, Catherine fell asleep.

The next morning she was in Dom's room looking down at him asleep. Sitting on the edge of his bed, she tapped him gently on the shoulder. Rubbing his eyes, he opened them . . . his voice deep from having been awakened, he said, "Hi . . ."

"Dom, I hope you'll forgive me for wakin' you up, but I've been burstin' with somethin' to say."

Sitting up, he thought, oh boy, here we go again . . . "Yeah . . . ?"

"Dom, darlin', I lay awake half the night, knowin' I had offended you by presumin' too much . . . I wish to apologize. You and Tish have a right to your own lives."

Dom smiled and kissed her on the cheek. "I'm happy you feel that way, Mama . . . I didn't want to leave with any hard feelings. I love you and I never want you to be upset."

"Well, my goodness, it's not possible to never be upset . . . but I thank you for the consideration . . . the trouble I guess is that mamas forget their children grow up . . . same as Grandma treatin' me like I was still a little girl . . . but I sort of like it and I always take her advice . . . not for one minute meanin' you should do the same, I hasten to say."

"You're great, Mama, really you are."

"Thank you, Dom . . . it's always nice to hear you're loved . . . now, any time you're ready, come on down for breakfast. There's so many things I want to ask about."

"Okay. I'll be down in a little while."

~

The day was hot, the air was filled with the kind of emotion that only such an occasion could evoke in parents when they saw their child grown to manhood, and now all the happy, carefree years were left behind and only the future, unknown, was before all the young men receiving their diplomas. Catherine wept, and Dominic remembered his youth . . . the years he had spent here in this very place, never dreaming at the time he would be sitting where *his* father had once sat, watching his son go through the same ceremony.

The feelings of each generation reacted the same. The pride . . . the enormous pride Dominic felt at this moment he knew was only an extension of what his father had known that day so long ago. He had been the same age as his son Dom . . . twenty-three when he graduated and how strange when he thought about how alike the patterns of their lives were. Dom, too, was getting married. Stranger even still, to a southern girl. For one brief moment, although the day was hot, he felt peculiarly chilled. But he refused to lean on the coincidence, knowing that was all it was. His mind moved on rapidly to another thought . . . thank you, Victoria, for all you have given me . . . perhaps if you said the right things, or maybe . . . thank you, my dearest . . . you knew it was right and it is. Dominic was brought up sharply as he heard . . . Dominic Rossi Jr. . . . Dominic Sr.'s heart raced a little faster as he turned around and smiled at *his* mother who sat in back of him, then caught a glimpse of Mama Posata shaking her head in admiration. Catherine clasped his hand in hers. They looked at each other, then to the platform below as the tears streamed down their cheeks.

The windows of the Georgian buildings reflected as they had for some three-hundred years on the milling crowd in Harvard Yard. Graduation caps were tossed in midair . . . parents embraced their sons . . . sweethearts kissed . . . brothers shook hands . . . flashbulbs blurred the eye and another day of memories would be stored away to be taken out, perhaps a generation later . . .

Dom heard his name being called dimly above the excited voices around him. He turned and saw Tish coming quickly toward him, waving her hand. He ran to meet her, and soon she was in his arms, saying breathlessly, "Dom . . . oh, Dom, I was so proud of you, you're beautiful."

Kissing her over and over again, he was unaware that the family was standing in front of them. Catherine felt put out as she observed Tish in her son's arms, a place she felt, as a mother, should have been her prerogative to first bestow her blessings, but she assumed the posture of the loving, devoted mother as she pushed the feelings aside.

Forcing a smile, she said, "Well, Dom, there'll be plenty of time for that . . . your family is waitin' to congratulate you."

Releasing himself from Tish, he turned and saw his mother. She kissed and held him to her, tightly. This was her son, her possession, her first born for which she suffered the pain of childbirth and had poured herself into the making of a man only to relinquish him to another woman who would become the center of his life. It didn't seem quite fair . . . now did it? The thoughts were swift, if not dismissed. She said with tears of a loss she could not quite accept, "Well, Dom, you made us all proud. I guess all the effort was worth it . . . yes, indeed, you made us all very proud."

Something in his mother's voice made him swallow the hard lump in his throat for all the years of his childhood and all the years of her devotion to her children. "Thank you, Mama, I hope I'll always justify that feeling."

"You will."

Now Dominic took his son by the shoulders as their eyes met. Everything Dominic felt was spoken more eloquently in that one moment than words could possibly have said. That deep and brief poignant exchange was broken as Dominic finally said, "I doubt if there was a father here today that was more proud and happy than I. I thank God you're my son. Congratulations."

"Thank you, Papa," Dom answered softly, as his father turned away to wipe the tears from his eyes. Then suddenly everyone was talking at one time . . . how well Dom had done . . . how happy they were . . . the grandmothers . . . the brothers . . . Gina Maria. Tish had been standing by, watching. What a marvelous thing to have such a family. Such love . . . and now she would be part of them . . . the feeling was filled with such joy. What a lucky woman Mrs. Rossi was. Tish knew at that moment how important a large family was and *she* was going to know the blessings of that experience one day.

Reverently, Dom took Tish's hand in his and introduced her to his family. She was more than her picture revealed . . . exquisitely slim with tawny, golden hair . . . the color of a lovely sunrise. Her violet eyes were fringed with dark lashes . . . her skin was the same as fine porcelain. She wore no makeup . . . only the most delicate tint of pink-peach which outlined the perfectly formed lips. Proudly, Dom said, "Tish, this is my mother and father."

She extended both her hands to Catherine. "I can understand why Dom speaks of you so glowingly."

"Well, he's said some pretty glowin' things about you, to be sure," Catherine laughed.

Then Tish turned to Dominic, "And you, Mr. Rossi, what a pleasure it is to finally meet you."

"This is the second time today I've been overwhelmed. Dom, you didn't do her justice."

Beaming, Dom answered, "Nothing could, except to see her."

Tish smiled, ". . . You're just prejudiced."

"That's true," he said, kissing her again. Catherine felt peculiar pangs . . . before dismissing the thought . . . go raise a son for someone else.

Driving to the hotel in one of the large rented limousines, Catherine sat between Tish and Gina Maria who had visions of some day looking and being what Tish Stevens was.

"Tell me, darlin', I suppose your Mama's terribly busy with the weddin' plans . . . how well I remember my own."

"Yes. But I think at this moment she's happy I'm an only child," Tish laughed.

"Well, I hope you're not gonna find us a little bit too much to handle bein' as many as we are."

"Oh, no, Mrs. Rossi. I'm so excited that Dom has a large family, being an only child."

"That's natural. We always want the thing we don't have . . ."

"Well, Dom has certainly provided me with what I've missed. I'm so thrilled with all of you."

"Why, thank you, darlin'. What makes me most happy is a silly little thing like you bein' from the south."

Tish smiled, "That is nice. It's almost like instant love."

"That's right . . . both being raised in the south."

"Most of my life . . . except when my family sent me away to school in Switzerland."

"That's why you don't have an accent."

"I don't?"

"No . . . but one loses it anyway. I know I've lost mine."

"I don't think so, Mama," Gina Maria said.

"I haven't? I thought I did, darlin'."

"No, you haven't, Mama."

"Oh, well, it doesn't make too much difference if your grammar's correct and besides I don't think anyone should be embarrassed about what they are . . . do you, Tish?"

"No . . . no, Mrs. Rossi. A person should be proud."

"My sentiments, exactly . . ."

There was an awkward silence as Tish sat uncomfortably, not knowing what else to say, but as the car sped along the highway, she had the peculiar feeling that Mrs. Rossi had not been too taken with her. It was something she couldn't put her finger on, but it was somehow in her manner. Still, Mrs. Rossi couldn't have been more charming with the little she had said, but it was as though there were hidden meanings behind the words that made Tish feel strange without knowing why. Her thoughts took her far afield until she was brought up sharply as she heard

Mrs. Rossi say, "Well, I guess we're here." And for a moment, Tish was never more grateful as they got out of the car and walked into the hotel lobby.

Lunch was served out on the veranda where they all relaxed, talked about the graduation, how proud everyone was . . . the wedding . . . how the Rossis couldn't wait to meet the Stevenses . . . Tish said how sorry they were not to be able to come, but Dr. Stevens was in New York on a case and Tish's mother was busy with next week's impending nuptials . . . she hoped they would understand.

"How does your Mama feel about you marrin' a westerner?"

Tish looked slightly bewildered, "I don't think my mother really ever thought about it."

"Oh . . . and you movin' out west doesn't bother her . . . your bein' an only child?"

"Well, I don't suppose she's thrilled about it, but she's never said . . . One thing my mother never did was make a career out of me. She's pretty independent," Tish laughed.

Well, I guess that's the difference between Italians and . . . and just plain Gentiles . . . why my Mama cried for weeks, Catherine mused.

That evening Catherine, dressed in pink chiffon, bedecked in her full regalia of rubies and diamonds, went to her mother's room. While Mama dressed, Catherine sat on the bed. "Mama, what do you think?"

"Of what, Catherine?"

"You know damned well what."

"Now, Catherine, you're gettin' up your dander . . . I'd be careful. Now, what do I think of what?"

"Of this girl."

"I think she's very beautiful . . . very well suited to Dom's temperament . . . as well educated . . . I think she'll be a great asset to him in the future."

"Do you really, Mama?" Catherine said sarcastically. "Well, I think she's a little . . . too . . . too . . . too non-Italian to fit into our family."

"Now, you listen to me, Catherine baby . . . I never lie to you, do I?"

"No you don't and I never get mad at you, do I?"

"No . . . because you know in your heart I never try to appease you . . . I like to try and make you see things as they are."

"And how are they?"

Quietly, Mama Posata said, "Catherine, you know what's happenin' to you?"

"No, what?"

"You got jealous Mama pangs."

"Why, that's a terrible thing to say to me."

"You may not like it, but it's the truth."

"That's ridiculous. Doesn't every mother want to see her children happy?"

"Why, a'course and that's just it in a nutshell . . . Dom is happy . . . he loves this girl and what's happenin' is you're havin' a reaction that most mothers have with sons."

A shocked Catherine looked at her mother. That *was* what she had felt today. Good Lord, was she that transparent . . . or was her mother psychic? "How do you know, Mama? You never had any sons."

"Well, a mother's a mother . . . I know if I'd had a son, I probably would be feelin' the same . . . thinkin' I'd raised my son for someone else's daughter."

Quietly, Catherine answered, "That's the truth, Mama . . . there's that little hurt that someone stole your property . . . it's silly, I know, but that's how it feels."

"Catherine, sugar, think about it this way . . . you had him all these years . . . now, if you're good and careful, you'll have 'im the rest of your life."

"Damned if Dominic didn't say just about the same thing."

"See, and he's a pretty smart man, Catherine."

"Alright, I admit I feel a little left out . . . but what about the other thing . . . her not bein' Catholic . . . I don't want Dom to be married by any Protestant minister."

"There again, Catherine, I'm just as religious as you are, but bein' married don't mean that she's got to remain Protestant all her life. I have a feelin' when she's livin' among the Rossis, she's gonna have second thoughts on how her children are gonna be raised."

"Well, that's somethin' I already thought about. Guess I get some of my gray matter from you, Mama."

"That's bein' disrespectful to your Daddy's memory."

"I didn't mean it that way, Mama, I meant your tolerance, your logic . . . just a smidgin rubbed off."

"Well, thank you. Now, go on back to your husband and I'll be dressed in just a few more minutes. What do you want me to wear . . . that printed chiffon or the violet taffeta silk I got last year in Paris?"

"The silk taffeta."

At seven-thirty, Dom walked in with Tish who looked enchanting in a white embroidered organdy dress, empire style, which even enhanced the silhouette of her graceful figure. Her tawny hair hung softly to her shoulders and shone in the dimly-lit sitting room of Catherine's and Dominic's suite. The family was all assembled . . . the men dressed in summer dinner jackets and Gina Maria looked every bit as lovely, thought Catherine, in her yellow tea rose silk organza that Catherine had also bought in Paris. They had hors d'oeuvres and drinks. At eight thirty, they went down to the exquisite outside dining room overlooking the lake. At nine, the music began. First, Dom danced with Trish as Catherine observed from around Dominic's arm. They were in love that pair . . . make no mistake about it, Catherine thought, wishing she could relive her romance, but this was different . . . nothing planned, no arrangements like hers had been.

Gina Maria took turns dancing with her brothers, then Grandma Posata who, for her age, danced with grace. She'll never grow old, thought Catherine. Then Dominic asked Tish, and Dom danced with his mother.

The evening was balmy and romantic . . . a night for love and lovers. When Dominic returned Tish to Dom's eager arms she said, holding his hand, "If I had seen him first, you wouldn't have had a chance, Dom . . . your father's more handsome and a better dancer than you are."

"I know, that's my problem," he said, smiling at his father, "he does everything better. I'm happy to be out of Harvard. You don't know what I had to live up to."

"Okay, thanks for all the compliments, it helps an old man's ego."

"Oh, Mr. Rossi, I only hope that Dom's the same kind of an old man when he's your age." She laughed as Dom took her to him and held her around the waist, whisking her away.

"Dom, I adore your father."

"I told you. Most everyone does . . . he's one of a kind."

They were playing "Tender is the Night." "That's our song, Dom . . . funny how songs make you remember things . . . in school, we were studying F. Scott Fitzgerald . . . one thing made me so beautifully sad."

"What was that?"

"You mean quote it?"

"Yes."

"Okay, let's see . . . 'The girls I once knew, with big brown eyes, real yellow hair in the fall of sixteen in the cool of the afternoon I met Caroline under a white moon. There was an orchestra—Bingo Bango, playing for us to dance the tango and the people all clapped as we arose for her sweet face and my new clothes'—life *was* like that after all."

"That's lovely, darling, and so touching."

"Talk about *touching* . . . shall we go for a walk or am I being too forward, Mr. Rossi, attorney at law?"

"You're being very forward, Miss PhD., but where would we be tonight if not for a little forwardness . . . remind me to tell you I love you."

"I intend to for the rest of your life."

He held her hand and led her to the table. Catherine looked up, "You both looked so pretty dancin'."

"Did we? Thank you," Tish said.

"Mama, Papa, if you will excuse us, Tish and I want to walk."

Dominic got up from his seat. "We probably won't be here when you get back so I'll say good-night now."

"May I kiss you good night, Mr. Rossi?"

"You may indeed."

She kissed him on the cheek, "Thank you both for having such a wonderful son." Then she walked to Catherine . . . "And thank you for dinner, Mrs. Rossi. Today has simply been one of the most unforgettable I've ever had." She kissed Catherine's cheek.

Tony said, "Don't I even get a peck? After all, I'm going to be your favorite brother-in-law."

Going to his side, she kissed him, then all the others and said good-night. As the two walked down the wide stairs from the terrace leading to the garden, then to the lakefront, Mama Posata said, "I think she acts rather Italian, don't you, Catherine?"

"What do you mean by that?" Dominic asked.

"Oh, nothin'. Mama's just tryin' to be smart," Catherine answered, looking at her mother sideways.

Dom looked at Tish in the moonlight. "You're so beautiful, darling. God, I love you," he said, holding her so close he could feel the rise of her breasts against him.

"Dom," Tish said, breathlessly, gently moving back, "I know this is not the time to talk, but I have to."

Holding her face in his hands, he kissed her, then asked softly, "Why now? Tish, let's go to my room."

"Dom, wait . . . I have a few things I have to tell you."

"Now . . . at this moment . . . can't it wait?"

"No . . . I want you as badly, but, darling, please sit here on the bench."

"I've never felt so rejected, not since my acne when I was a kid."

"Be serious, Dom."

"I am serious . . . if only you knew how serious . . . it's killing me . . . this better be important."

Taking his hand, she sat down . . . he moved closer. "Dom, move back or I'll never be able to tell you . . . please."

He slid over, away from her. "Okay, let's hear it because you're driving me crazy."

"Dom, I've done a lot of thinking."

"About what?"

"About our lives."

"And?"

"I've decided we're going to be married by a Catholic priest."

"What?"

"Yes . . . I've already spoken to him."

Dom was so stunned, he could not speak . . . moving closer, taking her hand, he asked, "You know what that means?"

"Yes . . . I've had a very long and involved talk with Father Daini."

"But, Tish, you were very adamant about this just a few months ago and we agreed to be married at your home by a judge so that neither of our parents would feel slighted . . ."

"I know, but I've changed my mind . . . it's a woman's prerogative."

"Why are you doing this?"

Gently, she said, "Because I love you, Dom."

"And you'd do this for me?"

"And for me . . . and for our children. I'm not converting . . . not unless I'm ready . . . but our children will be what their father is."

He shook his head, then held her. "How did I ever get so lucky . . . but I'm not going to let you do this."

"Of course I'm going to do it . . . it's been my decision. I've thought about it very carefully."

"Have you discussed this with your parents?"

"Yes . . ."

"And tell me honestly . . . what was their reaction?"

"They said that whatever I had decided was fine with them."

"I feel so selfish, but I'm so happy, I could cry."

"Then cry."

"You'd even encourage me to do that."

"Of course . . . I love little boys who cry." She kissed him and he returned the kiss too eagerly, too urgently. Again sliding away, she drew in her breath, "Okay, Dom, you heard the good news . . . now for the bad."

"Nothing could be that bad."

"Well, maybe, but no more sex until after we're married."

"You're right . . . that's bad news . . . but why?"

"Alright, Mr. Attorney at law, I threw my diaphragm away after speaking to Father Daini."

"*That's* a good reason."

Standing in front of Tish's door, Dom held her close . . . too close for comfort and kissed her too tenderly. Gently she removed herself from him, placing her hand against his chest. "Remember Father Daini," she said, breathing a little too rapidly.

"Couldn't we forget him just for tonight?"

"No, a little abstinence will be good for you. It will only make you want me more on our wedding night."

Bringing her closer once again, he said, "I never could want you more than I do now."

"Me, too, darling, but a deal's a deal."

"Well. . . I suppose I can't argue with logic like that. I'll probably have to take three or four cold showers during the night. But for a whole week? I'll be waterlogged by that time."

"The risks a girl takes when she marries."

They both laughed. "Good night, darling," he said,

running his hands up the nape of her neck, then under her hair, letting his fingers rest gently at the curled ends.

"Good night . . . I love you," she said.

He started to kiss her, but she opened the door to her room, slipped inside and closed it. With decidedly mixed feelings, he walked down the hall. As he turned the corner, he saw Dominic coming out of his mother's room. "Hi, Papa . . . been visiting with grandma?"

"Yes . . . she's so proud of you, Dom. That's all we talked about."

"Thanks, Papa, but I had a pretty good teacher . . . thanks for everything . . . you're quite a father."

Dominic looked at his son, remembering their talk that Thanksgiving day. What a young man, God, how much he had to be grateful for.

"What do you think of Tish, Papa?"

"I think you're a lucky man, Dom. She's quite a girl," he answered, taking Dom around the shoulder as they walked towards the suite of rooms.

"You have no idea how lucky, Papa . . . incidentally, that's all she talked about was you . . . anybody else, I would have been jealous of . . . I think the only reason she's marrying me is because of you."

Dominic laughed, "I doubt that."

As they approached Dominic's rooms, Dom said, "Papa, I have something to tell you and Mama . . . I can't wait."

Dominic looked at his son's beaming face, wondering what was so urgent. "If it can't wait, be my guest," he said, opening the door.

Inside, Dom asked, "Papa, let's have a drink."

Catherine's door was open. "What about me?" she said, sitting up in bed, putting down *Vogue* magazine. "I'll have Campari. I think there's still some ice left."

"Okay, Mama," Dom called out as he poured the drinks in the living room. Handing one to his father and taking his and Catherine's, the two went into her room. Dominic sat in the big chair. Dom handed Catherine her drink as he stood. Raising his glass, he said, "I want to drink to your health."

"And to yours," Dominic answered.

Catherine raised hers and said, "To your happiness."

"Thank you, Mama."

They sipped. "What a proud and happy day this has been for your Papa and me," Catherine said.

Dom looked at his mother and father, overcome with joy that they were together again. It all seemed so right . . . the circle had been closed. "Mama . . . Papa, I have something to tell you. Tish insists we be married by a priest." Catherine sat, stunned, then looked across the room to Dominic. "What do you think of that?" Dom asked, his voice almost hushed.

"I'm the happiest mother in the world," she said with tears in her eyes. "I simply can't believe it . . . did the talk we had when you were home make that much of an impression after all?"

Dom shook his head, "It had nothing to do with that, Mama. I never spoke to Tish about it."

"You didn't? . . . Then how . . . why did she change her mind? You must have said somethin'?"

"No . . . this was her decision. Her very own."

"I don't understand, Dom . . . you said she was just as devoted to her beliefs as we are."

"Well . . . it's a little embarrassing to put into words . . . but Tish said she loved me so much that she wanted the children we have to be Catholic . . . *imagine, because she loves me that much* . . . What do you think of a girl like that, Papa?"

He thought of Victoria. What a lucky, lucky man his son was, marrying a girl so like her. Shaking his head, finally, he said, "I'm at a loss for words, Dom. That takes a special kind of person to be that selfless . . . you're a lucky man, Dom, to be loved that much . . . and damn it, I hope you make her as happy. She's already given you a lot."

"I think she's lucky, too, Dominic . . . after all, Dom's no ordinary young man." But father and son were looking at each other and scarcely heard Catherine. The look did not go unnoticed by Catherine and the implications were all too apparent, but she shoved them aside. "Dom?"

"Yes, Mama?" shifting his glance to her.

"I don't know what really happened, but I can't tell you how thrilled this has made me . . . and your Papa, but darlin', she surely has been takin' religious trainin', I'm sure . . . realizin' the responsibilities of a Catholic mother?"

"No, Mama, Tish is not converting . . ."

"She's not?"

"No."

"But surely you must have . . ."

Dom interrupted, "Mama, this is something I never expected Tish to do . . . signing her rights away to me about how our children will be raised . . . I think she's done something so great . . . don't you?"

She's never satisfied, Dom thought, as Catherine said, "I do, indeed . . . but darlin', it would make us all so happy if she . . ."

"Now, listen, Mama . . . I'm not going to ask Tish to convert . . . suppose we think about her and her happiness for a moment . . . she does count, you know . . . and this decision didn't come easily nor impulsively and let's also consider her parents."

"Did they object?"

Christ, sometimes, he thought, the threshold of his mother's understanding was almost childlike. "No, they didn't."

"Well, I think that's very big of them."

"It's nice of you to recognize that."

"I do indeed."

"You bet, Mama." Dom took a sip of his drink.

Dominic picked up his glass and went to his son's side. Clicking glasses, he said, "Here's to long life with the loveliest girl in the world . . . make the most of it, Dom."

10

The day started in a flurry of excitement as all the Rossis boarded the plane for Atlanta. Dom sat holding Tish's hand. When the sign went on, he helped fasten the safety belt around her slim waist which he pinched, then his hand went just a little lower, "Ouch, Dom . . . stop being so Italian."

"Sorry, couldn't resist. How did you sleep last night?"

"I didn't. How about you?"

"One shower after another."

"No wonder you smell so sweet . . . Oh, Dom, I'm so thrilled . . . If getting married feels like this, let's do it more often."

"Okay, but only to each other."

"Are there any other people in the world?"

"No," he said, kissing her. He lay back against the seat as Tish snuggled close, putting her head on his shoulder. "I don't think you should do that or I'm liable to forget Father Daini."

"Darling, I spoke to my mother last night and told her all about your family . . . especially your father."

"When she sees us en masse, I hope she doesn't faint."

"She won't, you know my mother."

"I'm happy to say, yes, I do . . . you're going to be like her, Tish . . . I can just see it."

"And you're going to be like your father . . . in fact, you are."

"That's the best compliment anyone could pay me . . . Tish?"

"Yes, darling."

"You've never mentioned my mother . . ."

"Well, I . . . think she's very nice."

"You don't really, do you?"

"Well . . . she's very . . . beautiful and very . . ."

"Difficult to get to know . . . right?"

"Sort of, yes . . . but that doesn't mean I don't like her . . . some people are just easier in the beginning . . . like your father's charm. He's really about the most exciting man I've ever met. In fact, I can't imagine a woman not falling in love with him. He should run for president."

"He probably will. Don't press him too hard," Dom said laughing. "I can see my father sitting in the Oval Office . . . yes, connect me with the Vatican . . . they're out? Okay, the Kremlin."

"He's really involved in politics, isn't he?"

"Very . . . he's always been."

"How come he never ran for office?"

"Because of my mother."

"Why?"

"Well, my mother's a peculiar combination . . . when you get to know her, you'll understand her better. She's really a very private person."

"She doesn't give that impression . . . in fact, just the opposite. She seems very outgoing."

"That may be . . . but it's all surface. She has no

real friends . . . doesn't want any. Her whole life has been her children."

"I don't think that's such a good idea, Dom, do you?"

"No . . . but then, we are what we are and my mother likes her own private little domain."

"I hope you won't feel offended, darling, but I think that's rather selfish. I believe a woman has to assume the role of wife according to her husband's profession. Take my mother . . . my father's often away giving talks, or attending doctors' conventions, but God knows where, and when he comes home it's just like he never left."

"Does she go with him?"

"Sometimes. Not always."

"And she's never resented being alone?"

"Resented? How could she? It's my father's life . . . his profession. She keeps so busy, I don't think she has time to be lonely."

"That's wonderful. Would you?"

"Would I what?"

"Resent my going into politics?"

"Not if that's what you wanted to do."

"It's tough on a woman, you know."

"Are you trying to tell me something, Mr. Rossi?"

"No, just, one, two, three, testing."

"It's a little late for testing. A man should be sure before he asks someone to marry him."

Squeezing her hand, he answered, "I was sure."

"I hope so, Dom . . . I love you so much."

"And you know how I feel about you, even though I can't always put it into words."

"You do all right. I get the message . . . I have from the beginning."

They sat silently. Dom was deep in thought . . . Tish had no idea how careful he'd been before falling in love and why he related to Tish the way he did. She was all the things his mother was not. Remembering how he'd spoken to his father that day in Dominic's study, had taken his father to task for having a love affair ... what does she have that Mama doesn't, he had asked ... She gives me something I need so badly ... tranquility. That's what Tish had along with everything else. Of course, he had been enormously attracted to her sexually ... but it was even in those moments he knew that she was capable of giving herself completely. Yes, he knew what he had, and God, how he loved her. He'd learned a lot about marriage from his parents' mistakes. A sad way to learn, but at least not wasted.

He took her face gently and kissed her.

The stewardess coughed reluctantly as she stood at the side of Dom's seat, hating to interfere with what appeared to be a very personal moment in the life of Mr. Dominic Rossi, Jr.

"Uhhun ..." Dom looked up, trying to control his breathing.

"Yes?" he answered.

"Would you care for something to drink?"

"Tish?"

"I'll have a vodka and orange juice."

"Make that two," Dom said to the stewardess.

"Thank you ... you may remove your safety belts," she said, moving down the aisle.

They both looked down, then at each other and broke out in gales of laughter. "See what you do to me? We're probably halfway to Georgia by now!" Dom said, shaking his head.

Still laughing, Tish answered, "Well, no one can say we're not being disciplined with our chastity belts!"

"Hell, I need more, like a double jockstrap to hold me ... every time I kiss you, I get such a hard-on, I ..."

"Havin' fun?" Catherine asked on her way to the lavatory.

Dom looked at his mother, "Just terrific, and you?," he answered crossing his legs.

"Lovin' every minute," she responded, continuing on.

"Tish, I've got to go to the john."

"I'll be here when you come back."

Quickly, he hurried down the aisle.

On her way back, Catherine stopped and spoke to Tish . . . she hadn't been to Atlanta since she'd been about twelve, having gone with her Daddy. What she could recall was a most beautiful city.

"Thank you, Mrs. Rossi, it is lovely, but probably has changed since you last saw it."

"I'm sure, darlin'. From now on you're to call me Mama. Mrs. Rossi, indeed! Good Lord, I'm gonna be just that, when you come to San Francisco and live . . . how do you feel about leavin' the place of your birth?"

For some reason, Tish wanted to laugh. It sounded so strange . . . the emphasis she put on it . . . the place of your birth . . . Tish wanted to get up, salute and sing "I wish I were in the Land of Cotton" . . . "I don't have any qualms about leaving."

"But you'll miss it, I'm sure."

"Undoubtedly."

"Once you're southern, it's hard to be anythin' else."

"I've never thought of it quite like that . . ."

"You haven't . . . why, I'm surprised . . . I've never forgotten my heritage, *roots* goin' back four generations . . . my great-grandfather was a southern gentleman with a grand plantation."

"Well, that's the difference. My mother's from New England . . . very, very Yankee, I'm afraid. And although I was born in Atlanta, I somehow don't feel the same wonderful sentiment you do for the south . . . I love it, but—"

Catherine interrupted in amazement, "Your mother wasn't southern born?"

"No."

As though she was having difficulty trying to understand, "How did they happen to meet?"

"My mother was studying archaeology at Columbia at the same time my father was taking a postgraduate course in surgery, and when they met, my mother decided to give up digging." Tish laughed, "She said he was the best ancient ruin she'd ever find and traded in her shovel for a marriage license."

Catherine laughed too. "That's very cute." Then she frowned, ". . . strange, in a way."

"Strange? In what way?"

"My situation was similar . . ."

"Similar? You mean Mr. Rossi and you met at college?"

"Oh, no, darlin', I never went to college . . . livin' in the south at the time I was growin' up . . . nothin' derogatory meant by this . . . young ladies didn't go to college . . . simply wasn't the thing to do."

She sounded like Scarlett O'Hara thought Tish, but the thought went further. Somehow she found herself feeling sorry for Catherine . . . suddenly she realized her future mother-in-law needed to feel important, which being a southern belle gave her. That's rather sad, she thought, as she sat looking at Catherine, who rambled on about her meeting with Dominic. There was something pathetic about her that drew Tish closer to this woman . . . it must have been difficult to live in the shadow of a man such as Dominic Rossi and she couldn't compete. Suddenly it occurred to Tish . . . that's the reason for all the elaborate jewels worn even in the daytime. She was trying to be somebody and this was her way of trying to achieve it. Tish had not heard half of what Catherine was saying . . . only sat, watching the rouged lips move. Her thoughts were interrupted . . . "I didn't like San Francisco in the beginnin' . . . I hope your adjustment will be . . ."

Tish's mind moved away from the conversation again, remembering some of the things Dom had said about his mother earlier. Then and there she knew they were going to be friends . . . yes, she liked Catherine . . . in spite of her reasons being born out of pity.

"Is my mother trying to sell you the south?" Dom asked, returning from the lavatory.

For one moment, Tish felt a mild resentment, and

rather protectively she answered, "No, your mother was telling me about her lovely girlhood growing up in the south. We southern girls have a heritage to be proud of, don't we . . . Mama?" Tish smiled, looking at Catherine. In that moment, Catherine liked this reassuring girl . . . yes, indeed, she did.

There was a strength she admired which she had refused to see until this moment, "We do indeed, Tish."

"Well, viva la Dixie," Dom said as the stewardess handed him a drink, then reached over and placed a glass in Tish's hand.

"I'll drink to that," Tish answered.

The large aircraft swooped down like a graceful bird and came to a halt at 5:05 Georgia time. Dom and Tish, hand in hand, ran across the field with the Rossis lagging behind. Holding her hat with her free hand, Tish called out excitedly, "There they are . . . Mom . . . Dad."

Running even faster, soon they were embracing . . . Tish holding her mother tight while Dom shook hands with Dr. Stevens. His future father-in-law was an amazing man, Dom had thought from the very moment he had met him two years ago. He was a man of enormous warmth, which had come from his Irish ancestry . . . his Scottish genes had provided the handsome ruggedness . . . in fact, looking at him, one could not imagine from the size of his hands that those fingers could do the most delicate open-heart surgery. Once in surgery, someone jokingly said, if he hadn't made it as a surgeon, he could have become a dressmaker. His hair, abundant and totally silver, enhanced the handsome, square, tanned face. There was a twinkle in his green-blue eyes that seemed to change color. He was a magnificent specimen of a man with all the vigor and vitality of one younger than his fifty-three years.

"It's so good to see you, sir," Dom said.

"Good seeing you . . . *sir*, congratulations. Sorry we missed the big day," he said, with a soft southern drawl.

"It was my loss, I can assure you."

Then suddenly, Tish was in her father's arms, "Oh, Dad, I'm so happy to see you."

Dom turned around and embraced Tish's mother. Then holding him at arms length, Leticia Stevens said, "Let me look at you, Dom," in that frank, open way. She was beautiful, but not in the same way that Tish was, but the resemblance was there. There was an inner beauty that glowed in her slender freckled face. The angular bone structure was something an artist would understand. Her wide eyes were direct, warm and blue, the color of star sapphires. Her reddish hair was pulled nonchalantly into a topknot held with a rubber band. She wore a simple, sleeveless cotton shift which emphasized her slim, graceful body. Her mouth was ample and sculptured. When she spoke one became fascinated with her cadence of speech. There was a lilt to the Yankee, clipped voice. She meant what she said and she said what she meant . . . There was an air of inspiration in her honesty that made Andrew's Atlanta friends love and accept her and admire Andrew Stevens for having the good taste to marry and bring her as a bride to live among them.

"Well, well. So now all you have to do is a simple little thing like getting married and taking on the future . . . that doesn't seem too difficult now, does it?" she smiled that enchanting smile as her cheek bones rose and her eyes crinkled.

"No," Dom smiled back, "not when I have someone like Tish to work for."

"What a nice thing to say."

"Mrs. Stevens?"

"Yes?"

"I can't thank you enough for your having done what you did."

"And what did I do?"

"Allowing us to be married by a priest."

"Oh, dear boy, thank Tish for that. It was all her idea. But it meets with our approval. Ah, I see your family coming up the ramp, but before, make up your mind . . . think about it . . . either Mom or Leticia, one or the other." Before he could answer, the Rossis were standing in front of Leticia. "Now, introduce me to your family."

"This is my mother and father . . ."

Leticia held out her hand to Catherine, "I cannot tell you what a pleasure this is meeting Dom's mother at long last . . . and you, Mr. Rossi, were the topic of conversation Tish and I had last evening."

Dominic laughed, "That's very flattering, but you, Mrs. Stevens, have quite a girl."

"Why thank you . . . my name is Leticia . . . Andrew, this is Mr. . . ."

"Dominic . . ." he said, shaking Andrew's hand, "my wife, Catherine, my mother, Mrs. Rossi and my mother-in-law, Mrs. Posata . . ."

"Delighted," Leticia said, as Andrew stood by her side, smiling broadly. "Tish, don't tell me . . . let's see how good your descriptions were . . . you're Tory . . . Am I right?"

"Right," he responded smiling.

"The twins, obviously. For heaven's sake, don't forget which one either of you are or we'll all be in big trouble."

"That's no lie. I can't keep them straight after all these years and in September, they're off to Harvard," Catherine laughed.

"I can see why," Leticia shook her head. "And this is our artist . . . you've got a look about you . . ."

"So have you, Mrs. Stevens."

The way Roberto looked at her momentarily made her feel undressed, but she answered, "Thank you . . . now this is Gina Maria and last, but not least, Vincente . . . are we all present and accounted for?"

"We are," Tish said, holding Catherine around the waist.

. . . Isn't that nice, Leticia thought, as they all walked to the exit. Andrew had Dominic give the baggage tags to James who had driven Tish's car to the airport.

"You get all the baggage, James, then take a taxi back to the hotel. Have them taken to Mr. and Mrs. Rossi's suite, then you come on home."

"Right," he said.

Dominic thanked Andrew for his kindness and the men walked out into the parking area with the ladies behind them as the family followed. Leticia drove her Ford station wagon with Catherine, and the grand-mothers along with Vincente, Dominic, the twins, Tory and Roberto went in Andrew's large black Cadillac. Gina Maria begged to go with Tish and Dom . . . in her small car with the top down. Dom said to Gina Maria, "Honey, why don't you go with Mama?"

"No, Dom, I'd like to be with Tish and you . . . please?"

"Look, tell you what . . ." Dom started to say.

"No, Gina Maria's coming with us . . . get in the middle." Dom shot a glance at Tish, but she looked at Gina Maria, remembering when she was that age . . . how painful it was when her favorite and youngest uncle had gotten married. She felt positively sunk . . . secretly, she was so in love with him. Gina Maria was having confused thoughts, Tish knew.

When they arrived at the hotel just ahead of the others, getting out of the car, Dom said, "Thanks a *lot* for the ride."

"You're welcome."

Gina Maria said, "I loved it . . . this is such a beautiful city."

"I'm glad. That's why I wanted you along."

"Thanks, Tish . . . you're terrific."

"So are you . . . in fact, you're one of my favorite people."

Gina Maria was about to say something, but in-stead Dom said, coming around to Tish's side of the car, "We Rossis are like that . . . to know us is to love us . . .we grow on you." He bent down and kissed her, then whispered in her ear, "And I'd love to."

"To what? I'm afraid to ask."

"To grow on you."

She smiled, narrowing one eye. "See you later . . . sexpot!" Laughing, she drove off.

Turning into the circular driveway, Tish came to a halt in front of the sprawling southern Georgian mansion. Strange, she thought . . . you live in a house all your life and never think about how beautiful it is . . . or how much it means, or if you'll miss it. Those times away at school didn't count . . . I always knew I was coming home . . . but after next week, this will no longer be my home. Getting out of her car, she walked up the red brick path leading to the front veranda that ran the length of the house. Opening the front door, she stood in the enormous foyer and looked about her. How truly lovely this house was. That wide circular staircase. How many brides had walked down it since this house had been built in 1853? Andrew Stevens had inherited the house from his mother, who was a widow and failing in health when he carried Leticia over the threshold. For two years she almost willed herself to life to see her first grandchild born. With that accomplished, she died contentedly leaving Andrew and Leticia (whom she adored) a complete house filled with magnificent Victorian, Georgian and eighteenth-century antiques and paintings she had inherited from her parents. In the twenty-four years that Leticia had been mistress, the house remained much the same except for refurbishing. Tish walked into the enormous drawing room and looked out to the garden beyond the covered terrace. There was color everywhere bordering the expensive lawns. The pool sat cool and serenely blue among the profusion of bursting blooms, and down the wide brick path two tennis courts rested unoccupied. Like seeing it for the first time, today, everything looked especially enchanting. The oleanders, the hydrangeas and ferns that nestled among the huge oaks to shelter from the heat of a summer's day were breathtaking. In the distance the sound of water sprinklers could be heard. What a lovely, sleepy, lazy sound, Tish thought. Although she had always known she'd be married in this house, suddenly, she was overcome by the reality. *Of course*, she'd miss it and only yesterday she'd glibly told Catherine . . . *I have no qualms* . . . and brushed off twenty-two years of her life, just like that. My goodness what was wrong with her? She did love Dom . . . didn't she? Oh, come now, Tish, how can you ask anything so stupid. Suddenly for the first time in your life, you're all grown up and maybe you're having a few prenuptial jitters. Okay, as a psychology major, what's so unusual about that? Getting married is a very serious business, or was it something Catherine had said that at the time Tish took lightly, but right now . . . standing here, she simply couldn't sort out her feelings. Quickly, she went through the dining room to the kitchen where Jenny was finishing her pies. When she and James had come to work for Andrew's mother, they were both young and newly married. After Mrs. Stevens died, they stayed on. Jenny was now fifty-five and James about the same age. She was as small and light complected as James was large and dark. Tish came up behind her, putting her arms around Jenny's slim waist.

She turned around, "Good Lord, Tish, am I glad to see you."

"Me, too," Tish answered, kissing her on the cheek. "Oh, Jenny, it all smells so delicious."

"Feel like a glass of cold milk or somethin', Tish?"

"If I can have a piece of that pecan pie."

"Well, you just sit right down here." As Jenny walked across the large kitchen to the refrigerator to get out the milk, she noticed Tish looking rather pensive. Coming back with a filled glass in her hand, she sat down across from Tish. "What's wrong, baby?"

Tish looked across and smiled wanly. "I don't really know, Jenny."

"Don't wrinkle your brow like that."

"Was I?"

"Yes, you have a habit of frownin' when you're a little unhappy or ponderin' . . . now, what's wrong?"

"I'm not unhappy . . . just frightened . . . and sort of suddenly."

"What are you frightened of?"

"Making a good wife for Dom . . . being a good mother . . . cooking, taking care of a house . . . and I feel so . . . unequipped . . . it's a little late for second-thoughts, but I can't help it, Jenny."

"Listen to me, baby . . . just do what comes natural and you'll be fine."

"I hope so . . . really I don't know what's wrong with me today."

"I think you do, Tish."

She paused for a long moment, sighed and answered, "Yes, I do . . . it's knowing a part of my life that was so dear . . . is past . . . I didn't know I'd feel this way, but coming home today was so strange."

"Nothin' strange about it. Every bride that wants to make a success of her marriage feels that way."

"Were you, Jenny . . . ?"

"Was I? I was so scared, I thought I'd die, but I didn't. Only one regret I got . . ."

"What's that?"

"No children . . . that's kinda sad for James and me, but you have lots and lots of babies . . . Tish."

"I'm going to try . . . I love you, Jenny."

"I love you, too, baby. Now, go on upstairs and take a nice, cool bath and I'll bring up somethin' cold to drink in a little while."

Tish was just getting into the tub when she heard her mother's voice. With the towel draped around her, she called from the bannister above, "Mom, come on up. I want to talk to you."

"Okay, be up in a minute."

Going into the kitchen, Leticia dropped off a few last minute things Jenny needed, took out some cold lemonade, looked out of the open window and saw Andrew sitting under a shade tree. "Feel like a cold drink?"

"Little later . . . thanks," he answered, with his eyes closed.

She smiled happily to see him so relaxed, a thing he knew little of. He could have gone into his father's bank and there he would have known the quiet life instead of beating his rump off . . . but Leticia turned away, thinking maybe if he had, he wouldn't be the man he was. She went upstairs to Tish's room. Hearing the splash of water, she went into the bathroom, finding Tish lathering her arms with scented lemon soap. Taking a washcloth, she knelt down and washed Tish's back.

"Oh, that feels so good . . . you haven't done that for a long time."

"Um . . . I know."

"How do you like them?"

"The Rossis?"

"Yes."

"They're very nice . . . lovely family."

"And Mrs. Rossi?"

"Well . . ."

"You didn't . . . I take it?"

"I don't know her. Of course . . ."

"You usually have an instinct about people . . . I don't think you cared too much for her."

"I'll have to know her better, Tish."

"She was friendly enough, wasn't she?"

"Yes . . ."

"Then why the reserved judgment?"

"Because she's going to be your mother-in-law and I think, in this case, I'll wait."

"What were the outward impressions?"

"The truth?"

"Yes . . ."

"Like a Christmas tree."

Tish laughed, then reflectively said, "When I met her, I had the same impression . . . as though she were trying too hard . . . but something happened on the plane today . . . I found myself feeling terribly sorry for her . . . there's something so pathetic about her needing to be accepted . . . I don't know what it is, but I find myself liking her."

"I'm happy to hear that . . . it's important. You know, Tish, young people don't believe it, but when they marry, contrary to some beliefs, they marry a family and if they like one another, the marriage is so much more simple . . . less complicated. In-law trouble can be very difficult."

Tish's thoughts were suddenly filled with even more frightening questions than the ones she had revealed to Jenny. As Tish left the tub, Leticia noticed the beautiful violet eyes of her daughter grow dim. Following Tish into the bedroom, Leticia sat on the edge of the bed as Tish stretched out with her hands behind her head and looked at her mother.

"What is it, dear?" Leticia asked, although she suspected she knew the uncertainties her child was feeling.

For a long moment Tish remained silent, then softly said, "You know how much I love Dom?"

"Yes."

"You also know there's no one in the world I want to live my whole life with except him?"

"Yes."

"Then why am I questioning myself like this?"

"Because you know getting married is a very serious thing. If you were less in love, you wouldn't be questioning yourself."

"Maybe . . . but at this moment, marriage seems like such an awesome thing."

Leticia laughed softly at the serious expression on her daughter's face. Taking her hand, she said, smiling, "It's not quite as awesome as all that . . . To be taken seriously . . . yes . . . but it can be the greatest joy and bring a woman the greatest fulfillment."

"Yet just a few moments ago you used the words like 'More simple . . . less complicated.' Is being married *very* complicated?"

"It can be, but as in anything it depends."

"For instance?"

"Well, to begin with, the first thing to consider are the people involved. Love is great and I'm all for it, but it takes two very mature, yielding, giving, intelligent people to learn how to keep it alive. It's like my roses, they have to be nurtured or they won't thrive."

"It's pretty late in the game to begin asking all these questions and pretty stupid, I know ... but that's just the point ... am I all or any of those things?"

"Yes, you are ... but one thing I feel every woman should know and understand and I don't care what the feminist movement says ... it takes a woman to make a marriage ... of course, I'm not talking about world affairs or the role a woman should play in the labor market. I'm all for that kind of equality. What I'm saying is it's up to a woman. That doesn't mean she submerges her own self into her husband's personality or that she becomes submissive and says yes to his slightest command. But if she learns to know *her* man ... how to cope with *him* ... not the one on page seventy-nine, chapter twenty-four, but *hers*, then she's really a woman and being a woman is a very special thing ... maybe that's corny, but I believe if it's marriage she wants, then it's up to her to be smart enough to make it work." She paused, then added, "And incidentally Tish, backing up on what we were saying about Mrs. Rossi a few minutes ago, I sense she's a very lonely lady who needs a lot of love ... love her, Tish, love her a whole lot and I have a feeling she's got a lot to give back ... just instinct I suppose but I have the feeling she feels left out somehow."

Tish put her arms around her mother. "I only hope that I'm your kind of a woman."

"You bet you are."

Tish smiled, "Mom, I love you so ... and I can't be too immature to have picked a mother like you, can I?"

"I wasn't so dumb either ... look what I got."

Jenny knocked lightly at the open door with one hand while in the other she held a tray of lemonade and two glasses. "Interruptin' anythin'?" she asked.

"No, Jenny, come on in," Leticia answered.

Placing the tray down, she poured the pale yellow

liquid into the glasses and handed one to her mistress and the other to *her* precious child.

"Thank you, Jenny," Tish said. Then she noticed Jenny as she looked down at her . . . there were tears in her eyes. She placed the glass on the nightstand, got up and put her arms around Jenny's shoulders. "Jenny?"

"Yes, baby?"

All she could do was embrace her.

Tish then took Jenny's hand and led her to the other side of the bed across from Leticia, where she sat down with Jenny sitting near her. "Jenny, do you remember when you used to take me to your church some Sundays and after we'd go to Aunt May Belle's for lunch . . . I'll never forget those days or the time I slept there with you. It was James who taught me how to ride when I was five . . . in fact, he taught me how to drive a car."

"That's right and if I lived through that, I can live through anythin' . . . Good lawd, I just knew they'd be bringin' you both back on a stretcher . . . my, my, how I always worried about your growin' up. And here you are, all past the measles, the chicken pox, the mumps and all the other things that happen when you're gettin' to be a person." She shook her head. It all happened too quickly . . . life all seems so slow on the way up, but lookin' backward is only yesterday. "Well, enough of all the ramblin'. Those new relatives of ours is gonna be here for dinner before we know it and I'm not even half done. Miss Leticia, James got the flowers cut so anytime you want to make your arrangements, I got the bowls in the flower room." Getting up, she said, "Drink your lemonade while it's still cold."

After Jenny left, Tish said, "I'm just filled with all sorts of wonderful memories today."

"That's what it's all about . . . life . . . we have to first live it so that we can have the gift of that moment forever." Getting up, she said, "Now, darling, I've got a lot of little things to do."

On her way out, Tish said, "Mom . . . ?"

Leticia turned around, "Yes . . . ?"

"You're terrific."

Leticia laughed, "Ha . . . that's the understatement of the year."

———◡◡———

Leticia Stevens had a very disturbing effect upon Catherine . . . she found it impossible to sleep after being at her home for dinner earlier last evening. It was four o'clock in the morning and she had not shut her eyes. She struggled with the idea that Leticia was everything she was not. There was a graciousness that was inherent in Leticia that she resented, making her feel inadequate . . . depressed. Catherine wrestled with the whys of what made her what she was. My, she was just all full of conflicting questions in the wee hours of this morning. Getting out of bed, she went quickly into the sitting room so as not to disturb Dominic, who slept so soundly in the twin bed separated from her by the nightstand. She wouldn't for the world allow him to guess she was upset . . . or why. Look at him, sleeping without a care . . . Why was it that Andrew Stevens hadn't made Dominic feel inferior? Imagine . . . Andrew, whose heritage had been guaranteed from birth . . . One had been born into elegant gentry, while the other had pulled himself up by the boot strings and found a place he belonged in . . . he's achieved his goals and was exactly where Andrew was —accepted. Apparently, one's origins weren't nearly as important any longer in the scheme of things as Catherine had once imagined. The world had changed since she was a young girl growing up. . . . When family, the right kind, made all the difference. There was a time when Dr. Stevens would have never acknowledged Dominic as an equal . . . but from the way they had responded to one another, one would have believed they both had come on the scene from the same social class. My, oh my, how things had changed. Catherine was slowly having to realize the south was no longer the same . . . it had happened one day when that black girl refused to sit at the back of the bus. There were no more wops, were there? No more niggers? People became a little more cautious about saying things out loud. The signs that once had read "White" . . . "Black" were all gone. The world had changed and she hadn't even been aware of it. Where had she been while it was all taking place? Where? Totally involved with her children . . . her home. Where was she when Dominic got away from her and found himself in the arms of Victoria Lang? The thought had come into her mind painfully . . . but quickly she turned the pages of memory to Leticia. This evening had been devastating for Catherine. No one could possibly have guessed how ill-at-ease she was sitting at that lady's table, watching her . . . it was all so elegant, but with a simplicity. The china, the crystal, the silver, the monogrammed linen . . . all handed down from generations. You couldn't buy that, could you? No money in the world bought one that kind of inner composure. After dinner while all the men retired to the library to discuss politics (knowing Dominic she was sure that would be the topic of conversation), the ladies sat amid the quiet elegance of the dimly-lit drawing room, talking about the wedding. Then Catherine's eyes wandered to the picture album sitting on the large table. She got up and ran her hand over the lush, deep red velvet cover and read the brass plaque attached.

"Tish, may I see this?" she asked, forcing a smile.

"Would you like to?" Tish asked, getting up and handing it to Catherine. The two sat on the small settee and started from the beginning. Every important moment was recorded between the pages of that album . . . but when Catherine came to the picture of Tish's debut with her father at her side, Catherine's heart raced too rapidly. To all outward appearances she kept her inner composure intact, but inwardly, all the frustrations of her youth and rejection came back like a thunderbolt. No wonder Leticia and her daughter could feel the emotional security they had been privileged to in their lives . . . Junior League, the best schools, the best homes . . . the best people. Catherine's angry jealousy was almost more than she could subdue. Quickly, she continued on with the rest of the pictures, scarcely seeing nor caring. In spite of the lavish Balenciaga gown she wore and the enormous square-cut diamond she had on her left hand, she still felt that awful feeling of inferiority. After all these years, the rebuff still burned. Oh, well, no one had everything, did they? You bet they didn't. Soon Leticia Stevens would be left alone. Her only child would be married and living in California and what would she have? Her Junior League . . . president of the Garden Club . . . a big social lady in the community . . . the Gold Club? What the hell were they compared with what she had? Catherine Posata Rossi had seven children and she'd make sure she'd hold on to them . . . forever. Dom was definitely not going to open the law firm in Paris. She was going to make that perfectly clear to Dominic. They were her life . . . her Junior League . . . They were *hers*. Wearily, she glanced at the clock, it was five. Hidden thoughts could be exhausting. Good God, she had to get some sleep or she'd look dreadful this afternoon . . . and if she did nothing else, Catherine was going to make Atlanta, Georgia, and all of Leticia Stevens' *grand* friends know that Miss Tish Stevens wasn't marrying beneath her. Yes, siree, she was going to wow them this afternoon at the luncheon Leticia was giving at the Country Club at noon to introduce her and the other Rossi ladies to high society.

The following week was a frenzy of luncheons, dinner and cocktail parties, but Leticia took it all in stride, making the most of every moment. Wedding gifts were still arriving. Last minute fittings, last minute revisions with the caterers. She arranged things for everyone; while during the day the boys swam or played tennis, Dominic and Andrew played golf at the club which was a revelation for Dominic who learned a great deal about Andrew Stevens. Over lunch, they talked about everything. Dominic was impressed by Andrew's knowledge of politics and world affairs. He wondered when Andrew had the time to indulge in anything except his profession.

"Well, Dominic, no one can live in a vacuum . . . not in today's world. I spent my best years trying to save lives because I think there's a sanctity in life. I can still remember the first World War . . . everybody marching off as though they were going to some kind of jousting match. Until we began to hear about this one's son, or somebody's husband getting killed, war was a remote thing . . . we still lived in a world of innocence." He took a sip of water. "I remember as a small boy, somebody died and everyone in the neighborhood talked about it in solemn whispers . . . 'You know, John died.' It was very sad, someone dying. Then we had the second World War and we still felt pretty bad about young men dying, but it was in a damn good cause . . . we understood the reasons so it didn't seem so tragic . . . then all of a sudden, we had a little thing called Korea . . . of course, that wasn't a war at all, just a police action . . . well, what the hell, in a police action if some young kid gets shot up, it's not the same as if it was a war, so we didn't pay much attention to it. Then we get Vietnam. Congress never said we should be there, but every night we sat glued to our televisions and saw young men slaughtered by the thousands. Life becomes so unimportant, so expendable . . . so cheap. You wonder why the so-called younger generation didn't think much of what we fed them? Why they thought it was okay—even moral—"

"You're right, Andrew, but how the hell do you legislate conscience . . . morality . . . respect for life when you're dealing with human nature . . . men who only give a damn about getting elected."

"That's right . . . get elected at any cost. But unfortunately some of those costs are human lives and that's what I think the kids have been complaining about."

While Andrew spoke, Dominic thought about his sons. Dominic greatly admired Andrew, but Andrew was an idealist . . . Dominic was not. He was tough, but if he hadn't been tough his sons would be among the boys Andrew was now talking about. You bet it was heartbreaking to get that letter in the mail . . . "We regret to inform you that your son is missing in action." Well, he was damned happy that his sons weren't going to face that. It was the underprivileged . . . the Blacks . . . who mostly were taken. He'd move heaven and earth to spare his sons. Damned right, I'm patriotic, but I'm a father.

11

Leticia was a woman of enormous vitality, but this Monday morning, she indulged herself since she didn't have to see the Rossis off till four this afternoon. Having breakfast in bed was something she did only when she was ill and she hadn't been ill since she could remember. But after the past week's events which climaxed with yesterday's wedding, Leticia felt she had earned the luxury of a little leisure. Taking the last drop of coffee, she set the tray aside, snuggled back into the large pillows and relived the day . . . and what a day it had been.

Three hundred guests sat under the striped awning in that majestic garden holding their breath as Tish walked down the red carpeted aisle on the arm of her father toward the flower arbor where a nervous Dom waited with his brother, Tory, as best man. At that precise moment, Andrew Stevens was feeling the pangs of fatherhood . . . relinquishing his daughter into the care and protection of another man . . . a feeling he was not comfortable with. The thought that she would never be completely his again bothered him much more than he was willing to admit to himself. Suddenly his misgivings about Tish's marriage gave way to a flood of doubts. He set them aside when he glanced at the radiant young eager face beside him. There was that unmistakable look of love in Tish's violet eyes, velvet, shimmering . . . a look that made Andrew realize how unimportant he was. Slowly, they approached the white, satin-covered altar where he placed Tish's hand in Dom's, then looked searchingly at both of them, swallowed back the lump in his throat, kissed her gently on the cheek and took his place alongside of Leticia and held her hand. The gesture was more to comfort himself, thinking now there would be the two of them . . . but suddenly, his fears were dispelled as he saw his child kneeling alongside this handsome young man with whom she would spend the rest of her life. Yes . . . it all seemed so right when Dom reverently kissed Tish as they were pronounced man and wife after a solemn ceremony performed by Father Daini. A kiss of tender devotion as a promise of all their years to come. For a moment, they looked into each other's eyes, a look so tender, so poignant that it brought tears Leticia could no longer hold back.

When the sounds of music were heard, a smiling Tish, dressed in exquisite white organza and delicate reembroidered lace encrusted with seed pearls, walked back up the aisle, now on the arm of her husband whose face needed no interpretation. He could see nothing but his wife . . . My God, she was beautiful, in the veil that had belonged to her grandmother, so carefully stored away through all these years, and the Juliet cap framing her fragile face, making her look almost ethereal. Vaguely, as he heard the whispering sounds . . . she's positively magnificent . . . I've never seen anything so gorgeous . . . he felt the impulse to say out loud . . . she's mine.

The bridal entourage of ushers (the twins, Bobby,

Vincente and two of Dom's best friends from Harvard)
followed behind, walking beside the bridesmaids (the
most excited of all was Gina Maria who had been the
maid of honor) dressed in soft, tea rose yellow. They'd
finally taken their places in the receiving line and were
now awaiting the families. Catherine, dressed in
printed, flowing chiffon, extravagantly wearing her
diamond and emerald jewels (which shimmered daz-
zingly in the sun), followed with Dominic's arm on
hers. Smiling broadly for all to see, she looked at his
proud and happy face, thinking, I've beat you, Victoria
Lang . . . you bet. Although her mother walked behind
her, knowing looks of 'I told you so' were unnecessary,
Mama's thoughts and hers, at this moment, were one.
Leticia, dressed in an elegantly simple blue Christian
Dior, the same color as her eyes, held Andrew's arm
as she laughed softly, acknowledging the smiles of her
friends. From that moment on, events moved so swiftly
Leticia had difficulty trying to remember them all.
First, there was the reception line which seemed to go
on endlessly. Then the picture taking . . . first, the bride
and groom . . . then the newlyweds with each set of
parents . . . the grandmothers with Catherine and
Dominic . . . Catherine and Dominic and the two of
them . . . She could still hear the popping of champagne corks. How exquisite the buffet table was . . . the
flowers and, of course, the wedding cake . . . how many
tiers? Five . . . six? Well, no matter, what mattered
was the way Dom held Tish's hand when they took the
wedding knife and made the first cut. She remembered
dancing with Andrew and Dom and Dominic and all
those fabulous Rossi boys . . . Catherine was to be
complimented . . . she had certainly done a job, by
George . . . gentlemen, all of them. She had a right
to feel proud. And that daughter, Gina Maria . . . so
unspoiled, so lovely, so precious. It took a lot of doing
to accomplish that and Leticia could feel nothing but
admiration.

Then all too quickly the hours slipped away and that one special day that she had dreamed of all these years, seeing her daughter marry, was coming to an end as Tish went upstairs to change into her going away pink silk suit. Now all the guests were assembled in the drawing room and entry foyer, waiting for her to walk down the circular staircase with her husband at her side. Leticia recalled watching them as out of a dream and the reality of the culmination of all the years brought tears of joy. Quickly, Andrew handed his handkerchief to her as she wiped them away. There were then the sounds of good-byes amid handshakes and kisses, embraces and best wishes, and hand waving . . . and it was over as the Stevenses along with the Rossis and the guests waited on the front terrace watching the small convertible disappear. Leticia sighed . . . it had been a day long to be remembered. Now, after all the excitement, the house seemed so quiet . . . too quiet this morning. Then she smiled and thought it won't be so quiet in a little while . . . there are compensations to being Catholic after all . . . and suddenly, the idea of being a grandmother pleased her very much.

It was a tearful Catherine who stood waiting at the air terminal. Her family had dispersed until flight time. She could see the boys at the newsstand. Dominic, his mother and the Stevenses had gone to the coffee shop, but here she sat with her mother alone.

"Won't you please come on back and stay for just a little while longer, Mama?"

"No, darlin', much as I'd love to, I think it's time to go home."

"But why, Mama . . . I really miss you so and I need your comfort and companionship."

"I don't think you need me that much anymore,

283

Catherine, baby . . . we had a job to do and, with a lot of help from the Lord, we accomplished it, didn't we?"

"Not we, you . . . it was you."

"I only helped, but God was on your side."

"I don't know if he was or not . . . why kid ourselves, Mama . . . Dominic didn't come back because he wanted to."

"Well, even if that's the case, the point is you wanted him for better or for worse . . . now, be honest with yourself . . . how was it livin' without him? Isn't this better . . . in spite of the compromises?"

"I suppose . . ."

"Of course, it is. You were Mrs. Dominic Rossi at your son's wedding and you two were together . . . now, that was somethin', wasn't it?"

"I suppose . . ."

"Come now, Catherine, you've got an awful lot. You've got all the years ahead, watchin' your children go through what we saw this last week."

"I suppose I'm just not satisfied. I want Dominic to love me . . . really love."

"I think he does, Catherine . . . not like he once did, don't hope for that. But the point is, he's kind, and considerate . . . *livable* with, let's say, which is more than a lot of women have, livin' out their lives with some men."

"But Mama, I know he still loves her and *wants her, a woman just knows at those moments . . . in bed.*"

"Maybe, but she hasn't got him, you have . . . no matter how. Now, Catherine, when you get home, try and do somethin' . . . get interested in somethin'. If you do, then you won't be dwellin' about how much you're needin'."

Catherine sat with her hand holding her mother's . . . "Mama . . . I'm really so lonely . . . won't you come back for just a little while and then when you leave, I'll take your advice and get interested in somethin', but just for a while, come back . . . please?"

Violet Posata looked at her child . . . that's what she was, a child calling out in the wilderness.

"Just until Dom comes home from his honeymoon ... please?"

Violet sighed, "Catherine, baby, you have to understand everyone has to go home and I've got to go home. I have other children and I haven't seen Rosa Ann in a long time."

Catherine's lips tightened, "I'm furious at Rosa Ann."

"Now, that's not fair, Catherine. She couldn't leave her husband."

"Oh, now, Mama, she could have come to the wedding. Nick had his stroke a year ago. After all, I wanted my own sister present. There were *plenty of Rossis* who came."

"Maybe," Violet said, "but not when he's bed-ridden. I'm sorry, Catherine, you're wrong."

Catherine started to cry, "You're angry at me now."

Gently, she answered, "No, I just think you should be more understandin' ... try, Catherine ... for the love of God, Catherine, try and you'll be a happier person."

She took Catherine's head and placed it against her shoulder. "Don't cry, darlin', we have to learn to take the adjustments."

"I know, Mama, but sometimes it's not easy," Catherine said, trying to hold back the tears.

"I know, love ... but that's why we have to learn not to be tempted with dreams of what we would like life to be ... it's so much easier to accept it as it is."

Drying her tears, Catherine said, "You're right, Mama ... always so wise, you're my strength ... that's why I miss you so much."

"Well, sugar, as long as I'm still around, you've got me ... but darlin', you've gotta develop your own strengths."

"I've never learned ... learned how, and at this late date, I guess I never will."

"I don't believe we're ever too old to learn or to change if we want to."

Catherine heard the announcement, "Flight 82 will be boarding . . ." The voice trailed off as Catherine looked once again at her mother and the last remaining minutes were spent in good-byes as the family and the Stevenses now stood clustered around. Dominic shook hands with Andrew, kissed Leticia, as did the children, then Catherine embraced Leticia.

"It was beautiful . . . everythin' was beautiful . . . I'm so happy about the children and happy the Stevenses have been added to our family."

"What a lovely thing to say, Catherine, and the Stevenses are privileged to be a part of you."

At the immediate moment, all the foolish resentment was forgotten . . . the preconceived determination to dislike Leticia she found impossible. Holding Leticia's hand, she said, "Come and see us soon."

"We will, Catherine, I promise . . . the minute Andrew finds the time."

"Take care and . . . Leticia?"

"Yes, Catherine?"

"Thank you . . . thank you for everythin' . . . the weddin'. What I'm tryin' to say is thank you, for allowin' the children to be married by Father Daini . . ." Catherine heard herself saying things she hadn't been able to express till now because of pride . . . she would not allow the Stevenses nor give them the satisfaction to think they were bestowing a great favor upon the Rossis, giving Leticia a sense of superiority. But Mama's words must have mellowed and humbled her. Also, the Stevens's graciousness and hospitality had broken down her defenses . . . somewhere, deep down, the revelation had its reward. In spite of herself, she felt calmly happy. Catherine had made a friend in Leticia. Then things happened so quickly as Dominic took her by the arm and led her down the runway. Just before boarding, she looked back and saw the Stevenses standing with her mother. Grateful to them that they would wait and see Mama off . . . on her way back home . . . back to New Orleans. She walked up the landing steps with a feeling of foreboding . . . a

feeling she could not dispel, even after they were airborne, that this would be the last time she would see
her mother. The thought was too frightening to contemplate that one day, Mama would be gone and no
longer would she be anyone's child.

12

But thank God her fearful premonition had been an unfounded fantasy. A year and a half had passed since that day. "Mama," Catherine said, excitedly, via long distance, "your Catherine's a grandmother."

"Oh, darlin', I've been waitin' for this happy moment . . . you must all be walkin' on clouds."

"Oh, Mama, you have no idea . . . I'm so excited, I forgot to tell you we've got a precious little boy."

"Well, God bless you all. How's Dominic holdin' up?" she laughed.

"Like no one in the world's been a grandfather before . . . guess what Tish named the baby?"

"Dominic."

"That's it . . . Dominic Andrew Rossi."

"And Leticia . . ."

"Standin' right here waitin' to say hello." Catherine handed the phone to her.

"Mama Posata, how *are* you?"

"I'm fine and I don't have to ask how you are . . . tell me about Tish."

"Came through it like a Rossi . . . the only problem was Dom. I don't think I've ever seen a new father suffer so much . . . he just had the worst kind of labor pains."

They both laughed. "And Andrew?"

"Arguing with Dominic that the baby looks like him."

"Well, I won't say that was the worst fate in the world a child could suffer."

"Neither does he, but after twenty minutes, it's a little too early to tell."

"Keep appeasin' him."

"Not in front of Dominic, I won't."

"Well, God willin', I'm comin' out just as soon as I can."

"I probably won't be here by that time . . . Andrew's got to get back, but I know everyone will be thrilled to see you. Keep well, come and see us when we all simmer down . . . I'll say good-bye. Now, here's Catherine."

In the next few years there were many special reasons to keep Mama informed about activities that took place within the family. Tory no sooner graduated from Harvard, with his name added to the growing list on the door of the Rossi law firm, than he married a girl from Los Angeles. In spite of the fact that exotic, doe-eyed, raven-haired, olive-complexioned Joanna Razeni was Catholic and her Daddy very rich, Catherine found reason to vent her complaints. "Mama," Catherine said, holding the receiver in her right hand, "I'm not at all happy about this marriage."

"Why? What's wrong with the girl? From what I understood when Tory called and told me, she's just beautiful . . . lovely girl, fine family. What's your . . ."

Catherine interrupted, quickly, "Beautiful! Fine family? They're rich, but common . . . wait till you meet her . . . she's coarse and common . . . usin' all that eye makeup. You know as well as I that havin' money doesn't buy breedin'—and besides, she doesn't have the kind of warmth the Posatas respond to. She's not Tish, I'll tell you that."

"Well, you weren't too choked up about that in the beginnin'."

"*What!* Why, how can you say that? I was thrilled from the very beginnin' . . . I think you're a little confused."

Mama Posata smiled as she lay stretched out in the large bed in New Orleans listening to Catherine ramble on.

"My main objection was Tish's not bein' Catholic . . . now, you surely remember that?"

Mama stifled a laugh. "My memory's comin' back. But what about this one . . . she's Italian and Catholic?"

"So . . . that doesn't mean she's the kinda girl I would have picked for a daughter-in-law."

"Maybe . . . but it wasn't up to you, it was Tory's privilege to make his own choice."

"Whoa . . . now, you hold on for just a cotton-pickin' minute, Mama . . . remember? *Remember?*"

Across two thousand miles of telephone wire a bewildered Violet Posata asked, "Remember what? What am I supposed to remember?"

"How you influenced me into marryin' Dominic," Catherine answered, her anger mounting the more she thought about it.

Putting her hand over the mouthpiece, Mama laughed so hard there were tears in her eyes. Then she choked as the laughter began to subside. "You all right, Mama?" Catherine called through the phone.

Recovering her voice, Mama answered, "I'm fine . . . just a little coughin' spell . . . now what was this about me influencin' you?"

"Well, you did . . . didn't you?"

"I surely did and do you remember why?"

"You bet I do," Catherine answered, with mild rancor, "you were afraid I was gonna be an old maid

. . . and, Mama, much as I love you . . . there have
been a good many times, as you well know, I haven't
thanked you for pushin' me."

One thing Violet prided herself on was that she
loved Catherine in spite of all her faults, but a mother's
not a husband. You bet I was afraid. Dominic might
have had second thoughts findin' out about how tem-
pestuous you can really be, so I urged Cupid along a
little. . . . "I'm sorry you feel I influenced you badly,
Catherine . . . but let's not forget you were pretty much
in love with Dominic, as I recall. Even if it pleases you
to think you were pressured into marriage . . . knowin'
you as I do, I don't think a team of wild horses could
have stopped you from marryin' him . . . now, isn't that
the truth, Catherine?"

She didn't answer for a moment, then laughing as
though she'd been caught stealing cookies out of the
cookie jar, she said, "That's the truth, Mama."

"Well, then, Catherine, you've gotta put things in
their proper perspective . . . you can't go around
blamin' me for somethin' I thought was right."

"I know, Mama . . . it's just when I get all steamed
up, I sorta lose my straight thinkin'."

"Well, I suppose most of us are likely to do that.
Somewhere, down deep, it makes us feel better if we
think we've been victimized . . . now, tell me about the
other children."

"Well, the twins are fine. Of course, Dominic still
hasn't recovered from the shock of the twins goin' over
to Berkeley instead of Harvard. I swear, Mama, sometimes the reality of life does get a little bit too much
to handle . . . . now, don't be confusin' me by a lot
of logic about this. I don't understand the rebellion
that's goin' on with these young people . . . seems that
parents have lost their influence."

"I know, Catherine, baby, you just said I was too
influential with you and . . ."

"This is somethin' entirely different," Catherine interrupted, "I just had to put my foot down on one
thing."

"And what's that, baby?"

"No long hair . . . sandals or that dreadful thing . . . they call pot."

"That's sensible . . . just hope those outside influences don't creep into your good intentions."

"They better damn well not!"

"And if they do, what then?"

"Oh, I'll think about somethin' to do 'cause one thing I'm not gonna have is the effort I poured into those kids findin' no reward."

"I know you will, Catherine, you're a good mother . . . Roberto's fine, I hope."

"Yes," Catherine answered, slowly, "yes, but I'm concerned about him."

"Why?"

"Well, he doesn't come home as often as I'd like. Lives in that studio. I'm not sure that he eats right . . . or . . . oh well, the point is he's an artist and you have to give in to people like that. They're just different."

"Well, I'm sure Roberto's gonna make you proud . . . how's Dominic?"

"How's Dominic? Damned if I know . . . he's been workin' his tail off, tryin' to get this Senator DeKaye from Sacramento re-elected. Why, I'll never know, but one thing I'll tell you, Mama, he better have all those meetin's and conferences over by June because we're gonna take Gina Maria to Europe on her birthday. Imagine, she's gonna be seventeen."

"I just can't believe it."

"That's right . . . Good Lord, Mama, where'd all the years fly? Sometimes, I feel as though I just misplaced about half my life."

"Oh, come on, Catherine, you're still a young woman with a long life ahead. I'm gonna be seventy and I never think about it . . . never felt younger or better."

"That sure makes me happy, Mama, seein' as how we're so far apart."

"No one would believe it . . . you know we've been on the phone close to two hours?"

"Honest? My, oh my, how the time does fly when I talk to you . . . Oh, I almost forgot to ask. When you come out for the weddin' in June, we'll be leavin' right after for Europe . . . will you take Vincente back home with you?"

"More than thrilled about that . . . but why isn't he goin' to Europe with you?"

" 'Cause he doesn't want to go."

"Well, he will when he gets older. Now, Catherine, I'm just about runnin' outta steam . . . I'll be callin' in a few days . . . oh, and Catherine?"

"Yes, Mama?"

"About Tory . . . I'm just as sure as I can be, she's gonna turn out fine and you're gonna like her. I just know you are, Catherine."

"I sure as hell hope so, Mama, because at this moment, I'm damned disappointed I didn't have the influence over Tory that you had with me."

13

To see Venice for the first time through eyes of innocent youth was to capture all the romantic fantasy of a sheltered, overly-protected, seventeen-year-old Gina Maria. All the poetry of life with its extravagant sentimental imagery brought forth feelings that captured and untapped longings yet to be born. The first night of their arrival she stood on the balcony of her room and looked out to the Grand Canal, watching with breathless excitement the gondola passing below in the moonlight. She heard the rippling sounds of oars dip gently into the serene water and listened to the handsome gondolier singing songs that must have been sung for hundreds of years. The sights and the sounds conjured up images of Venetian ladies long since past being escorted by their dashing lovers to some rendezvous. Gina Maria could see them . . . almost hear them speaking . . . breathing . . . could almost reach out and touch the delicate silk gown . . . the soft velvet flowing cloak . . . the jeweled masks which hid the eyes in disguise from some jealous husband. Her pulse quickened as her mind moved back into time and glimpsed the ladies dancing at court . . . their ball gowns billowing out as the gallant gentlemen dressed in satin pantaloons, brocade waistcoats and powdered wigs, twirled them gently around the room to the sounds of violins. Perfume wafted through the air. The blackamoors, turbanned and plumed, stood at attention as the King and his Queen entered. There was a hush after the sound of trumpets blared announcing their arrival. The ladies curtsied and the gentlemen bowed gracefully, then with the wave of an imperial hand, once again the festivities began as the room reeled with twirling dancers and the violins played till dawn.

"Gina Maria?" she heard, calling her back from the grandeur of a once glorious Venice.

"Yes, Mama?" she answered, turning around.

"Enjoying the view?" Catherine asked, smiling.

"Oh yes, Mama . . . I've never been so happy or excited about anything in my life."

"That's the way I felt when my Daddy and Mama brought me here for the first time, but, darlin', you better get some sleep. We've got a big day ahead of us tomorrow."

"Alright, Mama, but first, I want to say good-night to Papa."

Dominic was sitting up in bed reading an Italian newspaper when Gina Maria bent over and kissed him. "Papa, it's so beautiful. I wish we never had to go back."

He laughed at her excited, exquisite face with the large brown eyes. Her hair was thick like strands of silk skeins that hung loosely to her slim waist, and the most beautiful soft lips kissed her father. "Oh, Papa, thank you so much for taking the time out to bring me here . . . it wouldn't have been the same without you."

"Did you think I would miss an occasion as important as seeing your face at this moment?" he asked, smiling.

Catherine stood in the doorway and thought, you're damned right you would have if I hadn't put my foot down.

But he continued, as though he were reading Catherine's mind. "No, Gina Maria, I wouldn't have missed this for *anything* or *anybody*."

Kissing him once more, she said, "Oh, thank you, Papa, again . . . I can hardly wait for tomorrow."

Climbing into the tall, oversized, draped four-poster Venetian bed, she turned off the bedside lamp and looked up at the starry blue night through the long French doors and thought that somewhere beyond those doors, her future waited. There was a world out there . . . How wonderful to be grown . . . finally . . . to be seventeen, in love with the love of life.

Early next morning, Gina Maria went down to breakfast alone, knowing her parents still slept and would have breakfast served in their suite. There was no one in the dining room yet. Apparently, it was a little too early even for the maitre d'. She hesitated, thinking perhaps she would wander around for awhile, then return at seven. But at that moment the maitre d' came out of the kitchen. Mildly startled at seeing a guest this time of the morning, he said, "Good morning. You're a little early."

"Oh, I'm sorry, I . . ."

"No . . . no . . . no, don't be sorry for such a little thing, please let me show you to a table. My name is Luigi."

She sat at a table looking out to the lagoon where she observed in wonderment the motorboat tied up along the short pier, unloading fresh produce. It was a delivery truck, Gina Maria realized, laughingly. Not quite like Guido's where Mama shops. His deliveries are made in a Ford pickup . . . poor Mr. Guido . . . with all due respect, Fords will never be as romantic delivering groceries as motorboats.

"What will you have, my dear young lady?" the dapper maitre d' asked in his most elegant broken English.

"What . . . ?"

"What is your pleasure . . . for breakfast?"

In Italian Gina Maria responded, "Coffee and a roll . . . please."

Astonished at her accent, he asked, "You are American and speak such Italian?"

"Yes," she said proudly, "because I am Italian . . . the same as you."

He answered with equal pride, "But I am not Italian."

She looked at him. "I thought you were."

He answered in tones of hushed reverence, raising one eyebrow, "No . . . I am *Neapolitan*."

"Well, that's Italy . . . Napoli, that is."

"True, geographically . . . but *I*, my dear young lady, am Neapolitan."

"In that case, I am Sicilian."

He looked for a silent moment, then added, "Because of your beauty . . . you can be forgiven." Smiling, with a twinkle in his eye, he adjusted the napkin with a great flourish across Gina Maria's lap and asked, "Now, I will have the waiter bring your coffee, rolls and a little cheese."

"Thank you, but the coffee and rolls will be sufficient."

"A little cheese with the rolls is good."

"No, I really don't care for the cheese."

"Yes, but a little cheese to start the morning with is good," he winked, shaking his head yes.

Waiting for her breakfast, she thought, we're wonderful, aren't we . . . Neapolitans . . . Sicilians . . . Romans . . . Venetians . . . all of us . . . how wonderful to be Italian . . .

After her breakfast of rolls, coffee and *cheese*, Gina Maria walked for blocks just beyond the hotel. The streets were still deserted except for the street vendors getting ready for the tourist trade. Here and there shopkeepers were washing down the sidewalks in front of their stores. How gorgeous the morning is . . . "I love you *Bella Venezia*," she said aloud, throwing her broad straw hat in the air, then ran to catch it. The cats, rummaging through the garbage cans, stopped and peered at her through slanted yellow eyes. They arched their feline backs and sneered.

"Stop being so disagreeable," she said, laughing. "I love you, too. Now, go back to your breakfast." Walking rapidly, she returned to their suite.

As she entered quietly, Dominic was coming out of the bathroom showered and shaved. Adjusting the sash around his dressing robe, he looked at Gina Maria. "Where have you been so early? I went to your room and you were gone. From now on, Gina Maria, when you go out, please leave a note, so I don't worry."

She laughed, "Were you worried, Papa?"

"Yes . . . a little . . . a foreign country, a young girl can't . . ."

Laughingly, she interrupted, "Papa, you're being so *Sicilian*."

Feigning a scowl across his forehead, he said, "That's right . . . I'm very *Sicilian* . . . very, when it comes to my favorite daughter . . . where were you?"

"You sound like you're going to lock me in my room and chain me to the bed for fear my lover may climb up and carry me off."

He laughed, "Maybe, that's not such a bad idea . . . at least I'd know where you were."

"I was downstairs having breakfast."

"Downstairs, having breakfast so early? I just called room service."

"But when I woke up, I couldn't wait to see Venice in the morning."

"Really?" He smiled at her radiant, fragile, fawn-like face, so full of wonder, not like so many unfortunate young girls Gina Maria's age who had the look of oldness about them, all the freshness of youth gone, never to be returned. By God, Catherine was a good mother . . .

"Papa, I have to tell you something funny."

"Yes . . .?" he answered, moving his mind away and back to her.

She told him about Luigi, the maitre d', refusing to admit that he was anything but Neapolitan. She repeated almost verbatim the conversation . . . "And when I said I was Sicilian, he forgave me." She laughed, "He simply wouldn't budge."

"Do you know why?"

"No, unless he thought being Neapolitan was like being the aristocracy of Italy."

"Not exactly . . . you see, it's a strange thing about us Italians . . . it wasn't until a hundred years or so that that Italy became a united country by a general named Garibaldi. For centuries, Italy was overrun by every other nation so that even now, Italians never say I'm Italian. Instead, they think of themselves as still belonging to the province or the city from which they've come. If they were born in Rome . . . they're Romano, or Genovese, or Tuscano."

"I didn't know that . . . we're fabulous people, aren't we?"

"You can't argue that with me . . . why, when the whole world was making war, we were painting the Sistine Chapel and producing the greatest art and artisans the world had ever known."

"Oh, Papa, I feel like the whole world is Italian today."

"Just wait until I show you some of the museums here in Venice. You'll feel even more so."

"Can we go right after you have breakfast?"

"Yes . . ."

"Terrific . . . *Bella Venezia*, here we come."

Catherine was just as excited as her daughter this morning, but for different reasons. She went off in a private launch to the Murano glass factory for a shopping spree. Catherine was never quite so happy as when she was shopping. After seeing her off, Dominic and Gina Maria walked the streets of Venice. By now, the city had become alive with activity.

"Well, Gina Maria, what do you think?"

"I think it's super, Papa . . . I *think* the expression is, see Naples and die . . . but after seeing this, the quote should be . . . see Venice and live . . . *live.*" They both laughed.

As they wandered through the crooked street, then up the narrow steps between the rows of shops, Gina Maria became aware of something that had not occurred to her until this very moment. "Papa?" she asked, "how do people raise their children here?"

"What do you mean?"

"Well, I just realized, there are no trees . . . no flowers . . . no parks."

"And you're curious about that . . . okay, let's take the motorboat and I'll show you."

"Can't we take a gondola?"

"This evening . . . but now, we'll go by water taxi, it's faster."

They got on at Pier One. Nothing went unobserved by Gina Maria. The Venetian housewives were on their way to market. With their string shopping bags, they stepped into the crowded water jitney and held on until they reached the pier they desired and disembarked. Finally, at Pier Nine, the boat stopped and Dominic helped Gina Maria down. Then the boat sped away as the two entered a stone foyer. The floor was slightly above sea level. Inside there was an inch or more of water that had slopped into the large hall. Unavoidably, Gina Maria's shoes were wet as they ascended the enormous marble stairs to the second floor. And what she saw made her forget her shoes. At this moment, she was all eyes that saw the most magnificent allegorical art in Venice. Silently, she stood before each masterpiece in complete awe. It was only when she paused for a long moment before the painting of the crucifixion, she clasped her hands in exaltation. Slowly she said, shaking her head in wonder without looking at him, "Papa, how could any human produce this? It's so beautiful, I could cry."

"That's why I wanted you to see this place. Now, let me answer the question about where people raise their children."

Walking to the French doors, they walked out to a balcony. Below was a secluded courtyard where trees grew tall and flowers bloomed in profusion. Stone benches sat on the lush green lawn. Between the stone columns statues stood regally. "Now, does this satisfy your concern about parks?" he asked, laughing.

Smiling back, she answered, "Yes . . . I thought Venice was only narrow streets and canals . . . but the Venetians didn't overlook a thing, did they?"

"That's right. This palace once belonged to a nobleman. It now belongs to the city . . . to be used as a museum."

"You mean this was someone's home?"

"Yes . . . try to imagine, if you can, the first occupants who lived here when this was built at the height of Venetian glory."

"It's almost too much to contemplate . . . The world is really so beautiful, isn't it, Papa?"

Poverty . . . hunger . . . wars . . . strife . . . human suffering ran quickly through Dominic's mind . . . but for Gina Maria? He answered, "Yes, it's very beautiful." He wanted to add, it could be if all the world remained seventeen, naive and untouched. But he dismissed all such thoughts . . . today, the world was young . . . as young as Gina Maria.

As Dominic and Gina Maria sat lunching at a sidewalk café in St. Mark's Square, the pigeons walked nonchalantly about. A moment later they took flight, ascending in midair as though their wings became one fluttering mass of white gossamer, then just as suddenly they were back once again walking imperiously among the human feet that promenaded. Gina Maria looked up from her salad and savored the sweet plump tomato she had just put into her mouth, when suddenly she stopped chewing. Her mouth still full, she was unable to swallow because standing not more than ten feet away, she saw the most fantastic-looking young man she had ever seen. Unable to take her eyes from him, she watched as he stood with the small group of tourists explaining the history of Venice. He gestured elegantly at the different buildings, pointing out the significances of the Square itself. When it was built, etc., etc., etc. He had repeated the same things every day to a different set of tourists for the last few years so that by now he reeled off the spiel as though it were a recording. Gina Maria finally swallowed the tomato and sat captivated by the sight of him. She could hear his voice . . . what he was saying in the most exquisite broken English, but all she was aware of was him . . . dressed in a beautiful Italian silk suit, Italian leather shoes, pink poplin shirt, paisley tie . . . dark glasses rested on his thick black hair, styled to one side and cut critically just the right length. He looked in the direction beyond where she and Dominic sat and Gina Maria saw his dark, languid eyes. For a moment, she thought she would faint. Then quickly, he moved on with his Americans tagging behind him until they reached the Cathedral. From where Gina Maria sat, she was able to watch the expedition. As the tourists went inside to browse and ooh and ah, he remained outside. Standing to the left of the entrance, he braced himself against the wall, took a cigarette from his gold case, tapped it, then lit it with a gold lighter. He inhaled the smoke deeply and slowly. Of all the places of interest, he loved the church best . . . not for reasons of religion, but because it gave him a short respite away from the clucking voices of the American hens who in the brief span of an hour expected him to teach them the history of a hundred years. Then there was always one in the group that said, quaint . . . everything was *quaint* . . . or simply *divine. Mama Mia!* What a way to make a living . . . well, it was better than being a waiter. At least being a guide afforded him the dignity of dressing in gorgeous silk suits, although at times he didn't have two nickels to rub together inside the elegant pockets of his trousers. It also had other compensations. After the sightseeing was completed, he directed his group to the best bargains where later in the day he collected his lire from the shopkeepers under the table. Now the group was standing together once again as he counted heads and like Garibaldi, he charged on to the Doge's Palace, walking erect and dashingly elegant across the square with the ladies trying to keep up with him. Gina Maria sighed as he was lost from sight.

"Aren't you enjoying the salad?" Dominic asked. "Gina Maria . . . ?"

"You're daydreaming . . . eat your salad. Venice will still be here tomorrow."

But, she thought, will *he*?

That evening at dinner, Catherine told Dominic and Gina Maria about the things she ordered. The conversation went on endlessly, with Gina Maria scarcely hearing a word, although Catherine was now speaking directly at her, ". . . Papa said."

"What, Mama . . . ?" Gina Maria asked.

"I said . . . Papa told me how you loved the museum."

"Oh, that . . . yes, I loved it."

"What's wrong with you, Gina Maria?"

"Nothing . . . nothing, Mama."

"Are you sure? You're actin' awful strange."

"No, I'm not," she answered quickly, her heart pounding.

"You feelin' alright?"

"Yes . . . yes, I'm great, terrific."

"I think you're tired."

"Yes, just a little."

"Well, you can't take it all in at one time . . . we're gonna be here ten days . . . now, you just slow down . . . hear?"

"Okay, Mama," she heard herself saying. Then suddenly in *he* walked, and went to the bar where he seemed to know everyone. Oh, Madonna . . . her pulse raced so, she thought she'd faint.

Dominic looked at her, "We better go back to the hotel."

"No, Papa, I don't want to ruin your evening."

"You're not ruinin' anythin'," Catherine answered. "Better pay the check, Dominic."

And from the sound in her voice and the wink in her left eye, he knew Gina Maria must be having her period.

That night, Gina Maria slept very little. For the next two days, she asked to have lunch at the same café, precisely at the same time, knowing *he* . . . whatever his name was, would appear with a different group. She forced herself to eat. As much as she loved and respected her parents, the idea of being so overly protected seemed positively ludicrous. But old habits were hard to break. Going to a Catholic girls' school hadn't helped emancipate her. She knew all about sex from her convent comrades. If only she could have told her parents the things that went on inside those cloistered walls, they would have been appalled. The girls smoked pot . . . slept with boys . . . read pornography . . . name it, they did it . . . but not Gina Maria and not because she was unlike them. There was only one difference . . . Gina Maria was afraid of disgracing her parents if she got caught. Also, she had inherited a devotional love so great that the thought of defying her father and losing his respect outweighed her desire to do things that were only natural for girls, so she became the oddball at school, a role she did not enjoy and until now had accepted. But suddenly, the urge became more than she could accept and in spite of all her love and the feelings of guilt, she simply had to be free to wander off alone. In this day and age she was being treated like a seventeenth-century princess . . . instead of a girl seventeen living in the twentieth century. But how could she get away for a day? What excuse could she give? Papa wouldn't permit it . . . not in a foreign country . . . that was some laugh, foreign country? Why, Mama even selected the movies she saw and the books she read. Thank heaven, none of the girls at school suspected why she *always* had a headache or a toothache . . . or . . . whatever else she could invent when she was asked to go with them. It was damned embarrassing . . . thank the lord for Roberto . . . he was the only one that spoke up to Mama . . . a book never raped a girl . . . a movie never seduced anyone . . . so where are you when I need you, Roberto? But suddenly she heard, "Gina Maria . . . I don't believe it. Of all places . . ."

Quickly, she got up, dropping her napkin as she greeted the most welcome face she could ever imagine. It was a sign from heaven. "Papa," Gina Maria said, "you know Pam McCormack."

Standing, Dominic smiled, "Yes, of course, how are you?"

"Fine, Mr. Rossi, thank you . . ."

"Won't you join us?" Dominic asked.

Pam looked at her wristwatch, then said, "Okay, but for just a few minutes. I have to meet my folks." She sat down.

Animatedly, Gina Maria asked, her eyes lighting up, "Last time I saw you at school, you didn't say you were going to Europe this summer."

"We didn't know until the last minute."

"Why's that?"

"Well, my Dad had to come on business unexpectedly and he thought it would be great if Mom and I joined him . . . so here we are."

Gina Maria laughed and thought that her guardian angel was here. "How long are you staying?"

"About a week, then we have to go on to London. This week is only the holiday part of it."

"When did you come over?"

"Last week."

"How come we haven't seen you till today? Seems everyone meets in St. Mark's Square."

"Because we just arrived here late last night from Rome. That's where Dad had business to attend to."

305

"Oh, Pam, I'm just thrilled to see you."

"Me too . . . it's so great bumping into a friend from home. Now I know I'm going to have fun."

Gina Maria laughed a little too openly. Checking herself, she answered, "I can't believe it . . . small world, isn't it?"

With the advent of Pam's arrival, Dominic and Catherine reluctantly allowed the girls to spend their afternoons together, so long as they didn't wander too far from the square. At this suggestion, Pam thought, the Rossis were square. Sitting at the café which had become Gina Maria's habitat, Pam asked, "What gives with your folks?"

"You don't understand, Pam."

"You're right, I don't. Explain it to me."

"It's too complicated . . . you wouldn't understand."

"What's there to understand . . . what are they afraid of?"

Hesitatingly, Gina Maria answered, "Of my growing up . . . I said it and I feel disloyal."

"I don't understand any of this . . . growing up? You are! We're both the same age and my folks wouldn't dare tell me . . . 'Stay on the square.' That's ridiculous. What is this . . . the dark ages?"

"For me, yes . . . no, it's not either . . . it's a traditional thing about Italians . . . fathers in particular."

"Well, you and I have never been what you'd call buddies at school, although we've known each other since grade one, I guess. We pal around with different groups . . ." Pam frowned, "Do you date?"

"Well, no . . . not exactly."

"Not exactly? What does that mean?"

"I don't date the way you do . . . I can go to parties . . . listen, Pam, I've got problems."

"You sure do."

They remained silent, then Gina Maria said softly, "Pam, can you keep a secret?"

She smiled broadly, "You're going to have a baby ... it happened when they weren't looking, right?"

"Be serious, Pam."

"Okay, I can keep a secret."

"I'm in love."

"In love? How can you be in love? You don't even date."

"I'm in love with someone who doesn't even know me. Someone I've never met."

Pam blinked. Slowly, she said, "I think this whole thing has really gotten to you ... I'd suggest psychiatry just for openers, then graduate to analysis."

"It does sound crazy, but it's true."

"You're weird ... honest."

"No, I'm not, Pam, let me tell you."

When she finished, Pam answered, "So, did it ever occur to you to meet him?"

"Yes, and that's why I was so happy to see you ... not that I wouldn't have been anyway."

"Got the whole picture ... we go to the Doges' Palace while Romeo's there ... right?"

"Right."

"Well, what are we waiting for? Let's go."

Blonde, blue-eyed Pam McCormack stood alongside of a trembling Gina Maria, standing at the back of the group listening to the brief lecture. As the dissertation continued, a surprised Sergio DiGrazia became aware of the contrasting beauties that had joined his group without paying, which ordinarily enormously offended him. Imagine, the nerve, getting his knowledge for nothing ... but these ladies ... oh well, they were young ... beautiful ... lovely, especially the brunette whose large eyes had not left him.

"Now ladies and gentlemen, the murals you see ..."

Gina Maria followed in a trance. Then suddenly, it was over ... the group had dispersed.

Pam said, "You're on your own," and split as Gina

Fairytales

Maria remained, standing dwarfed by the center of the enormous Throne Room of the Doges' Palace . . . as Sergio stood against the wall smoking . . . studying . . . wondering, should he . . . shouldn't he? He decided he should.

"You seem fascinated by these ancient murals."

For a moment she thought her legs were going to give way when she heard him addressing her. She tried to seem composed, but when she attempted to answer, she sounded like an adolescent boy whose voice was changing. Swallowing hard . . . and clearing her throat, she heard herself saying a most profound thing . . . "Yes . . ."

Her eyes deliberately wandered from one picture to the other as he walked slowly toward her. "You're interested in Italian art?"

Nervously the answer came, "Yes . . . yes, I love Italian art."

Now he was standing before her. If she could get through this without cracking up, she'd live to see the Hilton Hotel on the moon. He was gorgeous . . . her stomach was doing somersaults.

"Let me introduce myself . . . my name is Sergio DiGrazia."

Breathing in, then out, she answered quickly, "That's a lovely name."

"Thank you," he smiled, "and I can imagine someone as lovely as you has an equally lovely name."

"Gina Maria Rossi."

Smiling he said, slowly . . . ever so slowly as though it sounded celestial and unheard before . . . "Gina Maria . . . Gina Maria Rossi . . . that is more than lovely, it is beautiful."

Maybe she should never have come. "Are you staying long in Venice?"

"Not too long," she answered, moistening her lips. She had to get out of here. And what if her father walked in now?

"For how long?"

"Another few days . . . well, I have to be going

308

now . . ." After all, he was a total stranger and probably only the two of them were left in the palace.

She started to walk toward the door with him following her, "May I have the pleasure of your company for a capuccino?"

"No . . . no, thank you . . . I . . . I have an appointment."

"Oh, what a pity . . . another time perhaps?"

They were now outside where she felt safer. "Perhaps . . ."

"May I walk you to your destination?"

"Oh, no . . . no, thank you."

"I would like the pleasure of seeing you again."

"Oh, thank you . . . but . . ."

Before she finished, he looked at her and said quite seriously, "You're frightened of me . . . yes?"

"Oh, no . . . why do you say that?"

"Because you seem so tense, so ill at ease. I can assure you I do not bite."

A smile played around her mouth. Then he asked, "Why do you not want to see me again?"

She thought carefully for fear of hurting his feelings. "Because it's impossible."

"Why, are you betrothed?"

Only an Italian would be so poetic trying to pick up a girl . . . betrothed . . . what a grand word . . . American boy . . . you engaged . . . taxis are engaged . . . "No, I'm not betrothed."

"Then, why?"

Pressing her finger against her lips in contemplation, she finally said, "Because my father wouldn't approve."

"Ahh . . . the one I saw you with at lunch yesterday . . . I like that, especially for an American."

"You saw me . . . yesterday?"

"Yes, and you saw me. Am I right?"

"Yes . . ."

"You're not only beautiful, but honest . . . I like that, too."

"Thank you."

"You are most welcome. Now, what would happen if I were to ask your father for the pleasure of taking you to dinner this evening?"

Gina Maria laughed. "You don't know my father."

"True, but American fathers are not quite that formal . . . remember, I have met a great many Americans in my profession."

Again she laughed, "My father was only born in America, but when it comes to his children, he's very, very Sicilian."

"Ahh . . . *Sicilian,*" he shook his head as though he understood the total situation, "then, in that case, is this to be our one and only meeting?"

Sadly, she answered, "Probably."

"If I suggest something to you . . . you will not be offended?"

"First, I'll have to hear the suggestion."

"You were taught well, my compliments . . . now, my suggestion is . . . may I, in broad daylight, escort you in a gondola down the Grand Canal?"

"I'll have to think about it."

"I would prefer you say yes now, but if you must consider it . . . I will wait for fifteen minutes at Pier One, at three o'clock tomorrow afternoon." He looked deeply, searchingly into her eyes. She wanted to melt into his arms as he continued, "If you do not come, I will be filled with much regret . . . but life is full of disappointments . . ." he finished stoically. He took her hand gently and held it for a moment. She wanted to cry for reasons she could not quite understand . . . reasons that went beyond familial loyalty . . . guilt . . . or anything she had ever felt before.

Releasing her hand slowly, she said softly, "*Arrivederci . . .* Sergio."

"That sounds so final . . . to you, instead, I will say . . . *Arriverderla* . . . until tomorrow . . . *Arrivederla,* Gina Maria." She walked down the stone steps as he watched her go past the old arsenal and then disappear.

Pam looked up from her coke as a flushed Gina Maria seated herself at the table in the Square. "Well . . . ?" Pam asked, excitedly. But Gina Maria sat in a dreamlike trance. Pam snapped her fingers in front of Gina Maria's eyes. "You look like someone who's just, as they say, emerged from her first sexual encounter . . . did you?"

From an echo chamber, Pam's last words penetrated, "Did I what?"

Impatiently, Pam asked again, "Did he whisk you off to his Venetian pad and make violent passionate love . . . the word is sex . . . don't look so shocked . . . ever hear it before . . . or didn't anyone ever mention that nasty word in front of you?"

"Oh, Pam . . . what a thing to say."

"Oh . . . then, you have heard of it . . . but don't knock it if you've never tried it . . . it's worth the trip . . . terrific . . . I can assure you . . . clears up your hay fever, sinuses, frustrations . . . just to mention a few therapeutic reasons."

"*Pam!*"

"Well, you were gone long enough for several rolls in the hay . . . while I sat here fending off the Hun . . . what happened?" she now asked anxiously.

Gina Maria carefully repeated the entire experience, reliving every exquisite moment . . . "I just can't explain how I felt."

"Oh, my dear child, let Mother guide you through this most dreadful ordeal . . . what really was happening, sweet, innocent Gina Maria, you were having a mental orgasm . . . shocking, simply shocking, my dear. Oh, my, now, isn't that just dreadful to think that you . . . so pure, so naive could have wanted to share a rapturous moment lying in bed, between the blankets of love . . . as the Italians say *Amore!*," Pam gestured dramatically. A shadow of pink passed over Gina Maria's face as her eyes clouded with tears. "Oh, come on, Gina Maria, it's not as tragic as all that . . . coming to grips with the fact you're just a *human girl* that

311

suddenly discovered she's got sex urges, same as just us ordinary mortals . . . you did feel that way? Now, fess up, didn't you?"

"Yes."

"Ahh . . . we're making progress. Okay, first step in the right direction."

"But, Pam . . ."

"Yes?"

"I don't think I'm going to see him again."

"*What!* You don't think you're going to . . . I give up. After all I've taught you? Oh heavens above, what is this world coming to when a straight A student on the honor roll every year deliberately defies the twenty-four lectures on sex by Dr. Freud. That dear and noble man who dedicated himself to the proposition that all men and *women* are born sexy and that inhibition is bad for the soul. Of course, you're going on that little safari down the Grand Canal and make your maiden voyage into the sea of life. For if you do not, fair maiden . . . I'm going to be at Pier One at three tomorrow, because if you think I'm going to allow that gorgeous, hairy-chested specimen to go moldy, you're out of your mind. He's so groovy I wish I'd been here first . . . now, how does that grab you?"

"But, Pam . . ."

"What's the trouble now?" she said impatiently.

"I know you'll think it's corny . . . but it's a question of family honor . . . trust . . . it's like a betrayal of everything I've been taught."

"I don't believe this conversation . . . like they say, you had to be there to hear it. For Christ's sake, Gina Maria, get out of your playpen . . . screw what you've been taught . . . because, baby, I've got news for you . . . your folks are the ones with the problem, they betrayed you by holding you back so that you're afraid of being human—"

"What you're saying is . . . I should go, even if I know I'm doing something wrong."

"I give up . . . never encountered anything like

this. Just one more time, I'm going to try and save you. Believe me . . . by meeting Prince Valiant tomorrow, the worst that can happen is you'll have a little fun . . . and the best that can happen is you'll be seduced . . . but I hasten to add, only if you want to . . . because unless a guy's a goon, he knows when a girl's asking for it and when she's not . . . they're smart that way, Gina Maria."

That night there were two people in Venice who had difficulty trying to sleep. One lay in the most elegant bed, in the most expensive hotel in Venice, disquieted, trying desperately to rationalize away all her fears and guilt . . . while the other lay in the dark on an iron cot in a shabby room, trying desperately to evaluate his future and the direction it was taking. Sergio DiGrazia was a very thoughtful, unhappy young man. For all the pretense of enormous glamor, the external trappings of the silk suit were acquired by bartering his services (leading the men tourists into the best haberdasheries in Venice), he was recompensed for his loyalty by having the choice of accepting a few lire or selecting a suit which in some way had been slightly damaged and would have been marked down drastically . . . so he took the suit . . . whatever repairs needed were done by his friend Petro. And one thing Sergio had, if nothing else, was a great many friends because Italians were something like Americans in the deep south. It was not what you had momentarily, it was who, where and from what family you'd come. Italians respected titles. And Sergio DiGrazia's mother was a countess who lived in a broken-down villa in Tuscany . . . a proud and majestic woman who dressed for dinner each evening, wearing the same black lace gown that had been mended over and over again . . . but she wore it regally as she sat in the huge dining salon decorated with pink Pompeian murals and dined by candlelight in impoverished splendor. The food at her table was sparse and homegrown and what had to be bought was purchased with skillful frugality. But with the small government pension she received and by selling her objets d'art from time to time, which widened the silver streak in her otherwise shining black hair, she survived. Her household staff was small and the tenants who plowed her fields were reliable, until it came to rent payments . . . so she settled for whatever tokens they could give. But there were times in her loneliness and her aloneness she would walk to the family cemetery and count the handsomely carved tombstones. It was a place of peace where her loved ones and all the Milaneses that had come before, who had seen better times, slept. Her dear husband and two sons lay near by. When she looked at the pictures of those beautiful faces mounted on the marble headstones, there were times she could not hold down the anger of the despirable trickery of destiny. The world changed, it seemed to the Contessa Francesca DiGrazia, always in the wrong direction . . . one step forward . . . three steps backward . . . Now that the gentry were gone . . . what had changed? Nothing. And her Sergio was robbed of his heritage . . . to become what? A nobody living in an alien world. Had she seen him at this moment with his hands behind his head, staring up at the dark ceiling as though there he would find the answers, she would have wept. He was drifting. Twenty-two years old and there was no way to escape. For all it was worth, what did it mean being Count Sergio DiGrazia? Titles . . . coats of arms . . . what could be done with them? Flush them down the toilet . . . that's what.

Indeed it was a restless wind that haunted Sergio DiGrazia this night. How could one think about life without the thought of marriage? And for all his handsomeness, who needed him? The rich girls of Rome? No . . . they could pick and choose someone not only as good-looking, but someone in their own social strata. So the Sergio DiGrazias of the world were a dime a dozen. The question was as yet unresolved, however, for this Sergio . . . who did he marry? A peasant, a common nobody to bear his children . . . to give his name . . . to bring home to live in his mother's house? No . . . positively no . . . the pages of his mind turned over a leaf. There was Gina Maria Rossi . . . but could he, in all self-respect, marry for money alone? No, without love, the money could bring nothing. For some other impoverished prince or count, perhaps . . . but not for him. Could he fall in love with Gina Maria Rossi, with the soulful brown eyes and the gentle beautiful face? It was quite possible . . . it was very possible indeed because today she had stirred within him feelings of depth he had not felt for any of the other rich American beauties who had in fact pursued him. He had accommodated them by taking them to bed, but that was as far as his interest in them went. Had his desires been only monetary, the effort to achieve that goal could have been attained more than once. But he had resisted the temptation of them dangling their wealth in front of his eyes like a brilliant jewel, and in doing so, he had tested his own needs . . . and what he needed was someone he could love. And Gina Maria somehow ran round and round in his mind . . . could he love her? . . . Could he? . . . Perhaps . . . he wasn't sure that he didn't, although at this moment, she lived only on the periphery of his love . . . wasn't it possible to fall in love with a rich girl? It was, indeed, and if she decided to meet him tomorrow and she was not just the illusion of love . . . or the delusion of love, then he would know . . . and if his instincts guided him with the same feelings which she had awakened in him today, he would marry her . . . if not, then he would say *arrivederci*, because not for one moment did Sergio question his self-worth . . . he was not a cad . . . someone without character or scruples. No one can destroy another person without destroying a part of himself. This was a thing his mother had taught him. No, he would not . . . could not take this lovely young girl unless what he felt was love.

At three o'clock the next afternoon, Sergio saw Gina Maria in the distance, running down the slight incline. As she came closer, her run slowed to a walk as he waited for her. When finally their eyes met, they stood silent for a long, lingering moment. Smiling, Sergio took her hand and helped her into the gondola. When they were seated inside under the hooded enclosure and the small boat moved away from the pier, Sergio said, "I'm so happy you decided to come after all . . . Gina Maria."

"So am I . . . Sergio."

"I wasn't sure you would."

"Neither was I."

"Was the decision difficult?"

"Yes . . . very, I lay awake half the night trying to make up my mind."

"And I lay awake half the night hoping you would."

She smiled, "Did you really?"

"Yes." Then they sat, silently, feeling the nearness of each other without touching. After a while, Sergio said, "You're a lovely . . . lovely, young woman . . . so unlike most of the girls I see." And he meant it.

"Thank you, Sergio . . . and you're unlike anyone I've ever known."

"Have you known many men . . . young men, I mean?"

"No."

"You do not go steady . . . as they say in the States?"

"No," she said without hesitation. "If I tell you something, will you promise not to laugh?"

"I promise."

"You're the first man I've ever been alone with."

"Truly . . . ?"

"Truly."

"I thought everyone in the United States was very permissive," he smiled. "But you are so different, so fresh . . . like sunshine."

Their eyes met then, she looked away.

"Thank you, Sergio," she answered with obvious embarrassment.

"There, I've made you blush."

"Did I?" she said, moistening her dry lips.

"Yes . . . and most becoming . . how old are you?"

"Seventeen . . . going on eighteen."

He laughed, "I sincerely hope so . . . and much much beyond that . . . where do you come from . . . what city, I mean?"

"San Francisco."

"Ahh . . . I understand that is the most fantastic city in the United States."

"It's very beautiful . . . you've never been there?"

"No . . . but that is one place I hope to see one day."

"I hope so too . . . that is I mean I know you would enjoy it."

"Of that I am sure . . . tell me about you."

"Well . . . there's really very little to tell."

"You go to school?"

"Yes . . . to a convent."

"You have sisters . . . brothers?"

"Brothers . . . six . . . two married . . . my oldest brother has a little boy . . . they are expecting another . . . my brother, Tory, just got married . . . in fact, last week . . . they're on their honeymoon."

"What a wonderful family . . . and your father?"

"You mean what does he do?"

"Yes."

"He's an attorney . . ."

"And your mother is beautiful like you, I'm sure."

Whenever he used adjectives, she became terribly uncomfortable. "She's . . . she's very beautiful . . . Sergio, tell me about you."

"As you said, there's really not too much to tell."

"Were you born here in Venice?"

"No, in Tuscany."

"Is anyone ever born in Venice?" she laughed.

"Why do you ask . . . ?"

She told him about Luigi, the maitre d', and he laughed.

"That's true . . . that damnable Italian provincial pride."

"I think it's lovely."

"Do you really . . . and I think you're lovely."

Quickly, she answered, "Thank you, now tell me about yourself, your family . . . your job . . . do you like it?"

"I despise it . . . the only family I have left is a most gracious mother." Then he said, bitterly, "My brothers were killed in the war . . . my father died two years ago." Suddenly, his mood changed.

How painful it must be for those left behind, she thought. She wanted to kiss him, hold him . . . help him. The world was not quite so beautiful at this moment. After an awkward silence, she said, "I'm so sorry, Sergio."

He shrugged his shoulders, helplessly. "Well, that's life, I suppose . . . now are you enjoying your holiday?"

She did not answer, still touched by his grief, then she said, "Sergio, will you forgive me for saying this . . . I don't mean to pry, but I think there's a great deal to tell about your life."

"For someone so young, you're very understanding."

"I'm not as young as you think . . . and how old are you?"

"Twenty-two."

"What's happened in those twenty-two years?"

"Well," he answered, slowly, "if *you* promise not to laugh, I will tell you."

"I promise . . . I won't laugh."

"All right, then . . . I'm a tour guide because Italian counts are out of style this season."

"I don't quite understand . . . Sergio . . . counts are . . ."

"Okay, that's an American expression I picked up . . ." He began to tell her of the nobility from which his roots had sprung . . . about the four hundred years that went into his lineage . . . the poverty, the humiliation his family had suffered, losing their heads. When he finished, he said, *"Okay,* now you can laugh . . . I give you my permission. In fact, if it didn't make me so miserable, I would laugh."

"Oh, Sergio . . ." she started to cry.

Handing her his handkerchief, he said, "See, my mother can't get used to the idea we're obsolete . . . She still sends me monogrammed crests on my handkerchiefs and shirts." Gina Maria wiped the tears that would not stop. "So, why aren't you laughing . . . you don't think it's a funny story . . . from count to tour guide?"

"No . . . I think it's very sad."

"That's because you're too sentimental, not tough enough . . . Americans! I want to spit every time I see the television or read in the papers how much you criticize yourselves, all the things you despise in yourselves. Why, America is the only hope of the world. Americans don't begin to know what hunger is . . . and all the people who hate the system? So they get bombed out of their minds? And that's the way they're going to save the world? They're absolutely crazy . . . the only country in the world where someone can say they hate the President . . . shout the worst obscenities and don't get shot. If they don't like what's happening, the idiots have a chance to change it . . . to save it, it's worth saving . . . but how can you save anything when you can't save yourself? Getting bombed out of your skull is just a cop out . . . more American expressions I picked up. What chance did I have to save anything . . . I ask you . . . what? None . . . so, they got rid of *us,* the terrible ruling class, and replaced it with *what?* A tyrant who shot peasants in the square for complaining a little too loudly. Americans don't like America? They have no freedom? When was the last time the fascist police broke down your door in the middle of the night? Some people don't like the country? They should have had a Mussolini or a Hitler . . . *Mama mia*, why am I getting so wild . . . is this any way to romance a girl? With speeches? Forgive me, Gina Maria, I've made you cry. Oh, I'm so sorry . . . you're the loveliest creature I've ever met and already I'm making you unhappy . . ."

"No, it's only because I love you, Sergio, and feel that you've been so hurt . . . that's why I'm crying."

"That's why?"

"Yes . . ."

"You truly love me? Or are you infatuated with the first man you've ever been this close to?"

"No, I've loved you since that very first day I saw you standing in the square . . . in fact, I arranged to meet you . . . it was no accident."

He took her face gently between his hands. Softly, he said, "I'll tell you something now . . . I wanted to fall in love with you . . . but there's a difference between *wanting* and *loving* . . . I love you . . . I love you, Gina Maria . . . truly—you're everything I dreamed of . . . do you believe in fate?"

"I'm not sure."

"I do . . . I believe it was fate for us. I don't know what moves our stars . . . I will not even waste time asking, but this I know . . . we were meant to live our lives together . . . I love you, I can't believe it, but I do." He smothered her with kisses. Taking a deep breath, he said, "Now, we're going back. I'm afraid of my feelings . . ."

The next day, Gina Maria found it practically impossible to contain the joy she felt inside. As she and Pam sat at their table, Gina Maria said, breathlessly, "I thought you'd never get here . . . I've been dying to tell you what happened."

"Don't tell me . . . let me guess . . . you got laid, right?"

"*Wrong* . . . I got loved . . . if you never tried it, don't knock it."

Smiling, Pam answered, "Touché . . . big mouth McCormack, love object of the universe . . . so tell me, what happened?"

"Oh, Pam, he really loves me."

"Hmm . . . pretty fast workers, these Italians . . . how do you know he loves you? In any language, it's easy to make a pitch . . . did he make a pass?"

"I know he loves me, and he didn't make a pass . . . I know because he told me . . . Pam, he really does . . ."

"If you say so . . . now, where do you take it from here?"

"I'm meeting him at Pier One at three this afternoon."

"That's great . . . peachy . . . groovy . . . but you've got a problem . . . unless you can work something out with the warden."

"Why . . . what do you mean?"

"I mean I can't baby-sit with you any more . . . my Dad has to go to London today."

"Oh, no ! . . ."

"Oh, yes . . . he got a phone call late last night saying it was imperative he be there today. Government negotiations wait for no man, much less Cupid . . . so, sweetie, you've got a problem, unless you can hire a governess."

"Oh, Pam. . . what am I going to do?" Gina Maria was practically in tears.

"I don't know, cookie . . . I guess one of three alternatives."

"What are they?"

"Well, first, you could go to the board of directors . . . lay it on them . . . say, look Pappy, Mummy, I really dig this guy, and wait out the holocaust . . . or split . . . or the third is be a nice sweet adorable little chump and stop seeing Romeo . . . but let me remind you of what happened when Juliet tried that."

Gina Maria was in a state of shock.

"Come on, kiddo . . . don't carry on like the heroine in *La Boheme*. Life is not an Italian opera."

Then suddenly, Pam sat quietly and said, "Look, Gina Maria, I'm going to level with you . . . a lot of the things I've been telling you were to make you get angry enough to feel you're really underprivileged, but emotionally you're the most adjusted girl I know . . . in fact, you knock all the psychologists in the creek . . . why, you should be nutty as a fruitcake, but you're not . . . and what's so crazy about the whole thing is . . . your folks did all the wrong things according to Spock . . . but damn it, you're a terrific gal who *really* knows where it's at and I, dear Gina Maria Rossi, take off my hat to you. I really admire you in spite of all the rousting around, the advice, the glib loose talk I spouted. The truth is, you're the only *honest* nonconformist I know . . . because you held out and didn't run with the crowd like a bunch of sheep listening for the mating call. As my parting shot, the more I think about it . . . What the world needs now are more Sicilian fathers . . . *Ciao, bambino.*"

When Sergio saw Gina Maria, he ran to meet her. Taking her hand, they walked quickly to the gondola. Once inside the enclosure, Sergio kissed her tenderly, with restraint. He released her before his passion rose beyond his control. "Gina Maria, I dreamt about you all night . . . you touched me so deeply. The beauty in your eyes haunted and followed me everywhere I went . . . you're trembling . . . why? Are you unhappy you came today?"

"Oh, no, Sergio," she answered, half whispering as her eyes became misty.

"Then why are you on the verge of tears . . . I don't understand . . . I love you, you love me . . . then why are you so unhappy?"

"I don't know how to tell you this . . ."

"Tell me what . . . what is there to tell?"

"I don't think we can continue to see each other."

"We can't continue to . . . what do you mean by that?"

"It's simply no use . . . I mustn't allow myself to be in love with you."

"You *mustn't!* This is too much. Love is not a tube of toothpaste you can squeeze and stop. Yesterday I discovered love and today you tell me it's no use . . . my whole world is falling apart and you say it's no use?"

"I won't be able to see you . . . my friend, Pam, is leaving. She was my only excuse . . . from now on, my parents will expect me to be with them. What can I do, Sergio?"

"What can you do? It's quite simple . . . we will go to see your father . . . the problem is resolved."

"*No*, we can't . . . you know he doesn't have any idea I've been meeting you."

"So we'll tell him . . . since when is it a crime to fall in love?"

"But he doesn't know about us, don't you understand that?"

"Yes, I understand, but when we tell him, he'll know."

"Oh, Sergio, you don't know what you're saying. He'll get so angry, I don't know what he'll do."

"Why? He beats you? You don't look like a daughter who's been beaten lately . . . so what will he do? Scream . . . holler . . . rant, rave?"

"You can say that again . . . my father can get very angry. You don't know what he once did and said to my brother Roberto."

"Whatever Roberto did, I don't know, and maybe he had it coming to him . . . so what has happened as a result? Roberto hates his father?"

"No, he loves him."

"So? When your father gets over his anger and realizes I want to marry you . . . and this is not panky-hanky . . ."

"Hanky-panky, Sergio . . ."

"Ah, yes . . . hanky-panky . . . he'll relent."

"I don't think I have the courage to tell him."

"So if you don't have the courage . . . I will be your courage."

"Sergio . . . what are you going to do? Walk up to my father and say, Mr. Rossi, I want to marry your . . . what did you say before?"

"When? Before what?"

". . . marry . . ."

"Of course. What did you think my intentions were? If this was anything but true love, you would have been in my bed long before this. I am a very ardent lover as you will find out on our wedding night . . . it will be like Columbus day when they light the firecrackers."

"That's the Fourth of July."

"Ah, yes, the Fourth of July . . . I get confused . . . now, we will turn back and go to see your father."

"No . . . please, not today."

"Why not? Today is as good a day as any other . . ."

"Let's wait, Sergio. I don't think I'm up to it."

"You will not be up to it tomorrow or the day after . . . the time to do something is now . . . while you are frightened . . . it is then you show the true nature of your strength. . . . Turn the boat back," Sergio called to the gondolier.

Standing in front of the hotel, Gina Maria looked at Sergio, "This is going to be very difficult . . ."

"So . . . anything worth achieving is difficult."

"You'll have to wait in the lobby while I tell my parents . . . and that may take a very long time, Sergio."

"So . . . it will take a long time . . . I have waited before in my life for much less."

"I don't know what will happen, Sergio."

"I do . . . if you can't get to base first."

"First base! . . ."

"That's right, first base . . . then your father will have me to contend with . . . and my dearest, Gina Maria *mia*, he will have a very stubborn fellow on his hands."

Dominic looked up from the paper as Gina Maria entered.

"Well . . . did you get bored with Venice? This is the first time you've come back to the hotel so early."

"No . . . I . . . I . . . where's Mama?"

"Taking a bath."

"Oh . . ."

"Oh is right. Her feet are killing her . . . in fact, her feet are killing me. We walked from store to store all day . . . by the time your mother leaves, Venice will be out of merchandise." He laughed. "And what did you do?"

She was going to throw up. "Excuse me, Papa," she said, running to the bathroom. Once the nausea subsided, she went back and sat in the large chair opposite her father.

"Do you know, Gina Maria, since we've been here, I don't think you've felt too well."

"I feel fine, Papa."

"You don't look fine . . ."

"I'm okay, Papa."

"Really? . . . Gina Maria, do you have a problem?"

"What makes you think I have a problem?" she said, trying to keep her voice even and the nausea down.

"Because you're nervous and pale . . . and because you came back so early. Did you have an argument with Pam?"

"No . . ."

"Honey, whatever's bothering you, you can talk to me."

She looked at Dominic and bit her lip. "Could I really, Papa . . . I mean really?" She was asking, questioningly . . . searchingly.

"Why, you know you can."

"No, I don't, Papa . . ."

"What do you mean you don't . . . did you ever have a problem you couldn't come to me with?"

"No. When I've come to you with problems, you listened and helped, but, Papa, did it ever occur to you that I might have had problems I didn't think you would understand, so I kept them to myself?"

"No, because I thought you knew I'd understand anything that would be important to you."

"That's because I always discussed problems that never offended you."

"Never offended me? That's an odd thing to say. Obviously, you're trying to tell me something."

"Yes, Papa, I am . . ."

"But you don't think I'll understand."

"Yes, that's right, I don't think you'll understand."

"I feel badly about that . . . but test me."

"I'm afraid, Papa . . . I think you'll be very angry."

"Angry . . . angry . . . Am I such an ogre? What have you done that I couldn't understand or forgive? What is it, Gina Maria . . . tell me."

"I know you'll be very angry."

"I'll try not to be."

Clearing her throat, bracing her hands firmly on the arms of the chair, she said, "Are you ready for this?"

Dominic nodded yes as he ran his fingers over his dry lips.

"Okay, Papa . . . I'm in love . . ."

"In love!" he exploded, *"in love with whom?"*

"With a very handsome young man."

Catherine came out of the bedroom when she heard the shouting.

"What's this about a . . ."

"Stay out of this, Catherine. Now, where did you meet this handsome young man?"

"At the Doges' Palace."

"See, Catherine, I warned you Pam is not a chaperone. Two children alone in a foreign . . ."

"That's just the point, Papa, I'm not a child . . . you'd like to have me be one all my life, but I'm a woman."

"You're not a woman." Dominic's voice rose higher, "You're a girl of seventeen."

"No, I'm a woman . . . Mary Queen of Scots was the Queen of France when she was fifteen."

"I'm not interested in history. And this handsome young . . . this bum is not the King of France . . . who is he . . . what is he . . . what do you know about him? And you're *in love!*"

"In love!" Catherine now echoed.

"Yes, in love . . . in love and he's no bum. You don't have a right to say that . . . you don't even know him . . . he's a count."

"I can imagine, and I'm a cockeyed prince from Japan."

"See, Papa, I was right when I said you only helped with problems you accepted . . . Papa, I'm terribly disappointed in you . . . for the first time . . ." She ran from the room and threw herself on the bed and wept.

Dominic paced the floor and ranted. "See . . . guide your children, give them values, try to teach them decency and honor and look what happens . . ."

"Stop screaming, Dominic. I'm just as upset about this as you are, but you handled it in the wrong way."

"Sure, sure, I know you have no temper. You never raise your voice above a whisper."

"Why are you fighting with me? In this case, I happen to be on your side, but shouting at Gina Maria when she thinks she's in love isn't going to solve the problem," she said with no small amount of anger.

"So, what should I have said . . . Okay, fine, Gina Maria, if you want to be in love with some—"

Interrupting him, Catherine said above his voice, "You should have sat down quietly and listened, then asked to meet the boy. I'm no pushover, Dominic, and you know it, but we have to face the fact Gina Maria's at an age where she can't help being attracted to the opposite sex. She's a normal girl. We should go down on our *knees* that she's a decent, lovely girl who has never caused us a moment's anguish. And that's a hell of a lot more than most parents can say today."

"I find this pretty damned strange . . . your attitude about this, when all you did was bitch . . . bitch and find fault when Dom and Tory fell in love . . . and what gets me is they married girls from fine families whom we knew all about. I don't know what the hell's come over . . ."

"Listen, Dominic, if you really want to have a fight with me, I'm ready . . . but my Mama taught me a few things among which was if you want to lose, just oppose a child."

"Terrific, how much you learned from Mama, but her advice seems only to apply in this case. How come you didn't use the same philosophy a few months ago with Tory . . . answer that."

"Okay, I *will* . . . Tory's a boy . . . I mean a man . . . a man can't become pregnant . . . a girl can . . . that's why I want to meet this young man. At least we'll know what he's like and Gina Maria won't have to go runnin' off to meet him in some dark corner . . . for God's sake, Dominic, someone as smart as you shouldn't have so much trouble tryin' to figure that one out."

Dominic poured himself a stiff drink, went to the window and looked out . . . stood there for a very long time, thinking. Then he turned around slowly, trying to keep his voice even, with all his discipline, he asked, "Alright, Catherine, since you're so well versed on the subject of juvenile warfare, what do you suggest we do?"

"Not we . . . since it was to you Gina Maria came in the first place, I think you should go in and speak softly and fatherly and *now*."

He hesitated for a long moment, then half angry, half conciliatory, he opened the door to Gina Maria's room. He saw her sobbing and he knew how much she must have hated him at this moment. Sitting on the edge of the bed, he took her hand and said quietly, "Alright, Gina Maria, where is this young man?"

"Downstairs . . . he's been waiting for a long time."

Dominic bit his lip. "Okay, have him paged . . . let him come up."

"May I go down and bring him?"

Slowly, Dominic shook his head, "Alright, go down."

"Oh, thank you, Papa," she said, kissing him, then jumped off the bed, went quickly to the bathroom, washed her face as Dominic walked back to where Catherine sat.

Within seconds Gina Maria was out the door and running down the hall. As she got off the elevator, a nervous Sergio came to her. "Well?"

"My father wants to see you." She took his hand and together they went up in the lift without a word exchanged. Entering the large sitting room, they found Catherine seated on the settee while Dominic stood with his hands behind him. His face was set and unsmiling.

Slowly Gina Maria said, "This is Sergio DiGrazia . . . Sergio, this is my mother, Mrs. Rossi."

Sergio walked to her, kissed her hand and said, "*Charrrmed.*" The sound of those rolling R's . . . and the kiss on the hand too . . . Who did he look like? A young Italian Tyrone Power dressed in white flannel trousers, a raw silk pastel plaid jacket and the yellow open polo shirt exposed his brown hairy chest. Catherine was taken with him from that first moment. But she wasn't surprised, knowing Gina Maria would never have struck up an acquaintance with anyone less than this sort of young man. He was a gentleman . . . didn't have to go to Harvard to recognize that.

Very continental . . . bowing from the waist . . . kiss on the hand . . . the whole bit. However, no things went unnoticed by Dominic. Very schmaltzy, as they say back home . . . "My father, Mr. Rossi," Gina Maria said, leading him.

"My pleasure, Mr. Rossi," Sergio said, extending his hand which Dominic reluctantly shook, as though he were stroking a dead mackerel.

I think the count is already counting the money, Dominic thought as he said, "Please be seated, your *Highness.*"

For a moment Sergio's right eye narrowed, but he seated himself in a chair. Gina Maria cringed, embarrassed by her father's rudeness, but seated herself across from him. Catherine was positively incensed by the remark, as she listened to Dominic begin the interrogation . . . very slowly . . . very poised . . . very sure.

"Now . . . your *Highness*, my daughter tells me she is in love with you." Dominic paused for a moment, which gave Catherine the opportunity to think, no wonder he wins all those cases, he must scare the hell out of the witnesses. "But what are your feelings?" she heard Dominic ask.

Sergio answered with all the poise he possessed, "Your daughter, sir, is the only woman I've ever loved with such deep devotion."

Very good . . . also very clever and true to form. "Alright . . . now, being a European, brought up in the finest traditions, I'm sure, when I ask this, you will understand . . . what are your intentions?"

"Didn't Gina Maria tell you?"

"I didn't have a chance, Sergio . . ." she said, avoiding Dominic's eyes.

"Well, sir, my intentions are to marry . . . with your blessings."

Pretty smart cookie . . . Sure, I'll give my blessings along with my daughter and all the money that goes with it . . . in a pig's ass I will. "And now, your *Highness* . . . how do you propose to support my daughter?"

"Before I answer that, Mr. Rossi . . ."

Here it comes, boys!

"I am not an *avvocato* . . . I mean a lawyer, but neither am I stupid enough not to know when I'm being patronized. I do not wish to be rude, sir, but my name is Sergio DiGrazia."

Well, at least this one's not afraid of me . . . "If I gave that impression, I beg your pardon," Dominic answered, like the calm before the storm.

"I accept it, sir, in that spirit."

Very generous of you . . . "Now, Mr. DiGrazia, we've lost the question."

"No, not at all. You asked how I would support your daughter." Without flinching, he continued, "I regret to say not in the style to which she is accustomed because I am a poor man. But if Gina Maria loves me as much as I love her, then I think we can be happy . . ."

Dominic interrupted this time with obvious antagonism in his voice, "And how long do you think you'll be happy without money . . . it's fairly essential to love and happiness."

"No one need remind me of that, Mr. Rossi . . . I've known the best and the worst of both worlds . . . however, I was about to say that I am a young man with a great many visions. I will not remain in my present status all my life. That I can assure you, sir."

"Really, that's very commendable . . . and how do you expect to accomplish these . . . visions?"

"In America."

And my daughter's your passport, Dominic thought, but aloud, he said, "I see. And *you*, like so many, think the streets are paved with gold and all you have to do is dig it out . . . Am I right?"

"You are right, sir . . . only in so far as many people who believe the myth about America . . . I, however, am not among them."

"Oh? Then how do you propose to become rich?"

"Let me explain, Mr. Rossi . . . for a very long time now, I have realized that we Europeans possess a great culture, ancient and magnificent . . . and while Queen Isabella was counting out the money to give Columbus for the ships, your nation was inhabited by savages and in two hundred years . . . look what you, as a nation, have accomplished, in spite of all the dissenting voices and noises being made. Your greatness lies in the very fact that those voices can shout their dissent . . . but there is one word that holds the key that opens the door to that greatness . . . that word is called *hope*. If one has the *will* and the *inspiration*," he said, looking at Gina Maria, "then it is quite possible for me to, say, start as a busboy and wind up owning my own restaurant . . . It is the last frontier . . . it is the last place on earth where a man can still make his dreams come true."

Dominic appraised Sergio carefully. He was beginning to find his resentments . . . his defenses slowly crumbling. By God, this one had a hell of a lot on the ball. Charm . . . breeding . . . brains . . . but the testing had to go on and he wouldn't stop until he was convinced beyond the shadow of a doubt that Mr. DiGrazia loved his daughter whom he was not going to relinquish without a battle. "That's well-said, but let me ask you . . . Mr. DiGrazia, what made you fall in love with my daughter?"

Looking at Gina Maria first, then at Dominic, Sergio answered, "If you, Mr. Rossi, can answer why a king gave up a throne for a twice-divorced woman . . . or why the son of a tycoon such as Mr. Rockefeller fell in love with and married a Norwegian maid, then, Mr. Rossi, I will be able to answer. It is impossible to explain the chemistry that happens when two people meet and fall in love . . . but I must say, Mr. Rossi, it surprises me just a little that you should put the question to me in such a way . . . since you surely must be aware of your daughter's beauty . . . but above all, her tenderness . . . an understanding that goes beyond her years . . . her unworldliness in an age of such great permissive upheaval when all the respect for parents . . . for convention is a thing considered to be passé." He paused, looking lovingly at Gina Maria, and Dominic thought, he should have been an attorney . . . he pleads his case damn well. He was beginning to like the challenge and the fact that Sergio DiGrazia challenged him without backing off.

Standing up, Sergio walked to where Gina Maria sat and held her hand. "But you, Mr. Rossi, were not asking what made me fall in love . . . you were really asking me why. I know that both you and Mrs. Rossi have questioned my reasons and motives, which I surely can understand."

"That's very good of you, but yes, as long as you're being so open about it . . . yes, be perfectly honest . . . didn't the thought cross your mind?"

Gina Maria bit her lip and Catherine put her hand up to her head and shut her eyes . . . she could have killed him. "Of course, Mr. Rossi, it crossed my mind and I thought very carefully about it. But, Mr. Rossi, had I been tempted by money alone, I would not be so impoverished today . . . it may be difficult for you to believe, but a number of very rich American ladies have shown more than a passing interest in me."

"No, I can believe that . . . but how long have you and Gina Maria known each other?"

"For three days."

"You proposed to me the first day I met you, Dominic . . ." Catherine said, no longer able to merely sit by and say nothing, but Dominic answered quickly.

"No, as I recall, it was you who proposed to me." She was seething.

"It was Sergio who asked me, Papa . . . one can fall in love in a moment, time has nothing to do with it," Gina Maria said, angrily.

"I'll concede that . . . sit down, Mr. DiGrazia." Now, Dominic pulled up a chair and sat down. "Tell me about your background."

Gina Maria relaxed . . . if Papa wasn't interested in Sergio, he wouldn't have asked. Sergio told them about his mother, his family, repeating the story he had told Gina Maria, but hearing it retold a second time affected her in the same way. She started to cry. He took out his handkerchief with the crest embroidered in the corner with red, green and a gold wreath (which Catherine carefully noted) and wiped Gina Maria's eyes.

"Don't cry, Gina Maria *mia*, I promise never to tell the story again."

Dominic was touched too. By God, he *was* in love with her. But once more he would test him. "*If I were* to consent to this marriage . . . you know Gina Maria is only seventeen."

"Yes, sir, I know that."

"Alright . . . I will never allow her to marry until she comes of age, which is eighteen. That is one year and it will mean a separation. If after that time Gina Maria still wants to marry you, I give my blessings."

The two men stood up. Sergio walked to Dominic and extended his hand, which this time Dominic took as he would a son's.

"I thank you, sir, for the great honor and blessing . . . I will live only to make Gina Maria happy and to make you proud."

Dominic smiled. "No father could ask for more."

"*Grazie* . . ."

Catherine got up with tears in her eyes and said, embracing him, "Sergio, this is a very joyous day for us."

"And for me."

Gina Maria went to her father. "Papa, please forgive me for the things I said to you earlier . . . I love you, Papa."

Putting his arms around her. "We have to fight for those we love. Someday, you'll understand . . . you and Sergio. Now, I think we should celebrate . . . I'll order champagne."

"While you are doing that, I would like to go down and call my mother and with your permission, may Gina Maria come with me? I want to introduce them . . . since we are now betrothed."

"Use the phone here, Sergio."

"In that case, you, too, can speak to my mother."

Catherine couldn't believe it . . . her Gina Maria marrying into royalty. Wait till New Orleans heard about *this* . . . Wait until the invitations were sent.

What a sensation that was going to make. Nearly smacking her lips, she could see the look of shock on everyone's face when they opened the envelope and read:

> *Mr. and Mrs. Dominic Rossi*
> *request the honor of your*
> *presence at the wedding*
> *of their daughter*
> *Gina Maria*
> *to*
> *Count Sergio DiGrazia*

Let's see . . . the invitation would be white and gold . . . elaborate as possible. Damn . . . if only she could use the DiGrazia crest. Oh, well, on Gina Maria's stationery, Catherine would have the crest embossed in color on white. That would be her little surprise.

The rest of the week was one that found Catherine in a total state of thrilled intoxication. The anticipation of Gina Maria's impending nuptials was all she could think about. In spite of the fact that the culmination of that glorious event still lay a year off, she began planning it step by step. But the first step was to call Mama. To hell with how much it cost to call New Orleans. ". . . that's right, Mama, he's a *count*, but as plain and down-to-earth as an old shoe."

"But what was that you said earlier in the conversation about Dominic not likin' him?"

"You havin' a hard time hearin', Mama . . .?"

"It's just a little fuzzy, Catherine."

"I'll speak louder . . . How's this . . . can you hear me better?"

"Yes, just fine . . . now about Dominic?"

"I said he didn't like him in the very, very beginnin'. It was like you told me once about Dom . . . remember?"

"Remember what?"

335

"It's like when he was gettin' married . . . well, Dominic was havin' jealous pappy pangs, but now, you'd think he picked Sergio out for Gina Maria."

"Well, I just can't get over the whole thing, Catherine, I swear."

"You can't! Why, Mama, it's just like we're all floatin' in midair . . . and you should see the two of them together . . . the most handsome couple in the world . . . Gina Maria's in a complete cloud of dreams and Sergio can't take his eyes off her."

"I can understand that . . . we all knew she was gonna be a ravishin' beauty . . . I told you that a long time ago . . . now, tell me about the contessa. Is she uppity . . . do you like her . . . when did she arrive?"

"Hold on, Mama, you're about as excited as I am . . . no, she's not uppity . . . I'm simply wild about her, and she arrived here yesterday."

"What's she like . . . tell me, quick!"

"She's absolutely regal . . . like a countess should be. When she stepped off that plane, lookin' like nothin' you ever saw dressed in the most fabulous light gray silk suit and a white straw hat with a red chiffon scarf, gray and white shoes that I just know must have cost a fortune, and wearin' a heavy string of pearls with a diamond and ruby clasp, I swear I wanted to curtsy and you know I'm not about to bow to anyone . . . but she's somethin' else."

"What's she look like . . . tell me?"

"Oh, my goodness, Mama, you sound like you're bustin' out at the seams . . . I swear."

"And that's no lie . . . now, tell me."

"Well, she's got a skin . . . not a blemish, just as clear as crystal . . . gorgeous black hair with a silver streak like someone painted it . . . she's thin . . . about 110 . . . and wouldn't you know it . . . can eat like food's going out of style and never puts an ounce of weight on and . . ."

"Tell me who does she remind you of . . ."

"Who? Well, I'd say an Italian Merle Oberon."

"Oh, I just can't stand it. Tell me more . . ."

"Well, Mama, you should have seen when we took her and the children out to dinner last night. I really would have liked to take pictures. She's simply regal, wore a black lace dress . . . must of cost a fortune . . . with those pearls! She talks and walks like a queen."

"Oh, I'm gettin' goose bumps, Catherine, I swear."

"Me, too, Mama . . . but when she gave Gina Maria that emerald and diamond ring, I thought I'd die . . . it's an heirloom . . . been in the family for generations . . . I can hardly put it all together . . . them supposin' to be so poor and all . . . somehow I got a very strong feelin' they got a lot more than they're lettin' on to. She lives in a villa like a palace . . . she just let a word drop . . . Gina Maria and Sergio are gonna spend part of their honeymoon there . . . can't be all that poor . . . don't you agree, Mama?"

"I don't know and I don't care. We got ourselves a girl in love and I, for one, am the proudest, most excited grandmother this side of the Mason-Dixon Line. Now, what's gonna happen day after tomorrow when you leave? Tearin' apart a couple of lovebirds is gonna be a very sad thing to see."

"I hate to think about it, Mama."

"Well, darlin', Gina Maria will survive . . . now, Catherine baby, we better hang up . . . this is long distance . . . now call and let me know how things are progressin' . . . hear?"

"You know I always do, Mama . . . I'll call you the minute we get to Rome . . . now take good care of yourself and spread the good word around . . . be sure now. I want the whole of New Orleans to know that we Posatas can handle royalty."

"Leave it to me, Catherine baby . . . now, *arrivederci*."

"*Arrivederci*, Mama."

It was a tearful Gina Maria who disengaged herself from Sergio's arms as Dominic repeated, "Come
on, Gina Maria, or that plane's going to go off without
us . . . You'll call Sergio tonight."

"I will, Sergio . . . I love you . . . I love . . ."

"And I love you, dearest Gina Maria . . . I will live
only to hear your voice."

"I'll call every day . . ." she was still saying as
Dominic finally took her arm and led her up the landing step, then into the cabin where she took a seat by
the window and looked out to an already lonely Sergio.
When the plane was finally airborne, Sergio and his
mother walked back to the airport restaurant and sat
down. They ordered capuccinos.

"Well, Sergio . . . ?" the countess said looking at
her son.

"Well, what, Mama?"

"You've realized your dream . . . Huh, Sergio?"

"Yes . . . yes, Mama . . . it is no longer a dream,
but a reality."

"You truly love this girl . . . truly? With me,
Sergio, you do not have to pretend."

"With all my heart, Mama . . . yes."

"I am happy . . . I hoped . . . prayed that you
would find something rewarding in life . . . my prayers
have been answered . . . in fact, Sergio, we are the vic-
tors after all . . . they have not conquered us, have
they? Now, Sergio, redeem your gold cigarette case.
Here is the money."

Sergio looked stunned, "How did you know about
the gold case . . . ?"

"Because I am your mother . . . how else would
you have gotten the money to send me the plane
ticket . . . ?"

"And how do you have the money to pay it back?"

"Never mind how."

"You sold something. Yes? Now I know why you
disappeared for a few hours after you arrived. Why
did you do it, Mama?"

"Why did you pawn your gold case?"

"Because you mean more to me than a cigarette case . . . you are my mother of whom I am very proud . . . and I wanted them to see you and for you to know my future bride . . . she is so beautiful in my eyes."

"And in mine . . . you are indeed fortunate to have someone as exceptional as Gina Maria to love you, Sergio . . . be faithful, be constant . . . cherish her . . . what sustained me through my darkest hours was the gift of love your father left me . . . the greatest legacy a woman can have. So my clothes are old and shabby . . . so I was not as elegantly dressed in the newest Parisian styles as the dear Mrs. Rossi, but she accepted me as I was . . . a very lovely and charming lady . . . now, my dearest son, I must leave you."

"Stay for a few days . . . please, Mama. I have a friend who has a hotel . . . not the best, but it is not really too bad . . . you will stay . . . Yes?"

She smiled, looked at his face, then said, "Yes."

14

Two weeks in Florence would normally have been
considered too short a time for Catherine to spend
in the city she most loved, but Rome at the moment
was her most pressing priority, since it was there she
would select most of Gina Maria's custom-designed
china, crystal, hand-forged silver as well as the table
and bed linen, monogrammed with the DiGrazia crest
(all of which would require the better part of a year,
from the placement order to delivery). Also there was
a Roman couturier, renowned for specializing in
period wedding gowns. Although Catherine fully intended to take the expert advice of that master designer . . . still she had a few ideas of her own which
she would expect the maestro of the fashion world to
interpret. She could see it all now . . . Gina Maria
walking slowly down the aisle, dressed in a heavy pure
silk satin gown, the color of soft white candlelight.
The deep V-shaped bodice would be heavily encrusted
with tiny hand-sewn pearls, and the Juliet sleeves
trimmed in ermine would be traditionally Venetian . . .

long, gradually ending in slender points. From the bridal coronet (which was befitting a countess) would flow six yards of tulle, edged in the most delicate heirloom lace. At this moment, she could not concern herself with what the bridesmaids' gowns would be . . . let the maestro worry about that, but one thing she knew for certain was they should be dressed in exquisite simplicity, but carefully designed so as not to detract from the awesomeness of the bride. Catherine would insist upon their dresses being white and whatever color the maestro decided upon for sashes, she would acquiesce to. Oh, what a day that was going to be. Since this would be *her* only chance up at bat, having only one daughter, she was going to show the mothers of her daughters-in-law.

First, they would be married in the flower-filled Cathedral, then the reception would be held in the Venetian ballroom at the Fairmont Hotel. Five hundred guests, give or take. Of course, she fully intended to discuss all of this with Gina Maria . . . naturally . . . a little later. But now, the excitement of planning this extravaganza fired her imagination so that the momentum within her became so heightened she was becoming more than anxious to press on to Rome. However, she was reluctant to make the suggestion about leaving, thinking that Gina Maria would feel deprived, this having been her first experience abroad and the trip was, after all, planned entirely for her. But . . . so far as Gina Maria was concerned, there was only one place on earth she wanted to be and that was in Venice. She spoke to Sergio every day . . . wrote him letters, pouring out her unfulfilled love . . . her painful discontent over their being separated for a year . . . if only Papa would compromise, after all, what did it matter if she was a year older . . . her love could never be greater than it was now, and he responded with such speed that their letters must have passed each other in transit. And by now, Dominic was impatiently beginning to call the overseas operator more frequently as to what was going on at the office. So all in all, each for his own separate reasons was quite content to board the plane for Florence.

It was midnight when the Rossis arrived at the hotel in Rome . . . where they were less than strangers, having been guests here many times in the past twenty years.

"Ah . . . *Signora* and *Signore* Rossi . . . it is with the same usual honor I welcome you and your most beautiful daughter," said the distinguished manager in Italian. "We have been awaiting your arrival with most delighted enthusiasm."

"Thank you. With the same enthusiasm, we look forward to our stay here in Rome."

"Thank you, *Signore* . . . your suite is in order, now if you will register . . . I will turn you over to the desk clerk and for this evening I wish you good-night."

After Dominic had registered, the clerk said, "Ah, *Signore*, we have a message for you."

The young man reached into the tiny mail slot and handed it to Dominic. As he opened the envelope, Catherine asked, "Who's it from?"

"Dom," he answered as the expression on his face changed.

"What's wrong, Dominic?"

"Nothing," he said, trying to appear casual. But Catherine became worried.

"Here, let me read it."

"It's nothing, Catherine . . ."

Grabbing the cable from his hand, she read . . . Urgent . . . call immediately upon your arrival . . . Dom. Catherine grew faint. "Mother of God, it must be Tish . . . the new baby . . . somethin' must be . . ."

"Now, don't start imagining," he said, walking toward the elevator with Catherine and Gina Maria at his side, while the bellboy followed behind them, wheeling their luggage on a cart. Once in the suite, the bellboy was tipped and dismissed. Dominic went immediately into the bedroom, sat on the edge of the bed and called the overseas operator. Let's see . . . it would be eight o'clock in San Francisco, so Dom would still be at home. Catherine stood stiffly, trying to put down her fears. Why is life always so jealous . . . they had just come away from one of the most joyous occasions in their lives and now . . . her thoughts were interrupted as she heard Dominic say, smiling at the small voice at the other end to Dominic III who now always ran to the phone each time it rang. "Hello . . . yes, it's *nonno* . . . that's right, *nonno*, Dominico . . . *nonna*? She's right here . . ."

"Let me talk to him," Catherine said with tears in her eyes. Handing the phone to her, Catherine said, "It's *nonna*, darlin', . . . *nonna* . . . how's my baby, my little love? *Nonna*'s gonna bring you home a lot of presents and I . . ."

He was screaming because his father had taken the phone from him. "Mama?" she heard Dom say.

"Yes, darlin', I'm in tears, hearin' that sweet voice . . . how's Tish?" she asked anxiously.

"Fine, Mama sends her love and is so happy about Gina Maria as we all are. And you, I suppose, are on cloud nine . . . How are you feeling, Mama?"

"Couldn't be better, now that I know everythin's fine at home." There was a long pause. "Everythin' is . . . isn't it, Dom?"

"Yes, Mama . . . say hello to Gina Maria. Now, let me talk to Papa."

"Alright, here's Papa."

Handing the phone back to Dominic, she stood quietly listening.

"Yes, Dom . . . *what? Repeat that again.*" . . . his face had turned ashen gray.

"That's right, Papa, DeKaye dropped dead on the golf course this morning."

Dominic sat, looking at the receiver in his hand in stunned disbelief.

"What is it, Dominic? What's happened?"

He looked blankly at her, then in a whisper, he said, "DeKaye dropped dead today."

"Oh, dear God," she answered putting her hands up to her mouth.

Finally recovering from the initial shock, he put the receiver back to his ear, "I simply can't get over this, Dom . . ."

"Neither could we . . . no warning, no nothing . . . I think you better come immediately because you know what this means. We have no candidate for state senator . . . after the thrust, the money poured in promoting DeKaye as the *only* one who could help fight the city's problems from Sacramento. Not to be disrespectful to poor DeKaye . . . this leaves us with our candidates down."

"Naturally, nothing's been proposed as an alternative . . . what am I talking about . . . you and our supporters must have been in a state of shock."

"That's putting it mildly, Papa . . . but again in all due respect to DeKaye, we've been in conference all day . . ."

"And?"

"And, Papa, we've decided unanimously, there's no one that can beat Pat Douglas except *you.*"

Trying to measure the true impact of Dom's suggestion, Dominic answered slowly, "Me?"

"Why not, Papa . . . although DeKaye was a terrific state senator . . . who knows more about politics than you . . . knows more about and loves the city more than you . . . politics isn't anything new to you . . . you've worked behind the scenes of national politics all your life . . . you've got more friends, power and influence in the party than anyone is aware of. We both know this has been a secret dream of yours for a long time and maybe, Papa, this unfortunate circumstance was meant so that you would be compelled to take up the lance . . . do it, Papa."

Looking at Catherine, he said, "We'll see, Dom . . . we'll have to wait and see."

"I know you're really too big for the job. Washington is where you belong, but, Papa, for obvious reasons, it's a beginning. Take it."

"Let me think about it."

"Okay . . . but, Papa, you've got to come home immediately."

"I'd do that in any event . . . DeKaye was a very dear and close friend . . . I'll take the first plane I can get."

Dominic hung up and sat staring ahead of him. His mind was a jungle of conflicting thoughts. He lay back on the bed and stared up at the ceiling. Catherine sat on the edge of the twin bed across from him and watched the struggle he was having with himself.

"Dominic, what does all this mean . . . with election so near?"

He turned his head and looked at her without answering.

"Why you lookin' at me like that, Dominic?"

He said softly, "They want me to run for state senator."

"They what? Why, you've never held public office before. Why you?"

"Because Dom said the committee was in conference all day kicking around the idea of who to run and decided I was the logical one to salvage our loss."

"I don't know much about politics, but it's only three months away from the primaries, and as well-known as you are in certain circles, the man on the street doesn't know you from a bale of hay. You have no political record to back you up . . . after all, DeKaye was a state senator with a name."

Dominic smiled. "You know a lot more than you're giving yourself credit for. That's pretty damned close to the truth."

"Well, thank you, Dominic . . . now, what are you gonna do?"

"I'm going to think about it."

"And after you've thought it out, what then? How do you propose to get elected with all the strikes against you?"

"Well, it wouldn't be easy . . . but on the other hand, it would be a hell of a challenge."

"And knowin' your great feelin's about challenges, you'd walk right in where angels fear to tread . . . but challenge or not, how you gonna get the people to know you in so short a time?"

"Okay, if you're asking."

"I'm askin' . . ."

"Alright, it will mean public appearances constantly . . . luncheons . . . ladies' groups, organizations . . . I have a lot of support with the unions . . . business . . . I'm not sure about the newspapers."

"Is that enough?"

"To a large extent, but I think there's one big plus on my side."

"What's that?"

"Well, since the mayor endorsed DeKaye, and knows I was solidly behind him, I have a feeling he'd support me. After all, he knows I'm not exactly a novice."

"Well I'd certainly hope so. The way you worked for him when he was runnin' for mayor . . ."

"And I'd do it again . . . he's a good man . . . justified my belief in him."

"Okay . . . suppose he does help ya. That still doesn't answer the questions of how the public's gonna get to know you."

"Well . . . it takes exposure . . . if you want to get known in a real big hurry, television, radio. By God, Catherine, the more I talk about it, the more I think maybe we have more than an even chance . . . in fact, I don't have as many strikes against me as you think . . . it always appeals to the masses . . . from rags to riches . . . the same American dream that Sergio talked about . . . everyone likes someone who's made it on the way up . . . makes them think maybe they could do the same thing. I've already got the same organization together who were working their asses off for poor DeKaye. And it just occurred to me, maybe it's a plus on my side that I have no political record, in this case, nobody can point a finger and say he did that wrong. I won't vote for him because he doesn't keep his promises . . . it just might prove to be one of the most important assets in my favor."

"Then you've decided to run?"

"No, I'm still considering."

"Come on, Dominic . . . stop playing footsy with me. All I have to do is look in your eyes to find the answer."

"And if I did, how would you feel about it?"

"I wondered if you'd ever ask."

"Well, I'm asking . . . You could be a great asset to me, Catherine . . ."

"You're makin' it sound as though we went along with the package . . . like you'd be exploitin' us like television and radio. That's not very flatterin'."

"I'm sorry, Catherine, you felt it necessary to say that . . . a man needs his wife and children. I need you and if I do take it, I'm going to ask you to stand at my side."

"You really want this, don't you, Dominic?"

He ran his tongue over his dry lips. "You've known that for a long time, Catherine . . . this time, it's been handed to me. I never sought it, but since it has . . . yes, will you help me?"

She hesitated for a long time and thought carefully. Being the wife of the state senator from San Francisco was not the worst thing that could happen to a woman . . . in fact, it held a great many exciting promises. San Francisco was a city where foreign dignitaries visited . . . she might become the Perle Mesta of San Francisco . . . she would never have believed it but the idea suddenly appealed to her . . . New Orleans would be shocked out of their hominy grits . . . her, the senator's lady . . . but above all, Dominic would be so consumed with the senate he'd no longer be able to be in active private practice which took him away constantly, trying cases . . . no, sir, instead he'd be in Sacramento only fifteen minutes away from home. The children were gradually getting married and in a few years, they'd all be gone . . . maybe it wasn't such a terrible thing Dominic was doing, after all. It just might be the beginning of a very nice renewed relationship for them, him coming home every weekend and even during the week. Yes, sir, it just might be a whole new ball game . . . Okay, Victoria Lang, eat your heart out because I'm going to say, "Alright, Dominic, since you really need my help, I'm more than willin' to give you all I've got."

Dominic looked at her, never believing he'd ever hear her say that, then slowly smiled, "Thank you, Catherine."

"You're more than welcome, Dominic. It might just be like sharin' some of the good things we had between us once."

"I think it might, Catherine . . ."

She smiled back, then quietly she asked, "Now, Dominic, what are we gonna do . . . I suppose you have to get back for the funeral?"

"Yes."

"Since we and the DeKayes were never social friends, I don't think it's necessary for me to attend. I'd like to remain in Florence, not wantin' to deprive Gina Maria of her vacation. And since I'm already here, I'd like to get rollin' on the weddin'. So, if you don't mind, I won't go back with you."

"Of course, Catherine, I understand . . . now, I'll call the airport and make a reservation."

She handed him the phone.

By the time Catherine and Gina Maria did arrive back in San Francisco, two weeks later, she was shocked as they drove from the airport into the city. There were huge campaign signs everywhere. Seeing Dominic's handsome likeness smiling broadly from the blown-up posters and mounted atop the numerous headquarters buildings scattered about the city was a thrilling experience she hadn't thought herself capable of responding to. Each automobile that passed with a Rossi bumper sticker enhanced her sudden feeling of importance. Talking about this in Florence was one thing, but to see the campaign in full swing in San Francisco was more exciting than she'd ever imagined.

She found herself anxiously waiting and wanting to hear his voice being broadcast. When interviewed on television, Dominic conducted himself with such ease and charm, projecting the perfect image which he knew the people would relate to—saying just the right things at the right time was an instinct he was born with. Catherine was so mesmerized, she forgot for the moment he was her husband rather than some remote celebrity who she did not know. Hearing him . . . seeing him bigger than life on that screen, made her feel it would be impossible for anyone not to respond to his sincerity, his honesty, his devotion to the city of his birth. He worked tirelessly in behalf of the electorate. As their leader, their savior, their only way of repaying this selfless man was to render unto Caesar what was Caesar's . . . their vote.

However, as the campaign began to rapidly gather momentum and move into the final days before the primaries, Catherine began to feel the effects of campaigning and there were times (for all the promises she made earlier to Dominic for standing by his side) . . . she began to wonder if there wasn't an easier way to make a living. She was getting bored with smiling and hand-shaking, exhausted with the pace, never having a moment's solitude, and being on time was something she loathed and was never disciplined for. She was sick to death of fruit cup, unpalatable, dry, half-a-broiled chicken with green peas which were usually cold, ice cream and a small cookie, which was the standard fare for those donors who gave twenty-five dollars to hear the candidate make the same speech that he made at the dinners for hundred-dollar donors where tough roast beef was served accompanied by duchess potatoes, ahh . . . just mashed, made fancy . . . and for the five-hundred dollar donors, the waiters wore white gloves, but the food was just as bad (with a few variations) and the speech much the same (with

a few variations). Yes . . . Catherine was becoming
sick . . . *sick* . . . Had she not been so carried away
with the idea of being madam senator and truly if she
had realized how strenuous campaigning was, she
might have had second thoughts about all of this . . .
on the other hand, if she could ride the waves . . . get
through the primary and should Dominic receive the
nomination, then go on to become state senator (which
at the last poll-taking seemed more than likely) she
could go back to her former life of quiet and merely
enjoy the joys of hostessing for the dignitaries, which
it would be her pleasure to oblige Dominic with. Much
more than that, she was sure, would not be expected
of her . . . "I didn't know what I was lettin' myself in
for when your sweet pappy-in-law asked me to stand
at his side . . . Stand at his side! I guess I'm just about
ready to fall on my face," Catherine was saying on the
phone to Tish, who was now very large with child.

"Well, it's just about over, Mama. Tomorrow night,
you'll see how rewarding it is when Papa and you
stand up on the platform taking your deserved bows."

"Bows? I don't think I'll have the strength to have
my hair done."

"Yes you will . . . Mama." Tish laughed. "You've
been a brick through this whole ordeal."

"Is that what I've been? At this point, I should
have been twins . . . thank God for Gina Maria. She's
been workin' so hard and relieved me of a lot of
responsibilities, throwin' herself into this with Papa.
In fact, I think sometimes she forgets about Sergio."

"Maybe that's why she's worked so hard. It makes
waiting a little easier."

"I suppose . . . well, darlin', take care and don't
forget the whole family's gonna be comin' to dinner
tomorrow night and wait out the agony till post time."

"I'll be there earlier with a bottle of aspirin."

"I won't need it when I see my baby Dom . . . who
probably won't even recognize his *nonna* with the way
I've had to neglect him lately."

"He'll recognize you, Mama, you only saw him yesterday."

"Yea, sure, runnin' in and out of your house between the creamed chicken and mashed potatoes." Catherine laughed, seeing at least some of the humor in it.

After a good Italian dinner served in the Rossi family style everyone settled back and watched with nervous anticipation the jubilation that was going on at the main headquarters on Market Street. Every time the latest returns were announced that Dominic was leading by a wide majority, simultaneously the workers at headquarters across town screamed out *whee . . . wowee . . .* just as the Rossi clan did sequestered in the mansion overlooking the bay. By ten that evening, Tony said, "Papa, I think we've got it made . . ."

"Don't count your votes until they're hatched."

"Come on, Papa," the other twin said. "Douglas is running scared."

"Maybe you don't know this, Angie, but I remember going to bed one night, thinking Tom Dewey was President only to wake up in the morning, turn on the radio and cut myself shaving from the shock of hearing Truman was going to be the new tenant in the White House for the next four years."

"Yea, Papa," Vincente said, "but that was before computers. Look at the way those returns are coming in . . . fast . . ."

"Wait a minute . . . listen . . . keep quiet," Dom said at that moment when only he and Tory were glued to the screen. There was a hush as they listened to the announcement. . . . "And it appears that Pat Douglas is on his way down . . . however the speculation is that he'll concede the race . . . the majority now is so great in Rossi's favor and at this time, most of the precinct votes have been . . . wait, I have just been handed a note . . . Yes, Pat Douglas is now walking into his headquarters . . . we will now take you to . . ."

Dominic and the family sat rigidly, listening. The television switched over to a room that now projected the feeling of the city morgue where the camera zoomed in on the faces that resembled cadavers . . . expressionless, they watched a badly beaten Douglas mount the platform with his wife at his side. Trying desperately to hold down the anger, disappointment and tears, he stood for a moment staring at the people who had worked so diligently for him. Finally, he said, "First, I want to thank everyone who believed in me. That's a great honor for a man to know he's been trusted to lead . . . it's also a great gift to remember. I'm going to make this very short . . . the greatest kind of giving . . . is of one's self. If a man with five million dollars writes out a check for one hundred thousand dollars and gives it to charity, that's not nearly as painfully benign as when a poor group of people buy a rowboat for someone who's about to drown." He looked at this small group and thought, Christ, this wasn't a contest, a campaign, a fair fight, a match against wits, it was a blockbuster, a steamroller. I knew as soon as Rossi got into the race I was dead. They poured money into this election like the Russians were going to land in Burbank tomorrow. "So . . . Mrs. Douglas and I wish to thank you, each and everyone, for your help. . . . I'm conceding to Mr. Rossi and in November I hope the people that have helped me will throw their weight behind him for the sake of our great party. Now . . . God bless you all," he said quickly and made his exit. Losing was a very painful business.

The reaction at the Rossi home was equal to the workers at headquarters. They cheered, wept, screamed, kissed, hugged, congratulated. The phone began to ring . . . and ring. Dominic looked at Catherine. "Well . . ." he said, "remember all those strikes you talked about in Florence. Well, it didn't turn out too bad, did it?"

And she answered, "Instead of bein' so damned smug, Mr. Wonderful, I think a wife who wore herself out deserves a thank-you or two and maybe a kiss . . . ?"

"She sure as hell does, Catherine . . . thank you," he said, kissing her on the cheek, then quickly on the lips. "Okay everybody, I think they want us at headquarters."

When Dominic and his family walked in, a cheer went up. Dominic stood, trying to quiet the ovation for ten minutes with his arms raised . . . then he lowered them and laughed, holding his hand over the microphone and whispered something to different members of his family. Then once again he tried, but the crowd kept chanting . . . Rossi for president . . . Rossi for governor . . . Rossi for . . . the band struck up "I Left My Heart in San Francisco" . . . finally the crowd quieted down and Dominic addressed them. "This has been said so many times before that I wish, I wish I were eloquent enough to come up with something different, but I can't. I couldn't have done it without you." He looked out over the crowd and saw the mayor smiling broadly. The men's eyes met. There was genuine gratitude in Dominic's face. "Come on up, Mr. Mayor." The mayor moved through the crowd and took his place alongside Dominic. They embraced, then locked hands in a victory sign. "Your complete dedication to the party is unmatched," Dominic went on. "But the thing that especially touches me is that you took a chance on a man who until a few short months ago was an unknown quantity to most of you . . . and that leaves me with an awesome responsibility to justify your beliefs in me and never to betray the trust in the promises I have made." The applauding and whistling began once again, then died slowly away. "However," Dominic continued, "we're not home free yet . . . there's another harder task in the months before us until November which requires the same enthusiasm and dedication you have displayed in the primaries. When I go to Sacramento I promise you will have the greatest support this magnificent city has ever had. I'm going to listen to what it is that *you* want. With your help, let us work toward making our dreams reality."

Dominic put his arm around Catherine as she smiled. The children gathered around them and waved as the crowd responded. Catherine, still smiling, knew in her heart, which wept, that she had won—and lost —her bet on a dark horse . . . she had lost him to the crowd . . . They were replacing Victoria Lang.

15

The next four years found the checks and balances of their lives swaying decisively in Dominic's favor. Nobody had to be a political analyst to know after the tributes paid him the night of the primary he would be elected. And a damned good state senator he was, some said, and a damned bad one, others said, but good or bad nobody tried harder to do a good job and along the way to build a prestigious name for himself in the party. Of course having been an attorney of some international repute had scarcely left him a nonentity. At times some of the Rossi staff complained, knowing he was too big for the job and the effort he put forth was far and above the title. But his son Dom kept insisting it was only a launching pad for Papa. The Rossis brought to the hardly exalted office of state senator a kind of charisma the Kennedys brought to the White House. There was an elegance about them, even a glamor. But it also meant they lived in a glass house, because of the very uniqueness of the situation. They'd become public property. All privacy was gone, and Catherine was suddenly pushed into a position she thought she wanted and yet was overwhelmed by. She knew when Dominic won their lives would change . . . but as she looked back, in all honesty she had not expected the kind of critical exposure not only Dominic was getting but that she was subjected to as well. Wherever she went, people stopped her as though she were a celebrity. She couldn't even find privacy at the beauty salon without putting up with a million questions. Everything she said was quoted, most times inaccurately. The morning paper often had some juicy little tidbit about her, which hurt her. The way she furnished her home was criticized, and the criticism extended even to Dominic's office, which she had furnished elaborately, but Dominic's offices had always been elaborate . . . why should they be different in Sacramento? She wasn't trying to show off. She became more and more camera shy, more and more withdrawn, as if she would make them all disappear. She hardly belonged to herself. It was taken for granted she would appear with her husband. A thing he not only expected, but insisted on and for awhile, in spite of her dislike, she tried to do her duty, especially since the children more than once gave her to understand that she was not helping Papa the way she should. But she had to back away . . . restore her spirits, so she retreated to the Farm. But after a week, she would return to the same situation.

Nothing had really changed, even though the past few years had brought their changes. Dom and Tish were the parents of four sons. Tory had two little girls, and Joanna was expecting again. Gina Maria and Sergio had married and she was ecstatically expecting *her* second child. Sergio was more than an ideal and loving husband as well as a great success in his travel agency business . . . Tony had married Pam McCormack. . . . Angie, now the father of one, had married a Swedish girl he'd met at college . . . and Roberto was living with a Japanese girl in a garret in North

Beach . . . which left only Vincente at home, and soon he would be leaving to travel in Europe. He was as uninterested in politics and law as Roberto. So where did this leave Catherine? In left field. Dominic traveled even more now than he had in his private practice. Always going off to one place or another . . . especially Washington, D.C. Always tryin' to meet the *right* people. She'd said in no uncertain terms, "I thought you were supposed to be a state senator, not running the country." You'd think by now she'd know better than to go up against Dominic, especially now that he'd become a public figure. "I don't see any of the other state senators knockin' themselves out like you do," she said. "I don't know about them . . ." he said, "but I'm going to do anything and everything I can to serve my constituents." Who was he kiddin' . . . She had gone along with him in the beginning, but the Washington scene was just a thorn in her side. She also found political wives as ambitious as their husbands, which made her feel not only remiss but inadequate . . . *they* knew all the answers. They seemed to say all the right things at the right times and she seemed to say all the wrong things at the wrong times. It wasn't her intention to create any dissension, but somehow she always seemed to be a source of embarrassment. At a diplomatic affair given at the British embassy one evening, she wandered around while Dominic was off in some corner with a group of men discussing whatever the hell he discussed. She stood off by herself with a champagne glass . . . For want of a little human contact, she spoke to a gorgeously gowned woman also standing alone momentarily.

"My name is Catherine Rossi."

The lady replied as though the queen was deigning to address a commoner. "Vanessa Baden-Powell . . ."

"Oh . . . unusual name."

The lady made no comment. At that point Catherine knew she should say some profound things, such as . . . 'Well, it's been nice meeting you,' but the silence was so awkward that she said, "Were you born here? . . . I mean are you an American?"

"Oh, dear me, no . . . I was born abroad."

The lady was such a goddamned snob, Catherine couldn't resist. "*You sure were,*" she said, and quickly walked away.

Well, apparently the gorgeously dressed lady felt enormously offended and told whoever one tells about such things and the next morning in the Washington newspaper's gossip column, a small portion was devoted to the remark mentioning the outspoken Mrs. Rossi. It was the first time she'd made the Washington *Post.* She was getting up in the world, only Dominic didn't think it was so funny and said so. In no uncertain terms.

"Damn it, Catherine, you can't go around insulting people."

"*Insulting* . . . what should I have done . . . stand there like a dummy while she was puttin' on all those phony airs? I'll tell you one thing I'm not, for all the faults you find, I'm not—"

"You're not a diplomat, that I'll tell you, and if you want to get along—"

"I don't give a crap about gettin' along with a bunch of phony stuffed shirts and as far as I'm concerned, you know what you can do with all your diplomats . . . you can shove it . . . I'm gettin' the hell out of this city."

Upon arriving home without Dominic, she called her mother. "Mama, I really don't know how I can go on like this. I said one damned silly little thing and you'd think I bombed the Pentagon. My life is more lonely now than at any other time and if anyone wants to write a song about loneliness, I can give them the lyrics. I'm disgusted and fed up with the pressures, the cocktail parties I'm always supposed to give and go to . . . I mean, what for? So Dominic can have his fun and games? What the hell am I gettin' out of it but one great big fat headache." She took a breather, then went

on, "And what the hell does Dominic need it for? I
ask you . . . don't answer. I'll tell you, he eats it up.
All the power . . . the swoonin' over him by the ladies
like he was some kind of a god . . . in fact, at times,
I think he feels he is . . . and I'm left out like excess
baggage. I've got to laugh when people tell me how
lucky I am to be married to someone like the great
Mr. Rossi . . . lucky! Hell, I'd like to see how they'd
like bein' used as an ornament. He needs an official
hostess? Let him hire a pro. My house has turned into
Grand Central Station . . . and I can't find one little
tiny place in this great big universe where I fit. Now,
you're a smart lady . . . tell me, Mama, where do I go
from here?"

"Catherine, I can't argue. That's difficult, but if
you recall, I once mentioned you ought to involve
yourself in something worthwhile?"

"I remember, Mama, but that was before he himself decided to get into the deep blue sea and swim
upstream. How can I do anything when I'm always at
his beck and call?"

"Well, from what you said, Dominic's not home
so much . . . you could do things while he's away,
couldn't you?"

Catherine thought for a long, lone moment and
the embryo of an idea was beginning to take shape.
"Okay, Mama, I'm gonna take your suggestion . . . yes,
sir, I'm gonna do somethin' with my life to fill the gap."

But what Mama had in mind to occupy Catherine
was far from what Catherine had in mind. She took
the Ferrari out of the garage and drove downtown,
parked in Union Square garage, then stood across the
street from a building they owned on Post Street and
looked at one of the stores that was occupied but
whose lease had fortunately expired. In that moment,
she had made the decision . . . she was going to open
the most exclusive, most expensive . . . most fabulous
boutique in San Francisco. Why not . . . she wasn't the
first political wife to have a business . . . what about
Mrs. Javits . . . Mrs. McCarthy? . . . and then there's—

oh, come on, Catherine, you don't have to justify what you're doin'. It would make her feel important, using her maiden name, CATHERINE POSATA, standing out like a neon sign. She was going to be a someone with an identity of her own, damn it. In fact, she might even call herself Ms. . . . But most important, it would give her the reason not to be so available to accompany Dominic on his safari through the jungles of politicking which he was about to begin for a second term. Yes, sir, she was going to take Mama's advice in spite of the consequences. She was ready for battle.

The next morning, Catherine was up early. In between bites of toast and sips of coffee, she said, "Gina Maria . . . I'm invitin' the family to dinner . . . Papa's comin' home and I want everyone here."

"We'll be there, Mama."

"No later than six . . . now, I've got to call the others. Bring the children . . . you know how Papa misses them."

"I will, Mama."

Fights, confusion were something the Rossis had learned to recover from. The recent Washington incident was forgotten . . . if not forgotten, at least no longer a major issue. That night at dinner, especially with the whole clan assembled (except for Roberto and his Japanese mistress), Dominic was a contented man . . . for the moment. After dinner was served and the family was still seated, drinking coffee, cracking walnuts, passing the platter of assorted cheeses, the bombshell dropped.

"Alright, I want everyone's attention," Catherine said. "I'm gonna open the most gorgeous boutique in town."

Everyone stopped what they were doing and looked at Catherine, dumbfounded. Recovered from the first shock wave, all now rushed to begin to speak at the same time . . . you're what? . . . You've got to be kidding . . . this is crazy . . . you can't be serious. Everyone except Dominic, who sat staring at Catherine in total shock.

"That's right . . . I was never more serious about anything in my whole life," she answered, smiling defiantly as Dominic thought, she's got to be going through the menopause.

"When did you decide that?" Tory asked.

"Yesterday."

"I don't get it, Mama . . . why?" asked a bewildered Tony.

"Why? Because I'm tired of being useless, that's why."

"Useless?" Angie asked, his voice a little higher than usual.

"That's right, useless."

"How can you say you're useless when you're helping Papa?" Dom demanded.

"But that's just the point, I'm not helpin' Papa at all . . . I think I am hinderin' him," she answered, ignoring Dominic as though he were absent.

He scratched the back of his ear, then cupped his hand around his mouth and thought. This is just a little device to try and jolt me, even punish me for what happened in Washington . . . Okay, we'll handle this one. "Look, Catherine, this is something I believe you and I should discuss after the children leave."

"Anything you say, Dominic darlin'," she answered like a proper Sicilian wife. That's what he'd like me to be, Catherine said to herself, but he'll find out . . .

After the children left, Catherine and Dominic went into the study.

"All right, Catherine, now . . . what's on your mind?"

"Weren't you listenin' at dinner?"

"I was listening."

"So you must have heard . . . I want to open a little shop."

"Why?"

"Because I want to become a worthwhile person . . . as you suggested so many times in the past. And besides, I want something to do when you're away— not like in the good old days."

Dominic sighed.

"I see . . . and it doesn't occur to you that maybe it might embarrass me that my wife is running a . . . what's that name again?"

"BOUTIQUE."

"Yes, a *boutique*."

"You make it sound like a bordello . . . but to answer your question, I wasn't especially thinkin' about you . . . not anymore than you were thinkin' about me when you decided to throw your hat in the ring for a second term, as I believe the sayin' goes."

Trying to hold down his anger, he asked, "Maybe I should give that up and go to work for you running the boutique?"

"Might not be such a bad idea . . . at least, I wouldn't be left alone three weeks out of every four."

"That's not because of me—"

"You're sayin' it's because of me . . . right? But I can't live out of a suitcase. What's the use of all this talkin' . . . we've been this route for almost thirty years now."

"Why are you doing this to me, Catherine?"

"Because you have a life, and I need a life. I'm not so crazy about the one I got—"

"Okay . . . okay . . . open your damned store . . . and thanks a lot . . . you timed it perfectly." He went out of the room, slamming the door behind him.

Once Catherine had thought nothing ever changes . . . but was she ever wrong . . . and Mama ever right. *Her* shop was exactly the answer to an absentee husband. Seeing *her* name written boldly above the tall, slender, chic black shining double entrance doors with the heavy brass knobs, never ceased to make her pulse race just a little faster. Her name . . . CATHERINE POSATA . . . Yes, sir, that's the one she was born with, the one on her birth certificate. It would have made Daddy proud . . . Proud to see the Posata name perpetuated, especially since there were no sons. There would be little Dominic Rossis running around for generations. But not one boy Posata. Yes, sir, it was the least she could do as a livin' memorial to her darlin' Daddy's name.

Being a merchant was the beginning of a dream . . . the excitement, the challenges, left her excited, happy, anxious to reach the next day. Always something new, always something to anticipate. It meant short trips to Paris . . . Rome . . . New York, Los Angeles, taking along one daughter-in-law or the other for companionship depending on who wasn't pregnant or expecting momentarily. But she was never able to take Gina Maria . . . because Sergio was strictly against wives leaving their husbands for any reason . . . it was simply not the thing to do . . . "Go argue with a count!" But in spite of the joy it would have been taking Gina Maria, still she adored Sergio's jealousy (although he knew it was unnecessary). But that was marriage the real Italian style. He wanted Gina Maria with him. If only Dominic wanted her as much, there'd be no need for *Catherine Posata* to . . . oh, well, what the hell, she loved what she was doing. A career provided an exhilarated excitement she had not experienced till now. Catherine wheeled and dealed, speaking on the phone not only consumed her days completely, but the sense of importance it gave her was immeasurable as she pushed one button after the other . . . *"On Hold"* was her favorite . . . "I'll call you back." As she released the hold button, "Sorry I couldn't get back to you sooner . . . now, I want to order four dozen more silk scarves."

"But Mrs. Rossi, that seems to be quite a large order. The point is I don't want you to overstock. I'm not that kind of salesman and . . ."

"Look, I'm payin' the bill . . . send the order."

She ordered to her heart's content. To hell with it
... what if they never sold ... it was such fun to be useful, happy and fulfilled. The only problem she had was
the turnover in help. If her stock turnover was as constant as her employees, she's be making a great deal
more money than she was. But for some reason, the
help just didn't stay. It wasn't because she was sus-
picious about them stealing, it was simply one had to
watch carefully and the clerks seemed to resent that
... She kept the store open in spite of that, but stayed
home and conducted her business in the comfort of her
boudoir. Naturally, she called the store frequently
throughout the day to see if everyone was on their toes.
One could not be too careful. She wondered how
Dominic controlled such a large staff ... well, that
was his problem. The only problem she had to worry
about was her little empire.

The only thing wrong with Catherine's little empire
was her accountant, who constantly kept badgering
her. "Look, Mrs. Rossi, figures don't lie ... last year
we were in the red and this year ..." "Don't keep
confusin' me with a lot of small talk," Catherine interrupted. "Let's get down to the nitty-gritty of what's
wrong." The silence during the conversation was mis-
construed by Catherine as sullenness on the accountant's part, as he sighed (with his hand over the receiver), shook his head then wiped the perspiration
from his brow. He had explained it a dozen times
before but somehow it just didn't seem to impress
Catherine. "Now, Mrs. Rossi, we have to view this
thing logically ... it's as simple as this ... You cannot continue to run your business like ..." "Like
what ... ?" "Like ... like ... like it was all fun and
games." "Okay ... you're so smart, what's the solu-
tion?" "For one thing, you employ too many people for
such a small establishment ... with a volume of sales
such as Posata's you are overstocked ... even if ..."
"Hold on a minute ... we showed a profit last year."
"True ... but only on paper. The thing that clobbered
us was the floor tax ..." Interrupting, she jumped in,

"I don't want to hear about the negative, let's deal with the positive." "Alright, Mrs. Rossi . . . get rid of some of your help and have a storewide sale. You've got to turn your merchandise over." The word SALE was like waving a red flag. Sale . . . she'd let the stuff rot before she'd allow Posata's to become a schlock store, with sales and reductions like a Market Street operation . . . never . . . but the help was one thing she understood. The accountant was right about that . . . okay, she'd listen to reason. The next day without notice three of her five employees, as of that moment, were out of a job. She had a time clock installed. It was expensive but it would be worth it . . . time was money, and money was time, so Posata's was going to be run as all efficient businesses . . . on time, with her only two remaining employees checking in and out. In that way she'd know exactly what was going on.

As the election grew near, her appearances from time to time were necessary, and she attended as few functions as possible, but in some cases, at the last minute she simply refused to go . . . who missed her smiling face . . . and besides, she'd given a hell of a lot to her children, now let them return a little. Gina Maria proxied in her behalf as hostess, as well as Tish who had become more than a daughter to Catherine. Tish was her confidante, her friend and the only one she trusted. And for that loyalty, Catherine filled Tish's home with magnificent antiques she never failed to buy when in Europe. The other daughters-in-law she bought for but with a reluctant charity . . . anything to keep the family together and happy. In fact, everyone seemed to be thriving and forging ahead.

Hardly a surprise, Dominic was elected to a second term. And those brief times they had together, all she heard was money for education . . . housing for the poor . . . that's what the mayor kept begging Sacramento for, and if the mayor was beggin' for something, Dominic fought for it in the Senate. If she heard all that once more, she'd scream, and if she saw him on the television a few more times, she'd break it. But aside from those difficult moments, she was quite content. She was doing her thing . . . and he was doing his thing. However, of late, it seemed to Catherine that Dominic was beginning to show the effects of his pressures . . . he was less composed at times and a little more explosive . . . giving vent to his frustrations with the boys. Dom, Tory and the twins understood and did not take him seriously, but Catherine began to think, happily, maybe he was beginning to see the light. Who needed it? So one day Catherine pressed down the hold button, while a salesman waited, and said to Mama, "Dominic's got two years left on his prison term and then I think he's through with politics. I got that feelin'."

"What gives you that feelin'?"

"Well, a man can take just so much, Mama. I just know Dominic's simply got to get his belly full . . . he's havin' so much trouble with this union and that union and this ethnic group and all the loonies that constantly hound him. One of these days he's gonna say . . . look, I've had it and then just maybe we'll be able to settle down and live like human bein's do."

Knowing Catherine was deluding herself, Mama asked, "What about the boutique? You poured your heart and soul into it."

"To hell with it. When it outgrows its usefulness, I'll chuck it."

"Why not give it up now? Why don't you spend some time with Dominic—"

"In Sacramento! That hick town. Never."

"All right, Catherine, but you're losing lots of money and—"

"To hell with it . . . it's worth the loss for my peace of mind."

But Catherine's peace of mind was to be invaded.

"Catherine, they want me to run for senator," Dominic said to her before going to bed.

She looked at him. "You don't say . . . so what else is new?"

"I'm talking about a United States senator."

Having just bathed, she stood stark naked with her nightgown in her hand . . . and thought she'd go out of her mind. "When you gonna get over this drug you've been on, Dominic . . . this craziness? Haven't you had enough? Taken enough punishment? When in the hell are we gonna live . . . find time for livin' . . . don't you think by now I've earned the right to—"

"Let's not get started on that again . . . how many men get a chance to be a U.S. senator?"

"Not too many. Most of 'em are too smart and realize they need a home life—"

"Catherine, for God's sake, I'm asking . . . begging for you to understand. Won't you please understand how much I want this?"

"And then after senator, there's only one other job you just might like . . . president . . . right?"

He smiled. "Well, what the hell . . . you'd be the first lady."

"It sure as hell would be the only time I was ever first.

"Okay . . . okay, I guess there's no way to fight you on this. In fact, Dominic, I'm too tired to give a damn. If you want to run, run . . . but I'm not gonna live in Washington. No, thank you . . . but keep runnin' till you run out of steam."

16

It was with these blessings Dominic declared his intentions to enter the senatorial race. The competition was no pushover. Dominic's opponent had the most important piece of real estate pretty well tied up and that's where the votes counted . . . Los Angeles, Orange County, was where Dominic needed to make his greatest thrust. In fact, it was the whole southern half of the state where he needed all the help he could get, and Dominic got help from those whose voices meant something . . . the important members of the movie industry who pitched for him loud and clear were no small contribution. But there was a lot of territory to cover, so for six grueling months he stumped the state, concentrating his total energies in the southern cities. There was no hamlet too small . . . not a nook or cranny that was not familiar with the name Dominic Rossi. And this time, Catherine agreed to make as many junkets as possible. Dominic had pleaded with her (among a few other pressures brought to bear by her family and key members of the committee) that this race was not San Francisco, where their faces and names were household words . . . this was the big time . . . the whole state was involved and the more well-known *they* became as a couple, as a family, the better his chances. She was an integral cog in the machinery . . . more essential than she could ever imagine. One of Catherine's special and natural assets was she looked good in photographs. Her smile was enchanting and warm and that appealed to the ladies who read the morning paper over a cup of coffee. As long as it was not her wish to address the ladies in her husband's behalf, they were in good shape. Her appearances sufficed.

Eager to get on with the ordeal and the damned thing over with, an exhausted, apathetic Catherine flew to Santa Barbara, arriving there just in time to bathe and change into her fabulous gown and jewels. Where was Dominic, she wondered angrily . . . probably downstairs in his usual conference . . . God, how he loved those conferences—better than her, that was for sure. He didn't even respond to her page when she arrived.

Suddenly, he rushed into the room, pecked her on the cheek, mumbled . . . glad you're here as he rushed into the bathroom, showered, shaved and put on his tuxedo. Then like a hurricane, she was whisked out of the room with Dominic holding onto her elbow, walked rapidly down the hall and waited for the elevator.

The evening was a huge success. Even the mayor had flown down to lend a hand. Everyone had done their homework and it was apparent from the responsive applause. The crowd loved him . . . hung onto his every word . . . he captivated them with his sense of humor, his ability to reach the rich as well as the poor, and while he was speaking, the committee in San Diego was pushing like a panzer division. When the evening's festivities were over, as always before retiring he spoke to Dom who had his pulse on every statistic. Yes, it looked like they were leading. . . . "Out in front, Papa, but we've got to keep working, pushing."

The next morning, a confident and happy Dominic and his entourage flew to San Diego, with Catherine saying, "I'm gonna rest and meet you later."

But later never came ... she was now missing for two weeks.

The anxiety of Catherine's whereabouts during the interim of those days was only to be compared with the sinking of the Titanic. When Catherine did not put in her appearance ... nor show up prior to the banquet at the San Diego Hilton that evening, Dominic walked into the overcrowded ballroom with a feeling of foreboding, although he conducted himself with the same sure composure and knew exactly what he was saying. Still, he kept glancing around the room from table to table to catch a glimpse of Catherine sitting with members of the family, a portion of which was always present at all dinners, rallies or whatever the occasion demanded ... but as he continued speaking ... something kept whispering in his ear ... "We're in big trouble ... can't put my finger on it, but? Where the hell is she?" His stomach turned and churned nervously. When the family retired to Dominic's suite, speculations began. First Tory called the hotel in Santa Barbara only to be told that Mrs. Rossi had checked out that morning soon after the senator's departure. What did she do, take a taxi? No, it seemed the dear lady had rented a car. What kind and from where? The manager regretted to say he could be of no help since he had no idea. The bellboy that assisted Mrs. Rossi, was he on duty? Again, the manager regretted the man was off duty until tomorrow. Tory hung up the receiver with his palm sweating. Next step ... call the airlines ... No leads there.

"Christ, nobody disappears in thin air ..." a very apprehensive Dominic said.

"Now, wait a minute, Papa," Tory answered, trying to calm his father's fears. "Let's face it . . . if anything had happened, wouldn't we have heard?"

"I don't know, Tory. I have a terrible fear somehow that I've never had. I can't explain it."

"What, Papa? Say it."

". . . That something's happened to her."

"Come on, Papa," Angie answered. "You're over-reacting."

Dominic became angry. "How come you're so calm . . . all of you? This is your mother . . . she's missing. We called home—"

"We don't really know she's missing—"

"Then why didn't she show up tonight?"

Finally Tory spoke up. "Look, Papa, isn't it possible she just decided to drive home?"

"Without telling me? No . . . besides, why would she drive? Look, she's a public figure. Anything could have happened to her . . . especially with all that damned jewelry she wears . . ."

"Papa, just a minute," Dom said evenly, "let's back up for just a minute. Did you and Mama have words . . . an argument?"

"When? I haven't seen her all day."

"I mean yesterday."

"Yesterday? You mean in Santa Barbara?"

"Yes."

"No . . . she didn't arrive until late, then we went to the banquet . . ."

"Think, Papa, think . . . were her feelings hurt?"

"Hurt? Why . . . why should her feelings have been hurt. We hardly saw each other."

"Papa, Tish and I sat next to Mama last night and both of us got the feeling she was upset about something."

Bewildered, Dominic asked slowly, trying to sort out the events of last night, "Upset? It's no secret she's not exactly choked up over campaigning . . . but she's been more cooperative in this one than at any other time."

"Okay, granted . . . but something bothered her."

"What . . . . ?" Dominic asked, raising his shoulders and turning his palms up, "what . . . ?"

"I don't know," Dom answered.

"But you said she was bothered . . . what gave you that impression?"

"She got up from the table without a word as you were just finishing your speech and left."

"She did . . . ?"

"Yes."

"Okay, what else?"

"Well, this morning before we left, Tish said she'd stay on and take the plane with Mama later . . ."

"And?"

"And Mama said she wanted to be alone to rest and think out a few things and then come down later."

"And?"

"Well, Tish got the distinct impression she was very disturbed."

"Funny, I didn't get that impression when I left. In fact, she seemed . . . happy."

"Well, apparently she wasn't."

"Then how come neither of you said anything about it till now?"

"Because with all you've got on your mind, we didn't want to add to your . . ."

"You didn't want to upset me? If Mama was that upset why didn't you come to me . . . what am I, a cream puff? I wouldn't be able to take it?"

"The point is, Papa, Tish guessed Mama was upset . . . but that she wouldn't show up didn't even cross her mind."

Dominic was now silent, trying to sort out the pieces, then answered, "No, she wouldn't do that to me. Granted, she wasn't overcome with joy, but she promised to go along with me and she has." He paused, then asked, still disbelieving, "But . . . if she did, where would she go?"

"To the Farm. Where else?" Tory answered.

"Okay, but we called the airlines and no Mrs. Rossi took a flight out," Dominic insisted.

"She could have driven," Dom suggested.

"All the way to Arizona? Don't be foolish. She'd be afraid to drive that distance alone."

"Don't underestimate Mama . . . she's got more guts when she wants to do something than anyone I know."

"Alright then . . . call."

Dom picked up the phone, asked the hotel operator to place the call to the Farm, then hung up. They all waited. When the phone rang, Dom picked it up quickly as the silent family sat waiting and listening.

"Mrs. Rossi?" asked the night switchboard operator. "Why, no, she didn't check in today."

"She didn't?" Dom asked, repeating the question only out of disappointment, then continued, "Do you have a reservation for her at all . . . anytime this week?"

"Hold on, I'll look through the book." Scanning the pages, she said, "No, sir, I don't see her name down."

"I see . . . now, if she does come at any time, it makes no difference when, please call this number day or night." He gave the number to a very innocent operator, unaware that Catherine had been secreted away in a tower suite since earlier . . . so when she said . . . "Yes, sir, I have your information" . . . she filed away the slip of paper never dreaming it would in future have spared an overwrought Dominic plus seven children a great deal of anxiety. However, since a strict gag rule had been imposed by Mrs. Van Muir, the operator, who had no way of knowing, saw no need to even mention the call to the directress of the Farm. Dom hung up more disturbed than he pretended.

"Alright," Dominic said, his breathing labored, "she's not there."

"Not yet," Tory answered quickly to offset his father's fears.

Fairytales

"If that's where she was going, she'd be there by now," Dominic said adamantly.

"Maybe she stopped off somewhere . . . overnight."

Dominic looked at Tory. "You don't believe that anymore than I do."

"Fine, so where do we go from here?"

"To bed, if any of us can sleep . . . and in the morning, we'll call Santa Barbara, try and get some information about the rented car. That's the first step."

"Then . . . ?"

"Well, obviously she's got to turn that car in eventually. She can't keep driving forever and by now, she's too well known not to be recognized," Dominic answered.

However, for his peace of mind as well as the family's, such was not the case. For days the Santa Barbara police department with the aid of the San Francisco department, under the cover of complete secrecy, alerted the State Highway Patrol to look for a Mercedes Benz. They were given the license plate numbers. That was the only information they had so far been able to obtain. Even if Catherine decided to go incognito, using her maiden name, at least the car had been taken out in the name of Rossi and her driver's license bore that name . . . it was only another ambiguous clue, which up to now seemed to be unproductive. Dominic cancelled all his speaking engagements . . .

"What'll we give as an excuse, Dominic?"

"Any goddamned thing you can think of . . . but for God's sake, no excuses of sickness . . . that's all we need is to start a rumor that the candidate had a mild coronary."

When the news media asked why he had returned to San Francisco . . . "On very pressing official business which demanded my immediate attention."

Each day that passed, Dominic tried desperately to believe Catherine was safe and well somewhere as the family kept trying to brainwash him. Now his anxiety about her welfare outweighed any hostility

374

that might have crept into his overlapping thoughts. By the end of a terrifying week, he was unable to go to the Capital or function at all. He couldn't sleep or eat. There were dark circles under his eyes and he was beginning to lose weight. In the sightseeing bus that passed daily, the passengers heard the tour director say and point out, "Now, ladies and gentlemen, on your right is State Senator Rossi's mansion. It is considered to be one of the most . . ." None of them could possibly have known the gloom, the apprehension that went on behind those imposing double doors. The family never left Dominic alone. It was two weeks since Catherine's disappearance. Now Dominic finally said to his children, as though he were delivering a eulogy:

"I guess the time has come for us to announce publicly that Mama's missing."

Gina Maria broke down and sobbed. Quickly, Sergio drew her to him for consolation.

"Papa . . . should we give it another day or so?" Angie asked.

"What for," Dominic said with tears in his eyes, feeling all the burden of guilt heavily upon his shoulders. He had driven her to this. He wouldn't wish his dreams, his nightmares on any enemy. He could see her lying in some ditch in some remote spot . . . he blinked his eyes. "We've waited long enough . . . there's nothing to wait for. I've listened to many voices . . . Ricci's among the few that knows. So let the public think this is a grandstand play . . . to hell with the public . . . the campaign . . . who needs it . . . who wants it. . . . the cost is too high."

Gina Maria began to scream, running out of the room with Sergio after her. A very sober, subdued Tony said, "Papa, somehow, I just know nothing has happened to Mama . . . I just know she's safe . . . somewhere."

"No one hopes it more than me . . . go to church . . . pray, I don't want to add to all of your worst fears, but if Mama were safe, she would have called one of us by now." Dominic swallowed back the tears, got up from the table and went into his study, closing the door behind him. He was now prepared to have Chief of Police Howe make a statement publicly to the press. . . . With that decision, he picked up the phone and called. Hanging up, openly crying, he said to the silent room, Catherine, where in God's name are you . . . ?

———

Catherine at that very moment was luxuriating in a soft, lukewarm tub of fragrant blue bubbles at the Farm, lying back and thinking how much she had matured. She had survived this lonely ordeal longer than she'd ever thought possible . . . aside from the fact that she missed her grandchildren at times with a longing she had difficulty trying to control . . . It really hadn't been too bad. She also missed her children. Disappointments? She had a few . . . except for Tish. The boys had disappointed her by marrying girls she was not too fond of, and Roberto? Better to blind herself on that issue. But all in all, this absence would make her appreciated more. I'm finally an emancipated woman. I've *survived*. Getting out of the tub, she dried herself, put on her sheer chiffon gown and matching peignor, walked into the bedroom and waited for lunch which was soon to be served. Pouring herself a sherry, she thought what a joy Mrs. Van Muir has been . . . I'm never gonna forget how she listened to me pour out my achin' heart . . . those terrible nights when I couldn't sleep and she came up and played gin rummy till four . . . after all, I couldn't keep the poor dear soul here till dawn . . . I do have consideration for the workin' classes even if I'm not runnin' for public office . . . but I'm never gonna forget her kindness, sittin' with me, drinkin' a little brandy, joinin' me for dinner when I was so low in spirits . . . no, sir, I never forget a friend . . . let's see . . . I'm gonna buy her . . . ? A case of brandy. Catherine heard the soft knock as Mrs. Van Muir wheeled in the luncheon cart. Taking off the silver domes, Catherine said, "Looks positively luscious . . . just simply too beautiful for words. That salad's a work of art . . . and you got a raspberry napoleon this time . . . you darlin' . . . my very favorite."

Mrs. Van Muir smiled and hoped Mrs. Rossi was doing fine. "*Bon appetit . . .*" she said, as she left the room.

Catherine poured a glass of clear cold Chablis into the wineglass, held it up to the light . . . lovely, then took a sip . . . put the glass down, picked up a fork and stabbed a plump crab leg, put it in her mouth and savored it. A little music would go nicely . . . getting up, she turned the knob on the radio as the soft melodic strains of "Amapola, Pretty Little Flower" invaded the room. Returning to her luncheon, she seated herself again and contentedly continued to eat, humming in between bites. The song ended . . . another began . . . so pretty, she thought, when suddenly the announcer interrupted the melody. "We interrupt this to bring you this news bulletin. Senator Rossi of San Francisco . . . candidate for United States senator . . ." "Oh God," Catherine thought, "not again . . . now on radio . . . it's not enough I bashed in the television tube . . . what's that he's sayin'?"

". . . and she has been missing now for two weeks. The news has come as a shock to everyone. At this point, the police cannot make a definite statement as to the mysterious disappearance of Mrs. Rossi. The only clue they have is that she left Santa Barbara to join the senator in San Diego and has not been seen nor heard from since. The senator and his family are in seclusion at the Rossi mansion in San Francisco and none of the family have made a statement. We will interrupt this program for any further developments . . ."

The music began again . . . Catherine was dumbfounded, then excitedly happy, then frightened like a child about to dive off a high diving board. She ran for the phone . . . "Mrs. Van Muir, did you hear the news?" Catherine asked breathlessly.

"Yes . . . oh my, yes, Mrs. Rossi. Do you want me to come up?"

"I want you to get me a San Francisco paper."

"Immediately."

When Catherine read the entire account with her picture staring back at her, she was delighted. . . . Well, Senator Dominic Rossi, I finally made it . . . pushed you off the front page . . . for a little girl who came from New Orleans I gave you a pretty good run for your money . . . San Francisco, here I come.

She picked up the phone and called Gina Maria. "*Mama*," she screamed, then cried, "Where are you?"

"Never you mind about that . . . for now . . ."

"We've been going out of our minds . . . tell me something . . . anything . . . ?"

"Not now, all I'll say is I'm fine . . . couldn't be better . . . just had to get away and do some tall thinkin'."

"Why didn't you let us know?"

" 'Cause it wouldn't have worked."

"What wouldn't, Mama?"

"Straightenin' out your Papa."

"I wouldn't have told . . . if only you had let me know you were safe."

"Not intentionally . . . maybe, but if you'd seen him bein' a little concerned you'd have told him."

"No, I wouldn't have, Mama. We thought something terrible happened."

"No, sir, somethin' wonderful's happened. I'm gonna be a wife that counts and Papa's gonna be a husband that cares or there's not gonna be any senator named Rossi in Washington come November, 'cause there won't be any marriage . . . hear?"

"I hear . . ." Gina Maria answered between tears of grief and relief. "When are you coming home, Mama?"

"I'm not comin' home . . . that is, right away, but

I'm comin' back to San Francisco. When I get there, I'll call you from the hotel I'll be stayin' at. I'm char- terin' a plane so no need to find out about nothin' else. You've got my permission to tell the others . . . Gina Maria?"

"Yes, Mama?"

"How are my babies?"

"Fine . . . they've asked for you, Mama."

"Well, I'll be seein' them soon. Now give 'em a big kiss and hug from their *nonna*."

"I will, Mama, thank God you're safe and coming home."

"Me, too . . . nice to be wanted."

"We all want you, Mama."

"All? . . . well, we'll see."

When Catherine arrived in San Francisco, it was five in the afternoon and getting out of the airport incognito, then picking up the car she had reserved earlier under the pilot's name (a deed for which he was handsomely rewarded) was no problem, but how to get into the hotel without detection, incognito or not, was no easy task. She thought it out very care- fully. She drove into the hotel garage in the rented Ford (so as not to call attention via any gawkers), quickly accepted the parking tag and walked rapidly up the backstairs to the employees' entrance. Thus avoiding the main lobby, she opened the door care- fully to see if anyone was around. Fortunately, the maids going off duty paid little attention to her, if at all, since she was still wearing the dark sunglasses, bandanna and a simple cotton dress she had bor- rowed for this occasion from Mrs. Van Muir which was much too long and much too tight, but so far, she had not been recognized. Finding a house phone, she called the manager. When he answered, she said, enjoying all the suspense, "I'm not gonna tell who this is, but come to the second floor employees' entrance."

"Who is this?" he demanded.

"When you get here, you'll find out . . . and Fritz, don't bring anyone with you . . . hear?"

"Who are you? Fritz! . . . How dare you call me by my first name?"

"Because I've been doin' it for years . . . now get up here."

"I insist upon knowing who . . ."

"I'm tellin' you to get up here, then you'll know!"

He slammed down the phone and thought, should he take the security man with him? Well, of course he wasn't going to go without protection, but he would have security stay tucked away, out of sight, just in case this proved to be more than he could handle. "Now, Sam, if I don't come out in five minutes, you come in after me. Better keep the gun ready in case of any surprises," Fritz said to security.

"Right . . ." security answered, and stood back against the wall as his boss opened the door and went in.

"Fritz . . . how are you?" Catherine asked, taking off the glasses.

It wasn't security Fritz needed . . . it was the fire department's oxygen tank or mouth-to-mouth resuscitation. He looked like he was going to faint. "My God, Mrs. Rossi!"

"That's right . . . Mrs. Rossi . . . that's just who I am."

"But . . ."

"I know, they've had the mounties out lookin' for me . . . well, I just found out this mornin', but I don't want anyone to know I'm here . . . hear?"

Recovering sufficiently from his state of shock, he remembered Sam, who would be charging in at any moment like a bull. "Wait, Mrs. Rossi, security is outside. I'll be right back." He dashed from the room and returned within seconds. "Now, Mrs. Rossi, let me say how terribly happy I am to see you well and home."

"That's just the point, Fritz, I'm not goin' home just yet. I need a room . . . You're the only person other than my family that knows I'm safe." A bewildered Fritz stared with his mouth hanging open. "I'm not gonna explain, but you're not to breathe a word about this to a livin' soul ... Ya hear?"

"I understand, Mrs. Rossi ... you have my word on that."

"I sure hope so ... for your sake ... 'cause if the word leaks out, I'll know where it came from."

"Oh, Mrs. Rossi, you have my sacred word."

"I surely hope so, Fritz, 'cause we own a sizable hunk of stock in this fine establishment."

"Have no fear, my dear Mrs. Rossi ... now what may I do for you?"

"Well, first, I want a room ... then get my luggage out of the car ... it's in the garage. Here's the parkin' tag ..." Catherine handed it to him and added, "I want you and no one else to bring the luggage."

"Understandably."

"Fine, then I'll give you an order for dinner ... again, Fritz ..."

"I know, Mrs. Rossi, I will see no one knows. I will attend to everything personally ..."

"Right on ..."

Knowing this large, exquisitely furnished suite was only to be for a night, if that long, she hadn't bothered to unpack. She was sick to death of *rooms*. What she needed now after that long lonely retreat was her *home*. Catherine was going home come hell or high water ... hail or brimstone ... Dominic or not ... that house was *hers* as far as she was concerned, but first he was going to get out, if only temporarily ... If they couldn't come to a meeting of the minds once and for all, he could go permanently to hell. With each mounting thought grew the anger which had accumulated over a period of two weeks ... no, a lot longer than that. But she'd face Dominic.

Marching into the bathroom, she bathed, put on fresh makeup, slipped into a peach-colored sheer wool dress, put her size four and one-half feet into a pair of brown suede boots, pulled them up over her legs to just below the knee, then stepped back and observed

381

her image. After wearing nothing but cotton shifts or staying in a nightgown all day . . . everyday for two miserable weeks, she looked wonderful, like the Catherine of old had just come back among the living. First, she called Fritz to have her dinner brought, then phoned Gina Maria.

"*Mama!*" she cried, "I've been waiting all day."

"Well, I just got in a little while ago."

"I'm so relieved, Mama, where are you staying?"

"Where else but at my favorite hotel atop Nob Hill . . . watchin' the cable cars climb halfway to the stars."

"Mama, I'm so glad to hear you're happy, but we've all been under such pressure . . . Mama, don't you think the least you can do is call the family?"

"No . . . absolutely not. In fact, Gina Maria, if you tell where I'm stayin' I'll never trust you with another secret . . . I swear, as long as I live."

"I won't, but I don't understand any of this, Mama . . . why didn't you go home instead of to a hotel now that Papa knows."

"That's a question I'll answer later when you and Sergio get here . . . Gina Maria . . . ?"

"Yes, Mama?"

"What was your Papa's reaction when you told him yesterday . . ."

Gina Maria winced and swallowed hard. "You there? . . . Gina Maria?"

"I'm here . . . he looked like, he looked like a beaten, bewildered man," she answered, thinking, "I hope that satisfies you . . ."

"Okay, darlin', I'll see you later."

Going to the bathroom, Gina Maria opened the medicine cabinet, reached for the bottle of aspirin, unscrewed the top, took two pills out and swallowed them with a glass of water. Trembling, she held on to the edge of the pink marble wash basin to steady herself. She looked at her pale face in the mirror, but the image she saw was not of herself, but the recollection of her father's face which seemed to stare back at her.

Remembering his first look of total shock, too dumb-founded to speak. It was as though someone had just risen from the dead. In those few moments he ran the gamut from relief to rage.

"How could she have subjected us to this mon-strous anxiety . . . put us through this unforgivable kind of apprehension. It's inhuman . . ." he screamed as though he had lost all his senses. "What kind of a person in their right mind does a thing like that? I ask you, who?"

So outraged, he shook with the desire to strike Catherine . . . to retaliate, if only she were there at that moment, and Gina Maria was sure he would have for the first time in his life. The effects of seeing her father in such a state unnerved her so, she could not control the fears of what she anticipated the first meet-ing would eventually be like between her parents.

Gina Maria and Sergio sat together on the settee in Catherine's room, as she reclined fully dressed against the pillows, propped up in bed. After the salutations were out of the way, Catherine began, "You asked me before why I didn't go home . . . well, it's simple. I want your father to leave my house and I want you to tell him."

"Why, Mama . . . why?"

"Because I can't face him . . . and not out of fear."

"What has he done so dreadful," Sergio spoke up, "he is a man who has suffered painfully in your absence."

"Has he really?"

"Yes, he has asked over and over why you became so angry . . . he does not know in what way he of-fended you."

"Oh, doesn't he?" Catherine said. "That's just the point . . . he's so busy with his own affairs, he doesn't know I exist."

Sergio was not an American so it was impossible to understand how a woman could run off and aban-don her husband and children. What she had done, he considered absolutely unforgivable. But he was in no position to go against her since he felt his obligation to her keenly. It was Catherine who had insisted Dominic buy the travel agencies. It was Catherine who purchased the house for Gina Maria and furnished it while they were in Italy on their honeymoon for three months. Catherine gave so much, it became virtually impossible not to surrender one's self. He loved Gina Maria and he also loved his life, but it took a strength he did not have to reject the keys to the kingdom when they'd been handed to him . . . and Catherine always pulled the strings not only with him, but with all her children . . . and the string could be cut at any time. It was very fragile. One never knew. Guardedly, Sergio said, "But now, Papa is very much aware you exist. I think you should go home and find out."

"You sound like you're favoring him, Sergio, and I don't think that's bein' very grateful," she said.

Gina Maria took the initiative. "Mama, please listen . . . we're at a loss to know exactly the reasons you found it necessary to go into hiding, but since you did, then you must go home and face Papa," she said, her face set and strong. This was an attitude Catherine rarely saw in her daughter. But she did not delude herself . . . if Gina Maria were forced into a position, it would be with Dominic against her . . . and Catherine's daughter represented a loss she knew she could not endure . . . sons were sons. They now belonged to their wives, but a daughter always belonged to her mother. Catherine listened quietly as Gina Maria continued, "I refuse to take sides against my parents . . . I don't think you really want me to . . . I'm not going to say who's right or who's wrong but I am going to remind you that once when you and Papa were not together, Papa came home and faced you for all our sakes . . . and, Mama, I think you should be equal to that . . . now, go home . . . resolve what must be resolved . . . whether Papa's in the house or out, you're going to have to talk this out. You may not like the position, but the whole country is waiting to hear what happened to you because you have made yourself a public person and the responsibility of that falls upon you to explain. Papa is in the public eye and his situation is untenable. I love you both, but, Mama, you started something and you must finish it."

Catherine looked at Gina Maria intently, knowing in her heart she was standing in judgment.

"Gina Maria's right, Mama . . . it's the only way," Sergio said, pleadingly.

"You think so . . . do you?" Catherine asked without rancor.

"Yes, Mama . . . if you decide to take her advice, we will drive you . . . now . . . please."

"Alright . . . get my coat, Gina Maria, while I call to have my bags brought down . . . the backstairs. That's the way I came in . . . Now, onward christian soldiers!"

Fortified with the boldness of a Carrie Nation, Catherine strode up the wide marble stairs to Dominic's room. Without knocking, she flung open the door and found a Dominic who looked like he had turned to stone, staring at her as she stood with her hands poised on her hips, waiting for Dominic to make the first overture. She would know how to deal with him no matter which way he decided to pursue the subject. Pacing back and forth, trying with all his might not to give in to his desire to strike her . . . he continued to pace; at this moment his desire was so great it would have taken very little to incite him. The wrong word . . . the magic word . . . would have set him off into a rage of uncontrolled violence. He could see it now in large, black headlines: "Senator Strangles Wife." Finally he stopped short, stood very close to her. *"Why have you done this to me . . . ?"*

"To you! Who the hell do you think you are? The head of the world . . . So you're running for senator and what does that make me? I'm a person . . . your wife, and damn you I'm gonna be treated like a person or you and I are finished . . . you hear?" she struck back, feeling his hot breath on her face. She stood her ground, looking him square in the eye.

Through clenched teeth, he asked, "How could you have put your family . . . your children whom you're supposed to love so much . . . through that kind of hell, not knowing if you were alive or dead . . . did that ever occur to you? Or what this little donnybrook would mean to my chances? I may lose because of you."

"To the first question, the answer is yes . . . it did occur to me and I thought a little anxiety won't hurt them a bit . . . they'd appreciate me as a mother a little more for all my sacrificin' through the years . . . as for you, I honestly didn't give a damn about your chances . . . not after the way you treated me in Santa Barbara. I felt like a puppet . . . like a discard."

"Okay, what did I do to you that made you feel justified to go into hiding without a word, allowing us to believe you were kidnapped . . . dead . . . God knows what?"

"You really want to know? Okay, I'll tell you. You've gotten so impressed with your own importance . . . you forgot I existed . . . you're so pompous and self-inflated with all the attention, the adulation you've received, you don't need anyone unless they're useful to you and your cause . . . and I got fed up with bein' manipulated."

"When did I ever do that . . . ?"

"When! You didn't even have the common courtesy to see to it that I was sittin' alongside of you where I belonged . . . didn't you wonder where I was? . . . There I go, still askin' those stupid questions. When am I gonna learn . . . ? The least you could have done was to make me feel that maybe in some way I was worthy of a little acknowledgment. Goddamn it, Dominic, I'm your wife."

"And for *that* you had to go to such measures . . . I think what you did was unforgivable."

"Sorry . . . Mr. Rossi . . . strong medicine was in order, and I gave it to you."

"And you didn't think you could have come to me in the privacy of our room and said, 'Look, Dominic, you offended me and I'm sick of being ignored and I'm going away by myself for a while,' if you felt *that* offended . . . no, instead you're going to make me look like a horse's ass in front of the world . . . how the hell do I explain this . . . you've embarrassed me to the point I've no idea how I'm going to explain this—"

"Really? Imagine, anyone embarrassin' you at a time such as this. But you know somethin' . . . I did what I bet every politician's wife since Martha Washington has been wantin' to do for a long, long time now but maybe never had the guts. You bet I wanted a little attention . . . I played second fiddle to another woman for a while and that's been a little hard to take for a long time."

"But to have left without a word . . ."

"Why didn't you look for me if you were worried about what this was gonna do to your campaign . . . that's really what you were concerned about . . . wasn't it?"

"What do you think I was doing, and not for that reason, but because of—"

"Dominic. . . I was gone two weeks and the police couldn't find me? Well, in that case, I think you got a lousy department . . . I was smarter than that when you were carryin' on with your lady love. I found out where to look . . . I hired a private detective . . . didn't that occur to you?"

"Yes . . ."

"Then why didn't you?"

"Because we wanted as little attention called to this as possible, not only for our sakes, but for *yours* . . ."

"Sure you did," she said, bitingly, "you were afraid that just in the event I wasn't kidnapped or God knows what, I'd have to come home and explain where I've been and what forced me to take a hike for myself . . . isn't that just about the long and short of it? Well, I'm ready to meet the press and when I get through, we're either gonna be together in this or you and me is through . . . as they say down south."

Dominic paced the floor once again. Now, what did he do? He was going to come out the heavy. One thing he knew, he'd have to apologize to her. He stopped pacing and quietly said, "Alright, Catherine, I'll pull out of the race. There's no other way. That's what you want . . . that's why you did this."

"Wrong . . . I had a lot of time to do some tall thinkin'. At first I didn't want you to run, but now I do . . . but under these conditions, I'm gonna be Madam Senator . . . not the Senator's wife . . . I'm not a Nancy Reagan, grinnin' and smilin' behind her husband. I'm gonna have my say when I feel like sayin' it . . . No more bein' pushed into the backroom and forgotten until election night when you need me standin' up there smilin' like a robot."

"But you never wanted to participate."

"Well, now I do, but as an equal. I've changed, that's a woman's prerogative . . . and I want my fair share. I'm gonna be someone and somebody. No more of this sittin' in the shadows."

"But you hated politics before. Why now . . . why the sudden about-face?"

"I just got through tellin' you . . . I've changed. The idea of bein' Madam Senator suddenly appeals to me . . . I underwent a big fat change durin' my stay at the Farm. Did a lot of thinkin' and my thinkin' made me realize that I could become a leader in a new kinda cause. A cause that would liberate a lot of political wives who are just as fed up as I am, but have been too timid to say so . . . it would destroy the images of their lovin' husbands . . ."

Dominic began to sweat, afraid to ask . . . afraid not to. Finally, softly and controlled, he asked, "What do you plan to do?"

"Do . . . ? I'm gonna let it all hang out . . . as the sayin' goes . . . now you call a news conference for tomorrow. I don't know if I'll photograph as well as

Mrs. Alioto did at hers, but I'm gonna do the best with what I've got."

"Catherine, for God's sake, let's discuss this sensibly and make some kind of a plan . . . an explanation . . ."

"No, sir, Dominic . . . darlin' . . . we're gonna tell it as it is . . . and now, I'm goin' to bed . . . sweet dreams . . . see you at the press conference in the mornin' . . . Sleep well," she said, walking out of the room, slamming the door behind her.

While a victorious Catherine prepared for bed and a restful night's sleep (so she would look her radiant best when meeting the press in the morning), a frightened Dominic was on the phone half the night conferring with his key men, as well as Dom.

"What are we going to say? How are we going to get around this?"

"Jesus, Dominic, we really got ourselves one hell of a problem," his campaign manager, Ricci, answered.

"You're telling me . . . she's so damned unpredictable . . ."

"You must have tried to make her understand how crucial this could be to the election?"

"I tried, but winning a case with your spouse, mostly I've learned you lose the big issues . . . it's not like trying a case in court, and I at least realized to push her too hard at that moment would only make her more adamant . . . it could be the kiss of death . . . like sending me the black hand and kissing me on both cheeks . . ."

"Okay, let's cool it for a minute . . . calm down and think rationally . . . what exactly did she say she was going to do?"

"She said, 'I'm gonna let it all hang out' . . ."

"Okay . . . listen to me, Dominic. She was just sounding off. Now . . . later this morning, at breakfast, sit down quietly and reason this out with her . . . explain that perhaps she isn't aware of the situation being so crucial, what the repercussions of her showing *any* hostility in front of the press would be for the election . . . that millions of people are going to be listening to what she has to say."

"Sure . . . you don't know her like I do—"

"Maybe not, but I know enough about women . . . she's a smart woman, Dominic, and knows enough about politics . . . knows that something like this could ruin your chances . . . the speculation would be, if you can't control your domestic affairs, how the hell can you represent a state . . ."

"She's not thinking logically . . . but if she were? That still would leave us with having to explain what the hell happened to her for two weeks, and why none of us reported it in the beginning."

"Fine . . . think of a good excuse . . . that she was under pressure . . . not quite responsible for her actions . . . that she found—"

"Let me interrupt. First of all, she's not going to put herself into a position of looking like some kind of a ding-a-ling. Or that she had a sudden case of amnesia. Besides, you know no one's going to buy that."

"I still contend that after a good night's rest, a little sweet talk will change her mind. The most important thing is to get together on a story . . . alert the kids . . . stick to it and maybe this might not turn out too badly after all."

"I'll try."

"You've got to. There's too much at stake . . . now, get some rest, Dominic, you've got your work cut out for you." Hanging up and turning off the bedside lamp, Ricci said to his wife at four in the morning, "Laura . . . ? I'm damned glad Dominic uses an electric razor." . . .

"How'd you sleep last night . . . ?" Catherine asked cheerfully.

"I didn't."

"Oh? Well, you look fine, Dominic. That's one thing I admire about you, the ability to look so rested even with very little sleep. Now, take me, I need my eight solid hours."

He was scarcely listening . . . his mind was on much more pressing problems. "Catherine?" he said evenly, sure his pulse was at least 110.

"Yes, Dominic?"

"I want to speak to you as my wife . . . as my friend."

She smiled. "Yes, Dominic . . ."

"I've done nothing but think about our relationship . . . our lives together. I've tried to see what might have triggered off your indignation and—"

"That's one step forward for mankind . . . or should I say womankind?"

Keep the temperature down to a normal 98.6, Dominic cautioned himself. "That's a pretty profound way of putting it."

"Oh, you think I'm profound . . . do you, Dominic?"

"Sometimes, yes, I do, Catherine."

"That's really grovelling . . . you want that election so much, you'd promise me the Brooklyn Bridge. Well, I swear, that's the nicest thing you've said to me ever since I can remember . . . Dominic."

"Catherine, you and I *must* discuss this press conference . . . what you're to say is . . ."

"Dominic, I've already decided how I'm gonna handle my first press conference. You're not gonna put the words in my mouth."

Getting up from the table, he paced the floor with his hands clenched inside his trouser pockets. Stay cool . . . or you're going to be cut and quartered . . . Once again, he sat down opposite her. Taking in a breath, he began again. "Look, Catherine, I'm *begging* you, pleading with you, let's try to make this situation as painless as possible with as little sensationalism as possible . . . they're going to cut me to ribbons, don't you understand?"

"I surely do."

"Then can't you and I come up with a plausible excuse about why you . . . retreated for a little while?"

"Then surfaced like Aimee Semple MacPherson

did when she emerged out of the sea in Carmel about forty years ago . . . ?"

"Please, Catherine . . . please let's be mature sensible people—"

"Sensible mature people? Why weren't you those things when you left me sittin' there like some kind of a rejected gland?"

"I realize now how much I offended you, but for God's sake, Catherine . . . I apologize . . . It was thoughtless and you had a right to be angry, but I have been under a strain and I simply overlooked it . . . can't you understand that?"

"And can't you understand that it wasn't only *that* slight that forced me to do what I did. Look, Dominic, who knows you better than I? For thirty-two years I've been your wife . . . for better or worse . . . but the fact is . . . you don't listen . . . you're a man of action, that's what you understand, so I acted."

"Couldn't you have tried to talk to me?"

"What the hell do you *think* I've been doing all these years? Why do you think I opened that crazy store which I need like a hole in the head . . . How come you're so smart that you couldn't even get the message . . . ? I've been sendin' up smoke signals for years now, but you couldn't read them because you were too preoccupied with *you*. For years I wanted your love . . . I begged you to find time for me . . . for us . . . but your damned ambition . . . you know what our problem has been? You should have been married to an old-world Sicilian lady only too happy to sit back and never ask, 'When you comin' home,' and then you'd have a perfect mate. And now, you want me to make up some kind of a cock-and-bull story I went off my rocker temporarily so that you can come out of this smellin' like a rose? Well, I am not about to do that, not even to become Madam Senator, much as I'd like it."

Dominic got up once again, his face pale and paced the floor. Turning around, he asked, "I'm really confused . . . why your sudden interest in politics . . .

I'm happy that finally you are . . . but I can't quite put the pieces together . . . you want to be Madam Senator, but you also want to ruin my chances, and along with them, yours. You can't have both, you know."

"Let me stop you right now . . . you think I hate politics? I sure did. You think I hated them because it took you away much more than even before? You're right but once you decided to run for office for the first time, as much as I hated bein' in the limelight, I was proud of you. I wanted everyone to see how brilliant you really are. I don't underestimate you, Dominic . . . no one has to tell me what you are . . . the thing is, you never made my efforts worthwhile for me to take any interest in your activities. You have always made me feel superfluous . . . never important . . . really important, not from the day I married you and for the first time in my life, I've found my own worth, my own importance. Now, if you don't like it, Dominic . . . I honestly believe you were to blame. Sure you asked me to go with you . . . I tried that, didn't I . . . when you went to Washington, D.C. . . . remember what happened when I said one little thing wrong. Well, okay, this time I'm gonna have my say and not feel guilty. I've passed that point in my *maturity.*"

Dominic paced the floor again, this time with his hands folded behind his back and stared up at the ceiling. He stopped and stood, looking down at Catherine, "You're punishing me for all those terrible things . . . alright, you've done a good job . . . This will probably ruin me. You know that, don't you?"

Catherine stood, facing him. "If you'll excuse me, Dominic, it takes me about an hour and a half to get myself put together for special occasions . . . and after all this one is my *debut.*" She walked around him without another word and went up the stairs, as Dominic stood listening to the sounds of her footsteps echo on each marble tread.

Upstairs in her room, Catherine drew back the silk gauze curtain just far enough so she could peer out unseen and what she saw was an army of reporters, sound trucks and cameramen waiting out in front, champing at the bit to get inside so that the show could get on the road. Appraising herself in the mirror once again, she smiled at her reflection. Never looked better than at this moment dressed in her extravagantly expensive, shocking-pink print gown . . . the likes of which only Hanae Mori could create. She adjusted the heavy opera-length, ten millimeter string of pearls with the diamond clip around her neck, then put the wide diamond bracelet on her left wrist, slipped on the pear-shaped gem that looked the size of a ripe Bartlett pear hanging heavily on a tree, the diamond-and-pearl earrings came next and finally a cluster of diamonds the size of a walnut on her pinkie. She rouged her lips once again, put her hand up to her carefully coiffed blonde hair, which had been done an hour ago at home, the hairdresser leaving through the rear door, and pushed a small hairpin back into place. She was ready. Opening the door of her room, she heard the sound of voices below reverberating through the huge marble hall. Quickly, she walked across the hall, knocked on Dominic's door and waited. He came out, looking like a reasonable facsimile of a wax figure from Madame Tussaud's factory. He was pale, the color of gray-green putty . . . his chin was so set it looked as if when he smiled it would crack. Catherine grabbed his hand in hers, holding it firmly (like a warden), digging her nails into his palm. Head held high, chin jutting forward (like Gloria Swanson in *Sunset Boulevard*, she thought) Catherine made her grand descent, smiling broadly at the members of the press whom she recognized. Dominic thought any minute she was going to make the V-sign for victory. With no alternative in sight, he smiled too, but like a man who had plastic surgery, whose lips were stitched into a permanent upward curve. Before they were seated together on the sofa in the huge living room, the flashbulbs flashed (blinding Catherine temporarily). The questions came at her so fast and furiously she didn't have time to complete a sentence as the television cameras zoomed in on her, grinding out pictures . . . this would be documented for posterity. Now she thought she knew how Marilyn Monroe must have felt. The whole thing was becoming like a circus as a sheepish, miserable Dominic sat by her side. She heard fragments of questions thrown at her ". . . why did the senator . . . for two weeks . . . the story is, Mrs. Rossi, that . . . is it true you were . . ."

"*Hold* it . . ." she said. "I'll answer one question at a time. Now, who wants to ask first?"

Dominic began to perspire under his impeccably tailored suit. "Thank you, Mrs. Rossi," a woman reporter broke in. "Can you tell us what actually happened from the time Mr. Rossi left you in Santa Barbara until now?"

"I surely can . . . the night of the banquet I flew happily into Santa Barbara to be with my husband. A man runnin' for office needs the support of his wife standin' by his side. But that wasn't where I was standin'. No, that was not where I was . . . by his side." Her lip quivered when she began to recite the events of that evening. "No sir, I was sittin' with my children in some dark secluded corner as though we were uninvited guests. Well, I can tell you, that's a slap in the face of a wife who's worked, and given of herself through the strenuous difficulties of campaigning. I grant you, no woman deserves a medal for doin' her share, but she sure as hell thinks she deserves a little recognition . . . if the senator could thank his paid workers, the least he could do, I figured, was to acknowledge his unpaid worker . . . *his wife*, by givin' her at least the attention of a little introduction. Well, folks, I admit it, I just saw red. . . . and I got damned mad . . . and jealous. I wanted to punish him so I retreated to a place I have friends . . . I don't care if a man's runnin' for president, he mustn't get so carried away with his own importance . . . the sound

of his voice . . . the impression he's tryin' to make on
the public, that he forgets his family, which is just
exactly what my husband did . . . don't misunderstand
me, he's no worse than the rest of them . . . it's just
that *this* famous politician's wife decided to stand up
and do something about it . . ." She looked at Dominic
who was now sweating profusely under his collar as
the color of his face turned from putty-gray to bright,
bright pink.

The reporter then put the microphone up to
Dominic to ask him a question. Catherine quietly
spoke up. "I believe this is my interview, ladies and
gentlemen."

"All right then, what was your husband's attitude
when you returned home, Mrs. Rossi?"

"Well, we had a very understandin' little chat, at
which time the senator regretted his neglect of me and
the children, but like the fine man he is, he assured me
he's not about to underestimate me again. You see,
politicians are just human bein's like just plain ordinary citizens. They take their wives for granted and
sometimes a woman has to assert herself before she
gets noticed."

Again the reporter took the microphone and addressed Dominic, saying quickly, "Senator Rossi, how
do you think this is going to affect your chances of
becoming—"

But again Catherine spoke up. "Why you askin'
him that? Why should his chances be any more or any
less because I went away to think out my own private
thoughts? I'm just like any woman in private life. If my
neighbor did somethin' like that, you wouldn't all go
rushin' over to her house askin' if her husband's gonna
be demoted. The trouble with bein' in the public eye
is you can't even have a plain old-fashioned argument
with your husband without the whole world knowin'
about it, but we're just like the people next door. Politicians have fights and get mad at each other . . . but
they're not *supposed* to, and that's what's wrong with

the whole damned image thing. You people of the press get into the act and blow the whole thing right out of proportion. What I did was really between my husband and me . . . and grateful as I am for your concern, I think the time has come for my husband to get on with the thing he's doin' and let me go on helpin' him because he's gonna be the best damned United States senator this state has ever had, and I'm gonna support him . . . now, I'd say that just about ends the interview. . . . Don't you think so, Dominic, darlin'?"

He shook his head, still with that fixed smile on his face.

"Fine. Now, if you don't mind, I think my husband and I really do need a little privacy." She got up with Dominic's hand still in hers and together they walked back upstairs as the reporters ran from the room to the nearest phones. The television crew packed up their equipment. On the way out, one said to his associate, "You know why they held hands . . . ?"

"To keep the senator from belting her one?"

They laughed, slamming the back doors of the van shut, then drove away.

That night, Dominic lay awake in the darkness, feeling like a broken man. He'd been made to look like a buffoon, a stupid clown in front of millions of viewers. Not only were they seen on local television, but the whole nation had the privilege of watching the Catherine and Dominic soap opera . . . the only thing missing had been the organ music. The speculations ran from his being the unfortunate victim of a spoiled, jealous wife . . . to her being the poor, abused wife who'd sacrificed her life to help her ungrateful husband climb the ladder of success. The issue became so controversial that husbands and wives began having their own private little arguments at breakfast over their Wheaties.

"Let me tell you, Gladys, if a wife of mine did anything like that . . ."

"Oh, really Charley? Well, if I had a husband that went off and neglected me the way she'd been, and taken for granted . . ."

Although Dominic knew the public's reaction would be divided . . . it could be no more divided than he now felt himself . . . divided right down the middle . . . cut in half. One half asked how could he go on living in the same house with her . . . not only for what she'd done, but she knew how Italian husbands felt about being the strength and stronghold of the family . . . it was inbred, inherent in their nature for generations. This was a thing he could not come to grips with. Love her? At this moment he despised her. But on the other hand he so badly wanted to continue his career . . . he was forced to ask himself how else could he do it without her? Compromise, how else? To leave her would mean political suicide. It would only prove that he was an ambitious son of a bitch who put his own self-importance above wife and children. Well, if you can't fight 'em, join 'em. There were no options left, he would simply have to grin and bear it, take whatever she was going to dish out, handle it as best he could. Catherine had washed their dirty linen in public. He was surprised she had restrained herself . . . when she said . . . quote . . . 'I'm gonna let it all hang out . . . tellin' it as it is,' that she did not bring up Victoria Lang . . . whom he still loved and had never been able to forget . . . but he thought maybe I better not tempt the gods . . . Catherine might still say something, since she had now become a celebrity and had been asked to speak on the talk shows. Anything was possible.

The next week found a very shy, very embarrassed, very subdued Dominic being seen going to and from his office . . . and a very quiet, silent and taciturn Dominic had dinner at home each evening with Catherine. If he ever appreciated his children, it was that week. They at least seemed to understand his need not to be alone with Catherine.

As months turned to weeks, weeks to days, Dominic's spirits began to climb, and after more than one conference with his key people, it was decided the fiasco might even turn into a plus. He had to appeal to the women's vote . . . it was apparent from the mountains of mail Catherine was receiving from women both in and out of politics that she was the star, a celebrity made overnight. The letters all pretty much had the same sentiment. "Bravo for you, Mrs. Rossi" . . . "I wish I'd had the guts to do what you did" . . . "Many's the time I wanted to walk out for the same reasons you did" . . . "Been taken for granted for too long now" . . . "Bless you, Mrs. Rossi, you've given a lot of women a little spunk."

Catherine hired two secretaries to help with the mail, which she made sure was answered . . . every last letter. And Dominic took the clue. There wasn't a speech he didn't mention Catherine's name. When they walked into a room, the cry went up, 'Hurray for Catherine! Catherine for president!' Catherine loved it, and Dominic thought maybe he'd hit on a bonanza after all.

Now the dwindling days before the California primaries were quickly coming to an end, and the team of Rossi and Rossi had made the big time together, making the final campaign trek side by side. The day of the election, Catherine and Dominic voted early. They went to mass, then that evening the children came to dinner and waited patiently as they had done through three elections. At ten it looked like Dominic was lagging slightly . . . by eleven he knew the game was over. Catherine had never in her life felt as guilty, as filled with remorse as she did that night. She was certain she'd lost the election for Dominic, and in spite of all the efforts to reassure her, no one could come up with the magic word to console her. It was the first time Dominic had ever lost. She felt the burden of that. Also she had lost her bid to immortality as the senator's lady from California, which she now wanted to be as much as Dominic wanted to be the senator.

However, for all her remorse, there were other factors involved in Dominic's defeat. For one thing, Dominic had still not made the inroads in the southern part of the state that he needed so badly, also the eighteen-year-olds preferred the younger candidate, and theirs was a decisive vote.

Reading that, she could almost make herself feel better.

17

At eleven, a devastated Catherine left with a resigned Dominic for headquarters, with only Gina Maria and Sergio going along, leaving the others to remain until they returned later. When Dominic stood on the platform with his arm around Catherine (who had learned to smile in defeat, like a pro), she stood close, with eyes of admiration, looking at her husband. The cheers went up in spite of the fact he had lost. And a radiant, smiling Dominic, with all the magnetism he had ever possessed to captivate an audience, stood resolutely like the victor instead of the vanquished and addressed the crowd. Laughing, he said, "We didn't lose . . . we just didn't win. And when I was a small boy growing up in North Beach, I learned you take your licks, never complain and never look back. I thank you all for your help. Do the same for the man who's going to be our next senator. Now, good night . . . God bless you. Catherine and I are going on a well-deserved vacation. She really needs it because no one worked harder."

Dominic and Catherine walked into the living room as the family sat silent, not knowing what to say. Dominic stood before the fireplace and looked at his children, then laughed out loud. "What are you all so sad about? So I lost the race, but it was a hell of a good battle, and Sicilians cut their eyeteeth on survival or we would have been extinct long ago."

The family took no comfort in Dominic's bravado.

Once again he almost laughed out loud. "Look, you defeatists, do you remember I once told you about a man named Thomas E. Dewey? I went to bed one night believing with the rest of the country that he was a sure thing to be president. The next morning, I woke up and found out that you can't really fool the people most of the time. There was a little man named Harry S. Truman. An ex-haberdasher from Missouri . . . never had a chance, except he won, and turned out to be the best damned president this country ever had.

"Okay, Catherine, come on, break out the champagne and let's celebrate . . .

"We've only just begun."

ABOUT THE AUTHOR

CYNTHIA FREEMAN was born in New York City and moved with her family to California. She has lived most of her life in San Francisco with her husband, a prominent physician. They have a son, a daughter and three grandchildren. A believer in self-education, Cynthia Freeman has been determined since childhood to pursue knowledge for its own sake and not for the credentials. Her interest in formal education ceased in sixth grade, but, at fifteen, feeling scholastically ready, she attended classes at the University of California as an auditor only, not receiving credit. Her litarary career began at the age of fifty-five, after twenty-five years as a successful interior designer. "People seem quite shocked," she remarks. "It doesn't seem strange to me. You do one thing in life and then another. I'd been writing all my life—little things for Hadassah, plays for the Sisterhood. I never thought of myself as a writer, but the simplest thing seemed to be to put a piece of paper in the roller and start typing." That typing has led to her very successful novels. *A World Full of Strangers*, *Fairytales*, *The Days of Winter*, *Portraits*, *Come Pour the Wine*, *No Time for Tears*, *Catch the Gentle Dawn*, and *Always and Forever*.

THE LATEST IN BOOKS
AND AUDIO CASSETTES

DON'T MISS
THESE CURRENT
Bantam Bestsellers

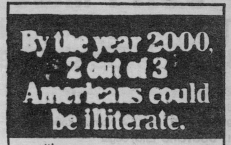
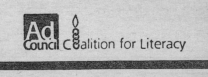

Now there are two great ways to catch up with your favorite thrillers

Audio:

☐ 45116-2 **Final Flight** *by Stephen Coonts*
Performance by George Kennedy
180 mins. Double Cassette — $14.95

☐ 45170-7 **The Negotiator** *by Frederick Forsyth*
Performance by Anthony Zerbe
180 mins. Double Cassette — $15.95

☐ 45207-X **Black Sand** *by William J. Caunitz*
Performance by Tony Roberts
180 mins. Double Cassette — $14.95

☐ 45156-1 **The Butcher's Theater** *by Jonathan Kellerman*
Performance by Ben Kingsley
180 mins. Double Cassette — $14.95

☐ 45211-8 **The Day Before Midnight** *by Stephen Hunter*
Performance by Philip Bosco
180 mins. Double Cassette — $14.95

☐ 45202-9 **The Minotaur** *by Stephen Coonts*
Performance by Joseph Campanella
180 mins. Double Cassette — $14.95

Paperbacks:

☐ 26705-1 **Suspects** *by William J. Caunitz* — $5.99
☐ 27430-9 **Secrets of Harry Bright** *by Joseph Wambaugh* — $5.95
☐ 27510-0 **Butcher's Theater** *by Jonathan Kellerman* — $5.99
☐ 28063-5 **The Rhineman Exchange** *by Robert Ludlum* — $5.95
☐ 26757-4 **The Little Drummer Girl** *by John le Carre* — $5.95
☐ 28359-6 **Black Sand** *by William J. Caunitz* — $5.95
☐ 27523-2 **One Police Plaza** *by William J. Caunitz* — $4.95

Buy them at your local bookstore or use this page to order:

Bantam Books, Dept. FBB, 414 East Golf Road, Des Plaines, IL 60016

Please send me the items I have checked above. I am enclosing $_____
(please add $2.50 to cover postage and handling). Send check or money
order, no cash or C.O.D.s please. (Tape offer good in USA only.)

Mr/Ms _____

Address _____

City/State_____ Zip_____

FBB—6/91

Please allow four to six weeks for delivery.
Prices and availability subject to change without notice.

1171